ghost ops

Dead to their pasts. Ghosts. No family ties. No connections.

Six men with a top-secret mission move to a small town where they have to navigate local life, protect their secret, and, above all, stay single.

Blaze "Shadow" Connolly
Chance "Wraith" Hughes
Seth "Phantom" King
Kane "Demon" Fox
Ethan "Dragon" Snow
Alex "Ghost" Bishop

PRAISE FOR LYNN RAYE HARRIS AND THE GHOST OPS SERIES

"**Get ready for a new HOT team**…
the Ghost Ops team has arrived…**and they
are everything fans love and more.**"
—Alphas Do It Better Book Blog on *Blaze*

"**I am dying for the rest of the Ghost ops guys to get
their stories** as Harris takes us on this journey through
the mission that was so top secret that the guys had to go
even more off the books than they were with HOT,
because it's bound to be an adventure for the ages."
—Michelle, Romance Witch Reviews on *Blaze*

"With **bad guys and suspense around
every corner** this book is a total page turner."
—H., Goodreads on *Chance*

"If you love **military protector romances, strong-
willed heroines,** and **emotionally complex heroes,**
you won't be able to put this book down!
It's definitely earned a spot on my favorites list."
—Anika, Goodreads on *Chance*

"**The banter is on point and
the snarky comments zing.**"
—Nikki's Book Nook on *Seth*

ALSO BY LYNN RAYE HARRIS

☆ ★ ★ NEW YORK TIMES AND
USA TODAY BESTSELLING AUTHOR ★ ★ ☆

★ GHOST OPS ★

Blaze

Chance

Seth

Kane

Ethan

Alex

★ BLACK'S BANDITS ★
HOT HEROES FOR HIRE:
MERCENARIES

Black List

Black Tie

Black Out

Black Knight

Black Heart

Black Mail

Black Velvet

HOSTILE OPERATIONS TEAM®
★ STRIKE TEAM 2 ★

HOT Witness

HOT Angel

HOT Secrets

HOT Justice

HOT Storm

HOT Courage

HOT Shadows

HOT Limit

HOT Honor

HOSTILE OPERATIONS TEAM®
★ STRIKE TEAM 1 ★

RECKLESS HEAT, a prequel story to *HOT Pursuit*

HOT Pursuit

HOT Mess

Dangerously HOT

HOT Package

HOT Shot

HOT Rebel

HOT Ice

HOT & Bothered

HOT Protector

HOT Addiction

HOT Valor

A HOT Christmas Miracle

★ THE HOT SEAL TEAM ★

HOT SEAL

HOT SEAL Lover

HOT SEAL Rescue

HOT SEAL Bride

HOT SEAL Redemption

HOT SEAL Target

HOT SEAL Hero

HOT SEAL Devotion

Check out Lynn Raye Harris' Online Store at

https://shop.lynnrayeharris.com/

for autographed books, HOT themed merch, and more!

Military Protector Romance

Top Secret Mission

Who can be trusted?

The World is at Stake

Undercover Black Ops Soldier Hero

FBI Agent Heroine

Enemies to Lovers

Sizzling Sexual Tension

Forced Proximity

Small Town Setting

Series Ender — it's the leader's turn to fall in love!

NEW YORK TIMES & USA TODAY BESTSELLING AUTHOR

LYNN RAYE HARRIS

ALEX. Ghost Ops, Book 6. First Printing, 2026.
Copyright © 2026 by Lynn Raye Harris®. All rights reserved.
For rights inquires, visit www.LynnRayeHarris.com.

ISBN 979-8-89117-115-2
Cover Concept and Design by Croco Designs.

Connect with Lynn Raye Harris online!
lynnrayeharris.com & hostileoperationsteam.com

AUTHOR'S NOTE

This book features a rape survivor.
Please be aware if this is something that upsets you.

FOREWORD

BY ALEX "GHOST" BISHOP

Well, shit. We all knew this day was gonna come, Hotties. I tried running from it…ran the whole way to Sutton's Creek, Alabama to be exact! I tried denial, and anger, and bargaining. Right now I'm hanging out in the depression stage of grief, but I can feel acceptance starting to creep in. Not that I'm happy about it. No, this is begrudging acceptance, at best. But I can't pretend I didn't know it was coming. I mean, if Brigadier General John Mendez himself couldn't get a reprieve, I knew that I — Alex "Ghost" Bishop — wouldn't stand a chance.

Shit. *Shit.* Do you even remember everything Mendez went through before getting his happily ever after? In case you need a refresher, HOT basically went underground and I wound up flirting with treason charges in order to run illegal ops out of a suburban basement to clear his name, while the good general high-tailed his ass across Russia, one step ahead of corrupted elements within our own government, with only the suddenly resurrected Russian operative whose "death" he'd been mourning for a couple of decades for company. I mean, it worked out in the end, but *damn!* Is that what I have to look forward to? Or something even worse? Oh no, it could always be worse.

I'm sorry, have I lost you? Wondering what exactly am I talking about? Well, my book, of course. The one you are about to start reading. I'm being paired off and put through the grinder. Raked over whatever coals Lynn has been formulating in that brilliant—but let's be real, more than slightly terrifying—mind of hers. And yes, if you've been a Hottie for a while, you may remember there was a time when I actually wanted a book and a love story of my own. I even talked to Lynn and Mr. Harris about it years ago, trying to jump the queue in front of Mal and Shade.

Let's just say that was before. Before I saw exactly how much my friends and colleagues were going through to achieve their own happy endings. Before I knew what was in store for Mendez and Ian Black. Somehow, the leader of the team always seems to get it worse, right? Who's the leader of Ghost Ops, again? That would be me. And yes, *of course* Viper and Ian will tell you it was all worth it in the end.

Blah, blah, marital bliss, 2.5 kids, a white picket fence and a yard, fucking blah. I would like to remind you, however, that both of them are married to particularly deadly women trained by Russian special intelligence.

Not saying they aren't happy, just saying it's in their best interest to keep their mouths shut if they aren't.

Ok, fine. I know they're happy. Disgustingly, nauseating, unendingly happy. It's just, c'mon! I'm a former HOT deputy commander. I've seen more than my fair share of danger and hardship. I'm not afraid of difficult choices and tough times. I'm also not strictly opposed to the idea of finding a good woman to help warm my bed, if nothing else...but does it have to be *this* woman?! *Really*? Of all the women in Alabama—all the women in the world—*her*?!

It's not enough I'm fighting for the security of the world at large right now, I've gotta fight with her too? And it will be a fight, you can count on that. You've seen us interact, we can barely maintain a civil conversation, somehow we're going to fall ass-over-boots in love? I'm not even sure she's got a heart under all those pristinely starched blouse-and-blazer combos. Forget about a woman to warm my bed, how about one that doesn't require a heating rock to maintain body temperature?

This is gonna get rough, folks.

You know what, I'm gonna stick with the depression stage of grief a little while longer. You? Well, you're probably excited about the current trajectory of events. Sadists. But I won't ruin your fun. Go on, read my book to find out what's in store for me. I'm gonna go ask Daphne is she still has that bottle of scotch hidden in her desk.

It's been real,

Alex

ghost ops
book six
ALEX

PROLOGUE

Seven years ago…

Her life would always be composed of *before* and *after*.

Diana dragged in a choppy breath, and then another and another. It was a ridiculous thought to have at such a time, but a distant part of her imagined it was the only thing keeping her from screaming.

Before and after.

Before, when she'd been a twenty-four year old working on her master's degree in international relations, a star student by all accounts, someone who was going places.

Oh, she'd have gone places anyway with a name like Adler. Her family was connected, powerful, a part of Washington DC political life no matter who was in office.

Her cousin had married a prince. Her grandfather was a cabinet member.

So many powerful people. So much influence.

None of it had saved her.

She was in the *after* now, sprawled on the couch in his office, a burn between her legs where he'd shoved his way inside her body.

She forced down the tears, the utter disbelief this could happen to her.

Diana Standish Adler. Wealthy, connected, privileged.

Violated.

By the man calmly tucking his shirt into his pants. His back was to her, and she thought what if she launched herself at him? What if she wrapped her arms around his throat and squeezed as hard as she could?

She could call her father. Tell him what this man—this guest lecturer, this betrayer—had done. He would deal with it.

But of course he wouldn't, that little voice whispered inside. The scandal, first of all.

Second, this man was someone who'd been to their house. He was liked, admired, applauded.

A supporter of humanitarian causes. A wealthy man who donated money to make things better in the world.

It was because of his ties to her family she'd thought him safe. She'd accepted his invitation to dinner, to his suite afterward, because he was a great man who cared. He'd been in town to give a speech at her university about supporting humanitarian causes. He'd spoken of how he was forming his own organization so he could send teams of aid workers to disaster zones faster. So his money would go farther and help more people.

Lives would be saved. Homes rebuilt. Families reunited.

She'd been proud of the connection she had to him. She'd sat in the front row, her chin held high, knowing that everyone was listening and admiring him. That she knew him personally—or thought she had, anyway.

She could go up to him after the speech, call him by name, thank him for taking the time.

She did those things, and he invited her to dinner at his hotel. To talk more about his new foundation and what kinds of things she could do as a student to help increase awareness and recruit others on campus to his cause.

"I have some materials in my suite you can use," he'd said after the meal. "Would you care to come up and get them before you go?"

She'd accepted. Why wouldn't she? It was a privilege he would consider her for such things. That he talked to her like she was an equal.

And now she lay on his couch, her skirt hiked up over her hips, her underwear torn and discarded, her body aching, her stomach rebelling. It had all been a lie.

He was a monster, not a savior.

He turned and gave her a cool look. "It's been a lovely evening, Diana. I'm glad you came to hear me speak."

She blinked. And then she scrambled to her feet,

yanking her skirt down to cover her exposed body parts, buttoning her shirt without attempting to fasten her bra. Her panties were somewhere, but she didn't care.

"I, um..."

"You are feeling surprised. I see this. Perhaps angry." He reached out to touch her cheek and she jerked away. He laughed. "You should not be so beautiful. And you definitely shouldn't go to a man's room if you don't mean to follow through on your promises."

"I didn't—"

"Ah, but you did. Looking at me with that hero worship in your eyes. Accompanying me here. If you had not wanted to fuck, why did you do it?"

She couldn't find the words. Later, she would hate herself for the lack. In the moment, she was stunned and confused, wondering if it *was* her fault. If she'd given signals.

He put both hands on her shoulders. "If you think to tell anyone you did not spread your legs willingly, I will not hesitate to ruin you, my dear. You and your family. The Adlers are wealthy, but theirs is but a drop in the bucket compared to mine. Remember this, and remember that everyone saw you with me. They saw you speak to me, leave with me. And you were seen willingly entering this hotel, having dinner with me, getting into the elevator with me at your side. No one will believe you if you claim you were forced."

"I didn't want this," she whispered.

He laughed. "I don't believe you."

He grabbed her coat from the back of the couch, tossed it at her. Diana shoved her arms into the sleeves and wrapped the coat tight, as if it were a layer of protection against him. She turned blindly for the door.

"Don't forget the materials you came for."

He handed her a folder. She should have thrown it in his face, but she hugged it tightly and fled. It was only when she'd emerged onto the icy sidewalk outside the hotel that she found the strength to drop the folder.

She stared at it lying on the frozen ground for a long moment, thinking of her life—before tonight and after.

It would be different now. Less hopeful. Less trusting.

Because her name hadn't protected her. Her family's wealth.

Nothing had. Nothing would.

The gold foil design on the front of the folder shone in the light, taunting her. There was a logo of a bear, and there was a name that would stay burned into her mind for the rest of her life.

A name that had stolen some vital piece of her soul.

His name.

The Dashevsky Group.

1

Present day...

He was going to die.

The cold crept through his limbs, numbing his joints, making his fingers and toes clumsy as he stumbled through the snow.

Everything was white. His breath. The trees and mountains and fields.

Ice as far as he could see. Behind him. Before him.

He'd never make it. He'd been stupid to leave. Stupid to try.

"No," he whispered. *"No."*

He stumbled onward, determined. He had to find a way.

Before the sun dropped behind the mountains. Before the temperature dropped another sixty degrees.

And then the wolf howled.

He stopped, his heart in his throat, his head jerking in every direction as he spun where he stood. Where was the wolf?

Another howl joined the first. A third, fourth, and fifth.

And then so many he couldn't count them anymore.

They were coming closer.

He started to run, his heart hammering, his eyes stinging as the moisture froze in them. His breath razored in and out, his blood beating in his ears.

So loud. Too loud to hear the wolves behind him.

He had to find a tree or a cave, somewhere to shelter. Somewhere to stay until the danger passed.

A branch snapped. He threw a look over his shoulder.

The wolf was big, white, with piercing blue eyes. Blood dripped from its teeth as it closed the distance between them.

"No," he panted, struggling onward, fear a cold thing inside that twisted his guts and made his heart leapt into his throat.

He stumbled on a root, his knees buckling, body sprawling in the snow.

The wolf was on him, jaws snapping. He lifted his arms, tried to fight. But the teeth sank into his tender flesh. There was pain, futility, defeat.

He was going to die—

Ghost snapped awake with a start, bolting out of bed and whirling, his pistol in his hand.

Nothing was there. Nothing at all.

Just him. Sweating, the taste of fear sharp and acidic on his tongue, his body aching from the accumulation of old injuries that wouldn't have bothered him just a few years ago.

"Fuck," he muttered, lowering the pistol to his side, and shoving a hand through his damp hair.

What the hell was happening to him?

The dream wasn't new. It was an old dream that happened sometimes when he least expected it. The feelings of helplessness from that time in his life had never completely gone away, and he hated the reminder of them. Hated the weakness.

He sucked in a breath and stalked to the kitchen for a beer. Maybe not the best way to cope, but it's what he was gonna do. The Ghost Ops mission would be over in the next few months. He had to stay focused. Get the job done, save the world, disappear somewhere. Not permanently.

Just long enough to get his shit sorted, stuff this dream back into the dark chasm it'd crawled out of, and figure out what the hell he planned to do with the rest of his life since his options had changed so dramatically when he agreed to this job.

Nothing he couldn't handle though.

Sure, he'd have to leave his team, the life they'd built in Sutton's Creek, and begin somewhere new. He got a pang at the thought, but it was no different than rotating out of one assignment and into another in the military. It's what you did, what you expected.

He was used to being alone. Used to moving on. He had no roots, no home. No family.

It's why he was here. Why they'd picked him to lead Ghost Ops.

He grabbed the beer, popped the cap, and took a long drink. Then he lifted the lid on the laptop he'd left on the counter and scrolled through the news. Not the most relaxing way to spend the early hours, but he wasn't getting back to sleep anyway. So why not?

President Willis smiled on the screen in one of the articles. That wasn't what caught his attention, though. She was overseas on another state visit and suddenly having to deny rumors of a new weapon the US was developing.

He frowned as he scanned the text. Sighed and rubbed his forehead. Fucking Athena Project. It wasn't a weapon, but it could be wielded as one by essentially giving whoever controlled it the ability to attack other countries without fear of retaliation. Nothing was getting through that shield, and that was a problem for people who were being asked to trust that the president wouldn't order a strike if she got pissed enough.

He understood the fear, but he also knew why the US needed the shield. It was revolutionary and meant to protect the citizens of this nation. And if they didn't develop it first, somebody else would. Then what? Could they trust Russia or China not to launch a strike if they had the technology?

He'd spent too many years in the military, too many

years preparing for war scenarios, to believe they wouldn't. The fact the project was actively being targeted by foreign operatives, resulting in Ghost Ops moving to Alabama to protect it, was proof enough.

Ghost snapped the lid shut and went outside, onto the screened-in porch at the back of the house. It was early September, and still hot as fuck during the day. But nights weren't bad at all. Not cool, but not sweltering either.

He liked the heat. Preferred it.

When he'd been nine, his dad had come home one day and announced they were moving to Alaska. His mom had seemed stunned, but she didn't argue. They'd sold everything, packed up what little they'd kept, and drove from Florida to Alaska over the course of three weeks. Mom had been optimistic and tried to make the trip fun. Dad had been jubilant, certain of their future. Certain that taking his family to Alaska was the right move to protect them from all the chaos he believed was coming.

Ghost sipped his beer as the memories crowded for space in his mind. He'd been a kid, excited about bears and caribou and seals. About the adventure of it all.

If only he'd known how bad it would get. How twisted his dad's mind would become.

He hadn't though. Probably a good thing since he'd been fucking nine and couldn't have done anything about it anyway. Some things were better not knowing.

Thanks to those years, he didn't trust many people.

His team. General John "Viper" Mendez.

That was about it.

If he didn't know he was adopted, he might have worried he could crack the way his father had. His parents had been good people, loving, but Desert Storm had triggered something in Calvin Bishop's psyche that never recovered.

Ghost finished the beer and took a shower, then headed up the driveway on foot. One Shot Tactical, the range and training facility he ran with his team, sat on a small rise about a quarter mile from the houses on the property. It was four in the morning and the moon was sliding across the sky, sinking toward sleep.

Some of the guys would arrive early to workout. Others would stay in bed with their women a while longer. He'd picked this team for their lack of relation-ships of any kind, and yet every last one of them was shacked up and planning to get married when this job was over.

If anyone had asked him back in December, he'd have said there was no way *any* of them would go against orders to form a relationship, let alone *all* of them.

Then again, it was a stupid fucking order some asswipe in Washington had thought was a good idea. Yeah, getting involved made them vulnerable to manipu-lation, but it wasn't enough of a reason. They were smart and capable—and special operators got married all the time. It wasn't the priesthood.

Honestly, the best way to blend in was to become part of the community, which is why he hadn't come down too hard on any of them. If the suits in Washington wanted to get pissy about it, Ghost would go toe to toe with them.

And if this operation went tits up and the worst happened, it could be the end for all of them anyway. Might as well enjoy life while they could. Fall in love. Feel those highs. Make plans for the future.

Even if the future didn't come.

He entered the range and locked the door behind him, then went down the hall to his office. Inside, he opened the door to what appeared to be a closet but was really a short hallway leading to the secure part of the facility. The SCIF was hardened, a place where classified information could be shared and discussed. When he was inside, doors locked behind him, he typed in his password and pulled up his encrypted messages.

There was one from Viper.

> **Viper:**
> It's a risk. You know that. But I'm with
> you. Do what needs doing. You were
> sent there to do what it takes, not to sit
> around with your thumb up your ass.

Ghost typed a reply, knowing Viper would get it the next time he logged in.

> **Ghost:**
> I'm not asking you to stick your neck
> out. You've got a family to think about.
> Just wanted you to know, in case it goes
> wrong, that I didn't actually go rogue.

He didn't expect a reply to ping back immediately, but he should have known Viper wasn't asleep. The man was always on alert.

> **Viper:**
> I'd know it even without you saying it.
> Time's running out. We still don't know if
> McCann passed your records to anyone,
> which means you need to be fucking
> careful.

Their official military records were sealed, hidden, and replaced with plain Jane assignments and histories that weren't theirs at all. All evidence of the Hostile Operations Team was gone. They were former Army Rangers. Special Forces, but not the kind of elite operators they really were.

Except that Paisley's ex-husband, Trey McCann, had seen them all in Sutton's Creek when he'd been stalking her. Since he'd been a former HOT operator himself, he'd gotten suspicious about their real purpose. He'd paid hackers to break into their files—but had he sold the information to anyone? Or had he died before he got the chance?

They'd never know because Ethan had shot the bastard before McCann could kill him.

Know that, Ghost typed. *I'll be careful.*

> **Viper:**
> You fucking better. I haven't liked
> anything about how this has gone down
> since you boys left here, but it's not up
> to me. I thought it was important or I
> wouldn't have asked you to go.

Ghost scrubbed a hand over his head. He'd made his choice and he wouldn't allow himself to regret it.

> **Ghost:**
> It is important. I'm not sorry we're here.
> But I wouldn't feel right about taking
> action without telling you.

> **Viper:**
> You've told me. Get the job done. Then
> come to Washington and we'll toast
> your success.

*HUA**, he typed. Once he knew Viper had seen it, he deleted the messages and logged off. Viper was deleting the ones on his end as well. Not even Seth "Phantom" King could retrieve them now.

Ghost took out the file on Viktor Dashevsky. All evidence pointed to Dashevsky being behind the attempts to steal the Athena Project's technology and use it for his own evil purposes. He was a Russian oligarch who ran a humanitarian foundation, but that was just a front for his real activities. He trafficked in weapons and humans,

---

* Heard, Understood, Acknowledged.

according to FBI Special Agent Diana Corbin, and he was amassing his own private army for purposes as yet unknown. But it wasn't good, whatever it was. Nobody formed a private army so they could give away more money than they already did.

To protect his humanitarian efforts in war torn countries? Also not likely since UN peacekeepers and private security often went into those places alongside the workers. So what was his objective?

Ghost continued to study the information on the Dashevsky Group's alleged members in northern Alabama, looking for connections he might have missed. Sometimes information had a way of slotting together suddenly when you looked at it, but no such luck yet. His team had been working hard to compile a dossier, but it was thin. Diana claimed she didn't have any more information than they did, but he didn't know if he believed her.

"Shit," he muttered as Diana's face lingered in his mind. Once she was in, it wasn't easy to push her out again. She was there to stay, in all her irritating glory.

He leaned back in his chair and studied the ceiling, thinking about the next steps he needed to take to move this mission along. It didn't help. She didn't fade.

Her long blond hair and sensible pantsuits—navy blue with white shirts, usually—lingered. He'd seen her in jeans, too. Off duty. She was shapely and beautiful, but icy cool. Like a marble statue.

She'd been a thorn in his side since this operation

began, gliding into his range with her partner, Clay Ackerman, and sticking her nose into Ghost Ops business like she had a right. He'd gotten her dismissed and sent to Kentucky, but she'd boomeranged right back again.

Because Diana Fucking Corbin was an Adler. The Adlers had been a fixture on the Washington scene for generations. Their influence and connections ran deep. She'd used those connections to return to her job at Redstone Arsenal.

And now it was ten times worse because she knew who they were and what their mission was. Knew and inserted herself into it. Pissed him off. Because everything he had, he'd worked his ass off for. He didn't know what it was like to be born with a silver spoon in his mouth, or what it felt like to snap his fingers and have shit happen.

When the Smiths had saved him from the hell his life had become in Alaska, they'd given him direction and encouragement, but the work had been up to him. He'd been incredibly far behind when he'd reentered public school, but he'd been driven. Because of that drive, he'd excelled. So much so that he'd gotten into West Point. If not for that, he wouldn't be where he was now.

All Diana had to do was call Uncle Stephen. Or Uncle Don (he assumed the FBI director was like an uncle to her, though they weren't related). And, boom, she got what she wanted.

He couldn't deny that she'd given his team information they'd been able to use—but she was still fucking infuriating. Her privileged existence annoyed him the hell out of him. The way she'd gotten involved in his mission like it was her right made him want to chew nails.

But the fact she made his balls ache? Now that didn't help his attitude in the least.

He hated that she affected him, but he had to admit she did. A man would have to be dead or gay not to notice how beautiful she was. With great tits and an ass he could hold onto.

Ghost growled as he closed the files. Diana Corbin was a walking, talking danger zone, and he wasn't stupid enough to wander into it.

No matter how fun it might be to peel off one of those staid pantsuits and discover the delights underneath.

He left the SCIF* and headed for the small gym they'd built in one of the bigger rooms. Nothing like a hard workout to purge an inconvenient attraction for a woman who'd slap him in cuffs if she got the chance.

And not the fun kind, either.

---

* Sensitive compartmented information facility.

2

Every time Diana drove along the short boulevard leading to the town square in Sutton's Creek, she thought about how perfect it was. How charming. The divided road wasn't long, maybe a half mile, but it passed beneath old oaks before spilling into a quaint downtown. The wrought iron streetlamps lining the boulevard were undecorated at the moment, but they'd sported miniature flags during the summer.

She could just imagine what kind of Christmas decorations the town would drape itself with. Wreaths, twinkling lights, maybe some carolers in the town square. She'd heard there would be hayrides and a pumpkin patch at a local farm in October.

Really, it was small town Hallmark movie perfection. And maybe real life wasn't that perfect, but a girl could wish for it anyway.

The Sutton's Creek Independence Day Fest had

certainly been a delight. She'd even approached the One Shot Tactical men and their ladies to say hello. They'd been parked on chairs in front of the Salty Dawg Tavern. The women had been friendly, but the men had darted suspicious looks her way.

Nothing she wasn't accustomed to. Working in a typically male-dominated profession, she'd had time to get used to hostility from the men she worked with. Not all of them, but enough. Not that the One Shot men were openly hostile, but their dislike was clear.

At least they didn't stare at her. Leer like she was an object of lust and not a professional colleague. If she had a dime for every room she'd entered in the course of her job where men thought they had the right to ogle her, smirk, say things about her body and then claim they were only joking... well, it'd be a lot of money.

Her hands tightened on the wheel. She didn't invite the attention. She rarely wore makeup, and definitely not on the job. Her hair was usually in a severe bun or a ponytail. Her suits were tailored, but modest. She wasn't trying *not* to be a woman. She was trying to be taken seriously.

Men didn't have that problem. If you were born with a dick, you were automatically considered more competent at some things.

Like being an FBI agent.

She wrinkled her nose. She'd been dealing with it for years. And maybe she wasn't as good as some of them, maybe she never would be, but she wasn't giving up. She had a purpose, and she wouldn't be deterred.

She'd finished her master's degree after Viktor's assault, barely, but she'd dropped out of the PhD program. When she'd informed her parents she was joining the FBI instead of finishing her doctorate or going to work for a senator or an ambassador, her mother had pressed the strand of pearls around her neck with a gasp of dismay.

"Why on earth would you want to do that, darling? You're an Adler."

"Justice," she'd said.

Justice. That elusive, desirable, addictive thing that got her out of bed every day and made her keep going even when she thought quitting would be easier. It wasn't just about Viktor, though. She wanted justice for everyone harmed by sexual assault—by any assault against their humanity—and though she was only one person and couldn't help everyone, she wouldn't quit trying.

One day, she would succeed in throwing him into prison for the rest of his miserable days.

She was getting closer to finding whoever was trafficking weapons for Viktor in Huntsville. She'd missed a huge opportunity when Jackson O'Malley came to town to sell Stinger missiles and the deal went down prematurely, but there would be other chances to find the people stockpiling weapons. And then, hopefully, stop them before they could sabotage the Athena Project.

Diana pulled into the parking lot behind the Sutton Building, staring at the three-story building with its age-worn brick. Then she dragged in a soothing breath.

She was going to do this. She was going to look at the

apartment for rent, though she considered it a formality, and she was moving to Sutton's Creek. It was a peaceful place, and she craved peace in her life.

Colonel Alex Bishop—sexy, infuriating, intense bastard that he was—would not be happy about it. Like she cared. It was *her* life. She might not ever belong to a tight-knit group like his team and their women, but she wasn't here for them. She was here for her.

He's going to think you did it to keep an eye on them.

Diana stepped onto the pavement and shouldered her purse. Of course being closer to the range and the men who ran it was a bonus for her investigation into Viktor's shady deals. But she'd have made this move even without their presence. Her lease to the apartment near Toyota Field was up, and she was tired of the traffic and hustle.

She wanted quiet. That elusive peace. Small town comfort.

Maybe she should find another small town to seek it in, but Sutton's Creek was perfect. Angels Cove, Sutton's Creek's sister town across the river, was also quaint and beautiful, but too inconvenient for commuting to work. There was no bridge close enough, only a sporadic ferry, and she didn't want to risk it.

Besides, she liked Sutton's Creek. The shops and charm, the historic buildings, the Southern hospitality. The only people who were ever cool and distant with her were the men of One Shot Tactical. She understood why and didn't blame them, but it was sure to make moving to this town a little more difficult.

She squared her shoulders and lifted her chin. Did she honestly care what Alex Bishop thought? What *any* of them thought?

Of course not. She had as much right to live here as they did. They weren't from Alabama either, but they'd made this town their home. She could do the same. There was nothing to stop her.

She selected the number she'd entered into her phone earlier today when she'd called it the first time.

"Hello, Ms. Corbin," a kindly voice said on the second ring.

"Hi, Dr. Sutton. Is this a bad time? I'm outside, but I can come back later—"

"Not at all. My wife is already upstairs, waiting to show you around. Just go up to the third floor and she'll meet you there. The back door is open. I'd join you, but I have a patient in a few moments."

Diana swallowed her apprehension. "I understand. Thank you so much."

"It's our pleasure. I hope you like what you see. If it's not for you, I understand."

"Thank you—but I'm sure it's perfect."

He chuckled. "My wife certainly thinks so. She's the one who knew how she wanted things done. Ask her about the kitchen cabinets. She'll talk your ear off if you do."

Diana laughed. "Sounds delightful."

His voice was warm. "Consider yourself warned. If you need to escape, don't compliment those cabinets. And definitely don't ask her about the floors. You'll be stuck for an hour."

"I'm sure I'll enjoy every moment," she said, and meant it.

She made her way up two flights of stairs, admiring the wooden banisters polished with time, the exposed brick walls. The hallways were wide. There were two apartments on each floor, so only four total since the bottom floor was the doctors' office.

Blaze Connolly and Dr. Emma Grace Sutton lived on the second floor. Someone else had moved into the other second floor apartment recently.

On the third floor, Daphne Bryant—previously known as Josephine O'Malley, the mafia king's daughter—had moved out to live with Kane Fox on the property adjoining One Shot Tactical. Daphne's apartment was available while the other had also recently been rented.

The door was open. Mrs. Sutton was perched on the wide windowsill, scrolling her phone, and Diana was in love.

Not with Mrs. Sutton. With the tall ceilings and original features.

"Oh, hello," Mrs. Sutton said, getting to her feet and coming over to shake Diana's hand. "I'm Ellen."

She was the kind of petite that always made Diana feel like a giant at five-nine. She wore a tailored cotton shirt dress and a hair band to hold back her blond hair, and she was so very pretty. Diana guessed her to be in her late fifties or early sixties, considering Emma's age, but she didn't look it.

"Diana Corbin." The name flowed smoothly from her tongue. It had been a little difficult at first to stop saying Adler, but she'd been using her mother's maiden name for years now. Her parents had been baffled at first. But like most things that didn't directly affect them, they soon got over it.

She'd wanted to succeed at the Bureau on her own merits, not those of her name. When she'd joined, Don Lewis, her dad's best friend from college, wasn't yet the director. But he was highly placed in the organization even then, and she hadn't wanted special favors. He knew she'd joined, because how could he not, but she'd stressed her feelings when they spoke about it. He'd nodded and said, *"You'll do a fine job, Diana. I have faith in you."*

Until Alex Bishop had her reassigned to Kentucky, she'd never once asked for a favor. And then, knowing that Viktor Dashevsky had his eye on Huntsville—but not *why*—she'd broken her own rule and went straight to the top in her quest to return.

"You're very pretty," Ellen said, and Diana blinked.

"Um, thank you."

Ellen laughed. "I'm so sorry. I realize that probably sounds like I'm buttering you up to rent the apartment, but I don't say things I don't mean. Are you new to the area?"

"No," Diana said truthfully. "I work for the FBI on Redstone Arsenal. I want to move somewhere quieter than where I currently live. I've spent some time in Sutton's Creek and I like the town."

"It's a very good place to live," Ellen said. "Historic, quaint, but not too far from Huntsville for commuters." She spread her arms and turned to encompass the large space. "This is a historic building. You would be facing the square here and you'd be able to walk to restaurants and shops. We have one grocery store, the Piggly Wiggly, but you can get to bigger ones if you want to drive a bit farther. We also have a thriving library, and a shooting range if you like that sort of thing. I'd tell you the men there also teach self-defense, but I imagine the FBI does as well. Though if I'm honest, I think most of the women in this town go to One Shot Tactical for the view."

Diana could well imagine. Those were six of the prettiest men she'd ever met. Even if they did glower at her like she was the enemy.

Which she supposed she deserved after the way she'd bulldozed her way into their mission.

Couldn't be helped though. She had a mission of her own, and she wasn't letting a little thing like a grumpy Army colonel derail her. In another world, he'd be the kind of man she was attracted to. Tall, muscled, with crinkles at the corners of his eyes and a bit of gray starting to pepper his dark hair. He was rugged, handsome, and he oozed competence.

All the One Shot men did, but Alex most of all. There were depths behind those pewter gray eyes she could only guess at. If she were honest with herself, he made her weak at the knees every time she was in his presence. Which made her work even harder to pretend she was indifferent to him.

She'd seen his military record. The real one. The things in there—my God, the man was formidable. A hero who wouldn't hesitate to give his life to keep his country safe.

Guilt pricked her. She wanted to succeed on her own merits the way he had. If she didn't have her connections to fall back on, would she be a failure? That's what kept her up at night sometimes, wondering if she'd made the right choices, if she had what it took to stop Viktor.

"We kept the original moldings in here," Ellen was saying as she strode through the apartment.

Diana focused on the tour, dutifully asked about the cabinets and floors, mostly because she liked Ellen's enthusiasm for the details. She was a warm and effusive woman. She seemed like the kind of mother who would hug often and say how much she loved you.

Diana didn't know what that was like, but she envied Emma for it.

"This way to the bedrooms," Ellen said, waving her along.

They toured two bedrooms and two bathrooms before returning to the living room with the wide-open space and the beautiful kitchen at one end.

"I'll take it," Diana said.

Ellen smiled. "That's wonderful, Diana. May I call you Diana?"

"Please. Yes. I'd like that."

"Well, then, I'll have the realtor send you the contract and the details, and you can move in whenever you like. Do you have a moment to come downstairs and meet my husband and daughter?"

Diana's pulse skittered. Emma would waste no time telling Blaze, and that meant Alex would know before she'd walked back to her car.

And she cared why?

She straightened her spine. Screw Alex Bishop and his way of looking at her like he wanted to throw her out whatever door they were closest to. He practically burned with dislike when they were anywhere near each other. It sparked from him with every look, every word. She imagined touching him, imagined that spark turning into a flame and engulfing her.

But, for her, it was flame of a different kind. The kind she felt between her legs and in the points of her nipples.

It was all the more shocking because he was an alpha male, commanding and confident, while she preferred beta males. They were biddable, lacked intensity, and they didn't make her feel like she had no control.

Alex, on the other hand, made her want to surrender.

Her control, her body, her fears. All of it.

Never.

"Yes, I'd love to meet them," she said. "That would be lovely."

3

Ghost was late to the Dawg. His guys were already there, probably knocking back beers and talking about how things had gone wrong that day.

It'd started innocently enough.

Daphne Bryant, their amazing assistant and the love of Kane's life, was determined to create an event space at the range. Ghost had—in a moment of weakness, he fully admitted it—agreed to let her start something small.

He should have asked for her definition of small. That was on him.

Because twenty tables had shown up, with twenty floor-length tablecloths, and what looked like a fucking truckload of flowers. There was also sawdust, twinkling lights strung everywhere, and a stage for a band.

When he'd first walked outside to see what all the noise was about, he'd felt like one of those cartoon characters whose eyes bugged all the way out of his head before snapping back again.

The noise had been a flipping truck dumping sawdust.

When he found Daphne, holding a clipboard and talking to a man in overalls, he'd managed to hold onto his temper. Barely.

But then she smiled at him, her face happy and full of enthusiasm, and he'd reeled his inner raging demon in, stuffing it into the hole it'd crawled out of. Hard to be pissed at Daphne, especially when she still held it over his head that he and Kane had once made an agreement about her life without consulting her.

Namely that Kane wouldn't touch her and fuck things up for the range because she was so damn good at her job and Ghost didn't want to have to find a new assistant when Kane broke her heart. He'd thought it was the right thing to do, but damn if Daphne hadn't let him have it when she found out. He didn't feel ashamed of much, but she'd gotten to him with her talk of infantilizing her and not letting her make her own decisions.

Which is probably why he had a soft spot for her now. Good thing he did, too.

Because there were twenty tables, a truckload of sawdust, twinkling lights, chairs, and an impending event happening tomorrow. When he'd asked Daphne what her definition of a large event was, she hadn't batted an eyelash when she very seriously told him five-hundred people would be a large event.

His guys had all sidled up at one point or another as

Daphne directed the anthill of workers that crawled all over the field near the range, raking sawdust, setting up tables, assembling the stage, and stringing lights.

"Damn, boss," Chance had said with a low whistle.

Kane had started shaking his head. "I swear I didn't know. She didn't tell me. She just said she'd booked a small event and it'd be a great test of her ideas."

Seth had snorted. "Even if she'd told you, you wouldn't have listened. Too busy staring at her a—"

"Don't say it," Kane growled.

"I was gonna say assets, but okay," Seth said with a shrug.

Ghost had to give him points for the save.

"Wait," Blaze said as another truck rumbled into the field. "Is that... are those goats?"

"Uh-oh," Chance said. "If they don't have a plan to keep those goats away from the flowers, this could go wrong real quick."

There was no plan, apparently. And it definitely went wrong. It would have been funny to watch Daphne shooing goats with her clipboard and shouting like a banshee if those fucking goats hadn't been trampling and eating what was certainly an expensive load of flowers.

They were supposed to be milling around in a pen, strictly for photo ops at what Daphne called a Small-Town Brunch Experience (capital letters on her clipboard) tomorrow, but the pen wasn't stout and the goats were determined. There'd been goat shit and the wreckage of flowers everywhere when Ghost left.

Daphne was still there with her hired help, still making calls and dealing with the situation. Kane had tried to stay with her, but she'd kissed him earlier and told him he was distracting her. Ghost stayed behind to deal with his own stuff. Now he was here, walking into the Dawg and trying not to think about one-hundred and sixty-ish women descending on One Shot Tactical for brunch tomorrow morning.

Where the fuck had Daphne found that many women willing to fork over eighty-five bucks a head anyway?

The mood around the table was a lot more somber than he'd expected as he strode over and dragged out a chair.

"Ordered you a beer," Blaze said. "Big Nikki's bringing it."

"Thanks." He looked around. "Where are the ladies? Group bathroom break?"

Blaze shook his head. "Emma's hanging out with Rory."

"Upstairs," Chance added. "Rory thinks she has to go over invoices. Theo tried to tell her he had it under control, but she's been feeling cooped up lately—so if it makes her happy..." He shrugged.

Rory Harper's pregnancy was progressing fine, but she had to be careful and rest. Her diabetes was controlled, and the fetus was healthy at all the checks thus far. But Rory wasn't the sort of woman who liked sitting still for long.

"She's smart," Ghost said. "She knows what she can handle."

"She does," Chance agreed. "Still worry though."

Ghost put a hand on Chance's shoulder and squeezed. "Of course you do. But Dr. Sutton is with her. She won't let anything happen."

"That's what I told him," Blaze said.

"Payz is still at the library," Ethan said when Ghost made eye contact. "Vivi's having a sleepover at Lily Park's house."

Seth took a drink of his beer. "Callie's working on a program for a client. Nik's at cheerleading practice."

"And we know where Daph is," Kane said with a grimace. "Fuck, that was brutal."

"Sorry, man," Chance said. "She'll fix it though."

"She will, but I know she's upset about it going wrong. She wants to prove herself so damn bad."

"She doesn't need to." Ghost accepted his beer with a wink when Big Nikki sidled up. She grinned and winked back before sashaying away. "We know she's good at what she does. Hell, she's damn good at talking me into shit before I even know what I agreed to."

The other guys laughed and made noises of agreement. Ghost was about to read over the specials when a familiar blonde walked into the Dawg from the back entrance. His gut twisted even as his balls tightened.

Fucking hell.

Diana Corbin found a table against the wall where she

could sit with her back to it and survey most of the room while she picked up a menu and looked it over.

"So," Blaze said. "Got some interesting news from Emma when I got home."

Ghost dragged his attention from the shining blond head and back to his friends around the table. Blaze was watching him warily. The hairs on the back of his neck prickled.

"What is it? Bad news doesn't get better with time."

Blaze forced a smile. "Emma told me somebody rented Daph's old apartment today."

"So? Isn't that good?"

The other guys studied their beers. Ghost's twitchy feeling intensified.

Blaze grimaced as he rubbed the back of his neck. "You'd think so, sure. But it's, uh…" He jerked his head in the direction of Diana.

Ghost's insides turned to ice. Well, why the hell not? This was just one more pile of shit on the shit sandwich this day was turning into. "You're fucking kidding me. She's moving to Sutton's Creek? Into your building?"

"Yeah. Emma's mom gave her the tour and Diana said she'd take it. She's moving in next week."

"For fuck's sake," Ghost grumbled.

Not that he cared what Diana did, but she was as persistent as a bloodhound. They were working on the same side these days—correction, they'd always been on the same side. But Diana hadn't known what the Ghost Ops mission was until she'd used her family connections to find out. Now she thought she could demand information at will.

When she'd found out they'd been surveilling Brent Gannon, the retired Air Force colonel with the sketchy background, she'd wanted to know everything. Since they hadn't learned much of anything, other than the guy liked beer and babes, he'd told her. Then he'd told her to go watch the fucker herself if she wanted more.

She'd glared daggers at him before she'd left his office that day. It was the last time she'd dropped in unannounced. He'd thought she'd found something better to do.

But this? Moving to Sutton's Creek? She'd be up his ass all the time.

And that was *not* what he needed right now. Not when he was about to do something he wasn't authorized to do.

He picked up his beer and made his way to her table, his gut churning with simmering frustration. Damn woman had no right getting involved. He didn't want her in his op, didn't need her in it.

They were a spec-ops team, the best of the best, and he didn't want to be worried about the FBI screwing anything up. Or about Diana Fucking Corbin getting into a situation she wasn't prepared for.

Not that he didn't think she wasn't well-trained, but nobody was trained the way a special operator was. Through the years, he and his teams had been sent into foreign locations to rescue alphabet agency employees at least once a year, which didn't give him confidence.

Because when those alphabet people got their asses into trouble and couldn't get out, who did it for them?

SEALs. Delta Force. The Hostile Operations Team.

He didn't want to have to do it with her. Didn't want her in the way and didn't want her distracting him.

Especially now.

She must have sensed him because she looked up from her menu, her eyes darting over him apprehensively before she managed to drape herself in that icy mantle she wore like a second skin.

He dragged out a chair and sat. "Why are you here?" he growled.

She blinked. "Hello to you, too."

He ignored her.

She broke eye contact first. "I'm getting a burger if you must know. What does it look like?"

"Not what I mean, Diana."

Her blue eyes flared. Her chin tipped up like she was a debutant at a ball and he was the hired help. "It's a free country, colonel."

His body went rigid. "Don't. Not here."

A flush crossed her face. She knew she'd fucked up. "Fine. Alex then."

"Better," he grated. But was it really? Because the way she said his name was like a soft stroke across his senses. He wanted her to say it again. And he wanted her to go away.

"I assume you're talking about my new apartment." She set the menu down and folded her hands on the table.

"I like this town. I don't like where I live now. Too noisy and busy. My lease is up, and I needed a change. Satisfied?"

"No. Not in the least. I don't trust you."

Was that hurt that flashed across her features?

"Trust who you like. It doesn't affect me. We're on the same side, but you go ahead and be all growly and mean if it makes you feel better. I'm not here for you. I'm here for me."

Before he could respond, Amber materialized out of the crowd to take Diana's order. She asked for water and the special cheeseburger with truffle fries and aioli.

"And you, Alex?" Amber turned to him with an expectant look. "You want to order something too?"

"I'm at the usual table, but sure. That gonna mess you up?"

"Nope. I'll deliver it wherever you're sitting when it comes out."

"Thanks. Then give me the steak. Medium rare."

"You want to change the sides or are the potatoes and salad good?"

"They're perfect. Did Theo make his special ranch dressing?"

"The smoky one? Yep. You want extra?"

"Always."

When Amber was gone, he met Diana's gaze. She was as cool as ever, naturally. Something inside him wanted to shatter that cool. He wanted to see her burn. For him.

No. Definitely not.

"How's life at the FBI?" he asked.

She drew in a breath. "Fine."

He waited but she didn't say anything else. Had to admire that. He'd learned in training that silences were uncomfortable and the best way to get someone to talk was not to speak first. She'd probably had the same training.

He decided to concede. "Sounds exciting."

She snorted. He thought she probably didn't mean to because she blinked. Then she smoothed her features into the same careful mask she always wore. Shrugged.

"Terribly."

"Care to elaborate?"

"No."

He sipped his beer. "You're full of sunshine, aren't you?"

"And you aren't?"

"Sometimes. Not today."

"And not with me. I get it. You don't like me, Alex. I don't like you either. But we've got an important task to accomplish, and I'm not about to let your bad attitude stop me from doing it."

"No, *we* don't have anything to accomplish. I do. Whatever you've got going on is peripheral to my task. And I think you know by now that I'm not letting you get in my way. So don't try it, Agent Corbin."

She spread her hands. "I'm here to eat, not argue with you. If you're going to keep glaring and threatening, then you can march right back to your friends and leave me out of it. I didn't ask for this and I'm not putting up with it. You aren't the first man to try and intimidate me and you won't be the last. So be nice or go away. Those are your choices."

The last thing he should be feeling in that moment was turned on. But damn if he didn't like her fire. She displayed it so rarely that it was always a surprise.

He leaned back in his chair and folded his arms over his chest. Diana's gaze dropped before snapping back up again. Ghost chuckled on the inside. Most women couldn't resist that move. Emphasized the size and definition of a man's arms and chest. He resisted the urge to flex, but only barely.

"I tried to be nice. Asked about your job and everything. You gave me monosyllabic answers."

"I'm not the one who started glaring and demanding answers to questions I don't have a right to ask."

"Not this time. But you demand answers all the time."

She waved a hand at him. "You're giving me a headache."

He scraped his chair back and stood, snagged his beer. "I'll leave. Happy to work with you when it's mutually beneficial—but don't think moving to town's going to get you invited to join every conversation I have with my boys."

She gave him an exaggerated frown. "Aw, and here I thought we were going to be such great friends. Cookouts, sleepovers, reindeer games. Now I'm sad."

Like hell she was. And now she had him thinking about sleepovers, damn her.

"Stay out of my business, Diana. That's all."

"Heard you loud and clear, Fred."

"Fred?"

Amber dropped off a water and shot him one of her flirty grins before heading to the next table. Diana picked up her drink and sipped daintily from the straw.

"Flintstone," she finally said. "A famous cartoon caveman from the sixties, I believe. Since you seem to think telling a woman what to do in a growly voice is all it takes to make her heed your command." She tilted her head to the side. "Or maybe Conan the Barbarian is more like it. Which do you prefer?"

He wanted to kiss that smart mouth, shock her into speechlessness. Probably shock himself too, come to think of it. "Guess you do have a sense of humor. Who knew?"

She shrugged. "I'm full of surprises."

"That's what I'm afraid of, ma'am. Enjoy your dinner."

He tipped an imaginary hat and walked away before she got even further beneath his skin than she already had.

Before he really did kiss her right here in front of God and everybody.

4

Diana didn't mind eating alone. She was used to it, but the chaotic energy of the Salty Dawg Tavern—all the people laughing, talking, and eating—made her feel like she was on the outside looking in. She'd picked a table in the corner, against the wall, for a reason, and she watched now with all the hunger of someone eager to be invited in but knowing they didn't fit.

She'd rented the apartment and she was moving to town, but maybe she was wrong about how it was going to make her feel to live here. Maybe she'd always be the outsider, her face pressed to the window, wanting to belong to the happy group on the other side.

The town wouldn't embrace her. She wouldn't walk into Miss Mary's diner and be greeted like a local. Nobody at the Dawg would know her regular order. Paisley Allen wouldn't call to tell her the book she'd wanted had arrived at the library. She wouldn't be invited to join the altar guild at the First Methodist church, and nobody would ask her to bake a cake for the annual bake sale.

She pushed her burger away, her stomach suddenly churning too much to finish it. Why did she do this to herself? Why did she build up a happy future in her head only to tear it down again and again?

Joel had accused her of pulling him in only to push him away. Repeatedly. Until he'd finally broken up with her. She'd thought he'd be back, but he hadn't been. He hadn't called. She hadn't called him either.

And, really, she didn't want to. Yes, she was lonely. But Joel had never been a serious boyfriend, even if he'd wanted to be. He was FBI, too, but he worked a desk as an analyst. He wasn't a field officer. When she saw him at work these days, he was polite. Distant. Like they'd never been naked together.

They could have made it work, probably, if she'd been different. She had trouble letting anyone in. Trouble believing she could have the things other people did.

Love. Happiness. A man who worshipped the ground she walked on same as she did for him.

She was damaged. Viktor had done that for her. And not just him, not really.

The way she grew up, with parents who didn't know how to show love, hadn't helped at all. She'd always tried to earn more crumbs of affection from them, but it'd never been enough. Now she just accepted that some people didn't get what they craved from others.

She sipped her water and watched the Ghost Ops table beneath her lashes. Alex didn't look her way again. He sat with his buddies, eating and laughing at something someone said. The women joined them until the table was full and the laughter was continuous.

She envied them for the friendship they had. For the relationships. She'd never been that close to anyone. She'd grown up going to a private girl's school, and then she'd entered college and been too busy with her studies and the Adler Foundation's charitable work to nurture rela-tionships with women her age. Maybe if she'd had a friend, she wouldn't have been alone when she attended Viktor's speech. Wouldn't have gone to dinner alone, wouldn't have gone to his apartment.

So many *wouldn'ts*, and she didn't know if she was right or it was simply wishful thinking. Mostly, she didn't think about it, but when the loneliness got to her deep in her soul, she let all her sorrow leak into her brain.

She needed to pay her bill and go home, start orga-nizing boxes for the move. She didn't have a lot of stuff, but she had enough. A couple of antiques she'd gotten from her grandmother. Some artworks. Books. She really loved books.

She waved at Amber until the waitress walked over to her table. She didn't look exactly hostile, but she didn't look friendly either.

"You need anything else, hon?"

"No, just the bill. Thanks."

"Sure thing." She slapped the tray with the slip onto

the table and moved away before Diana could get her credit card out. Then she swung back by and picked up the tray without a word. Diana took out her phone and checked her messages.

The laughter from the Ghost Ops table reached her in her corner, and her heart squeezed.

Really? Was she that pitiful she had to envy other people instead of finding her own friends?

She sucked in a breath and let it out. Yes, she was that pitiful. She didn't have friends. Not really. She had Ackerman—her partner—and she'd had Joel. Women didn't like her because she was too much like her mother, too distant and reserved, and most men only wanted to get into her panties.

Amber dropped off her receipt with a pen and said, "Have a nice day, ma'am," before moving on again.

Diana wrote in a big tip and scribbled her signature, then got to her feet to make her way to the rear parking lot. The back hallway was blocked by a group of men waiting to snag a table. Four big men around age thirty or so, talking loudly and leering at the waitresses and other women standing nearby.

An odor of beer emanated from their midst. Not overwhelming, but enough to know they'd been drinking.

Four pairs of eyes homed in on her like lasers as she approached. Sliding down her body and back up again.

Diana sighed. Men like them didn't frighten her. They were pack animals, filled with testosterone, and clearly trying to outdo each other.

"Hey, baby," the cockiest one said when she reached them. "Where you going?"

"Home," she said mildly, despite the churning anger in the pit of her stomach. "Care to get out of the way?"

She looked pointedly at the hallway behind him. His gaze was insolent, sliding up and down her body. He grinned. "Now, honey, no need to be so uptight. Come party with us for a while, let me loosen you up. You'll feel better, promise."

"Thanks, but no."

He laughed and looped a hand around her upper arm as if he didn't hear her. She batted it away. His expression changed from friendly to confused, and then angry in a heartbeat. Like so many men, he thought he was entitled to touch her because he was being *friendly*. Because, so long as he smiled, he wasn't being aggressive or inconsiderate or presumptive at all.

"No need to be such a bitch about it. I'm just trying to be nice."

Diana glared. She was tall, but he topped her by about four inches. "You aren't being nice, dude. You're being misogynistic and entitled, and you need to check your attitude. Women don't want to be leered at. They don't want you to grope them or tell them to be nice because you're nice. And none of them want to be called *baby* or *honey* when you've never met before and you don't even know their fucking names."

His eyes had grown wide. His buddies' eyes were

wide. The people nearby had stopped talking to dart their gazes between her and this idiot.

She had hopes that he'd get it. That he'd apologize for calling her *baby* and *honey* and trying to touch her.

But of course that was never how it was going to go.

His expression hardened. And then he stepped forward, into her space. "Somebody needs to teach you a lesson about talking back, you know that?"

She tipped her head back to look up at him. "Oh yeah? You think it's going to be you, huh?"

He grabbed one of her arms and dragged her over to the wall so her back was to it.

"Hey, man, let her go," somebody said. "That's not cool."

"When does the lesson start?" she whispered, her eyes locked with his.

"Right fucking now, bitch."

"Oh goody, I'm so thrilled."

He started to move again, presumably to drag her into the darkened hallway, but he never made it. Diana did what she'd been trained to do. She took the bastard down to the floor with a knee to his balls, hooking a leg behind his knees to finish him, and a twist of his wrist to neutralize him further.

When he lay on the floor gasping in pain, she glared at his buddies. "Anybody else?"

The other men were red-faced, angry, but they were smart enough not to pursue it. "You made your point," one of them said.

Had she though? Men like these would never understand why they weren't entitled to a woman's rapt attention and enthusiastic agreement to their demands.

Diana looked at the jerk on the floor. She dropped his wrist and he cradled it to his body, glaring at her.

"Never touch a woman without her permission, *baby,*" she growled. "Or bad things can happen."

The women nearby started to clap. Diana flushed. When she turned to find the purse that'd fallen off her shoulder, she collided with a hard male chest. Six-foot-three inches of pure alpha male gazed down at her with a thunderous look on his face. Alex Bishop held out a hand, her purse dangling from it.

"Thank you," she said, shouldering the strap and holding tight to the bag like it was a lifeline. Because of the way he made her tremble inside, not because of the four assholes grumbling and shooting her looks.

A little voice told her to take him home, get him naked, and let him do his worst. That would cure this itch she got whenever she was near him. Or it'd make it worse.

A possibility she wasn't willing to risk.

"You're welcome. I thought I was coming to rescue you. Got here a little late, but to be fair you dropped him rather quickly."

She tipped her chin up. "Thanks for the thought, but I'm capable of rescuing myself."

"I see that." His gaze was hot and mysterious as it raked over her. "That was... masterful."

Her flush deepened. Thankfully, it was dark enough

she didn't think he could tell. "Thank you. I think. Though maybe I should be insulted that you sound so surprised."

"Yeah, maybe you should. Got to admit I wasn't expecting it."

"Again, this feels like an insult."

He grinned, and her heart turned over. Why did he have to be so damned gorgeous? She was a moth dancing too close to the flame, but it was warm and glowy and it felt good.

"Yeah," he said a bit sheepishly. "Sorry about that. You've just always seemed like a woman who doesn't like to get her hands dirty."

She rolled her eyes, falling back on humor because it was the only way to keep him from seeing more than she wanted him to see. "Oh boy, Alex Bishop, you're really digging a hole here, you know. First the performance at my table when I was minding my own business and now this."

"I know. I'm delightful that way. Come join us for a drink?"

She wanted to. She imagined being invited into their group, being accepted. But she knew how it would go. The awkward silences from the men. The resentful looks. "I need to get home. Long day."

"Okay. Then let me walk you to your car." He held up a hand before she could tell him no. "Not because you can't take care of yourself, killer. But those boys are pissed and back up is never a bad thing. I'll be your Agent Ackerman for a few minutes, watch your six."

She didn't know how to refuse without sounding ungrateful or, worse, willfully stupid. "Thanks."

He held out a hand to indicate she should go first. "After you, ma'am."

Diana clutched her bag tighter and led the way.

5

host followed Diana out the back door of the Dawg and down the steps to the parking lot, fighting his swelling cock the whole way. Why the fuck was he so turned on? He taught women how to take down guys bigger than they were all the time. It was nothing new to see it happen.

But the way she'd so coolly looked the guy in the face and then slaughtered his pride would be etched in Ghost's brain for weeks. Like butter wouldn't melt in her mouth.

He'd gotten up to head her direction when she'd slapped a hand away from her body, but he hadn't realized the situation would turn so quickly. Or that she'd drop the douchebag like the sack of shit he was before Ghost could even reach her side.

He'd seen red when the asshole pushed her into the wall. He'd nearly been there, ready to break some bones, when suddenly she was in motion. Boom, boom, boom. Man on the floor, buddies in shock, Diana in control.

She'd gazed at those men with enough ice to freeze the surface of the sun, and they'd shrunk from it the moment they realized what she was capable of.

He wondered what had made her so cold. What had happened to her? Or was it just the way rich people were raised? Probably all that time in drawing rooms with government officials and foreign ambassadors. Learning which spoon to use, whether to curtsy or not, if it was long gloves or short ones—or none—for the opera that night. Things he didn't give a shit about, but which had probably been a part of her life for years.

The air was a little cooler tonight. A cold front had moved in, but it wasn't enough to stop the daily temps from reaching the eighties. Just enough to make nights bearable.

The parking lot was crowded because it was Friday. Voices carried over the cars as people arrived. It was dusk, the light fading quickly, the sky a brilliant salmon and purple to the west. He easily caught up to Diana. She marched forward like she was on a mission, and he kept pace with her.

"You have to do that often?" he asked.

She shot him a glance. "What? Drop grown men to the floor?" She snorted. "Not as often as they deserve, probably."

"What did you say to him?"

"Which time?"

"When he backed you into the wall."

"He said somebody needed to teach me a lesson. I asked when the lesson started. Then I put him on the floor when he tried to pull me into the hallway."

"You damaged his pride. He won't forget it."

"He was warned. I asked them to stop blocking the exit, but men like that don't listen. If he tries again, the same will happen."

"Probably should have shown him your badge so he doesn't try to fuck with you again. Rednecks like that won't respect you, but they will respect that you're a Fed."

"I was a little busy, Alex. Seemed like a moot point by the time you handed me my purse. He comes at me again, I'll make sure he knows." She strode up to a navy-blue BMW and unlocked the doors with a click before turned to face him. "Though I shouldn't have to use a badge to get a man to leave me alone, should I?"

"No, you shouldn't. But it's smart to use it with people like that."

Her jaw worked. "Next time. Thanks for the escort. You're right that back up was smart."

Ghost pushed his hands in his pockets. It was that or touch her, and he already knew she could kneecap him. "You're welcome. You sure you don't want that drink?"

She snorted. "Positive. Didn't you just tell me earlier that you don't like me and to stay away from your guys?"

Shame dug into him. "I was pissed."

"Because I rented an apartment in Sutton's Creek. I remember."

He rubbed the back of his neck. "I don't trust people when my team's safety's at stake. Not you and not anyone. It's not personal."

She nodded, two spots of color high in her pretty cheeks. He'd only just noticed because the lights in the parking lot buzzed to life, illuminating her beneath the glow.

"Suspicion is part of our nature. It's what makes us good at the job." She sighed, looked past him like she was staring at some far-off thing on the horizon. "I respect what you're doing. I know it's important. It's not my intent to interfere with the successful completion of what you came to do. But I've got my own thing I need to do, too. I'm not just ping-ponging between targets with no plan. I'm competent, and I'm good. I won't stand in your way. But please don't get in mine either."

Again, he wondered what had made her this way. Woman like her should be soft and pampered, but she wasn't. Not that he thought women needed to be soft or pampered unless they wanted to be, but in his experience it took a rough kind of life to turn someone into the type of hard ass he'd become.

Guess being wealthy didn't guarantee an easy life after all. Or maybe some people were just wired to be hard.

"Not the plan," he told her.

"Good."

She opened the car door and he grasped it while she sank into the leather interior. She gazed up at him, a wounded look on her face. Or maybe he imagined it since it was gone in an instant.

"Thanks for coming to rescue me. It was nice of you."

"Unnecessary though," he said softly.

She smiled and electricity zipped through him. What would it feel like to lose himself in her? To slide into her body, her arms and legs wrapping around him, and let go of all the pent up frustration he'd held onto for the past few months?

"It was. But still nice of you."

He had the oddest urge to bend down and take her mouth with his. He straightened instead. Pushed the door closed. She didn't break eye contact for a long minute. Then she turned her head, started the car, and drove away without looking at him again.

6

aphne poked her head into his office. "Diana Corbin's here to see you, Alex."

His gut tightened. He hadn't seen Diana since that night at the Dawg over a week ago, but he'd thought about her. Specifically, he'd thought about the look in her eyes when she'd said she had her own mission.

She'd always been reserved, but that night was different. Maybe it was the adrenaline surge from kicking the ass of a big man who'd crossed her, but there'd been emotion in her voice. He wasn't accustomed to that coming from her.

Made him think about her a lot lately. Not only the emotion, but the absolute turn on it'd been to realize she'd taken down a man twice her size and hadn't broken a sweat.

He'd be lying if he said he hadn't availed himself of the charms of his own hand a few times since. Always while thinking of her, wondering how much heat lay beneath that layer of ice. Wondering what made her tick, and why she was such a contrast beneath the surface.

"You mean she didn't follow you down the hall like she usually does?" he asked, dragging his mind from thoughts of a white-hot Diana in the nude. Wearing a gun.

Jesus.

"Nope, not this time," Daphne said, oblivious. "She's waiting in the conference room. Didn't even argue with me about it."

"Wonders never cease, I suppose."

Daphne gave him an exaggerated smile as she stepped into his office, her chest puffing with pride. "You mean like how I pulled off that brunch after a disastrous beginning and made a buttload of cashola in the process?"

Ghost snorted. "Yeah, like that. Didn't I already congratulate you on the save? Pretty sure I've mentioned it every day this week."

Daphne batted her eyelashes. Too funny, this woman. Kane was a lucky man, though he already knew it. "You have, but a girl never tires of hearing how indispensable she is."

"I feel like you're setting me up for an even bigger favor at some point soon." Ghost got to his feet and came around the desk. "What does Kane see in you anyway? You're a giant pain in the ass."

Daphne laughed. "First things first—I did all of *you* a

favor with that event. And second, maybe he likes a little butt play. You ever think of that?"

"Jesus. I'm sorry I asked."

"Butt play?" Kane had magically appeared in the door. He looked confused and Ghost had to hold back a guffaw. That's what happened when you walked in on a conversation you weren't a part of. Though Daphne had probably known he was close by when she said it.

"Honey buns." Daphne whirled around and stood on tiptoe to kiss his cheek. "I was just telling Alex here how much you loooove you some butt play. You like a little pain in your ass, right?"

Kane sputtered. "What the fuck, Daph? I do *not* want pain in my ass. I don't want *any*thing in my ass."

"Relax." Ghost laughed because damn, why not? "I said she was a pain in the ass and I didn't know what you saw in her. She said you liked butt play."

Daphne snorted. "You guys are so much *fun*. It's ridiculously easy to wind you up."

Kane growled. "Daphne, swear to God I'm gonna spank *your* ass one of these days."

"Promises, promises, Grandpa."

Ghost held up a hand. "I don't even want to know what kind of crazy shit you people get up to, but don't do it here. Take it back to your house if you're getting kinky. I'm going to find out what Diana wants."

The sound of muffled gunfire came from the range as he strolled through the building. The door to the conference room was open and Diana stood at one end, looking out the window that had a view of the field and two farmhouses beyond. The old Johnson farm belonged to Ghost and his men on paper, but it didn't really. The money for it came from the US Government, and they were going to want it back when this was over.

He'd miss the place, but he tried not to think about all the things that would happen when the mission was done. Mostly because it wasn't finished yet. The timeline might be rapidly shrinking, but success wasn't a guarantee until Athena was live and doing the important job it'd been assigned to do.

Diana turned when he tapped on the door frame to warn her he'd arrived. She moved away from the window, and he got his first good look at her without the light turning her into a dark shadow against the glass.

His tongue felt thick in his mouth as he took her in. She wasn't wearing one of her FBI uniforms, aka her plain pantsuits, today. He'd seen her in jeans when she'd been off duty, but he'd never seen her like this.

In a loose white t-shirt and black leggings. She was also wearing a pair of sneakers, which he was pretty sure he'd thought she didn't own, and her hair wasn't tightly controlled for a change. It was perched on top of her head in a messy knot, strands of silky blond dangling around her face. Like she'd been interrupted while working out and came racing over here without changing.

"To what do I owe the pleasure today?" His voice was a growl, but he couldn't seem to help it. She'd been in his head too much lately. He didn't like it. Didn't like seeing her face or imagining her body beneath the tailored pantsuits every time he closed his eyes.

Her eyes flashed with anger. "Pleasure? I'm pissed, asshole."

His gaze narrowed. It wasn't just her eyes. Her cheeks were flushed, and so was the exposed skin of her clavicle. Her shoulder appeared as her t-shirt slipped down. He saw her bra strap, the hint of lace. He was riveted. Took him a moment to drag his gaze back to hers.

"What about?"

"Like you don't know," she grated.

He held out his hands, palms up. "I don't. What the fuck are you talking about?"

She closed the distance between them until he could smell her. Lavender. Roses. A hint of sweat.

Fucking intoxicating.

She stuck a finger in his face. "You did this. Somehow, you did it."

He shook his head, torn between fascination at her passion and bewilderment. "You have to tell me what it is I did. Spell it out, Diana, because I'm at a loss here."

She whirled from him with a growl. Put distance between them. Popped her hands on her hips, tilted her head back and yelled a few choice words.

He was utterly fascinated. And alarmed. He moved to close the door. Kane, Daphne, Blaze, and Chance tumbled from the hall at the back, probably because of the yelling. They crashed to a stop when they saw him. Ghost shook his head and closed the door. Then he turned back to the enraged woman standing on the other side of the table.

"Okay, Agent. Tell me in clear terms what the fuck I did to piss you off so much."

"Don called me."

"Don?" It took him a second, mostly because he was so fascinated by her anger. The fire of it. The way she was lit from the inside and ready to spark into a roaring flame. Just like his fantasies, only those featured less anger and more passion.

"Oh, yeah," he drawled when he understood. "Uncle Don, your good family friend. And that's my problem why?"

Her jaw clenched. "I've been told to leave the subject of the Dashevsky Group, the weapons, the militia—and most especially the *project*—alone and concentrate my efforts on other things more in line with my position and rank in the organization."

"I see."

"I bet you do."

She could have bit a railroad spike in two. It was arousing as fuck to see her so pissed. And it bothered him, too. Because she was passionate about her work, and she was being told she wasn't on the case anymore. He knew how that could feel, but before he could think of something suitable to say, she kept going.

"I was told to leave the investigation to you and—" She waved her hand in the general direction of the range. "Your people."

And now it was coming clear. The reason she was here. The reason she was angry. "You think I got you removed from the case."

"Didn't you? Wouldn't be the first time."

"Not this time, no."

She popped her arms over her chest. "I don't believe you."

"Believe what you like, sweetheart, but it wasn't me."

Her eyes narrowed at the endearment. Maybe he shouldn't have done it, but her reactions were quickly becoming an addiction.

"Well, *sweetheart,*" she shot back. "Who else could it be?"

"I don't fucking know, but if I got you removed from this mission—again—I wouldn't care if you knew it was me. What are you gonna do? Drop me with a knee to the balls as you sweep my legs out from under me?"

"I'd love to," she growled.

He stepped around the table until there was nothing between them but a few feet of space. "So do it. Come and drop me. If you can."

Her nostrils flared and he could tell she was considering it. In the end, he knew she wouldn't. Her shoulders deflated, her spine curving inward in defeat.

She continued to glare, though. "I really, *really* hate you. All that nice guy stuff when it suits you, cooperating with me, taking information I gave you to do your job— demanding I fix things for Daphne so she could stay here with Kane. Argh!" She spun away and threw her arms out before facing him again, hands on hips. "I did that to be nice, because it was clear they had feelings for each other and I didn't want to see them torn apart. I wanted to *help* you, all of you, because I know you're doing an impossible job. But you hate me. You've said it from the first, and you've never wanted to work with me. Only for what you could get out of me, not because you trusted me or respected me or thought I could be a good partner for what you're doing."

"Diana—"

"No," she grated. Her cheeks were pink, her eyes flashed, and her messy bun was listing to one side. "Don't make excuses. Don't lie to me and tell me you appreciated my help, or that you don't actually hate me. None of you like me. I can see it every time I'm here. Or when I see you at the Dawg, or the Independence Day festival. The way you look at me—"

She shook her head. All he could do was watch her, stunned and, yeah, probably a little bit ashamed too. Because he'd openly talked of disliking her, his men didn't like her either. None of them were friendly to her. He'd never encouraged it, but he hadn't actively discouraged it either.

Asshole.

Yeah, he had been. And he wasn't proud of himself right now. Not when she seemed hurt by it. He'd have sworn she didn't have feelings, but he knew better. Everybody had them. Sometimes they just buried them beneath a mountain of pain that made them seem numb on the outside.

He should know.

"Fuck," she muttered, slicing a hand beneath her eyes, wiping away the tears that'd glistened there only a moment before. Making him feel even worse than he already did. Pond scum was a higher form of life than he was. Pond scum wouldn't make this woman cry for no good reason other than she irritated him.

"Diana." His voice was rough.

She shook her head. "It's okay, colonel. Alex. I'm used to it. You don't have to apologize for not liking me. It's my problem, not yours. I'm not likable. I get it. I was born with a silver spoon and all the advantages, and most people don't like that. Especially in a job like this where they think I don't care, that I'm just playing around, and I can leave as soon as it's not fun anymore. Slumming down in the trenches." She blew out a breath. "But doing this to me? Taking this case away from me? You have no idea what you've cost me."

He could handle it when she growled and accused and hated. He was helpless against her despair.

"I didn't do it. I swear to you on my oath as an officer in the United States Army that I didn't get you taken off the case. If I had, I damn sure wouldn't hide it."

She frowned at him for a long while before deflating even further. He had the strongest urge to wrap her in his arms. "I think I believe you. But it doesn't matter. You're still happy I'm out of your way."

He huffed a breath, thinking of what to say. But he would tell the truth because she deserved that much.

"Not gonna lie and say I'm not glad you won't be poking around in my business. You're right about that. I've got a job to do, and I don't need the distraction of you and your investigation getting in the way. There's too much at stake here. Not just for the world, but for my men too. Our lives are on the line, and though I know you're competent and determined, you aren't an operator. You have no idea the trouble you cause me just by demanding to be included. I can't spend time I don't have thinking about what you're going to do, worrying how it's gonna affect us here. So, yeah, I'm happy. But I'm not happy you're upset."

She scoffed. "You don't care how I feel about it. You're probably having a party inside, can't wait to tell your guys. All of you swaggering into the Dawg later, laughing about me getting thrown off the investigation." She drew herself up, her spine straightening, eyes flashing with determination and fury. "Go ahead and laugh. Have your fun. I'm out for now, but I'm never out for good."

She breezed past him on her way to the door. It was everything he could do not to reach for her.

When she got to the door, she turned to look at him. "I've read your file—the real one—and I know you're one of the good guys. So trust me when I tell you that Viktor Dashevsky wants the project. What's going on with the militia is tied to that. If he gets control... Well, it won't be good, I promise you that."

His belly tightened. "I don't intend to let that happen."

"I know. I could help you, but I have a feeling you won't accept my participation, especially since I'd be going against the orders I was given. But if you change your mind, you know where I live."

There was nothing he could say. Because she was right, he wasn't going to let her into his mission. What he was doing now was too dangerous. He hadn't involved his team and he wasn't involving her.

Because if it came crashing down, he intended to be the only casualty.

7

One month later...

Diana drove down the long dirt road, searching for the turn off, her heart thumping the closer she got.

Was she really doing this? Was she really attempting to join Viktor's followers? To become one of them?

Yes, she was. This gathering on a remote farm was a recruiting event, and she'd managed to get invited by a guy who'd been trying to get in her pants. He'd wanted to ride together, but she'd said she had to work and she'd meet him there. Thankfully, he'd texted her burner an hour ago to say he'd been called in for a shift and he wouldn't be there after all. One less thing to worry about.

She didn't know exactly what she was looking for today, but she hoped to be invited back—and not by the guy trying to get in her pants. Nobody would openly talk about the real plan at this gathering, and she suspected there would probably be just as many people present for the shooting and partying as for the real cause.

Disgruntled people became converts, and converts were what Viktor's movement wanted. She had no doubt he had his own people watching and sorting through the prospective members, deciding who had staying power.

Who could be groomed. Turned.

You shouldn't be doing this.

It wasn't the first time she'd heard that voice in her head, and it probably wouldn't be the last.

But what choice did she have? She'd been told to leave the investigation alone, that it was shifting to Washington where they had more resources to spare, that they were happy with all she'd done, *thankyouverymuch*, but it was time to move on.

A delicate matter, Don had said when he'd called her out of the blue. *You understand,* he'd said. *You're a fine officer, and we're proud of you, Diana. But this one has to be handled with kid gloves.*

Because Viktor was rich and powerful, and most of the world thought him a good man with his charitable organization. He gave money to causes, and she had no doubt some of his causes were sitting in the US House and Senate. And they were eager to protect him. It only took one of them to make a call to the FBI and demand her investigation stop.

Diana dragged in a breath. It'd been a long month since she'd been told to stand down. A long month since she'd bolted to One Shot Tactical and practically had a meltdown. Alex had been utterly unmoved by her emotional outburst, but in the end she'd believed him when he said it wasn't him who'd gotten her taken off the case.

She might never know who'd made the call, but she wasn't letting an anonymous asshole protect yet another rich man who thought he was untouchable.

She'd played the game in the weeks since, gone to work every day, did the mundane things she'd been asked to do. She'd moved into the Sutton building, but she never went to the Dawg when Alex or his friends were there. She saw Emma sometimes. Emma was a bubbly, friendly person and she invited Diana for drinks, but she always found a way to refuse.

She knew Emma only did it because she was kind, raised by a kind mother and father, but Blaze wouldn't want Diana in their home. So she said no.

Now she was out here on her own, deep in the wilds of Alabama, looking for a gathering of the Dashevsky Group's followers. Nobody knew what she was doing. She hadn't told her partner, and she certainly hadn't told anyone in her chain of command.

Not after the spectacular blow up she'd had in the director's office recently. A blow up that'd resulted in some enforced time off, in fact.

Now she was just a woman with time on her hands, driving around looking for a farm where some folks were getting together to shoot and then party. She didn't think she was in danger, but if she managed to get deeper into the organization after today, she could be. Depended on how deeply they looked into her background.

And whether or not Viktor took a personal interest in this particular group.

She found the turn and continued through the woods. The trees were turning, the leaves a brilliant orange, yellow, and brown. In Sutton's Creek, they were preparing for the Fall Founder's Fest and Halloween. Colleen Wright, proprietor of The Mystic Chick with her friend Reba, was in her element these days. She wore black exclusively and gave cemetery walking tours, intoning the scary parts in a deep and sonorous voice before doing something silly like screaming.

Once, Reba had fallen into an open grave, and that resulted in a lot more screaming than usual. Diana heard all about it at Miss Mary's Diner the next morning as people snorted into their coffee and tutted about the poor dear. Colleen tried to pretend it'd been on purpose, but the fact Reba refused to go on the next few walking tours told another story.

At least according to Miss Mary. It was never dull in Sutton's Creek, that's for sure.

Diana drove into a small valley, her heart squeezing at the sight of all the cars parked there. She could still turn around. It wasn't too late. Maybe she should have told Ackerman what she was doing. He was older than she was. Not enough to be her father, but he was fatherly to her despite being recently divorced—again—and dating. She liked him. He didn't leer or make snide remarks. He treated her like a partner should be treated, and he smoothed the way on the job by being far more personable with people than she was capable of.

If she'd told him what she was doing, she risked fatherly disapproval—and she risked tainting him with guilt by association. He'd already moved on from chasing after illegal weapons and proving a militia connection to Viktor Dashevsky. He didn't know she hadn't let it go. That she couldn't.

She parked and steeled her nerves, then opened her door and stepped onto the grass. She'd worn jeans and hiking boots, a flannel shirt over a black t-shirt, and her gun was visible on her hip because that's what these people did. Her hair was loose because she hadn't wanted to look too much like her FBI persona, and she'd put on lip-gloss.

She locked the car and started toward the staging area where they'd roped off part of the field. There were targets set around the field, and a berm at one end. At least somebody was concerned with safety.

"Hey, Diana! You made it." A woman waved at her, a can of cider in one hand and a 1911 on her hip. Probably a 9 mil. The .45 was iconic if a bit strong on the recoil.

Diana waved back and pasted on a friendly smile. "Hey, Tessa. Haven't seen you around Big Mike's lately."

Tessa came over and they did a side hug. "Yeah, I been busy working at the salon and haven't been out much. Dwight's been on the road a lot, but he's home now. I'm fucking stoked to be here! Gonna do a little shootin', a little drinking, maybe smoke a little weed. Then I'm gonna get laid."

She threw her head back and laughed, and Diana laughed with her.

Tessa elbowed her in the side. "I thought you and Teddy were heading that way. He seemed sweet on you."

"Nah, we're just friends. He couldn't make it today. Had to work a shift last minute."

"Aw, poor guy. Gotta get paid, though, right? So you gonna find you a man out here, huh? Somebody to take home and warm the bed?"

Diana's heart kicked. "I might. Depends on if I see something I like."

Tessa waggled her eyebrows. "Plenty to choose from, hon."

"Tessa! Get your ass over here," a big man hollered. He wore camouflage and had an AR-15 slung across his back.

"Oh, Dwight's calling. Gotta go! See you!"

"See you."

Tessa trotted over to Dwight, who wrapped an arm around her and pressed a possessive kiss to her mouth before grabbing her ass and squeezing. Tessa swatted his ass in return and the two of them disappeared in the milling crowd.

Diana shrugged to loosen tight muscles. There were a lot of people today, mostly men, though some women too. The odor of cooking meat filled the air. Smoke rose from a couple of big grills and there was a table with plates, utensils, and sides. Coolers held drinks such as cider, beer, sodas, and water.

She wandered over to the food, hoping to strike up a conversation there. She'd been hanging out at Big Mike's lately, though she didn't see anybody she knew from there besides Tessa. It was a bar in Huntsville where people who were connected with the group spent time. There were other locations around town, but she'd chosen that one precisely because it wasn't where Brent Gannon, the former Air Force colonel who worked at the Missile Defense Agency, hung out. Alex and his people had surveilled Gannon, and though he'd said they didn't find anything interesting, Diana wasn't taking a chance he'd been lying—or that one of his people would still be watching and then he'd confront her about what she was doing.

She imagined him, darkly handsome as he'd stared at her the day she'd accused him of getting her taken off the case. He was always darkly handsome, always enigmatic enough to tug at something deep inside her that craved his approval. The Ghost Ops men were accomplished, lethal, and committed to their oaths. All of them were formidable.

But Alex was something more. He'd run an operation against orders to rescue Colonel—now Major General—John Mendez from a conspiracy. In the process, a vice president had been implicated and removed from office, and Alex had been promoted to full Colonel—at a younger than usual age—and restored to his duties along with Mendez and the entire Hostile Operations Team.

He'd been intended to take command of that organization one day, but then he'd been chosen to lead the Ghost Ops team and had to give up that career path. He was a complex man, that's for certain.

She wished he'd let her in when she'd offered to help. That he would have said, *yes, of course I'll work with you. You'd be an asset to us.*

Instead, he'd been happy to see her sidelined. So she'd taken a page from his playbook and started her own operation. Which had brought her here.

Diana nibbled the inside of her lip as she circled around the groups of people. She almost wished Teddy had come, despite the awkwardness of having to refuse his romantic overtures. At least he knew people, and he could introduce her.

She grabbed a drink from the cooler and found a place to stand so she could watch the shooting. Men eyed her, some leered, but she couldn't bring herself to give any of them encouragement. There were a few hours to go before the event was over, and she wasn't that desperate to talk to people yet.

She would pick a group soon, introduce herself, strike up a conversation. But first she wanted to observe.

Just then, a tall man in dark clothes moved through the crowd, a rifle slung over his broad shoulder, his dark hair silvered in the afternoon sun peeking through the clouds.

Diana's heart skipped as a shiver skated down her spine. She straightened, staring. There was no way that confident swagger belonged to who she thought it did. It was simply another tall, commanding man with the kind of presence that tickled her senses.

He reached a knot of camo-clad men and started talking. She crept around the crowd, trying to get closer without being seen. She had to know. Because it could *not* be Alex Bishop standing with those men, acting like he belonged. Laughing like they were old pals.

When the guy next to him clapped him on the back, he turned, laughing, his features fully exposed.

She couldn't contain her gasp. It was too noisy for anyone to notice, but she clamped her lips shut anyway and ducked into the crowd. Her heart tripped and stumbled before racing to catch up.

How the hell was he here? What was he doing? Had he been ordered to start surveilling the militia up close? She didn't believe for a second that he'd joined them, but stranger things had happened. Never assume you knew a man.

Never assume.

Fuck, fuck, fuck.

She put a hand to her chest, forced herself to breathe deep. To think.

This was a disaster. An absolute disaster.

Alex was here. If he saw her, he could expose her. People who joined the militia came from all walks of life, including law enforcement, but she was new and she didn't know many people. She hadn't proven herself. A word from him and she could be frozen out.

Or worse.

Diana shuddered. She had to stay far away from him. She couldn't let him see her. If she stayed on the perimeter, avoided the men he was with, she should be okay. But how was that going to help her get invited to the next gathering?

She stalked toward her car. If she could sit and think by herself for a few minutes, she'd come up with a solution. She had to.

"Hey, hey, lookie here, Jeff. It's that cunt from The Dawg."

Diana crashed to a halt. There were three of them dressed in camo, smirking at her. They had pistols at their sides and AR-15s slung across their chests. Recognition slammed her. The man glaring at her the hardest was the one she'd dropped to the floor.

"I think I owe you something, bitch," he grated.

Diana lifted her chin, her hand straying toward her pistol. "Do you really?"

"Oh yeah, sure do." He nodded toward her hand. "You shoot me, Jeff's going to shoot you."

"But you'd still be dead." She smiled though her heart throbbed a million miles an hour.

"Maybe, or maybe you aren't good enough to hit me before I take you down. Most people aren't that great a shot."

"I am. You want to try?"

He hesitated. She didn't draw because there were three of them and they were armed to the teeth. Drawing was a sure way to get shot. But if he thought she might, she could use that hesitation to return to the gathering.

"You're a mouthy bitch, you know that?"

Fuck you. That's what she wanted to say, but she didn't. She was outnumbered and in unfamiliar surroundings.

"If you'll excuse me, gentlemen, I better get back to the gathering." She hooked a thumb over her shoulder, backing up as she went.

The smirks didn't change, and her pulse dialed higher.

She was just about to turn and sprint when her body collided with a solid form. Before she could step away, two rough hands grabbed her arms, squeezing hard.

Then a sweaty cheek pressed against hers before a rough voice spoke in her ear. "Go ahead and scream. Nobody's coming to save you."

Diana swallowed as she sorted through a deck of options in her head. Nothing was good. Nothing was going to work if these pricks took her farther from the gathering. There were four of them that she knew of.

They were armed and smug, certain of their power and willing to do whatever it took to punish her.

Screaming was still the best option, no matter what the Neanderthal holding her said. That and fighting dirty.

She had to act.

Three, two...

The click of a pistol being cocked penetrated her brain, stopped the internal countdown. And then a hard, growly, beautiful voice said, "Boys, this one's mine."

8

"**B**uddy, there's four of us and one of you," the man holding Diana said.

Diana fucking Corbin. Here, in the midst of this gathering. Her eyes were wider than usual, and her pulse thrummed in her throat, but she wasn't terrified. If anything, she'd been about to do something that would have probably gotten her killed.

"I see that," Ghost said mildly. He was livid and not in the mood. "But I tell you what. I'll take on all four of you at once. Whoever wins gets to keep her."

The assholes exchanged a look between them. Ghost slid a pair of zip ties from his back pocket. "You can use mine or yours, but tie her up if you're worried she'll escape." He nodded at the weapons. "Only thing is, no guns. You can use knives though."

The man who'd assaulted Diana at the Dawg snorted.

"Are you serious? You really think you can take on four of us armed with knives at the same time?"

"Yeah, I really do. You in or out?"

They exchanged a look again before one of them spoke. "Man, it's your funeral. Why not?"

"Great. Secure her arms and let's go."

He holstered his weapon and tossed the zip ties to the man holding onto her. Diana's gaze was an inferno as the man wrenched her arms behind her back and secured her. Then he shoved her down in the grass. "You try to run away, bitch, and I'll find you and make you pay."

Diana looked as if she could chew nails, but she didn't respond. The four men put their pistols away, took off their AR-15s and laid them in the back of a truck before they drew knives. Ghost sighed. Then he reached into his boot and pulled his own knife, a KA-BAR combat utility knife that'd seen him through countless missions before he'd gone to the command level and had to move teams across a map from DC instead of being in the field with them.

"Come on, old man," the first asshole said, grinning and waving his knife like a douchebag in a Hollywood action flick.

"Old man? Really? You think because I'm older than you, you can beat me with youth and stupidity?"

"You talk a lot for somebody about to get hurt," the second asshole growled.

The first asshole—the one who'd held Diana—gave his friends a hand signal. Then he lunged. Ghost stepped out of the way, wrapped his arms around the guy's extended one, and twisted. The knife dropped, the arm broke, and the man screamed. For good measure, Ghost smashed one of his knees and let him fall.

The second man hurtled toward Ghost, knife held low. Ghost slid into the grass, kicked his opponent's legs from under him, and had the dude's own knife at his throat before the other two could blink.

The remaining two stared wide eyed at the carnage. One of their friends cradled his arm and blubbered like a baby and the other's throat was a breath away from being sliced open. The one beneath him was breathing hard, sweat rolling down his face. Ghost grinned at him.

"Having fun yet, sport?"

"Fuck you."

"Not my type, but thanks for the offer." Ghost let the knife slip into the man's skin. Blood trickled from the wound as he started to beg for his life.

Ghost let him, then pressed the knife a little deeper before pulling it out and tossing it into the grass. Next, he took the fucker's pistol and dropped the magazine into his hand, cleared the chamber, and dropped the gun onto the guy's chest before he pushed to his feet and glared at the other two.

"Who's next?" he growled.

Asshole number three went for his gun.

Ghost drew first, because he was that much better, and leveled the pistol at his target. His temper frayed at the edges, and he was itching to drop these motherfuckers.

Not a good idea, but he wanted it. Been a long, frustrating few months on this mission and he was tired of the bullshit.

"You really want to play this game? Spent twenty years in the Army, most of it with special forces. Been in combat situations you can't begin to imagine. You want to throw down with guns, you better know that I'm gonna blow your fucking heads off, one right after another. I don't hesitate, and I won't miss. Not a nervous shooter, not someone who only target practices a few times a week, not a man who's never had to shoot and kill an enemy combatant. So, I'm gonna need you to think about this, scooter. You want to start blasting away with those odds? Or you prefer to walk away and live another day?"

Asshole number three, the one who'd assaulted Diana at the Dawg, finally shook his head. "You know what, ain't no uppity bitch worth this kind of hassle. You can keep her, man. I ain't got no beef with you and I don't want one."

"Smart choice. While we're talking, you try to come after me—or her—after this, and I won't be so polite about it. I will put you down like a rabid dog, and I'll use my connections in law enforcement to walk free. Not only that, but anything happens to me or her, you're the first assholes they'll come looking for. You hear me, Tyler Long?"

The man started. "How the fuck do you know my name?"

"Good question." Ghost pointed at each of them in

turn, reciting their names as he went. After that incident at the Dawg, he'd put Seth onto finding out who they were and where they lived in case they ever went after Diana again. Didn't know it'd come in handy today, but he was glad he'd done it.

"Holy shit, you a cop?" Jeff Stout asked.

"Not quite, but I know people. We understand each other?"

"Absolutely," Jeff said. "Clear as crystal."

The others agreed with nods and, at least in the case of one of them, whimpers of pain.

"You'll need to get Brad some painkillers, maybe set that arm. His knee isn't permanently damaged, but it's gonna hurt. Cason here could use a Band-Aid for his cut. Not sure where his knife has been, but maybe check his shot records for tetanus while you're at it. And one more thing, boys. The right way to approach a woman is with respect, not entitlement. You'll get a lot farther that way."

He stalked over to where Diana sat in the grass and held out a hand. She took it because she'd broken the zip ties, which he'd expected, and he pulled her to her feet. Then he hustled her into the trees. He didn't expect those four assholes would change their minds—they had good jobs working at the Toyota plant in Greenbriar, and incarceration didn't come with the same benefits package—but he hadn't lived through some of the shit he had by taking chances.

He got Diana into the woods, a good distance away

from the crowd gathered to shoot targets, and let her go. She spun around to glare at him.

"Are we alone?"

"Yes."

She huffed a breath. "What the fuck are you doing here?"

He stepped into her space, unaccountably angry and ready to throw her over his shoulder and spank her damn ass. "What the fuck are *you* doing here? And keep your goddamn voice down when you answer me. We're alone, but voices carry."

She bared her teeth as she closed the remaining distance between them, until they were practically chest to chest. She had to tip her head back to meet his eyes, but she wasn't short and her mouth wasn't all that far away.

Fuck me. Why was he thinking about her mouth at a time like this?

"Don't you tell me what to do. You absolute *asshole*," she hissed. "Why are you here with these people?"

He snorted. "Am I to take it by the way you just sneered at *these people* that you aren't a convert?"

"Are you?"

His dick was getting hard. He wanted to kiss her, and he wanted to fuck her until she screamed his name. There was too much adrenaline in his system, too much fury and need. He stepped back before he did something stupid and raked a hand through his hair.

"Have you been spying on me? Is that why you're here?"

She lived in Sutton's Creek now. She'd been removed from her investigation. What better thing to do than watch his range? His men? Him?

"What? No! I had no idea you'd be here. How could I? And not only that, but are you fucking insane? You could have gotten us both killed when you put down your gun and offered to fight. You had the advantage, and you gave it up."

He laughed. "Did it look like I gave up the advantage to you? Those boys don't know what they're doing. They're gravy SEALs, nothing more. No combat experience, no real training. They'd prefer a fight to a shootout because they think they're badasses. Besides, they believed the odds were in their favor, and that's all I wanted."

"They had *guns*, you jerk. They know how to shoot."

"Yeah, and they weren't going to do it. They get off on the idea of it, the power behind it, but they aren't pulling a trigger. Don't get me wrong, if they thought they'd get away with it, they absolutely would. But with three hundred people milling around nearby? Not happening. If they were inner sanctum, knew the others had their backs, yeah, sure. But that's not what today is, and that's not who they are—even if they want to be."

She stood stiffly, hands curling into fists at her sides. "You are absolutely infuriating."

"True, but so are you. And you still haven't told me what the fuck you're doing."

"I don't have to. We aren't working together, remember?"

He sucked in a breath, blew it out. "So how about you tell me because I just fucking saved your ass, okay?"

Her nostrils flared. "Thank you for that," she said after a long, silent moment. "I wasn't sure how I was getting out of the situation."

Anger flared bright again. "You weren't getting out without backup. They had overwhelming strength and they had you captured. Those boys might not pull a trigger, but they *would* have raped you. Wouldn't have had a qualm about taking you somewhere remote and taking turns. Probably would have beat you up, too."

She trembled and he felt like shit for making her, but she needed to know she had no business out here alone, trying to insert herself into a fucking militia group. It was insane. She was a beautiful woman, not a seasoned operator like he was. Those men would have hurt her, and he'd have had to kill them. If she stayed, he'd always be thinking about how to keep her safe.

"I'm aware of how it works, thanks. Don't you think I know that some men think they're entitled to take what they want by force? That every day I dare to do anything alone, if I'm in the wrong place at the wrong time, I'm a target? Trust me, Alex, I am well aware of how the world works when you don't have a penis."

"Good thing, because you need to get in your damn bougie-ass car and drive out of here. Right damned now, before somebody else decides you need to be taught a lesson."

She put her fists on her hips and glared. "I'm not leaving. I got invited, same as you, and I want to know more."

This damn woman. She was going to drive him crazy.

"Does your boss know you're here?"

The flare of apprehension in her eyes told him all he needed to know before it was extinguished and replaced by determination. "None of your business."

"I take that as a no."

She didn't respond so he took her by the arm and started to march her back toward the field where the cars were parked. She dug in her heels and wrenched free.

"Stop," she hissed at him. "You don't get to decide what I do. I'm staying. You either need to get used to it and leave me the fuck alone, or you can work with me."

"This isn't a game, Diana," he growled, stalking her until she backed into a tree. "And you don't know if I'm working or not."

Her eyed widened a second, then narrowed into slits. "You're not one of them. I've seen your record."

"People change."

He didn't know why he was pushing, but damn her for thinking he was incorruptible. The irony of it was that this group, their mission to avoid government oppression, aka anyone telling them what to do even if it was good for them, was something his dad would have bought into hook, line, and sinker. He *had* bought into it, in fact, until he got too paranoid and decided going off grid entirely, in as remote and frozen a place as possible, was the best plan.

Diana's glare didn't change. "Bullshit. You're trying to get me to go away, but I'm not doing it. I'm going back to that gathering, and I'm taking my shots at those targets when it's my turn. I'm talking to people, and I'm going to the next fucking level. You think you're the only one who gets to go off book and do what they want? Not even close. Just stay out of my way, and I'll stay out of yours."

She pushed past him to stalk away but he caught her arm and dragged her back. She collided with his chest, her hands coming up to curl into his flannel shirt. She wore flannel too, and jeans, but it was her hair that fascinated him. Long and loose, messy now that he'd dragged her through the woods and they'd been fighting.

"What now, asshole?" she grated.

But she didn't push away. He almost laughed, except he was too busy telling his dick to stay down like a good boy. "You shouldn't be here, Diana. But you are, and you fucking won't listen. These people are dangerous, and you're in over your head."

She sputtered but he kept going.

"Not because you aren't good at what you do, but because you don't have the kind of training I do. Or the background. I know how these people tick because my dad was one of them. It's like dropping into his head again to be around this shit. I know what's expected, what's required, and I know how to say what they want to hear. Guaran-fucking-tee you don't."

Her mouth dropped open, but nothing came out. She closed it again, her blue eyes troubled.

"You need to go home. It's safer." He was gentler this time, hopeful she would see the sense in what he said.

Her eyes closed before snapping open again. "I can't give up. It's important."

"I know it's important," he growled.

Leaves shuffled and twigs snapped as someone approached. Ghost listened hard. It was one person, not three or four, and they weren't making an effort to hide their approach.

"Hey, Alex, you in here, man? Got somebody wants to meet you."

"Fuck," he muttered, tugging Diana closer. "Just remember you wanted to be here. Now go along with me or it'll be both our asses in a sling, you got me?"

She nodded.

Then he dropped his mouth to hers and kissed her.

9

Every nerve ending in her body blazed to life. She stiffened but he made a noise in his throat, reminding her this was a performance. For whoever was stomping through the woods toward them.

Big hands cupped her jaw more gently than she'd have thought him capable of being. Diana put her hands on his wrists, her heart hammering as his mouth slid across hers. She tried to stay aware of her surroundings, but she'd been plunged into the middle of a forbidden fantasy come true and it was almost impossible.

Alex Bishop was kissing her. She'd imagined it more often than she cared to admit. In every single dream, he took control and kissed her with the kind of fire she'd thought was probably a lie. Just one of those things romance novelists exaggerated but did not truly exist.

It was not a lie. His mouth on hers was perfection. His lips teased and tormented, gliding over hers. When he sucked her lower lip, an answering tug bloomed in her center. She was wet immediately, her body melting like wax against his as he held her and stroked his tongue across the seam of her lips.

She opened to him without thought, and he slipped inside, a groan in his throat. Flames licked her from the inside out. She wanted to throw a leg around him, rub herself against that burgeoning hardness pressing into her. The fact he was affected too? Made her wetter.

"There you are—shit man, sorry," somebody said.

Alex's entire body stiffened for a moment, and then he broke the kiss and took her hand firmly in his. Did he think she was going somewhere? She was too dizzy to walk.

"Hey, Brent, sorry 'bout that."

A chill rolled through her. Brent?

"Damn, man, don't blame you. Haven't seen this hottie before or I might have beat you to it."

Brent Gannon, former US Air Force colonel, leered. She wanted to glare at him but she managed to keep her expression as vacant as he expected it to be. Blond hair was handy sometimes.

Alex wrapped an arm around her. "Sorry, dude, but we have history. On again, off again kind of thing. Ain't that right, baby?"

If she kneed him in the nuts right now, would she regret it? Probably.

So she smiled and wrapped her arms around his waist, pinching his side for good measure. Not that it was easy to get any flesh. The man was hard-muscled and gorgeous.

"That's right, sugar britches. I just can't resist scratching this itch even though you piss me the hell off."

Gannon laughed. Alex squeezed her—a warning?—and chuckled too. Gannon held out a hand and Diana accepted. His grip was sweaty and soft. She wanted to wipe her hand on her jeans, but she kept a smile fixed on her face.

"Brent," he said, winking. "You get tired of this lame old stud, you can come see me, baby girl. I'll take care of you right."

"You're too kind," she said, while secretly wishing she had an excuse to shoot him. He was such a douchebag he didn't even bother to ask her name before he dropped her hand and looked at Alex.

"Came to find you because we've got some people here want to meet you."

He'd dismissed her as arm candy at best. Fucker.

"Sounds good, brother."

Alex tugged her along as they started to walk toward the field. Brent didn't say a word to her, just talked to Alex about the men who wanted to meet him. Two guys from Europe. That was the only useful thing she got. The rest was about guns and his grievances with the Air Force.

Thankfully, she'd never interviewed Gannon during her investigation because she'd had no cause. She'd wanted to catch him in the act, but that got blown all to hell by the man currently holding her hand.

She'd suspected Gannon was the missing buyer when Jackson O'Malley tried to sell Stinger missiles a few months ago, but she had no proof. The meeting never took place because Jackson was a loose cannon who'd taken a hostage and tried to hurt Daphne. Alex and his team had burst into the warehouse and put an end to it before the buyer arrived, and that particular line of inquiry dried up like a drop of rain in a drought.

They made their way toward a knot of men standing at the center of the line of shooters. Their target was the middle and farthest one. Someone moved and Diana got a good look at the gun they'd set up. A Barrett M82A1 50 cal rifle sat on a bipod.

Great.

A powerful semi-automatic sniper rifle with a wicked range, used to take out enemy materiel at long distances. The bullets fired from this puppy could pierce parked aircraft and vehicles. Not a weapon to be fired casually, hence the fortified berm at the end of the field. She hoped it was good enough because a bullet fired from that monster could go right through it and keep on trucking.

Alex called to Brent that he'd be right there before he stopped and turned her to face him. "Go get some food for us, baby," he told her. "While I meet these guys."

She thought she'd crack a tooth she gritted her teeth so hard. "Now why would I do that, baby? Can't I meet your friends, too?"

"Best if you don't," he said, his voice low and growly.

He dragged her against him again, kissed her like he owned her, and dammit if her body didn't start to soften.

His mouth brushed her ear. "I'm begging you, Diana. Let me do this. Alone. I'll share the information if I get anything good."

She dropped a hand to his ass, snorted softly at the way he jumped. "I really, *really* fucking hate you right now."

"I know. But trust me on this, okay? I'll explain later."

She wanted to tell him to go to hell. But what if she went with him and ruined the meet somehow?

However he'd gotten here, he'd done it with far more success than she had. She was still tiptoeing around the rim of this thing while he'd plunged in with both feet. Brent Gannon called him Alex and wanted to introduce him to people. She was still trying to make Teddy understand they weren't dating and talking about getting laid with Tessa.

"Fine. But you *will* explain. Or I'll knee you in the nuts when you aren't paying attention."

He nipped her earlobe and she gasped. "Heard and understood. Don't go anywhere alone."

"I know that, Fred. Do you really want food or was that an excuse?"

He stepped back and grinned. "I'll take a burger. Mustard, no mayo. None of that fucking iceberg lettuce shit either."

She cocked a hip, put a hand there. "Anything else, your reverence?"

His gaze dropped to her breasts before sliding back to her face. If anyone else had done that, she'd be annoyed. Instead, a thrill tingled to life beneath her skin.

"You, baby. On a platter, naked and spread wide for me. But that can wait until later." He gripped her chin in his fingers and kissed her again. "Smile, Diana. Look like you like me. People are watching."

She smiled as he let her go, her heart thumping at the vision he'd put in her head. "You got it, dumpling. I'll just go get your burger. Should I bring it to you or wait for you to come get it?"

"Wait for me like a good girl. Be about fifteen minutes or so."

Oh, she was going to kill him. As soon as she got over the way her body responded to those two words coming out of his mouth. She'd been called a good girl before, and it was always patronizing. This? It was like he had a direct line to the pleasure centers in her brain because they were firing like crazy, sending sparks to her pussy, her nipples, making her long for him to say those words again—while they were naked.

Gah, what was wrong with her? She liked beta males. Nice, biddable, apologetic. Not an alpha who made her body clench greedily with nothing more than a heated look and some dirty words.

She stalked to the closest ice chest, reaching in to grab a cold bottle of water. She wouldn't go so far as to roll it over her cheeks and neck so she could cool the heat he'd stoked. But it was a thought.

10

Alex followed Diana home, her taillights a comforting red glow as they drove back to Sutton's Creek. The parking lot was crowded tonight but he found a spot and joined her at the door to the Sutton building. She looked small and vulnerable in the bright light shining onto the stoop from overhead.

Or maybe he was the one feeling vulnerable after everything that'd happened today. When he'd thought he caught a glimpse of her moving through the crowd and followed her to the parked cars, he hadn't expected to find her about to be attacked by four small-minded men with revenge on the brain.

He hadn't expected to fight for her, or to kiss her, or to claim she was his in front of witnesses. But he had, and now he had to deal with the fallout.

But at least she was safe, and they were here, and he wasn't leaving until he got her upstairs and found out what the utter fuck she'd been doing at the farm today. She'd nearly ruined everything by bumbling in, and he still wasn't over it.

She didn't speak when he joined her. A sure sign she was fighting her own tangled emotions. She simply turned and inserted her key in the lock. He followed her inside, checking that the door locked automatically behind them, and then trailed her up the stairs until she stopped at her apartment on the third floor and unlocked it.

They went inside—he shut the door and shot the bolt —and she set her purse on the kitchen island before throwing him a look. "Anything to drink?" Her voice was like snow—cold and light.

"No. Thanks."

Her apartment—formerly Daphne's apartment—was sparsely decorated. A tower of boxes sat in one corner of the living room. Not enough to fill the space once emptied. Unless she'd stashed the rest in one of the bedrooms. Surely a rich girl like her had more belongings.

She opened the fridge and took out a bottle of white wine, poured some in a glass, and put the bottle back. Then she toed off her boots and walked over to the couch to sink onto it with a sigh. She took a Faraday bag from the side table and dropped her phone in it, then held it out to him. He dropped his inside and she closed it before setting it on the table.

She reached over and flipped on a white noise machine. He was impressed. It didn't turn the space into a

SCIF, not even close, but they could talk around topics without having to go to the range and duck inside the secure space there.

"Well, are you going to tell me what I want to know?" she asked, fixing him with an expectant look. "Or was that a lie to get me to do what you wanted?"

He hadn't exactly lied, but he didn't intend to tell her everything either. It was safer that way.

"How about you tell me what you were doing there first." He joined her on the couch, because it was the only piece of seating she had, taking the opposite end and leaning into the corner to watch her.

She swigged wine, swallowed. Her eyes flashed. "Think I did plenty of compromising earlier when I let you order me around like your servant girl."

He supposed he should feel guilty, but he didn't. Still, he'd give her this much. She'd been remarkably cooperative when he'd asked for it. She could have refused. He expected they would have both walked away from that field with their lives, but he didn't think they'd have been invited back. And he needed to go back, find out what those fuckers plans were. The two men he'd met were European, military men, much slicker than most of the people there today.

They had an agenda, but they were subtle. It'd been a risk, meeting them, but he'd had to do it. They hadn't shown even a flicker of recognition at his name. Didn't mean they didn't know who he was, though. He hadn't hidden his special operator background from Gannon. If

Dashevsky's people had gotten his team's records from McCann, then it did no good to lie. Better to be open—in the cagey way of special operators—and let them draw their own conclusions.

"Okay, you did. Guess I'll go first," he added with a grin. She didn't even crack a smile. So much for charming her into compliance. "You said you read my record. You know what happened when Mendez had to flee the country and we were ordered to stand down."

She nodded. "Yes. You didn't. You took a core group of operators and ran a mission to clear him."

"I don't do well being told not to act." It was an understatement. The part of him that would always hate what his father had done to their family was incapable of inaction. Not after what'd happened in Alaska. He didn't sit quietly and play with his toys while others told him everything would be fine. He didn't trust others to keep their word. Not when the lives of those he cared about were at stake. He'd lost people because of inaction. Wasn't ever happening again.

"Are you saying you've been told to stand down?" she asked, her brow furrowing.

"No, I'm not saying that. I've been told nothing of the sort. In fact, I've been told *nothing*. I'd hardly say the powers that be don't care anymore, but I think they've got a lot on their plate. And maybe they're wavering with the pushback they're getting lately."

She frowned. Sipped more wine. "I've been tracking

that. Somebody leaked its existence. It's the only explanation for why it's suddenly everywhere."

"Agreed." He suspected the president and her people might be considering delaying the completion of the project. Or maybe they'd scrap it entirely. There were certainly those in government who'd been calling for it to happen. They said Athena was too expensive and couldn't possibly work the way it was intended. They'd whipped up anti-war sentiment among the public, and now people were crying for government accountability. It was the usual Washington bullshit, different day.

"But you don't intend to wait for someone to tell you what to do."

He liked that he didn't have to spell it out for her. The woman might annoy the shit out of him, but she was no dummy. Even if she sometimes made stupid decisions.

"No. We know this movement is tied to Viktor, and we know his people were involved with Callie. Or so I suspect since you didn't actually confirm who broke into her house."

"That's what I think, but I didn't have enough information. Smirnov was masquerading as Mikhail, and we know he worked for Viktor. Unfortunately, since we traded him back to the Russians and never heard from again, we can't ask any further questions."

They both knew what'd happened to Smirnov. Anyone who double-crossed the Russian intelligence service the way Smirnov had wasn't long for this world if they got their hands on him. Smirnov was probably wearing concrete shoes at the bottom of the Black Sea.

"If it wasn't Smirnov who busted in and tore the place up, it was somebody from the militia. Maybe they thought she'd have a fucking notebook with what they wanted to know, or maybe they were just having fun. Smirnov wasn't delivering what he'd promised, so somebody in the organization could have decided to go after Callie's place as a warning. Maybe it wasn't even meant for her—could have been meant for him since they knew he was likely watching her." He shoved a hand through his hair. "These are theories, none of them particularly a favorite. But it all comes back to the militia."

She nodded. He could see she was processing it. She drew her knees up to her chest, one arm around her legs, the other holding her wine glass, and frowned. She looked less polished than usual, more defenseless. His protective instincts twitched. "How did you manage to get invited?"

"Told you, I speak the language." He hesitated, let the words stew inside him. "My dad was a separatist and a prepper. Mostly, he was a paranoid son of a bitch, but he was involved in this kind of bullshit for a while before he lost what was left of his mind and took us to Alaska."

He didn't know why he'd told her about Alaska, but it was out there now. Not the horror of living remotely, surrounded by ice and snow and wild animals, never knowing if he'd escape. He didn't say it because nobody who hadn't lived it could understand. Especially not someone who'd been born into generational wealth and influence.

He thought of the day she'd told him she had her own mission—the passion and pain in her expression, the raw emotion in her voice—but whatever had happened to her, he didn't think she could comprehend the horrors of his childhood.

She didn't offer any bullshit platitudes or express sorrow he didn't want to hear, and he appreciated that about her.

"I started drinking at the brewery," he continued, "made contact, and told him what he wanted to hear. Doesn't hurt we're both military men, both colonels. That's another language we have in common. I may have suggested I was forced out, too." He shrugged. "The short version is that I got myself invited to their meet up, and I made contact with a couple people in the hierarchy."

"Yes, and you certainly made sure I didn't get to talk to them when you made me wait with your food."

"They wouldn't have talked if you'd been there. Besides, you already drew enough attention between Gannon and those fucknuts from the Dawg. I didn't want to be distracted by the need to protect you if anything went wrong."

Color flared in her cheeks. "You do realize that I didn't set out to draw anyone's attention, right? It happens because men think with their dicks too much."

"As a man, I can confirm. But that doesn't mean it didn't happen, or that there weren't other kinds of danger out there. I couldn't take the risk, Diana. I needed you safely away when I made contact."

She bared her teeth. "I'm going to pretend that's sweet of you instead of pointing out how very patronizing it is to think I can't defend myself—not against four men in an ambush, not saying that, but in general. Did you learn anything useful from them?"

"Not yet. They wanted to meet me, talk about my background." Men in particular were always interested in knowing what kinds of things he'd done. He was vague, always, because it wasn't a fucking role-playing game, and he wasn't their entertainment. But these guys wanted to know if they could use him, which meant he had to be a bit more forthcoming if he wanted to go deeper. "It's possible I won't get any farther than this. There are reasons, but I'll have to talk about those another time."

He wasn't going to talk openly about the breach, or that Trey McCann had said there were powerful people who knew their names before Ethan put a hole in him.

She nodded and he knew she understood it was something requiring a more secure location. "Then we need to make that happen."

"I've told you what you wanted to know. Think it's your turn now. Why were you there, Diana?"

She dropped her gaze to her wine glass, her body vibrating with emotion. Anger? Or fear?

Could be the adrenaline rush of having survived today finally catching up with her. He waited, determined not to let her off the hook.

"Because I need to know," she said in a small voice. "I don't care how often I'm told to leave it alone, or who orders me to move on—I can't."

Her eyes collided with his. The emotion boiling in their depths stunned him. It was the most feeling he'd ever seen her display. Even beyond the day she'd accused him of having her removed from the case a second time.

This Diana was alive, a raging tempest of emotion. Fucking beautiful. So arresting that his chest ached with the urge to touch her.

"It's personal," she grated. "But I won't stop until that bastard is finished."

11

iana waited for him to ask the question she dreaded. Her fingers scissored the wine stem, her heart careening down a raging river of emotion. If today hadn't been so damn stressful, if she hadn't been cornered by men intent on revenge, if she hadn't had to pretend to be this man's lover—so many ifs, but *if* those things hadn't happened, maybe she'd have a better handle on herself. As it was, she simply tried to avoid the shoals as she bobbed along, helplessly angry.

He studied her, his handsome face creased in thought. As if he was trying to find the source of her anguish. She decided to save him the mental gymnastics.

"My family has a charitable foundation. Viktor is more than a family acquaintance, less than a friend. My parents have hosted him for dinner in the past. He's been to foundation events, and he's donated huge sums. He..."

Her throat knotted. "He hurt someone close to me. I want him to pay for it."

"I'm sorry, Diana." His fingers traced a seam in the arm of the couch. Back and forth, back and forth. He did not ask what happened, or who was hurt. She was grateful for it.

"It was a long time ago. But I have not forgotten or forgiven."

"And now you've been ordered to let it go by the director himself."

"Yes. Not that Uncle—*Mr.* Lewis," she corrected, though not soon enough if the flicker in his eyes was any indication. "Not that he knows what happened, or to whom. And even if he did, it wouldn't change anything. That order came from higher up. Because Viktor has bought and paid for people in very high places. Or he has dirt on them, which is the same thing. Honestly, I'm surprised I got as far as I did for as long as I did."

She'd thought about it a lot over the last month. It was possible he didn't know that Diana Corbin was Diana Adler. A random FBI agent poking her nose into his doings in a small Southern city was probably not worth his notice. Until it started to impact his plans. Or he knew it was her and he'd found it amusing to give her enough rope to hang herself.

Alex still hadn't said anything. He just watched her with those wolf-like eyes. Studying. Cataloging. Judging her, no doubt. Words clogged her throat. She knew she shouldn't say them, but she couldn't contain the weight of holding them in for a single moment more.

"I won't stop. No matter what you say, I'm not going away."

She wanted to ruffle him. Wanted to see his eyes narrow, his nostrils flare, the line that formed between his eyes when he was furious. She needed him to feel as chaotic as she did.

He refused to comply, his gaze glacial. "The choice isn't yours, you know. It's theirs. The militia's. And they may not invite you to the next level. Then what?"

Her heart thumped. "I'll date one of them. Brent Gannon. He seemed interested."

"No."

"Newsflash, my dear colonel. You are not the boss of me."

And there was the spark of temper she craved, flaring in his eyes. "Leave it, Diana."

"I don't intend to. But maybe there's a better way…"

"What is that?" His voice was a growl. It seriously did things to her insides. Things she couldn't afford to think about.

"We could keep up the fiction you created today. I'll go with you to meetings, help you investigate. I'll fetch your food and pretend to be a dumb blonde, but I can watch and listen. I might catch things you don't."

"No, not happening. No fucking way."

Anger flared in her belly, flashed heat through her

limbs. She hadn't really expected he'd agree, but it hurt that he dismissed the idea so vehemently.

"Then I guess it's Plan A. Dating Brent Gannon. Or maybe Teddy, the guy who invited me today. Sadly, he had to work so we didn't get better acquainted. You know what," she said, leaning forward, wanting to irritate him as much as he'd irritated her, "there are a lot of guys at Big Mike's who'd be interested in a tall blonde with a nice rack. I imagine I can get one of them to take me to the next meeting if I dangle the chance for sex."

"No." The word whipped in the air between them. Violent as a tornado. Hard as a boulder.

And thrilling for some stupid reason she didn't know.

He leaned toward her now, body stiff with outrage. He wasn't accustomed to his orders not being obeyed. Well, too damn bad. She wasn't on his team, as he'd made abundantly clear, and she didn't take orders from him.

"You're playing with fire, Diana. Did what happened to you today not penetrate that thick fucking head of yours? Four men were willing to drag you away from the crowd and brutalize you. There was nothing you could have done about it. They'd have stuffed your mouth with something so you couldn't scream, and they'd have taken turns violating your body because they thought they could get away with it. And even if I'm wrong—even if rape wasn't what they intended—they were going to beat you and humiliate you because you stood up to them in the Dawg."

Fury and fear dripped through her veins in equal

measure. "And that means I have to quit? Because they might try again? Even more reason for us to pretend to date. If I'm with you, they won't touch me. Because you scare the shit out of them."

He stood with a rough sound. "No. I won't risk it. This is my fucking mission, my team, and I'm not taking on an untrained rich girl with a vendetta simply because she doesn't have the sense to quit."

Diana shot to her feet, went toe to toe with him. She had to bend her neck to look up at him. It pissed her off. So much so that she poked a finger in his chest.

"You *dick*. You motherfucking *dick*. You have no idea what I've been through. You think because my family has money that I'm somehow immune to pain or injustice? Or that I bought my way into the FBI and didn't have to do anything except show up and get my badge? Do you really think I've had no training whatsoever? What is *wrong* with you anyway? Do you hate women in general, or is it just me?"

"I don't hate you," he said through gritted teeth. "I'm trying to protect you. I'm a special operator, Diana. But you already know that. I don't need a gun or a knife to defend myself. I don't need weapons to kill someone. I can live off the land for weeks at a time, and I can make my way across this country without being tracked. That's what I'm talking about when I say you're untrained. You can shoot, and you can take down an opponent when they aren't expecting it—but can you fucking survive when you don't have a weapon or the advantage of surprise? Can you live in the wilderness for weeks at a time without starving? I'm talking about survival training, and combat training—you don't have either one. I can't be watching your back and worrying you'll get hurt while trying to get deeper into the group."

Her heart pumped. He wasn't wrong, but she wasn't letting him leave her behind. "I can be an asset, you Neanderthal. I'm blond. I'm female. I have tits and an ass that men like to stare at, and I can act dumb as a rock. They'll think I'm giving it to you so good you don't want to quit me. They're the kind of men who believe a woman's place is serving her man, and I know how to act like a good little woman who wants to please you. Two heads are better than one, and you need someone to watch your back, too. You aren't fucking invincible."

"No. You've just told me that Viktor's sat at your damn family dinner table. Do you think he has absolutely *no* fucking clue what's going on with his people? Especially here? Your name in his ear would blow what we'd be trying to do all to hell, don't you think?"

"He won't know. I'm Diana Corbin to these people, not Adler. They aren't asking for a job application, and they don't run every single fucking name past the man at the top, not at first. Call me your old lady or the old ball-and-chain. Call me whatever you like, but I'm not giving up. If you don't let me in, I'm heading to the bar where Gannon hangs out and getting to know him better."

"Diana." His voice was rough. His pupils dilated, his

gaze dropping to caress her mouth. "Why are you so fucking mule-headed?"

He caught her around the waist before she could answer, jerked her close. Maybe she should have pushed him away, but she fisted her hands in his shirt instead. His mouth hovered above hers, and a tingle of lightning sizzled to life in her core. Just the anticipation of it was enough.

"Are you going to kiss me or stare at me?" she finally whispered, the moment stretching between them like fine-spun thread.

"I'm thinking about spanking you."

Maybe she should have been afraid of that alpha threat, but a shiver rolled through her instead. "Only if I get to spank you, too."

"Jesus," he muttered. "The things you say."

Then his mouth crashed down on hers and the world tilted on its axis.

12

The first time he'd kissed her, it'd been in the forest, surrounded by silent trees and watchful birds, and she hadn't been prepared. He'd kissed her because Brent Gannon was coming, because he needed a reason for them to be alone in the woods, and that'd been a good one.

She hadn't thought for a second that he'd really wanted to kiss her. She'd known for months that she wanted to kiss him, however. Every time they'd clashed over his mission or her investigation, every time their gazes caught and tangled across a room, she'd thought about what it would feel like to have his mouth against hers, his body naked beneath her fingers.

She'd often suggested to Joel that they go to the Dawg for one of their dates, knowing Alex Bishop would be there, glowering at her like she'd stolen his puppy. She'd gone to the Independence Day Festival for yet another chance to look at this man and dream about what it would be like to belong to someone as self-assured and gorgeous as he was.

She'd admired him in his One Shot Tactical polo shirts, the armholes of his short sleeves stretched around his biceps, the fabric hugging his chest. She'd practically drooled over the narrow waist of his faded jeans, imagining the flat belly beneath and the muscles—dear God, the muscles—that adorned his torso.

She was not prone to fantasies about men she met, but this one had been the exception. For months now, he'd been an unwelcome exception—and a complete distraction.

She didn't know why, other than he oozed competence and strict adherence to a moral code she understood. He didn't display one face to the world while wearing another beneath it the way Viktor did. The way so many criminals she'd encountered in her job did.

His mouth demanded, his tongue danced against hers, and her body dissolved into bonelessness as she clung to him. There was no time to think because thinking would mean stopping.

And she didn't want to stop.

Diana tugged his shirt from his jeans, her hands slipping beneath the fabric to caress taut skin. He swore against her mouth, then pushed her flannel shirt off her shoulders before ripping her T-shirt over her head.

Thank heavens she'd worn nice underwear. He cupped her breasts in his hands, his thumbs caressing her nipples over the silk, his mouth still doing devastating things to hers.

She went for his belt, tugging it free, leaving little doubt what was on her mind. His mouth left hers, trailed along her jaw and down her neck. He unsnapped her bra with the finesse of an expert and tugged it off to drop it on the couch. Then her naked breasts were in his hands and his tongue laved around one taut peak and then the other before he sucked a nipple into his mouth with a strong pull that had her gasping and squeezing his arms.

A moment later he pulled back, gazing down at her. "What are we doing, Diana?"

She unbuttoned his jeans. "I thought it was obvious."

His eyes slipped to her breasts, lingered, before making the return trip to hers. "Feels obvious, but I need to be sure. And I probably should mention I don't exactly keep a box of condoms in my pocket."

"I've got that covered. But I really need you to stop talking and go back to what you were doing before I lose my nerve."

He frowned. "You need nerve? Because I'm thinking that's a sign we probably shouldn't be doing this." He took a step back, started to button his jeans, but she moved into him until they were skin to skin.

"I want this, Alex. I need nerve because you make me nervous, not because I don't know what I want. And if you think I want to fuck you so you'll take me to meetings, you'd be wrong. I'm going whether we fuck or not."

He swore and laughed at the same time. "Of course you are. Jesus, you piss me off."

"Same here. Also, I hate you. In case you were worried I'd think of this as a marriage proposal."

"Damn, baby, you're wounding my male ego here. A man likes to think he's so irresistible a woman wants to capture him." But his hand was on her jaw, threading into her hair, and his mouth inched toward hers again. Her heart careened like a butterfly.

"I'm not interested in capturing you," she murmured, her gaze on his mouth. "But I can think of other things to do with you."

He grinned, his mouth a whisper away. "I can't wait to find out."

She thought he'd kiss her but instead he dropped his mouth to her breasts again. He pushed them together in his big hands, sucking each nipple into a tingling point before he went to his knees and unbuttoned her jeans. Her nipples glistened from his attention, peaks taut and aching. She wanted him to suck them some more, but he pushed her jeans down her hips instead.

"What are you doing?" she gasped.

"Whatever I want. You got a problem with it?"

"Uh, no," she said, her blood beating a tattoo in her veins. This was new territory. She'd never had a man take the lead like this one. And never, ever had she thought he might do something she'd never experienced before. Not that she knew what he planned, but God it was exciting to think about.

When her jeans were puddled on the floor, she stepped out of them as directed. Alex leaned forward to press a kiss to her panties, and she had to strangle the cry that wanted free. *Dear God....*

"I, um, should get those condoms... we can go to the bedroom, and—"

"Don't need any yet. Got other things I want to do." He pulled her panties off, and she stepped out of them until she was naked. His fingers trailed down her body, gliding between her legs. "Damn," he groaned. "You're soaked for me."

"Alex," she gasped as he traced a finger over her clit. Her hands curled into his shoulders. Confusion and desire warred for space in her head.

What was he doing? Why wasn't he naked? Why wasn't he inside her, pounding deep? She wasn't accustomed to talking during sex, or to a man playing with her body like he did.

When he pushed her back on the couch and spread her legs, she thought she understood. His shoulders kept her spread open, his gaze fixed on her glistening sex, and her heart nearly stopped. Time seemed to stand still.

"I've been thinking about tasting this pussy," he said, fingers skimming her clit. "Watching you fall apart, seeing your cool facade crack and dissolve while you beg me for more."

"I—" She didn't know what to say. She wanted him to do that, badly, but telling him? She wasn't used to wanting like this. Wanting so much it hurt. Sex was supposed to be pleasurable. It wasn't supposed to consume you.

"What do you want, Diana? This?" He leaned forward, swiped his tongue through her juices, and settled back again.

She realized she was whimpering. Bastard. "Yes. Please. Do...that."

He grinned. "Do what, honey? Lick your pussy?"

"Yes. Please."

"You sound so pretty when you beg."

She vaguely thought she should be angry at the way he said those words, but she wasn't. If she thought he believed her to be less than he was because she was a woman, it'd be a different story. But, right now, she'd beg him for anything he wanted.

"Please, Alex. Please lick me."

"I thought you'd never ask."

He settled between her legs and began to take her apart at the seams with his tongue, teeth, and lips. Diana gasped as lightning streaked through her body, sizzling into every pore. She lay against the back of the couch, her body curled forward so she could watch what he did to her. His dark head between her legs was erotic as hell. His tongue was magic, licking, swirling, sucking. But when his glittering eyes met hers, she thought it was the sexiest thing she'd ever seen.

She wanted to ask questions, wanted to tell him what he did to her, but speech was impossible as he slid two fingers inside and fucked her while his mouth continued to do indecent things. Those fingers were distracting, but not distracting enough. She wanted it to last, but the tension spiraled out of control, until her body flew apart with a cry and her limbs shook as he held her down and licked her through the most intense climax of her life.

She stared up at the ceiling, her heart pounding, her world permanently skewed. Why had she never demanded more from a lover? Why had she performed oral sex but let others get away with not doing it to her?

Alex kissed her inner thighs gently, then worked his way up her body, sucking her nipples lazily, his fingers tracing furrows of pleasure against her skin. Everywhere he touched her lit up, seeking, craving.

It wasn't enough.

She touched him back, lifting her body to press her mouth to his neck, to taste his skin. His fingers drifted between her legs, and she gasped as he strummed her body, as heat built anew.

"You need to get naked," she said.

He kissed her, his tongue delving deep, tasting like her arousal. It was shockingly intimate, but she didn't mind. She tugged his shirt until he shrugged out of it, until the expanse of his golden skin was bared to her questing fingers. Her mouth found his shoulder, sucked the skin there, her hands dropping to his zipper.

He stopped her. Before she could protest, he was on his feet, sweeping her into his arms like she weighed nothing. He carried her to the bedroom and set her down and she attacked his jeans with renewed vigor. She was past caring how crazy it was that they'd danced around each other for months, barely tolerated each other, and now she craved him like she craved air.

She got his jeans off and pushed him onto her bed. His cock rose straight and proud—and big. It was thick, beautiful, and he hissed in a breath as she wrapped a hand around him. She'd never had a man go down on her before, but she'd done this. She bent over, swirling her tongue around the crown, and he groaned.

Then he patted the bed next to his head. "Up here, honey. Straddle my face while you suck my dick so I can eat your delicious pussy again."

How the hell was she supposed to say no to that? Diana did as he told her, moaning when he buried his face between her legs and sucked her clit. Her juices dripped down the insides of her legs and her body shook with the effort not to come as she took his cock in her mouth.

She rolled his balls in one hand and tried to take him deeper, but that wasn't going to happen. Instead, she teased the rim of his cock with her tongue and sucked on every upstroke.

His control was far better than hers, though. She soon forgot what she was supposed to be doing, her body winding tighter beneath his tongue and fingers. When he slipped the tip of a finger into her back entrance, she flew apart with a sharp cry, trembling like an earthquake rolled beneath the bed.

Alex licked the juices from her thighs with a chuckle.

When he smacked her ass—not hard, just enough for a light sting—the aftershocks of her orgasm intensified for a few seconds before subsiding again.

She tried to get back to what she was doing, but he managed to flip them until she was on her back, and he was free. "Condoms," he said.

"Nightstand," she managed.

He found them and rolled one on, then crawled up her body, settling between her legs. "Not what I expected today, but damn, you're amazing," he whispered to her, his mouth dropping to hers.

One touch of his lips and she was on fire again. His tongue delved deep, his cock nudging her entrance. She was too wet for him not to slide home easily. He filled her up, stretching her, and it was delicious.

They moved together like they'd always done so. It was slow and easy at first, but it changed, became intensely, hotly, frenzied. She thought, if they kept on like this, it would wreck her. Not physically, though she was going to feel it tomorrow, but something deeper that she wasn't prepared for.

Diana Standish Corbin Adler did not need anyone. And she wasn't about to start now, even if she'd never felt this crazy hot for a man in her life.

Alex dominated her body. It was like he knew what she wanted, what would light her up and make her writhe and pant and demand. She didn't think she would come again. She never came while being fucked. It was always before or after, with direct stimulation.

Until she did. Until the pressure wound tight and then exploded in a shower of sparks that left her breathless and filled with wonder.

"So fucking beautiful," he growled, stilling in that moment before his cock jerked deep inside her.

When he was done, he slipped from the bed and went to take care of the condom while she pushed upright and tried to decide if she was ready to move or if she needed to lie in bed and recover. Alex returned from the bathroom, and she let her gaze drop over him, enjoying the view. He was a tall man, muscled, with the kind of definition that would make most men cry.

His abs were a thing of beauty. The V from his shoulders to his waist could make a woman stupid. The happy trail of dark hair from his belly to his groin was guaranteed to do it.

His dick was still hard, still jutting proudly from his body, though maybe not with as much enthusiasm as before. Such a beautiful sight.

She could stay in bed with him, cuddling close and exploring his magnificent body, but she sensed that asking him to crawl between the sheets and hold her was too much like clinging, so she didn't do it. Instead, she swung her legs from the bed and stood, stretching.

"That was lovely. Thanks so much," she said, sashaying over to him and caressing his cock. It leapt at her touch. "If you want to do it again sometime, I'd probably be willing."

"Probably?" he rasped, his voice all deep and growly.

Delicious.

She shrugged. "I guess it depends on how much I dislike you that day."

He snorted and shook his head. "You're not like anyone else, you know that?"

"Aw, thanks. I guess you mean that I'm not suddenly a puddle of mush begging for this magic cock, hmm?"

He caught her wrist and stopped her from stroking him. "Magic, huh?"

"That's what you took from what I said? Just the magic part?"

He grinned. "A man likes to hear his cock is magic. What can I say?" He lifted her hand to his mouth and kissed the inside of her wrist. "I had a good time, Diana. More than good. Doesn't mean I like you interfering with my mission any less though. You need to stay out of it."

"I already told you I'm still going, whether you let me go with you or not. Your choice, big boy. I can be your hot girlfriend who craves your magic cock, or I'll cozy up to Gannon and pretend to crave his."

Shock painted his face. And anger. The rumble in his throat thrilled her. "You'd fuck him just to get into the militia?"

"Probably not," she said truthfully. "But if I had to, if it was the only way in, I think I would. Are you telling me you wouldn't fuck a woman to do the same? And if you dare to tell me it's not the same thing, I'm going to clock you."

He bared his teeth. "Only if I had to."

"That's what I thought. So, what's it gonna be, Magic Man? Am I your girlfriend or not?"

Her heart thumped as she watched the emotions play across his face. He glared at her, his teeth grinding, his jaw taut. "You fucking infuriate me."

"The feeling is mutual. Except for the last hour. That was a much more pleasant feeling."

His gaze dropped over her naked body, back up again. "Agreed."

"Time's wasting, lady killer. Are we working together or not?"

He closed his eyes, swore six ways to Sunday before opening them again. "On one condition."

"Being?"

"You do what the fuck I tell you when we're there. No questions, no arguing, no disagreements. You want to take it out of me later, when we're alone, you can. But I tell you to do something, stay out of something, go the fuck away while I do my job, you do it. If you don't, I'll find a way to freeze you out and make sure you can't come back. You understand me?"

Her pulse zipped. "Oooh, so bossy. Okay, fine, you've got a deal. But you're going to share everything you learn with me. You aren't keeping information to yourself, and you aren't making decisions without me—unless they have to be made on the fly while we're undercover, and we can't talk about it. You're also including me in your team meetings about this subject—"

"No can do, honey. Not the team meetings."

"Why not?"

His eyes glittered like jewels in the sun. "Because they don't know what I'm doing."

Her jaw dropped. "You mean you're operating alone?"

"Aren't you?"

She frowned. "Well, yes. But I don't have a choice." She also didn't have the kind of relationships he did. "I thought that's what your people were here for."

He huffed a breath. "They're in love, getting married, making lives here. Not involving them in something that could blow up everything they're building. Not unless I have to."

13

Diana stared up at him, her body maddeningly close, her tits begging to be sucked again, the peaks of her nipples straining toward him. Of all the conversations he'd had with a woman, he didn't think he'd ever had one like this while completely naked. And certainly not with a woman who managed to piss him the hell off nearly every time she opened her mouth.

"I'm trying to decide if that's sweet of you or crazy," she finally said, her brow furrowed.

"Neither one. I'll tell them if I have to, but for now I'm making an approach. If nothing happens, if I don't get any deeper into the organization, no need to involve them."

He'd debated it, because Phantom, Demon, Dragon, Wraith, and Shadow were the closest thing to family he had, but in the end he'd decided not to. Viper knew, and that was enough for now. If he needed his team at any point, he'd brief them. They'd be pissed as hell at him for keeping them in the dark, but he could handle it.

And if things went wrong and he got caught, he'd go down alone.

Except he wouldn't because this maddening woman would be there, going down with him.

Fuck.

She threaded her fingers in his, oblivious to his inner turmoil, and squeezed briefly before letting go. "So, the deal is you tell me what you learn and I follow orders whenever we're embedded with the militia. Correct?"

Everything about this deal rubbed him the wrong way. He didn't want her there because what if he couldn't protect her? What if it went wrong? He'd kept his team out of it because he didn't want them hurt. He didn't want her hurt either—but she wasn't going to stay out of it.

"Yes," he grated. "That's the deal."

She nodded. "Okay, then. You'll call me when you hear something from Gannon, and we'll go back together. I'll hang on your every word and gaze longingly at your ass while pretending I don't have two brain cells to rub together. Sounds fun."

"You have yet to tell me how you're gonna drop every-thing and go with me if you're actively working a case. It might not always be a weekend meeting."

She shrugged. "An administrative leave of absence. Didn't I tell you I was told to take some time to myself after I expressed an opinion about my investigation being taken away? No? How negligent of me."

He stared at her as she turned away, gliding to her closet like a frigging queen in her throne room, sliding the door open and rummaging around for something to wear.

She'd been out there on her own, nobody at the FBI knowing where she was, trying to find information to bring down Viktor Dashevsky because he'd hurt someone close to her. She'd been told to leave it, to take time off, to do nothing—but she was actively trying to insert herself into the militia.

She was as suicidal as he was. Maybe more since he at least had the training and know-how to deal with these bastards.

Ghost snatched his own clothing off the floor, dragged on briefs, jeans, and his T-shirt before shrugging into the flannel button up he'd discarded. His temper was raw despite the languidness of his limbs. Damn stubborn woman.

By the time they were both dressed, silence lay like a shroud over them. He refused to look at the bed and so did she. He didn't know why she wouldn't, but if he looked he'd have her panties off and his face between her legs again just so he could hear her beg.

Need thrummed beneath the surface, despite how recently he'd sated it. Despite how annoyed he was that she'd maneuvered him into letting her join his op.

He needed to get out of here, go home, clear his head. And then he had to figure out how to keep her alive when he took her into the militia's lair. He almost hated her for it, except it was impossible to hate her when he'd just spent the last hour craving her.

She walked him to the door, arms folded over her chest, looking small and alone in a way she hadn't before. He nearly dragged her against him and held her, but that was too much like a relationship.

"Thanks for the sex," she said as he pulled the door open. "It was nice."

He turned back to her, arched an eyebrow. How did she manage to throw him off balance so easily?

"Nice?"

She shrugged. "Nothing wrong with nice, Magic Man. But if you insist, I'll do better. It was great. My legs are shaking and I'm going to collapse the second you're gone."

He took her chin in his fingers and tipped her face up. Then he kissed her hard and deep. "Next time, I'll make sure you can't walk straight for a week. Or sit still because your ass is gonna be so damn red."

It was after ten when he left her apartment, and all he could think was that he could still be in bed with her, his cock buried deep in her tight pussy. There were still so many things he wanted to do to her, but he'd needed to go. Needed to get home and clear his head of her so he could think.

He parked beside the farmhouse, checked that his

security was operational and tight, no breaches or attempts, and went inside, shedding clothes and stepping into the shower to wash Diana Corbin off his skin. If he didn't, sleep would be hell because all he'd dream about was every moment of being with her tonight.

Fuck, she was hot. And somehow innocent at the same time. That's what he didn't understand. How a woman could be both those things at once.

Thinking of her, remembering how his skin had tingled with electricity everywhere she touched him, remembering her hands wrapping around him, her lips, the taste of her—

Jesus. He stroked his cock, groaning as it swelled beneath his fist. Wishing it was her he fucked instead of his own hand. He came with a moan, panting, pressing his face to the tile to cool the fever beneath his skin.

How the fuck was he supposed to operate with Diana at his side? How the fuck was he going to take her into danger and concentrate on what he needed to do when all he wanted to think about was getting her naked again?

"Not the first time you've faced a difficult mission," he muttered to himself.

No, but it *was* the first time he'd ever wanted to fuck his teammate. Which added a whole new level of difficulty he wasn't accustomed to.

He finished showering, dried off, and went to bed, sliding naked between cool sheets, forcing himself to think about the things that'd happened at the gathering.

Aside from the unwelcome surprise of Diana's presence.

The two men he'd met, Dashevsky's men, had been friendly enough, but they hadn't shown any particular interest in him. That's how it worked, though. They watched, assessed, debated. If they thought he was ripe for their cause, they'd be in touch. They wouldn't pull him in yet, but they'd take him a little deeper, watching for pushback, for a lack of commitment.

He'd shot several weapons today, but it was the 50 cal that'd drawn the most attention. He'd hit the target dead center every time he pulled the trigger. People around them had stopped to watch. He'd half expected Diana to show up, though he'd told her to stay away. He'd been grateful she'd listened for once.

He would have to find a way to cut her out of any future meetings with Gannon and the Europeans. He just had to do it in such a way she didn't get suspicious and decide to make contact on her own.

Because he had no doubt she would. She was driven by what had happened to someone she cared about.

He understood that feeling all too well. His mother might be alive today if his father hadn't lost his mind and isolated them from civilization. If Ghost had been stronger or bigger or braver, maybe she would have survived.

He'd failed her, though. He hadn't fought hard enough, and he would never do that again.

His phone buzzed with a text. He picked it up from the nightstand.

> **Diana:**
> Got a message from Gannon. He wants me to meet him for a drink tomorrow night.

He couldn't hit the dial icon fast enough. She answered on the third ring. Taking her sweet-assed time, no doubt.

"Hey, Magic Man. Couldn't stop thinking about me?"

That voice. Honeyed sweetness dripping down his spine, knotting his balls.

"What do you mean you got a message from Gannon?" he growled. "How the fuck did he get your number?"

"Hello to you, too," she said with a sniff.

"Diana."

"I may have talked to him while you were making those Europeans hard with your mad weaponry skills."

Fuck. "You were there?"

"I stayed in the crowd. I wanted to see what was happening. He saw me and came over to talk."

He closed his eyes. "That's exactly what I didn't fucking want. You didn't think to mention it earlier?"

"Well, no. Besides, you weren't exactly keen on working with me. I needed my own way in."

"He wants to fuck you, not give you the keys to the clubhouse."

"I know that, Fred. I'm blond, not stupid. Which is also why I gave him my number. You've been thinking about how to freeze me out of this mission from the moment you saw me, so don't pretend to be all offended that I took my shot when I got the opportunity. And don't pretend you haven't been thinking about it since you left here, either."

He was impressed. Aroused. Pissed as hell.

"What did you tell him?"

"I said yes."

"Diana," he groaned. "What the fuck?"

"Think about it, Alex. I go see him, have that drink. He might tell me something."

"Yeah, he's gonna tell you something all right."

"Meaning?" She sounded prissy.

"Meaning he's going to tell you whatever it takes to get you into his bed. That's what he wants from you. The man is a sexist prick."

"Once more with the things I already know." She huffed. "I think I can avoid being carted off to his bed against my will. And maybe I'll gather some information because men like that love to brag. Can't hurt."

"If you've made up your mind, why are you telling me?" he grated.

"Because, like it or not, we're partners. I thought you'd want to know my plans."

"That's not the only reason."

"No, it's not. You need to understand how important this is to me. You might think you've addled my brains with your magic penis and wicked tongue, but I won't be deterred. You can't redirect me, throw me off the scent, or pretend to work with me while blocking me from my goals."

"I thought we'd settled this. I said I'd take you with me if I got the callback."

"I know you did. And I'm sorry, but I don't believe you. I'm going to work my own angle, see which of us gets in first. That person will bring the other along. I still need your help, and I think you need mine. Even if you're too stubborn to admit it. But I'm not going to rely on you to keep your word when I know you don't want me there."

How did she make him feel like shit for wanting to protect her?

"I don't," he said. "But I want you dating that fucker even less. The good old boy network let him retire from the military instead of prosecuting him, but he was accused of forcing a young female airman under his command to engage in sexual relations. The key word is *forcing*, Diana."

"Heard you, Magic Man, and I appreciate the warning. But I've got this. Now if you're finished with the lecture, I'm going to bed. It was a long, tiring day and I'm beat. Not to mention boneless. You do know your way around a female body, that's for sure."

"Diana, for fuck's sake—" he started to say.

But she wasn't there. She'd already hung up on him.

14

Diana dressed with care. No short skirts, no low-cut tops, nothing to encourage Brent Gannon to leer or touch. He would anyway, but she wasn't planning to make access easy.

She chose a pair of tight skinny jeans that tucked into black ankle boots, a long-sleeved rust-colored top, and a black leather bomber jacket. She applied makeup. Just enough to highlight her eyes and lips.

Her hair was long and loose, curled at the ends. She liked the look, though she hated wasting it on Gannon.

She'd far rather it was for Alex.

A curl of heat unfurled in her belly. Damn the man. She'd thought he would show up today, try to talk her out of meeting Gannon, but he hadn't so much as texted. She'd actually spent the day in a state of half-arousal, expecting him to storm up to her door like a thundercloud.

And then expecting him to strip her naked and take control the way he had last night. Ordering her not to meet Gannon while attempting to fuck her into compliance.

She still wasn't over the things he'd done to her body. The way he'd taken her to places she'd never been before. She wasn't sure if he was joking about spanking her or not, but she half thought she'd let him if he tried. Just to see if it was as exciting in reality as it sounded when he growled the words.

She was more tender between her legs than she'd expected. It'd been a couple of months since she'd had a man in her bed, though she had to acknowledge that Joel was no Alex Bishop. Joel was the perfect beta male, and that's what she liked. Or thought she'd liked until last night.

Why had she accepted the diet plate for so long when she could have had the whole damned buffet? And how was she supposed to go back to safe, acceptable beta males ever again when she'd had a bossy, growly, ultra-competent alpha between her legs?

It had been stupid to allow her desire for him to override her common sense. She blamed it on all the things that'd happened yesterday at the militia gathering, and on her gratitude to him for saving her from the assholes who wanted to hurt her.

If not for those things, surely she could have resisted the itch that bloomed beneath her skin every time Alex

Bishop sauntered into a room looking good enough to eat with a spoon.

After a last check in the mirror, Diana slipped her handbag over her shoulder, placing the strap diagonal across her chest so she could have her hands free. There was a Glock 23 inside her purse and a Sig P320 at her back. Gannon would notice it, but that was the point. No dumb blonde act tonight. Just competence and confidence combined with manufactured interest in his manliness.

She locked her door and headed downstairs. The building was quiet, the only sounds muted televisions behind apartment doors. The sun was dropping behind the horizon and dusk stretched pink and purple fingers across the sky as she emerged into the parking lot.

The leaves were beginning to turn colors on the trees, but it was the barest hint. The days were still plenty warm, though the nights were starting to cool considerably. Diana hit the button to unlock her car, slipped inside, and started the engine. A motion at her window nearly made her leap out of her skin, but it was only Colleen Wright in a black kaftan and turban, both of which sparkled with silvery stitches made to resemble spider webbing. She motioned for Diana to lower the window.

"Hi, Mrs. Wright. Did you need something?"

"Hello, dear. I wanted to tell you about our cemetery ghost tour specials." She thrust a flyer through the window and Diana took it. "Ten dollars off your first tour. No guarantees we'll see a ghost, but it does happen."

"Thank you so much. I'd love to join a tour one of these nights."

She wasn't lying. Small town quirkiness was her jam.

"The spirits have guided me to tell you something, dear." Colleen put a hand on the windowsill, bent closer so that Diana could smell the stale cigarette smoke wafting from her. "Open your heart. Love will come."

Diana hesitated. Pasted on her best debutante smile. "Thank you so much. That's very helpful."

Colleen laughed. "No, it isn't. But you're sweet to say so." She rotated her hand with a flourish. "I but pass on the messages I am told. I'm not here to make sense of them, but the spirits know what they're doing. Open your heart, dear. The love and acceptance you seek is very close or the spirits would have said nothing. Oh, good gravy," she said, snapping upright like a rabbit sensing danger. "Reba is tottering about on the back stoop again. I think the kombucha is still too strong. Ta!"

Diana couldn't help but smile as Colleen trotted toward The Mystic Chick. Reba was indeed weaving about on the back stoop, though Diana wondered if it was perhaps bourbon rather than kombucha she'd been imbibing. Falling into an open grave in the dark would addle anyone's wits, especially when your bestie was continually hollering about ghosts and curses every night as you walked through the cemetery. Not to mention the seances and alien sightings.

Though she wished she could go explore the Chick, maybe sign up for one of the alien communicating courses Colleen taught (using the produce aisle at the grocery store, no less), Diana had more immediate things to do.

It was a half hour's drive into Huntsville to the bar where she was meeting Brent. The fact Alex hadn't tried to talk her out of it again weighed on her, but she pushed thoughts of him out of her mind and cued up an audiobook instead. It was a sci-fi story and it was good, but she found herself wanting to listen to one of those steamy romances she'd heard Emma Sutton and Aurora Harper teasing each other about.

She'd read romance in college, and then lost her taste for it after Viktor's assault. Now she listened to a lot of true crime, sci-fi, and self-help books about attitude and how to keep people from fucking with your head. All good things, but not as stimulating as a steamy romance novel.

Maybe she'd swing by the library one of these days, get some recommendations from Paisley Allen, Sutton's Creek's librarian. Paisley had always been friendly to her, though she was currently living with one of Alex's men. Ethan Snow was courteous whenever she saw him, but he wasn't exactly friendly. None of the men were.

She didn't have to guess why. As the leader went, so went the pack. And Alex had never made his dislike of her a secret.

The drive seemed to go faster than she wished, but she was soon parking in front of the bar and letting out a slow breath. Psyching herself up. She was good at the mental game, at shutting down her emotions and doing what needed done. It was what she liked about her job. She had to take herself out of her own head, figure out how to approach people, how to get the most out of them.

It hurt to be sidelined from the job, but she'd made her choice when she walked into the Huntsville director's office a couple of weeks ago and told him it was a mistake to let Washington have control of the Dashevsky investigation. He'd very rightly pointed out he had little choice in the matter, same as her, but that's where things went astray.

Nobody liked being called a coward and a bootlicker. Not her finest moment, that's for sure.

But hey, she'd found herself with all kinds of leisure time while she took the mandated time off, and that'd helped her pull the trigger on her plan to join the militia. She'd already been hanging out at Big Mike's and chatting people up, but an enforced absence from work was just what she'd needed to take the plunge.

She locked her car and went inside the brewery and bar that had been built in an old school building in Huntsville. There were a couple of breweries, restaurants, live music venues, and other businesses in the Campus 805 complex. It was a favorite hangout of Gannon's. He went to Big Mike's on occasion, but this was his staple, probably because it was closer to home and a bit higher class than Mike's.

He perched at a table in the corner, scrolling through his phone, a pint of beer on the table in front of him.

Diana watched him for a moment before scanning the crowd for familiar faces from the farm. She didn't see any, but that didn't mean they weren't there. Her powers of observation were pretty good, but a lot had happened yesterday.

Gannon looked up and saw her, a smile breaking over his face. He waved and she went to join him, pasting on her own smile.

"Hey, sexy lady," he said as she took a seat beside him.

"Hey there yourself," she purred. "What're you drinking?"

"An IPA. Seasonal brew. Really good." He picked up his glass and held it out. "Want a taste?"

"I'm good, thanks." She said it with a smile, and he didn't seem to take offense. She picked up the drinks menu and scanned it.

"I wasn't sure you'd come."

"Oh? Why not?"

"You and Alex seemed close. Wouldn't want to poach his woman."

Like hell he wouldn't. She laughed. "He's good for some things but he pisses me off most of the time, so yeah, we aren't exactly exclusive."

Gannon put his arm across the back of her chair, leaning toward her. "That's really good to hear, baby."

Ugh. She didn't seem to mind when Alex called her *honey* or *baby,* but this was like nails on a chalkboard the way it scratched the inside of her brain.

"Yeah, it is, right?" A waiter arrived then, thankfully,

and Diana gave him her order. She got a beer, but she planned to nurse it while she endured this man's company for the next hour or two. Maybe he'd keep drinking and she'd get something useful out of him. She'd come prepared for it anyway.

Once the waiter was gone, Gannon leaned back again and took a drink of his beer. "I don't think you ever said what you did, Diana. I'd guess supermodel, but not sure there's much call for that around here."

She tried to giggle, honest to God she did. And maybe she succeeded because he grinned.

"You're too sweet. I'm in law enforcement, actually."

She said it bluntly because she wanted to see the look on his face.

She wasn't disappointed. His eyebrows climbed his forehead. "Wow, really? Are you an officer?"

"FBI. I met Alex through the range. But I don't know how much longer I'll be there, quite honestly. I've been put on administrative leave while they investigate an incident." She finger-quoted the word incident. "Total bullshit, but you know how it is these days. The pussies in charge are all about political correctness, blah blah blah."

Gannon looked interested. "Yeah, I do know. So tell me, what did you do?"

She made up a story about arresting someone and the bosses saying the evidence wasn't good because she'd collected it illegally, even though they all knew the guy was a scumbag. Then she ranted about criminals getting away with too much, and about the kinds of people who should be thrown in jail and/or shot without costing taxpayers the money for trials or feeding and housing them.

Gannon ate it up. She'd thought about saying she was with a sheriff's department somewhere, but if she got into the organization and they did any research on her, they'd uncover that lie pretty quickly. So, FBI it was. Lots of people who joined militia movements came from professions like the military and law enforcement. They were usually white and male, but women and people of color joined too.

Gannon ordered more beer, got progressively tipsier and more handsy. Diana endured it, but she wanted to break his fingers every time they caressed the underside of her breast on the pretext of touching her arm.

"Women shouldn't be in charge," Gannon said when they'd been talking about President Willis and how the country was worse off under her leadership. "They don't have the stomach for it. No offense, baby. You are clearly the exception."

Diana simpered. "I think I'd do all right, but it's better if a man leads. People respect a man in a way they don't respect a woman."

That part was true, and it pissed her off. Men weren't automatically better leaders, but they were often treated like it.

"Too right. Damn, you're a reasonable woman. Fucking gorgeous, too." He leaned in to kiss her. Diana turned her head, so his lips landed clumsily on her cheek.

She took a sip of her beer as he straightened, glassy-eyed, weaving a little in his seat. She was on the same beer, not the fourth like him. "Tell me about you, Brent. I'm so impressed that you were a colonel, and you work in Missile Defense."

He grinned at her, downed the rest of his beer, signaled the waiter for another, and launched into the Brent Gannon show where he was the most capable dude ever and the rest of the world was against him for being so fucking competent. Oh, and his wife was a bitch for leaving him. His daughters were ruined by their mother, and they didn't speak to him either.

Her stomach twisted at the delusions this man labored under, but she had to keep him talking. See if anything useful popped out of that disgusting brain of his.

"You know, baby, if you wanted to take this somewhere more private, I could tell you some things you'd fucking love to hear about."

Diana perked up. It could be bullshit, but it could also be that Gannon talked too much when he was looking to get laid. "Oh, really? Like what?"

"Shit's happening, baby. Big shit. Can't talk about it." He put a finger to his lips with an exaggerated *shhhh* sound. He was weaving and slurring, but the worst of it hadn't hit yet. She'd like to get something out of him before it did. "But it's gonna happen here. Right fucking *here.*"

Her heart tripped. She deliberately pretended to misunderstand. "In the brewery?"

"No, baby." He leaned toward her. She stiffened but forced herself not to pull away. "The Arsenal," he whispered.

A chill rolled down her spine. "Oh my."

"Yeah, oh my is right." He put a hand on her leg, skimmed upward. "You ready to go? My place is close, and we can talk more privately. While naked."

"Well, I..."

His head snapped up, focusing on something behind her. She could tell the moment the shutters went down and the walls went up. She spun around to see what'd spooked him.

And came face to face with Alex Bishop. Dark, delicious, infuriating Alex Bishop.

"Hey, baby girl, what're you doing here?"

15

"I could ask the same of you," Diana said, her voice dripping with frost.

Brent swayed in his chair as he picked up his beer and drained it. "Alex," he said, offering a hand. "Didn't expect you."

Ghost resisted the urge to squeeze the man's fingers off, but only barely. "Hey, Brent. Getting cozy with my girl?"

"I'm not your girl," Diana snapped, her eyes flashing fire. "As you reminded me yesterday, I might add."

She widened her eyes at him, clearly telling him to back off. But he wasn't gonna. He'd waited as long as he could before making his presence known. He'd been in the back, by the wall, hat pulled low, nursing a beer of his own. He'd aimed a small listening device at them and caught most of what they'd been saying. He'd been content to let her work this angle on her own—until Brent wanted to maneuver her back to his place.

"Aw, baby, don't be that way. I know you're mad at me for looking at that waitress last night, but she put her tits in my face. What was I supposed to do?"

Her jaw worked. "I don't know... push her away, maybe? Not drop your eyes into her cleavage or swat her on the ass as she walked away?"

He laughed as she took his lead and sold it. *Good girl.*

Maybe he'd get to say those words to her later. While buried deep inside her, feeling her walls clench around him.

"Man, I didn't know," Gannon slurred, raising both hands. He seemed to be getting drunker by the second. "She gave me her number and I thought that meant you two had an arrangement or somethin'. Wouldn't have asked her out if I'd known..."

Ghost put a hand on Gannon's shoulder. "Relax, dude. I know it's her fault, not yours. She likes to make me jealous. Bitches, am I right?"

"Too right."

"Alex," she growled. "I'm going to murder you. Slowly and painfully."

"Nah, baby, you love me too much." He wrapped an arm around her waist and tugged her in for a kiss to the temple. Her hair smelled like flowers.

"I really don't," she muttered, putting a hand between them to push him away. He didn't let her.

"I should go," Gannon said. He got to his feet and

swayed before dropping like a rock to his chair. He looked shocked. Ghost turned an eye on the woman beside him.

She shrugged, and he knew she'd put something in Gannon's beer because the asshole was drunker than he should be.

"Maybe we should get you home," Ghost said. "I'll drive your car. Diana can follow us and then bring me back for my truck later."

"Okay," Gannon replied, because he wasn't really capable of anything else.

Diana paid the bill and Alex hefted Gannon to his feet, wrapping an arm around his waist and propping him up as he walked him outside to the silver Porsche SUV parked near the entrance. Even if he hadn't known which vehicle was Gannon's, the colonel's wings on the front plate would have given it away. Some dudes just couldn't let the rank go.

Ghost got him inside, buckled in, and shut the door.

Diana stood there with her hands shoved in her front pockets. She was a frigging wet dream with those tight jeans and all that silky blond hair. Blue eyes studied him, and she nibbled the inside of her lower lip. He wanted to suck it like a cherry.

"What did you give him?"

She shrugged. "Nothing that'll kill him. Just a little roofie."

"Poetic."

Gannon had been accused of roofie-ing female subordinates when they were TDY together during his active-duty days and taking advantage of them. One had finally made a formal complaint which had resulted in his being asked to leave the military. Not good enough, in Ghost's opinion, but it was better than sweeping it under the rug and letting him continue in his position.

"That's what I thought. I wanted to lower his inhibitions, get him to talk. Which he was doing until you showed up."

There was a hard edge to her voice. He shrugged. "I heard it. Big event. Arsenal."

Her cheeks bloomed with two pink spots. "You dick," she grated. "You were listening in. How long have you been here?"

"Since before you arrived. Did you really think I'd let you meet this asshole alone?"

She frowned. "You didn't text or call or show up at my apartment beating your chest—so yes, I thought you were going to let me go alone."

"Not happening, honey. Like it or not, we're in this together." He pointed at her. "Which was your choice, I'll remind you. You barreled your way into my op, so don't be surprised if I barrel my way into yours."

"Fine, but you've just detonated a bomb in the middle of it. He was about to tell me more."

"He wasn't. He only wanted to get you back to his place so he could get you into his bed. He wouldn't have told you anything."

She crossed her arms over her chest. The move served to push her breasts together. He dragged his gaze back to her face. She might be covered from her collarbone to her toes, but she was still sexy as fuck. Besides, he knew what she looked like under all that fabric.

The ivory skin, the pink nipples, the way her pussy glistened when he spread her legs and gazed his fill.

Damn but he wanted to see it all again.

"You don't know that, Magic Man. You only think you do. I could have gotten more out of him if you'd stayed out of it."

"Yeah, well, I didn't. Follow me back to his place and let's drop him off the balcony." He shook his head with a grin. "I mean let's tuck him up in bed like a good little boy. Maybe he'll talk while we read him a bedtime story."

She rolled her eyes. "Let's go, caveman. Before the damned roofie wears off."

It was a short trip to Gannon's place near Bridge Street. Ghost parked the vehicle and waited for Diana to join him. Between the two of them, they got Gannon out of his car and up the stairs to his apartment. Ghost unlocked the door and hefted the almost deadweight of the former colonel through it.

Gannon kept mumbling apologies about Diana, and Ghost kept telling him it was okay even though he wanted to punch the man in the mouth so he'd shut the fuck up.

Gannon's apartment was sleek, modern, and minimal. He had his military shadow box prominently displayed, and there were framed photos of him in uniform with various dignitaries on the walls. That's what a stint at the Pentagon could do for ya.

Ghost had met plenty of dignitaries in his job as deputy commander of HOT, but he damned sure didn't take pictures with any of them. The last thing he wanted was a bunch of photos of his face plastered all over anyone's walls. Not in his line of work.

Diana trailed him inside and shut the door. Ghost dropped Gannon on the couch and tossed a blanket over him.

"Go to sleep, Brent. You'll feel better in the morning."

"Gotta piss," Gannon said.

Ghost frowned. Diana shrugged. As far as he was concerned, the man could piss himself. But that wasn't going to ingratiate him with Gannon once he'd slept this off. Assuming he remembered anything.

"All right, buddy. I'm not holding your dick, though."

Gannon laughed. "She can," he mumbled.

"Sorry, sweet cheeks, I'm not holding your dick either," Diana said. "Maybe next time."

Like hell.

Ghost knew she said it to annoy him. He didn't respond, just dragged Gannon to the bathroom and fisted the back of his shirt while Gannon fumbled for his dick and then pissed half in the toilet and half on the floor.

When he was finished, Ghost shoved him toward his bed and Gannon fell face first onto the mattress. Then he started to snore.

"Thank fuck," Ghost grumbled before he started opening drawers and closets. It didn't take long since Gannon was neat and had minimal possessions, other than his *I love me* stuff all over the walls. Oh, and the stack of porn magazines beside the bed.

When Ghost went into the living room to help Diana, she was going through a desk and muttering to herself. She looked up when she heard him approach.

"Anything?" he asked.

"No. You?"

"Not yet. You dumb fuck," she swore. "He was about to tell me about something happening at the Arsenal. And then you had to tromp in like a bull in a china shop."

He felt the sting of those words. She wasn't wrong but fuck him if he'd been planning to let her go home with Gannon alone.

"The man's a rapist. And he was asking you to come here with him. You think he planned to talk like two besties on a girls' weekend? Or was he planning the full court press to get you naked?"

"He wasn't going to get me naked, you Neanderthal." She pointed toward the bedroom. "Is he dangerous now?"

"How was I supposed to know you'd drugged him?"

Those two spots of color were still in her cheeks. "You weren't, but you could also just trust me to take care of myself."

"You mean like yesterday at the farm?" he snapped.

Her chin went up, her spine stiffening. Her icy blue eyes stabbed daggers at him. "I admit I didn't see that one coming, but how was *I* supposed to know they'd be out there, huh? We both know you saved my ass, and I'm thankful for it. But that doesn't mean I'm stupid or that I'd have let Brent maneuver me into leaving with him. All I needed was a little more time. Which I won't get now because he's too scared of you to ever meet me for a drink again."

"Good."

She closed her eyes and shook her head. "You know what? Just help me look so we can get out of here."

They systematically went through Gannon's belongings. His laptop sat on the desk, plugged in to charge, but there was no getting into it without Phantom's help. Ghost snapped it closed again. He was tempted to take it, but he couldn't rely on Gannon's memory failing him so completely he wouldn't remember who'd taken him home and poured him into bed.

Diana flipped through a notebook she pulled from one of the drawers, her brow furrowed as she studied the pages. Her features hardened before she handed it to him and tapped a page.

The Greek goddess Athena was the patron goddess of heroes. She was also a protector of cities, particularly Athens. A symbol of freedom and democracy. Also a symbol of victory. Victory is ours. Victory is necessary to save us all from the evil of those who would see us weakened, who would negotiate with terrorists, who would lay down arms and give away our birthright as leaders of not just the free world, but the whole world. It is no accident that a true leader has come forth to forge a new world order. The mighty will be victorious. The weak and useless will no longer steal our power and our resources. Those who lied about me will rue the day when I lead our army to victory.

"Jesus."

"What are the chances he's really interested in Greek mythology?" Diana murmured.

Ghost scanned the page a second time. "None whatsoever."

"He said something big would happen at the Arsenal. But what? When?"

Ghost took his phone out and screenshotted the page. "I don't know, but that's what we need to learn."

"Should I point out again that I might have found out what it was if you hadn't gone all caveman protector on him?"

"Nope, don't need the lecture. Let's get the fuck out of here. Take me back to my truck, then head to my place. It's more private, and if we need to discuss something sensitive, we can go to the range."

She arched an eyebrow. "You aren't worried about Kane and Daphne seeing my car?"

"Are you?"

"I'm not the one who has to explain it to them. So, no, I don't care a bit."

Oddly enough, neither did he.

16

She'd said she didn't care if they were seen, but that wasn't exactly true. Diana followed him down the long drive toward the two farmhouses that sat on the property where One Shot Tactical was located. Alex went to the bigger of the two, parking beneath a massive oak tree that grew near one side of the house. She parked beside him, glancing at the smaller house.

There was a light on inside, but no curtains twitched to indicate someone spying on Alex returning from a night out. Diana didn't exactly expect anyone to storm onto the porch and demand to know why she was there, but she felt just about that unwelcome.

Daphne had been nice enough the last time Diana was at One Shot, when she'd been emotional over losing the investigation and certain Alex was at fault. And though Diana had given it her all to protect Daphne—aka Josie—

from the consequences of being an O'Malley, she wasn't sure Daphne's appreciation went so far as having Diana involved with Alex.

The men and their women were protective of each other. She admired it, wished she had it for herself.

But she didn't.

Alex waited on the wide porch that led into the house. Diana walked up the steps, breathing in the cool night air, willing her pulse to slow down.

Looking at him spiked it into the danger zone. Not only because she was pissed he'd interfered, but because she was still thinking about the things he'd done to her just yesterday.

She'd slept ten hours afterward, waking this morning feeling refreshed and sore. But happier than she'd been in a long time. Which made no sense. Her job teetered on the brink—Don wouldn't save her this time—and Viktor was about to walk away without consequences. Just like always.

But she'd been happy, dammit. Satisfied and happy.

And eager to do it again, no matter what she'd said to Alex when she'd intimated she might or might not be interested in a repeat.

She was definitely interested.

Alex stood with hands in pockets, watching her approach. He was a moody, gorgeous bastard, and she wanted to climb him like a tree. He'd worn dark wash jeans and a black henley tonight. He looked like the devil himself, if the devil was handsome and sullen and had just a little silver at the temples. Did the devil also have beautiful hands that made music on his lover's skin? If so, then Alex Bishop was definitely the devil.

He let them inside and locked the door behind him, then walked toward the back of the house. She followed, glimpsing beautiful hardwood floors and tall windows before emerging into the kitchen.

The kitchen was old, with white painted cabinets and Formica countertops. It was a time capsule of taste from a century gone by. She'd seen houses like this before, usually when she questioned people in rural areas. There was something charming about a house built last century and untouched for so many decades.

Chintz curtains would have hung in the windows, braided rugs on the floor. It would have been a homey kind of place. She imagined kids with skinned knees, laughter, dogs, and love. It was sheer fantasy, not necessarily true, and she knew it.

But she'd grown up in a much less inviting space. There were Persian carpets and priceless antiques, most of it curated by a designer. She and her brothers were never allowed to sit on the furniture, upholstered in watered silk, when they were children. And running through the house, chasing a dog?

Her mother would have fainted.

"Beer? Water? Soda?" he asked, opening the fridge.

"Water, please."

She'd only had one beer at the brewery, but she didn't want another.

He took out a bottle and handed it to her. He twisted the cap on a bottle of his own and tilted it back. She did the same, wanting to wash away the taste of beer and the stink of treason they'd encountered in Brent Gannon's notebook.

After carefully perusing it some more, she'd put it back where she'd found it. They'd made sure everything was in its place, looked in on Gannon to make sure he was still breathing, and locked up before heading back to Campus 805 to retrieve Alex's truck.

She was irritated with him for interfering with her interrogation, but finding that notebook cemented a few things. Gannon was definitely involved in whatever was planned, though to what extent was the question. Not that she'd truly expected him to spill all, but she might have gotten a little more out of him before Alex meddled in her business.

"Why didn't you tell me you'd be there tonight?" she asked when he still hadn't said anything.

He was looking out the window, jaw set in a stubborn angle, like he was thinking about something he had no intention of sharing. She wanted to touch him, slide her palm down his arm, squeeze his hand.

Ridiculous.

One did not pet a man like this one. If you wanted to soothe him, you dragged his mouth to yours and spent a pleasurable couple of hours letting him have his way with you.

"I didn't want you to know."

"I gathered that. Why not?"

His gaze slid to hers, eyes sparking. "Because I'm not in the habit of discussing what I'm doing."

"Not even with your team?"

"Not on this one, no."

She sighed. "I get why you want to cut them out of it, but don't you think they could help? At least in the background?"

He shook his head. "They need deniability. If this goes wrong and I get caught being a part of a group actively trying to overthrow the US Government, I don't want them near it."

"They already are," she said softly. "You're here together. They work with you. How will it not affect them?"

Temper flashed in his eyes. "It *will* affect them, but they won't go to prison over it."

"I don't understand you."

"Not asking you to."

She huffed. "Fine, then what are we doing about that notebook? Since we don't know the something big, or the when, all we've got is circumstantial evidence that he knows more than your average bubba hanging around Big Mike's. Maybe you could get your guys to surveil him again without telling them what you're doing?"

"No need. I dropped a bug in his apartment. I'll listen each night, see what I can pick up."

She was only somewhat surprised. Not that he'd done it, but that he'd been prepared to do it. "Or you could ask your team to listen. Seth King is your IT expert. He could probably write a script to isolate keywords."

"Know that, too, but this is how it's going."

"Fine. What if Gannon's too pissed at us after tonight and we don't get invited back to the next gathering?"

"I don't think he's in control of that. And he's not going to the powers that be and explaining how he got drunk trying to seduce you, or that we took him home and poured him into bed so now he doesn't like us anymore. Makes him look like a liability. He won't want that because liabilities have to be dealt with."

She folded her arms over her chest. "Okay, you're probably right. Especially since he intends to lead their army. Won't want to look incompetent to the higher ups."

"Right. Not sure he wasn't engaging in some wishful thinking with that army business though. But who knows?"

She thought back to last night when they'd talked about their reasons for being at the gathering. *Before* they'd ended up naked. "You said there was another reason you might not get invited back."

He hadn't told her what it was at the time because he'd said it wasn't safe, but they were in his space now. It wasn't a SCIF, but it was far more secure than her apartment. And if he wanted a SCIF, they had only to go the short distance up the hill to have access to one.

He shoved a hand through his hair. Such a sexy move. Made little sparks light in her belly. And lower.

"Our records were sealed when we left Washington.

They were hacked and stolen a couple of months ago. Trey McCann was behind it, but he said there were powerful people who knew our names. Which means he passed the information, or he was intending to. No way to know which one. Or who he would have passed it to, except he did jobs for Dashevsky quite often."

"Oh."

"Yeah. Dashevsky's people might know the truth of who I am, though not the mission. That wasn't in the record. They could let me into the group to keep an eye on me, or they could deny me. They could also let me join so they can kill me when it's convenient—after trying to torture information out of me, of course."

"Of course."

Diana chewed her lip. She knew about Trey McCann because they'd had to send a bomb squad to a farmhouse before it detonated and scared people across three counties. People in northern Alabama were used to explosions from Redstone Arsenal—rocket testing and ordnance—but a middle of the night fireball would have initiated hundreds of panicked calls to 911.

She hadn't known that McCann had stolen the team's records, though. That certainly added a new level of uncertainty—not to mention danger—to joining the militia. If the leaders knew his history, they'd be suspicious from the start. Didn't mean they wouldn't let him in since they'd be able to keep a close eye on him, but they'd never let him know their real plans.

And they'd eliminate him if he learned anything he shouldn't.

"If you're thinking you'd rather not work with me on this, I wouldn't blame you. Let me do it alone and I'll keep you informed."

Everything inside her rebelled at the idea of letting him go back without her.

"No, sorry, you aren't getting rid of me that easily. If anything, you're going to need backup."

"Diana," he said, his voice tight.

She held up a hand. "Not a fainting flower, Alex. And unless you decide to share this with your team, I'm all you've got. I won't abandon you."

"Fuck me," he muttered, shaking his head.

Yes, please. But, also, fuck him for thinking she wasn't a worthy partner. For thinking that going it alone was preferable to having her by his side.

"There's the gratitude," she said, keeping her voice light though emotions boiled inside.

"It's not that I doubt you. Much," he added, and she had to credit him for the honesty. "I know this mission could be my last. I'd rather not take anyone else down with me."

"You fucking idiot," she growled. "You've spent years going into combat situations with a handful of men, and you didn't balk at that. So maybe Viktor's people know who you are. You have a plan, or you wouldn't be doing this. Tell me what it is."

He studied her for a second, then shook his head and

laughed. "Goddamn, you're a ball buster. I'm not sure whether I like that about you or not."

"Just accept it, Alex."

He leaned against the counter and folded his arms in an echo of her posture. "Okay, fine. Here's what I'm thinking. It's possible McCann didn't pass the information. He was totally the kind of bastard to play two sides against the middle. He might have been negotiating, waiting for more money. Or he told Dashevsky simply for the pleasure of knowing he'd be causing shit for us. Even if he did pass the information, I didn't lie to Gannon or anyone else about who I am. I told the truth, or most of it, because they'd know a lie if they already have the truth. But if they believe I'm as disillusioned as I've claimed, then I might get to the next level anyway. I'm one guy, raging against the machine. How am I a danger to their operation?" He shrugged. "Like I said, I know the language and the culture of splinter groups. It helps."

She wanted to know more about him, but she wasn't sure he'd tell her. Still, why not ask? Worst he could do was refuse to answer the question. "You said your dad took you to Alaska. Was he part of a militia group there?"

He let out a breath, studied the floor for a long moment. "For a while," he finally said. "Until he decided they were ineffective and the best preparation against tyranny was to go remote."

"Remote?"

"The wilderness. Alaska has a lot of it, and much of it's inaccessible for months every year. When I tell you that no mission I've ever been on has equaled the hellscape my father created, I'm not kidding. I'd sleep on a thousand desert floors with scorpions and snakes crawling everywhere, and I'd face a thousand enemy soldiers before I'd ever relive even a moment of that life in the Alaskan wilderness. You don't know what cold is until you live like that. Or fear."

Her heart throbbed. "How old were you?"

"Nine when we moved. Eleven when he took us remote."

"How did you end up in the military?"

She knew he'd gone to West Point, but it wasn't simply a matter of filling out an application and showing up at the beginning of the year. You had to have fantastic grades and test scores, and you needed a Congressional endorsement. Not easy to get when you lived remotely.

"I had help from adults who cared. I didn't have access to school for most of those years, but when I got out at fifteen, a family took me in and gave me what I needed to succeed. They helped me get into West Point."

"I'm glad you had them."

"Me too. They were old enough to be my grandparents at the time, but they didn't hesitate. They've passed on now, but I'll always be grateful."

"Are your parents still...?"

His expression was flat. "Dead. Mom died when I was fourteen, my dad a few years ago."

"I'm sorry."

"Wasn't a big loss when my dad went. My mom,

though… She was the glue that held him together. Mostly. When she went, so did the rest of his mind."

"That must have been terrifying for you." He'd been fourteen. A kid. Not tall and broad and jaded with years and experience like he was now. Just a kid without the skills and confidence he had as an adult male grown into his own power.

"Wasn't fun." He straightened and walked toward her. "I'm done talking about it. No more questions."

He pinned her to the counter with a muscled arm on either side of her body. "Here are your choices, Princess."

She bristled even as her limbs softened because he was so near. "Princess?"

"You're a princess to me. Remote, beautiful, untouchable for a peasant like me. But here I am, about to touch you." He nuzzled her neck, his lips traveling up to her ear where he gently nibbled her lobe. "You even smell expensive, you know that?"

"It's, um, soap."

"Soap." He chuckled, the sound resonating through her body like a gong. "Fancy soap."

"French."

Honestly, why was she talking about soap? *Shut up, Diana.*

"Like I said. You're a princess. And I want to touch you. Everywhere."

Her hands curled into fists in his shirt as a sigh escaped. She'd been called princess before, but never had it sounded so sexy and tender.

"Your choices," he said, dragging her back from that blissful place in her mind she'd been sailing toward.

"Yes?"

"I can walk you to your car, put you in it, and say good night." He dragged her shirt free of her waistband with one hand, slid his palm beneath it, glided slowly toward her breast, branding her skin with fire. "Or I can peel these clothes off and take you to my bed."

She shivered. "And what would you do there?"

He chuckled again. "Whatever I want, Princess. But I promise you'll be satisfied."

"Let me think about it," she said just to make him laugh. She wasn't disappointed as it rumbled in his chest.

"Think about this, honey. My face between your legs, my tongue in your pussy, eating you good. I'll make you come fast the first time, then we'll take it slow, make sure all your needs are met."

Her body was on fire. Her pussy ached. She needed him to touch her.

"I've thought about it," she whispered, looking up at him, the intensity in his gaze turning up the fire. "And the answer is yes."

He gripped her chin in his fingers, tilted her face up. Stopped when she could feel his breath on her skin.

"I never doubted it," he growled in the moment before his mouth claimed hers.

17

Ghost wasn't accustomed to needing a woman like he needed air, but anytime he was near Diana Corbin, his body became hyperaware of her every breath and gesture. Of her scent, her expressions, the way she frowned when she was annoyed with him, the way her breathing changed when she was aroused.

She squeaked when he swept her into his arms and carried her to his bedroom. This house had two bedrooms on the lower floor and four upstairs. It wasn't a huge house by modern standards, but the Johnsons had had a lot of kids and plenty of land, so they'd built on as need be.

Alex carried her to the bed and dropped her on it, crawling over her to kiss her thoroughly before he moved on. Her tongue was his, her mouth, her body pliable and soft beneath him.

She responded to every swipe of his tongue, every tug of his lips on hers.

Listening to her with Gannon tonight… it'd been everything he could do not to interfere sooner than he had. And maybe he'd jumped in too fast, but damn if he was letting Gannon get her alone.

Everyone thought Diana was an uppity, cold-hearted robot of a woman. Not him. He knew she burned hot beneath the mantle of ice.

Thing was, he wanted that heat for himself.

Without a word, they each knew when it was time for more because hands moved to buttons and hems. They stripped each other frantically, though he got there first when he tugged her jeans off and settled between her legs. His were still on but the fly was open. He'd lost his shirt though.

Diana propped herself on an elbow, her expression torn between hope and need. He spread her with his thumbs and licked her from bottom to top.

"Oh my God," she groaned, falling back on the bed. "Why are you so good?"

"Because I like doing this to you." Her tits stood at attention, firm nipples pointing toward the ceiling. He wanted to suck them, and he wanted to stay right where he was and make her beg for his tongue. "So fucking sweet," he said, licking her again.

"Alex," she gasped, fisting a hand in his hair. "Please don't stop."

"Don't intend to."

He sucked her clit, tugging firmly. Diana moaned, pulling harder on his hair. He didn't mind the pain. Meant she was so into it she couldn't think about anything but the pleasure he gave her.

He sucked and licked her clit in turns, sliding one finger into her tight channel and then another. He fucked her that way until she exploded beneath him, his name a sharp cry on her lips.

So fucking sweet, that sound.

He didn't stop. He ate her again, driving her into another orgasm and then another before she pushed at his head and begged him to give her a break.

He crawled up her body, feeling smug, lavishing attention on those beautiful nipples while she lay boneless beneath him. Her fingers twirled in his hair, soft hands holding his head gently to her as she sighed and moaned.

Made him crazy with need.

When he couldn't take another second, when his dick ached to be inside her, he reached for the box of condoms he kept in the nightstand. He'd never brought a woman back to this house, but he'd been prepared to. Just never found anyone he wanted in his space before.

He kicked off his jeans, got to his knees between her legs and rolled a condom on while she stared up at him with a dazed expression. He touched her pussy and she gasped, her eyes closing as she bit her bottom lip.

So fucking sensitive.

He stroked her slowly, building her up again.

"Alex," she whispered, and his heart juddered at the

way his name sounded. She reached for him, positioning him at her entrance, stroking his length in a way that sent a quiver through him.

"I still don't like you," she whispered, her gaze fixed on his. "Just so you know."

He pushed forward until they both groaned. "I don't like you either. Love this pussy though. So hot and wet, Princess. Perfect."

He dropped to his elbows, and she wrapped her legs around his hips, her arms around his neck. "You're kind of perfect yourself," she said. "For a jerk."

He laughed despite himself. Then he flexed his hips and pushed deeper.

"Oh my God," she groaned. "Why you? Why?"

"Because I know how to please you. Because I believe your pleasure comes before mine. Because," he said, pulling out and driving back in until he was seated deep and her back arched to display her tits to perfection. "This feels forbidden—and that makes it hotter."

"So hot," she gasped as he started to move with intention.

There was nothing but the two of them in the entire universe at that moment. It was them, this bed, this room. They strained together, bodies seeking, tongues tangling and dancing, flesh shuddering with sensation. Ghost was determined she would come first. He stroked into her long and hard, short and sharp, driving her to dizzying heights.

One moment she was climbing and the next she cried

out, her body straining beneath him, limbs squeezing him tight, pussy walls milking his cock as she came, gasping and telling him not to stop.

When she subsided, he drove himself deep and detonated, his heart thudding as he poured himself into her. She put a hand on his cheek, stared into his eyes as he gave her that essential bit of himself. It was one of the most intimate moments he'd ever shared with anyone, though he couldn't say why.

It was sex. Great sex, but just sex. So why did he feel this way?

He dropped his head to kiss her softly, then disentangled his body from hers and went into the bathroom to dispose of the condom. When he returned, she was sitting up and gathering the clothes they'd scattered across the bed. It wasn't until she started to shrug into her bra that his brain kicked into gear, and he realized she was planning to leave.

And maybe she should, but he didn't want her to.

"Do you need to go?" he asked.

She glanced up, arrested in the process of putting on her bra. "I don't have to, but I think it's probably best."

He gently took the clothes from her and dropped them on the chest at the end of the bed. Then he climbed in beside her, back against the headboard, and pulled her to him until she draped an arm and a leg over his body.

"I think you should stay."

She sighed, her fingers tracing the line of muscle beneath his pec. "For how long?"

"As long as you want."

"Alex."

"Yeah?"

"Be straight with me for a second. Do you want me to stay, and how long? Are we talking showering together and breakfast? Or are you hoping for another round before you send me on my way?"

He skimmed fingers down her arm, over her hip, back up again. "How about another round in a bit, then sleep, shower, and breakfast?"

She tilted her head back to look up at him. "Why?"

"Why?" Honestly, he didn't know. Not that he intended to admit it. "Because what we do together feels fantastic. I don't do dirty secrets, Diana. We're supposed to be dating when we go to militia events, which means we should date now so nobody around here is suspicious when we spend time together—or go away for a weekend."

A line formed between her eyes. "Why do you have to make sense?"

"It's what I do. Stay, because I'm not sneaking around like sex is illegal. Unless that's what you want. I won't like it, but I'll do it if it makes things easier for you."

Her mouth pressed to his shoulder, a soft kiss that sent a shiver through his body. "You're strangely honorable for someone who doesn't like me."

"I don't have to like you to respect you. But I'd be lying if I said you weren't growing on me."

He said it lightly, but it felt a lot more impactful than

that. He did like her. Mostly. He'd figured out that a big part of the problem was that they were too alike. Take-charge loners with strong beliefs who wouldn't be deterred from their objectives. It created friction when they didn't agree on how to do things.

It also made sex more exciting.

"You're growing on me too," she said softly. "But is it a good growth, like a pretty flowering vine? Or is it more of a fungus? That's what I'm not sure about yet."

He snorted. "Ball buster."

"Neanderthal."

"I like Magic Man better."

"I bet you do."

18

Diana woke to a hand between her legs and a hard cock against her hip. The dim light of early morning slanted through the blinds. She turned toward him, slinging a leg over his hip, giving him better access to her body.

His fingers strummed her into a shattering orgasm and then he rolled on a condom and pushed inside to the hilt before pinning her to the mattress beneath him. She made a sound that caused him to still.

"Did I hurt you?" His voice was a soft rumble against her senses.

"I'm a little sore."

He swore. "I should have asked first."

When he started to withdraw, she gripped his hips with her knees and held him in place. "It's a good kind of sore. Don't stop."

Later, when they'd both come and he'd gone to dispose

of the condom, he returned with a warm washcloth and gently stroked it against her tender flesh. She bit her lip to keep stupid tears from falling.

No man had ever thought to bring her a washcloth before. Joel had always gone to the bathroom to remove the condom and turn on the shower. He never returned to cuddle in the immediate aftermath, never kept touching her the way Alex did. He touched her like he enjoyed it beyond the sex part, and that made her heart squeeze.

"You okay?" he asked.

"Of course. Why?"

He looked unhappy. "Your eyes are red. Did I hurt you that much?"

"I'm fine. Really." She sniffed and his gaze sharpened.

"Diana."

She hesitated. But if she didn't give him a reason, he'd persist in believing he'd hurt her. She didn't want him to feel that way. "You're thoughtful. I haven't had much of that. My own fault for choosing poorly, I guess."

"It's not your fault." His voice was rough at the edges. Almost angry. Not with her, but *for* her maybe?

"Not sure how you can say that."

"Because other people's lack of consideration isn't your fault. You can care about making sure your partner has a good time and isn't in pain, or you can be an asshole. I choose not to be an asshole. At least not about this."

She couldn't help but smile, which she thought he'd intended. "So, you admit to being an asshole."

"Most of the time, sure. Lived too long and seen too much not to be."

Including whatever had happened to him in Alaska. His mother died when they were living in the wilderness, and he escaped sometime in the next year. Just a kid. He was forty-two now, and she did not doubt he'd lived through some rough things. He was a special ops commander, not a raw recruit on his first mission.

"I've never been with someone like you," she admitted. "Not just the thoughtful part. You genuinely seem to like the things you do to me."

His gaze sharpened. "Are you telling me the guys you've been with haven't enjoyed making you come?"

She looked away as he finished soothing her body with the warm cloth. "I don't know if it's that, exactly. Maybe? I don't know."

He gripped her chin gently and turned her face to his. "Diana, what are you telling me? Spit it out."

"Oral," she squeaked when he didn't let her go, the heat of embarrassment crawling over her skin. "You're the first, uh... The first."

"Are you fucking telling me," he growled suddenly, "that no man has eaten your pussy before me?"

She put a hand over her face. Which was on fire. Why had she said anything? Why let him know how pitiful her sex life truly was before he'd shown her what she'd been missing?

"Oh God, this is so humiliating. Forget I said anything."

He pulled her hand away, forced her to look at him. His face was thunderous. Her heart hammered.

"Diana—baby. That's—Jesus, I want to kill the men who didn't treat you the way you deserved. How any man could *not* want to bury his face between your legs and listen to the sounds you make—I'll never understand it. You're perfect. Gorgeous. You piss me off, but I'd never consider not diving in there and licking my way to heaven. Fucking hell, Princess, I'm sorry you didn't get what you deserved."

She blinked at him. Then blinked again as tears threatened. "I didn't know I could ask for more. I should have."

"Maybe you should have, but it's still not your fault. You understand me? It's the men who were too selfish to take care of you before they took care of themselves."

She pushed up on an elbow. They were both naked and she felt the stirring of desire again. How could she want this man so often? She'd endure more soreness just to have him inside her. But she had a feeling he wouldn't go there yet. He'd want to give her time to heal first.

"You drink coffee?" he asked, his gaze finding hers after perusing her body again. His dick was throbbing to life, but he was trying to be considerate. Distracting himself.

"Naturally."

His grin fired off sparks in her belly. "One more thing we have in common then."

She arched an eyebrow. "Did you think I drank the blood of babies each morning?"

"Something like that." He stood. "I'll go make coffee. Gonna have to take a raincheck on the shower sex, unfortunately. Not that I don't want to, but you need to feel better."

"Like you said to me, it's not your fault. You didn't do this—okay, you did, but not on purpose. I don't have to go to the hospital or get a sling for my crotch, okay? It's just a little sore from all that banging around in there you've been doing."

He nodded. "I like banging you, Princess."

"I like banging you, too."

"See? There is something we like about each other."

He dragged on a T-shirt, jeans without underwear, buttoned the fly, and sauntered out of the room, whistling all the way to the kitchen. Diana headed to the bathroom and took a quick shower. She found an extra toothbrush in a package, used his comb to untangle her wet hair, and threw on her clothes from last night.

When she went to join him in the kitchen, Kane Fox stood at the counter. He frowned at Alex as he poured coffee into two cups. When Kane looked up and saw her, the corners of his mouth tightened.

"Morning," she said, going straight to bright and friendly since there was no excuse on earth he'd believe about why she was there, other than the correct one.

"Morning, Agent Corbin."

Her stomach tightened. "Call me Diana. Or don't if it makes you uncomfortable."

Whenever she felt backed into a corner, she went for

icy calm. People didn't know how to take someone who never got ruffled. She did get ruffled, but she was good at pretending she didn't. She'd learned the skill at the feet of a master—her mother. Mary Anne Corbin Adler never showed an emotion she didn't think about first.

Including love for her children.

The front door opened and closed. A moment later, Daphne Bryant walked in. Diana went rigid, waiting for the condemnation in the other woman's eyes, but Daphne only smiled like a cat who'd happened upon a bowl of warm milk.

"Morning, Diana. Sleep well?"

"Always," she said coolly. "How about you?"

Daphne cut her eyes to Kane. "Eventually," she said. Kane managed to blush, which was interesting.

"What do you want in your coffee, Diana?"

Alex held her gaze. He acted like this was a perfectly normal occurrence for her to be standing in his kitchen, wearing her clothes from last night, wet hair hanging down her back.

"Cream, if you have it. Milk if you don't."

"I've got half and half."

"That's perfect."

He took a carton from the fridge and poured in a healthy splash before stirring and bringing her the cup. Instead of walking away, he slipped an arm around her, kissed her temple, and faced the other two. It wasn't what she'd expected, but she was oddly grateful for it.

Then again, they were supposed to be dating. For all to

see. So it would make anything they did together less suspicious. It surprised her how quickly he embraced the idea. There was no easing his friends into the idea, no gentle introduction. He was going for full-frontal assault. Hit them with overwhelming force and conquer.

She should have known what his choice would be. He wasn't a brilliant military commander for nothing.

As expected, Kane's brow furrowed. In contrast, Daphne looked delighted. She went over to the cabinet and grabbed a mug. She was clearly at home here.

"I can see you have questions," Alex said, his voice a cross between mildly bored and diamond hard. "The answer is that it's none of your business."

"Boss," Kane began, but Alex must have given him a look because the man went silent.

"Considering what I've had to endure with the five of you going against orders to form attachments, I think you can acknowledge you have no right to question me about this."

Kane nodded. Daphne hip-checked him after pouring herself a cup of coffee, splashing in cream, and lifting it to her lips. "Mmm, good coffee. Kane forgot to buy beans." She smiled. "For the record, I'm happy to see you, er, enjoying yourself, Alex. I've always thought you were too uptight. A little lovin' will do you good."

"Babe," Kane muttered.

But Alex only laughed. "Thanks, Daph. Appreciate the vote of confidence."

"You're welcome. So, Diana... do you read romance novels?"

Diana blinked. Not what she'd expected. But Daphne was watching her expectantly. Eagerly.

"I, um, haven't read one in years."

"But you *do* read, right?"

"Yes, definitely."

"Good! Then you can come to book club. It's this Tuesday at the library." Daphne smiled. It wasn't entirely guileless. She was up to something. Diana could guess what it was, too. An interrogation.

"Shouldn't you check with your book club before inviting me?"

"Nah, we're a very welcoming crew. Besides, if you're planning to date Alex, then you should get to know the others who're crazy enough to fall for one of these guys."

"Babe, you make us sound like we're weird or something," Kane said before Diana could say she hadn't fallen for anyone and had no intention of it either.

Even if she was still having some feels from the conversation about the kind of men she'd slept with before Alex. Those feels were a bit of a problem if she were honest. She wasn't used to this, and she didn't want sex with him to mean more than it should.

I despise him. I despise him.

As if repeating that phrase would protect her. Especially when she could feel the warmth of his body at her side, his arm looped casually around her back. She felt protected and safe beside him.

"Not weird. Besides, Diana knows some of your shit already. She helped me get my life back. She knows you aren't normal."

Diana couldn't help the small smile that played on her lips as she took a sip of coffee. She liked Daphne. This girl was no nonsense, and she'd certainly gotten Kane in line. He'd been somewhat of a serial dater before Daphne, but now he was obviously devoted to her. It was sweet. And it filled her with envy.

"I should probably go," Diana said, setting her mostly full cup on the counter as the silence stretched.

Alex's grip tightened around her waist. "No need. These two were just leaving. And I promised you breakfast."

"Yeah, sorry, have to go," Kane said, taking the hint. "We're opening up the range. Just stopped in because, uh…"

"She knows why you're here," Alex said. "No need to make something up."

Kane glanced at Daphne. She shrugged.

"They saw your car," Alex told her, not waiting for the explanation. "And they wanted to know if you'd popped in spontaneously to harass me about something, or if you spent the night."

"Oh, I definitely just popped in. My shower wasn't working, so I thought, hmm, who would let me take a shower? Alex was the first person I thought of."

He snorted softly. Daphne laughed and set her empty cup down before looping an arm in Kane's. "Come on,

Candy Kane. Time to go. Let this lady finish her morning routine and get some breakfast before she has to go to work. If you want to come to book club," she added, "it's at six o'clock on Tuesday. We're reading about blue aliens with two penises this month, and Callie is about to die because Nikki suggested it."

"Thank you for the invitation," Diana replied, because she'd been raised with manners. She wasn't sure she'd go, but she kind of wanted to. Blue aliens with two penises? One seemed to be quite enough when attached to a man who knew how to use it, but the possibilities were intriguing.

"Nikki is Callie's little sister," Alex murmured in her ear as Kane and Daphne started toward the door. "She's seventeen going on forty, so it's probably okay. But yeah, sounds cringey as fuck to me."

Diana's heart beat faster than it should for such a mundane conversation, but it was how the conversation made her feel. Included. Part of the circle. It was a false feeling. She needed to remember that. She wasn't part of this group, not really.

"I remember Nikki," she said as they drifted after Kane and Daphne, coffee cups in hand. "She stomped on Dima Smirnov's instep when he held her hostage."

"She sure did. Nearly took ten years off Seth and Callie's lives, but the kid is made of strong stuff."

"Bye now," Daphne said as they went out the door. "Take your time, Alex. We've got nothing exciting happening this morning. I mean I may have ordered some decorations for Halloween, but nothing to worry yourself over. I'm sure the guys can put the skeleton together without you."

Alex stilled. "Skeleton? Daphne, what did you do?"

But she was already through the door and Kane pulled it shut behind them. A bark of feminine laughter came from the porch before footsteps sounded on the stairs.

Diana turned to Alex. He was stiff as a board, jaw working as he stared at the door. Then he shook his head and laughed. "Damn that woman. She's probably ordered a giant skeleton—and God knows what else—so she can host some kind of Halloween party. Never should have encouraged her ideas for an events business."

Diana was intrigued. "You let her start an events business?"

"It's supposed to be a small one, but damn if she didn't manage to sell a shit ton of tickets to her small-town brunch thing last month. Made a helluva profit." He groaned and dragged a hand over his face. "I told her she could use the profits to fund the next event."

"And that's a problem why?"

"Because Daphne possesses a singular talent for pushing envelopes. She'll have a damned carnival parked in that field before she's through."

Diana laughed. "I don't know. Sounds kind of fun."

"You ever read a book by Ray Bradbury called *Something Wicked This Way Comes?* Or watched the movie?"

"Can't say as I have."

Alex shook his head. "Yeah, well, carnivals in October aren't always fun. My luck, that's the one Daph will book. Cooger and Dark's Pandemonium Shadow Show, parked in my field and wreaking havoc on Sutton's Creek."

She was still laughing as he led her back to the kitchen. "Aren't you being a tiny bit dramatic?"

He sat her down at the small kitchen table and then pulled out eggs and bacon from the fridge. "There was a time when I'd have said maybe so, but that was before I moved to Sutton's Creek and everything I thought I knew turned upside down. Drama's in the water here."

"I think it's charming. I'll admit Colleen Wright is a bit kooky, though."

"She materialize beside your car yet when you'd have sworn nobody was there?"

"Oh my God, how did you know?"

It was his turn to laugh as he put bacon in the pan. "How do you think? She does it to everyone, and I'm no exception. Which is unnerving as hell considering what I do for a living. Not being aware of people approaching your position is a recipe for disaster. But she got me. Once anyway."

"And did she have a message from the spirits for you?"

"Nope. Did she have one for you?"

If she told him what Colleen had said, it would feel too much like exposing a piece of her soul. And she'd already done enough of that when she'd admitted he was the first man to go down on her.

"She wanted me to take a ghost walk tour. Offered me

a discount and then had to run because Reba was stumbling around on the back porch."

"The kombucha," he said sagely.

"Or the bourbon."

"Probably the bourbon." He grinned and flipped bacon, and her heart thudded.

"I could help you with that."

"Nope, got this." He cracked eggs in a bowl. "Drink your coffee and think about how much fun you're going to have at that book club."

She watched him beat the eggs with a fork. Now that she knew he'd spent a few years in the Alaskan wilderness as a child, she wasn't surprised he was so competent at cooking. She wasn't, but then she'd been raised with a cook and staff. What had he said last night about being a peasant unworthy of touching her? The memory made her stomach tighten, and not in a good way.

"I'm not sure I'm going," she replied. "She only invited me so they can grill me about you."

He gave her a look that said *duh*. "You need to go, Diana. You wanted in, you're in all the way. If we're supposed to be dating, it means you're coming to the Dawg for dinner, you're going to Rory and Chance's place for cookouts, and you're going to the book club. If you don't do any of it, it's suspicious."

"They don't like me."

"The guys don't, and that's on me. But the ladies— well, nobody tells them what to do, not really. Daphne likes you. I expect Kane does too since you made it possible for them to be together. He thinks he's taking my side by acting like he doesn't. Out of all of them, the only one whose dislike you've earned is Seth's. Because you ambushed Callie with that photo of Dima Smirnov and he hasn't forgotten it. But if Callie doesn't hold a grudge, and I doubt she does, he'll accept you."

"And when this is over and we aren't pretending to be together anymore?"

It was hard to think of not being with him, which was weird because they'd only given in to this attraction two nights ago. But she had to keep reality front and center. They weren't compatible long-term. Even if the sex was addictive, it wasn't enough when the foundation wasn't there.

He carried over a plate with eggs and bacon and set it in front of her. "I'll make sure our breakup is my fault, okay? They won't blame you, and you can still go to the book club meetings if you like it enough."

She arched an eyebrow even though her heart squeezed at how casually he mentioned their inevitable breakup. "It's two-dicked blue aliens. Of course I'll like it."

If for no other reason than how outrageous the subject matter was.

"You'll go?"

"I suppose I have to."

"Good girl," he said with a wink before he walked away.

She liked those words a lot more than she should. She liked *him* a lot more than she should.

19

"Respectfully, sir, what the hell is going on?"

Ghost sighed. It was Seth, of course. The other four members of the Ghost Ops team looked uncomfortable, but Seth appeared ready to shoot lasers from his eyeballs.

They were in the SCIF*, a place where they could talk freely. Nothing was off limits here, though he was beginning to think he should have made Diana off limits.

He'd been in such a good mood when he'd walked in, too. He'd cooked breakfast, eaten with the woman he'd spent the night with, and walked her to her car where he'd kissed her hot and deep just because he could. They hadn't made any plans for getting together again, but it was inevitable. Maybe not tonight since she was sore, maybe not tomorrow night.

---

* Sensitive compartmented information facility.

But soon because he needed to taste her again. Needed to show her how much he loved burying his face in her pussy and making her come. What kind of fucknut didn't want to take care of his woman's needs? And how had she gotten to the age of thirty-one and never had a man go down on her? If he taught her nothing else in their time together, he'd teach her how to accept only the best when she took a man to her bed.

His insides turned sour at the thought of her with another man. But that's what was going to happen because this was temporary. He wasn't the kind of man could do long-term. His shit went too deep, and he never knew when the cracks would form, when any woman who tried to stick with him would realize he wasn't worth the trouble. It was safer to be alone, to find comfort and companionship in the short-term and keep his life his own in the long.

Lonely sometimes, but that was the price he paid for his peace of mind.

He aimed a look at Seth that was somewhere between annoyed and mildly amused. "It's called chemistry, Phantom. I think you know what that's like."

"But with *her?*"

"Yes, with her." He glared equally at everyone as his temper jumped the tracks. "Not taking any shit from you guys. Not over this. Every damned one of you agreed to the mission. You showed up here with your gear and your oaths to this country, and yet one by fucking one, you got involved with a woman. Not just *let's fuck* involved, but *I love you, you're my everything* involved. Which makes you vulnerable, and you damned well know it. That's why the order to stay unattached, which you also know, even if you think it's unreasonable. You didn't have to take the assignment. So if I happen to find a woman who knows our secret—who has high-level access of her own and isn't nearly as risky to get involved with, by the way—if I find her sexy as fuck, not a damned one of you is going to say a word. Not. A. Word. Understood?"

They all stared at him with equally shocked expressions. Hell, he was shocked too. He hadn't meant to come out swinging quite so hard but fuck it. What he did with Diana in the privacy of his bedroom—or hers—was none of their fucking business. Not only that, but she wasn't the ice princess she presented to the world. She was far more vulnerable than she appeared, and she roused his protective instincts.

He still didn't know who in her life Viktor Dashevsky had hurt, but the pain in her eyes when she told him it was personal was something he wouldn't forget anytime soon. If he could help her put an end to that asshole's sick empire while achieving his own objective, he'd happily do it.

"Yes, sir," his team said in almost perfect unison.

"Excellent. Now before we go any further, I want it understood that when I invite Diana to join us at the Dawg, or anywhere we gather, I won't tolerate anyone making her uncomfortable. That's for you guys because your women are nicer than you are. They won't make her feel like she doesn't belong. Got it?"

Another chorus of agreement echoed in the room. Tension ebbed from his body. They might not like it, but they damn sure wouldn't disobey. It was a lot easier to ignore Washington's edicts than his. He was right here, in their faces, and he knew them well enough to know his opinion mattered. They may not technically be active-duty military anymore, but the structure still mattered—and he was in charge.

"Down to business then." He tapped his pen against the table. It was that or break it in two. "The update from Washington is more of the same. Delays, problems, obfuscations. Athena is on schedule, or not on schedule, depending who you talk to and whether the moon is in Virgo or some such shit."

Blaze groaned. "For fuck's sake."

"Know you want to marry your girl, Shadow, but it's gotta wait a while longer."

Blaze and Chance both had kids on the way, and their women were growing bigger with child. They had engagement rings, but no wedding date in sight. Both Emma and Rory seemed happy enough, planning their nurseries and reading baby books together, but he knew it had to chafe. Especially for Emma, whose parents were pillars of Sutton's Creek society and active in their church. Neither Dr. Sutton or his wife were pressuring Blaze and Emma, but he knew they'd probably like a wedding so they didn't have to keep fielding judgmental looks or snide comments from certain quarters.

Chance and Rory were engaged too, but Rory didn't give two fucks about other people's opinions and her parents were long gone. Her brother, Theo Harper, whole-heartedly supported her in whatever she wanted to do, so that wasn't a problem. No judgement there.

Still, Ghost imagined both men wanted to marry soon. Ethan and Paisley, who already had a child together, as well as Kane and Daphne, and Seth and Callie would probably like the freedom to plan their futures too.

"When do they say it'll launch this time?" Seth asked.

"January is the target date."

There was a collective groan in the room. Ghost didn't like it either, but in some ways it was better because he had more time to infiltrate Dashevsky's militia group. If it was up to the suits in Washington, he'd be sitting around waiting for intel and orders until the next ice age.

He was done sitting around. "You realize some CIA agents spend years on one mission, right? Infiltrating, assimilating, becoming part of the community. If all you have to do is run this range and the corporate security business while living with your women and forging lives here, is that so damn bad?"

"No," Kane said. "Other than not being in control of our own lives—no taking off for vacation, or a honey-moon, or doing anything that takes us outside a fifty-mile radius of this place—it's freaking fantastic. No disrespect meant, just pointing out the limitations."

"Understood. Still a small price to pay compared to what you used to be asked to do. Weeks downrange, stinking of sweat and shit and living rough while you waited to take out the target or rescue the hostages. This is a fucking fantasyland picnic in a field of wildflowers."

He understood the frustration. He really did. These guys were chafing under the restrictions, ready to kick some ass and take some names so they could move on with life—move on with their women—but they couldn't yet. Because Ghost Ops had them in a chokehold.

"You're right, boss," Ethan said, frowning at the others. "I know it sucks. But if we hadn't come here, I wouldn't have Paisley and Violet back. I'd still be the shell of a man I was before she came into my life again, and if I have to stay in this area and never step foot outside of it for the rest of my life, I'm gonna call it a damn fine bargain."

"Look, nobody said you can't ever go anywhere," Ghost told them. "Three of you can't go out of town at the same time, but we can operate with four if we need to. You can go to the flipping Gulf Coast for a romantic weekend. Athena will launch. It might not be as soon as we want, but it'll happen. Until then, we keep our ears to the ground, listen for rumblings around the project, and wait for orders from Washington. We've got a lot of contacts in the defense contractor community at this point. We've done security jobs for half of the companies in Research Park. We know where Athena will be controlled from, and we've got access to the building through our business. If we get intel from Washington about a threat, we'll act on it."

"What about the Dashevsky Group?" Chance asked. "They seemed to be our prime suspect for a while, what with Smirnov trying to get the code from Callie. Seems like Washington's swept it under the rug lately. And we still don't know if McCann gave them our records or not."

"We don't. And we aren't likely to unless they make a move in our direction." It was part of the reason he'd decided to infiltrate. Stop waiting and start doing. Give them someone to focus on instead of letting them target his team. He'd lain awake nights thinking of Dashevsky's people going after the innocent women and children belonging to his men. He wasn't letting that happen.

"We know that Diana's been told to leave the Dashevsky Group investigation to FBI HQ in Washington. Either somebody's pulling some strings to shift attention off the man and his organization, or the FBI's got it under control. Unfortunately, we're being kept in the dark on this one. But we've got a bug in Gannon's office at Eagle Tech, and we're listening. If something comes up, we'll do what needs doing and fuck politics."

He leaned back in his chair. He could tell them he'd put a bug in Gannon's apartment but then he'd have to tell them how he'd gotten in there. Wasn't ready for that yet. If something shook loose, he'd bring them in. Until then, better if they stayed separate from the risky shit he was doing. "What's on for today?"

"Blaze and I have a security assessment at King Solutions in Research Park this morning," Kane said.

"The long-range target group is coming at one," Chance replied. "I'm checking the field, making sure the targets are reset and the berms are good."

"RSO duty this morning," Ethan said. "Self-defense class after lunch."

"Combing through the local dark web for keywords," Seth said. "It's possible I'll find something about Athena or Dashevsky we can follow up on, but most of it's a lot of dudes in their mommies' basements trading conspiracy theories."

"Typical," Ethan said. "You know, if people who sit around thinking this shit up would actually do something productive, like get a job and work for a living, the world would probably be a better place. Fewer dumbasses believing everything they read online and causing trouble for the rest of us."

"But what would we do if everyone was happy and productive?" Kane asked.

"Find a new profession," Blaze said.

"Never happening," Seth told them. "So long as people click on crazy headlines, the advertisers make billions. They have no incentive to hold anyone accountable for the crap so long as the clicks make them rich."

Ghost got to his feet, signaling an end to the meeting. "Okay, think we're done here. If anyone needs me, I'll be grilling Daphne about her plans to erect that giant skeleton I saw in the warehouse this morning."

Seth snorted. "What about the giant spiders? Did you see those, too?"

"Aw, hell, really?" Ghost asked. "Musta missed those."

Kane managed to look contrite. "I swear I didn't think she was serious when she showed me the website."

"You knew about this?"

"Not entirely," Kane muttered. "To be fair, she distracted me."

Chance let out a bark of laughter. "I bet."

"Like you have room to talk," Kane clapped back.

"None of us do," Ethan replied as they filed out of the room. "Paisley wants anything, she knows just how to talk me into it. Not that I ever refuse her what she wants. But we both have fun with the talking me into it part."

Ghost snorted a laugh along with everyone else. He liked hearing them talk this way. Liked that they were happy. Nobody deserved it more than men who'd lived through the kind of shit they had. Taken the kind of shit they had so they could keep this country safe. Not just in the past few months, but their whole careers.

Despite everything, they were still willing to take a load of shit for their country. That's what made them who they were. Made them trustworthy and good. The kind of men who would sacrifice their own happiness if it came down to it, just so they could save people.

They hadn't changed. He had. Because he was no longer willing to let them. He'd take the shit himself, shoulder the load. If there was a sacrifice to be made, it was going to be his.

20

Diana didn't know what to expect when she walked into the library at ten after six on Tuesday night. She hadn't seen Alex since yesterday, hadn't talked to him. They'd texted briefly, but that was because she'd broken down and sent him a message to ask if he'd heard anything from Viktor's people.

He'd taken his sweet time answering, and then he'd told her no. She'd asked if he was lying to keep her in the dark. He'd said no. She couldn't think of anything to ask after that, so she'd put the phone down, screamed a little in frustration, and gone back to unpacking boxes.

Where she kept thinking about every moment of their night together, her stomach swooping and soaring, her heart racing, her pussy aching with need as memory after memory crashed against the shores of her mind. The box unpacking hadn't distracted her enough.

She'd thought he might knock on her door or call and tell her to come to his place, but she'd gone to bed frustrated. She'd taken care of herself, shattering with a moan as her fingers worked her clit, but it wasn't the same.

It wasn't *nearly* the same.

How had she accepted such unsatisfactory experiences before him?

She'd had another text this afternoon, but it'd come from Daphne, telling her that Alex had given her Diana's number and reminding her that book club was at six. Diana had responded that she'd be there, but only because Alex had impressed upon her the necessity of it.

So here she was, walking into the Sutton's Creek library in a pair of jeans with ankle boots and a thin cashmere sweater. A wiry older man, wearing a pink T-shirt that said *SOMETIMES FANCY, ALWAYS SCHMANCY* in a circle around a unicorn, stopped to stare at her. He had a stack of books under his arm, and she thought he might be wearing a touch of eyeliner.

"Are you here for the Bookalicious Besties?" he asked.

"Um, yes?" She knew the book club was called Bookalicious Besties, because Daphne had told her so, but now that she was here, she didn't feel like she belonged. Maybe she should just turn around and go...

"Great! Miss Paisley said you'd be here. I'll show you where it is. I'm Hiram Watson."

"Diana Corbin."

"Well, Diana, I run the murder mystery book club on Thursdays, and we use the same room. Follow me and I'll show you. We're the How I Met Your Murderer club if you like mysteries," he tossed over his shoulder.

She chuckled. "I do like mysteries."

"Then you should come join us sometime. Here we are." He stopped and knocked on a door, then pushed it open. "I've brought your new member, ladies. Y'all have fun."

Diana thanked him. Six women waited inside the room, paper plates piled with nibbles on the table in front of them and notebooks off to the side. Daphne jumped up. "Diana, you made it! Come on in. Grab a plate, get some food. We can't have wine, but we have soda and waters if you'd like something. I think you know everyone here..."

Diana pasted on a smile as a bought of nerves hit. "Yes, hello. Thank you for inviting me."

She didn't sense any hostility as the women welcomed her. It wasn't until she got a few crackers and some cheese and took her seat that the room when quiet. They were all watching her. Took everything she had not to squirm in her seat.

"Soooo," Aurora Harper said. "You and Alex, huh?"

These women did not waste time. She'd expected polite chitchat, book talk, and then an attempt to find out about her and Alex once she'd lowered her guard. Rory went straight for the jugular.

"We've been dancing around each other for months. I think it was inevitable."

"I would have sworn you didn't like each other,"

Daphne said, looking gleeful. "Then bam, there you were yesterday morning with wet hair and that satisfied look in your eyes."

Had she looked satisfied?

"Daph," Callie said, cutting her eyes at seventeen-year-old Nikki. Who rolled *her* eyes and bumped shoulders with her sister.

"I know the drill, Cal. Like you and Seth aren't making the beast with two backs on the regular."

"The what?" Callie asked, whipping her head to Nikki.

Nikki giggled. "It's Shakespeare. *Othello*."

Callie put her forehead in her hands. "Oh my God. I've done a terrible job. First the, er, blue alien book and now this."

Nikki slung an arm over Callie's shoulders. "Relax, Cal. You didn't think I thought you were playing board games in your bedroom, did you?"

"No," Callie mumbled. "But the visual you just gave me."

Diana couldn't help but grin along with everyone else. She already knew the Crowell sisters' history. Their parents had died, and Callie left her job in Poland to return and take care of Nikki who was still a teenager and going to high school. They'd ended up in Sutton's Creek because their parents had been nearly bankrupt, and everything had to be sold. When Griffin Research Labs had offered Callie, a brilliant programmer, a job, she'd leapt on it and made the move.

Nikki rode horses competitively and they'd needed

somewhere to keep her old horse that she no longer showed, so Callie had rented a small farm near Sutton's Creek. After someone locked her in the lab and nearly killed her, she'd gone to One Shot Tactical for help.

And met Seth, who'd ended up falling in love with her. Now they lived together on the farm with Nikki, a cat, her old horse, and a cream puff of a Belgian Malinois named Luna who was fiercely protective of her people, but also a lap dog who didn't quite understand she was supposed to be a scary military dog.

"Aaaand back to Diana," Daphne said when everyone was done laughing and Nikki was patting Callie's shoulder and saying, "There, there. It'll be all right, sissy."

Diana took a bite of cheese and found her calm. It was easier to do now that the tension had been broken by Nikki and Callie.

"There's nothing more to say, is there? We didn't like each other for a long time. Now we do. Guess we'll see how long that lasts."

Rory patted her belly. "Guess that's true. You never know what'll happen. I didn't like Chance, and he didn't like me, but then we did like each other just long enough to do this." She sighed. "I still thought I didn't like him, but I knew I liked being with him, if you get what I'm saying."

She did. She really did.

"Anyway, Chance was smart enough for both of us when the hormones were driving me crazy, and I didn't know what I wanted. He insisted on being part of our baby's life and he wouldn't take no for an answer. Then he wore me down with his patience and love—and here we are."

Emma reached over and squeezed her friend's hand. They'd been besties since they were toddlers, and it was clear they loved each other a lot. Emma was also sporting a baby bump, which Diana imagined meant the two of them were having a blast preparing for their children together. Their kids would also be best friends, and the cycle would continue.

Diana didn't know what that was like. She'd been isolated from other children growing up, other than her siblings, and she'd never formed those kinds of attachments. Connection was hard for her, and she thought it probably always would be. Whenever she tried it, it didn't stick. Since she was the common denominator, it had to be some flaw in her.

"I appreciate what you ladies are doing, and that you've included me," she said, her throat a little tight. "I don't know what the future holds, and it may be that you've invited me here for nothing, but, uh, if Alex and I stop seeing each other, I won't hang around and make this awkward."

The women exchanged a look. Daphne was the one who spoke because she was apparently the nominated spokesperson for the group.

"We don't know what the future holds either, but you're always welcome. I mean it helps if you like reading romance novels, since that's what we do, but if you and Alex break up, you don't have to break up with us."

Daphne reached over and put a hand on her arm. The touch was shocking and comforting at the same time.

"You did a huge, huge thing for me, Diana. You didn't have to do it, either. Trust me when I tell you that I will always be grateful for it. If Alex isn't smart enough to hold onto you, that's his problem. I will never let you go because I like you and think you're awesome."

The lump in her throat was huge. Tears stung, but she didn't let them fall. She also had to be honest.

"Thank you. I wanted to help you stay here with your man, and I'm glad it worked. But it might not have. It wasn't all me. I had help."

"Still, if you hadn't asked for it, it wouldn't have happened. I'm free from that part of my life because you did." Her smile grew. "And my father and brother are locked away for good, so that makes me doubly happy. You rock in my book."

"Okay, ladies," Paisley said, "I think we should get on to discussing the book, if we understand each other now."

"I think we do," Daphne said. "Diana?"

Emotion knotted her stomach. "Yes, I think so. Thank you all for including me. I almost didn't come, because I thought I didn't belong, but Alex encouraged me."

She didn't need to tell them why. Just that he had.

"He's a good guy," Daphne said. "Even if he's a bit of a hard ass." She guffawed. "Oh my God when he saw the skeleton and the spiders today. I thought he was going to kill me!"

"You really like to push his buttons." Emma shook her head.

"Honestly, I wouldn't do it if it wasn't a tiny bit of payback."

Diana didn't know what she was paying him back for, but she thought it was probably a good idea not to piss off Daphne Bryant, former mafia princess.

Everyone else nodded sagely, clearly understanding. She wasn't going to ask, but Daphne turned to her and explained that Alex and Kane had an agreement about Kane not asking her out—because Alex had been afraid Kane would break her heart and she'd quit her job.

"So, he deserves it," she finished, snickering. "Trying to interfere in my life like that. Making agreements about me without my knowledge. He's lucky all I do is irritate him with my little surprises. He puts up with it because he still feels guilty, heh."

Diana had to admit it was funny. "What about Kane? He agreed to it, too."

"Oh, I don't let him forget it," Daphne said. "But I love him so I'm nicer about it. Okay, onto the book. I got us sidetracked again. Sorry, Payz."

"It's fine," Paisley said, waving a hand. "This book club isn't strict. The main reason we're here is discussion. Oh, and making our reading journals." She placed a hand on the notebook beside her. "We'll tell you all about that after we discuss the book, Diana. And now I officially yield the floor to Nikki since she picked this one."

Nikki was practically bouncing in her seat. "Oh my God, you guys, this book! Did everyone read it?" She held up her e-reader to feature a cover with a shockingly blue man on it. With horns.

Callie pushed a paperback toward Diana. "You can borrow mine if you want to read it," she whispered.

"Er, thanks," Diana whispered back, taking the book, because it would be rude not to, and studying the blue man and his big horns. When she'd decided she wanted to try steamy romances again, this wasn't quite what she'd had in mind. But the cover was intriguing. Maybe diving into the deep end made more sense than trying to find a steamy novel about ordinary people.

"It was, er, hot," Rory said delicately. "Surprisingly so."

"Tell me about it," Callie muttered. "I still can't believe...."

"Get over it, sissy. All the girls are reading this at school."

"Do their mothers know?"

"Some probably do. Look," Nikki said seriously, waving her hands around. "It's not about the sexy bits— though they're very sexy—it's about how he *cares* for her. How he respects her and helps her navigate this new culture. He protects her from harm, but he also lets her make her own choices. He's the kind of guy any hetero woman wants—sexy, caring, protective. He's proof you don't have to put up with a guy who puts you down or just wants to get in your pants—or doesn't care about your needs as well as his own. If the dude doesn't respect you, then he's not worth your time."

Callie's mouth dropped open. Shut. "Wow."

"Exactly. You were so focused on the sex and the fact I read it that you missed the bigger picture. Romance novels can teach you things, Callie. Good things. You got lucky with Seth, but not every women gets so lucky to find a guy like that. Girls need to know not to settle."

"Well, damn," Rory said, folding her arms. "I just thought it was a smut fest. Turns out it's a life lesson."

Diana turned the book over in her hands. She could have used that lesson about not settling years ago. Maybe she wouldn't have spent so much time thinking mediocre sex was not only normal, but acceptable. And it wasn't just the sex. She'd never asked a man for emotional support, never expected it, but according to Nikki, the man in this book was all about supporting his woman *and* giving her fantastic orgasms. Who knew a woman could have both those things simultaneously?

"I may not know a lot about relationships yet," Nikki said, "But I know every single one of you has the kind of guy who would do anything for you. We all deserve that, and we should want to do anything for them in return. It's supposed to be mutual, not one person trying to keep the other happy. That's what I'm learning from these books."

When the book club was over and the ladies were preparing to go the Salty Dawg to meet the men, Diana slipped the two-dicked blue alien book in her bag.

Apparently, she had some reading to do.

21

The guys were kicked back at a table in the Salty Dawg, eating wings and drinking beer while they waited on the women to finish with their book club. After what'd happened a couple of months ago, when Trey McCann and his hired men broke into the library to kidnap the women, the men stayed close. Not only that, but they'd beefed up the library's security system to make sure nobody could break in again. If anyone breached those doors, six phones would squeal with alerts.

Wasn't likely to happen ever again, but none of the guys were taking chances. The fact they'd loosened their holds enough to let the women meet in the library after that—as if they'd had a choice—was only due to the heightened security.

When eight o'clock rolled around and the women

strolled into the Dawg, Ghost could see the collective release of tension in the faces of those around him.

Callie's sister made a beeline for Nikki the waitress, and they performed some kind of complicated handshake thing that featured slapping and popping and waving in unison. It was their thing, started when they were christened Big Nikki and Little Nikki because of their shared name.

He thought for a minute that maybe Diana hadn't come with them, but she appeared when the women split to go to their men. She'd been standing at the rear of the group. Ghost rose and took her hand, tugging her into his arms.

He told himself he did it for show, but the truth was he'd missed feeling her body next to his. He dropped his mouth to her ear.

"You survived it."

"I did," she said, turning toward him.

He took the opportunity to kiss her. She stiffened only a moment before melting against him. His dick began to throb, and he broke the kiss before it got any harder. He did not need a stiff dick in front of all these people. That was for Diana alone.

How had he gotten from wanting this woman to go away and stay out of his business to thinking about getting her naked and making her come at every opportunity.

"More of that later," he murmured. "If you're feeling up to it."

She stepped into him, went on tiptoe, and whispered in his ear. "Can't wait."

It was everything he could do not to take her hand and pull her through the crowd to the rear door and then up to her apartment. He preferred his place for security, but hers was closer.

She sank into a chair beside him, and he put an arm across the back of it, daring any of his guys to say anything. Naturally, they did not. There were no awkward silences, either. The women had embraced Diana, and they included her in their chatter about the book they'd read and the one they'd chosen for next month.

She didn't say much, but she smiled whenever anyone looped her into the conversation. She seemed to genuinely be enjoying herself, and not just pretending for the sake of their shared mission.

He wanted to tell her he'd talked to Gannon, that the dude was okay, if incredibly hung over, and that nothing more had happened as far as getting invited to another meeting. He hadn't asked, and Gannon hadn't offered. If it happened, it happened. If it didn't, he'd find another way.

Because he wasn't letting Athena fall into the wrong hands, and he wasn't allowing any of the people he cared about to pay the price it would cost if he did.

"Well, I'll be damned," a male voice said to his left. "Colonel Bishop, how the hell are you?"

He swung his head around to encounter a face he hadn't seen in a long time. And then he was on his feet, embracing the other man, slapping backs and laughing before breaking apart again.

"Asher McCrae. I'm good. No longer a colonel, though. What are you doing in this little town, huh?"

"Ash?" Rory said, standing up. "Is that you?"

Chance blinked at his woman. Asher's gaze slid to Rory.

"Ror! Hey, girl—whoa, look at you."

"Yeah, got knocked up by this Mr. Handsome Pants right here."

Asher and Chance exchanged a look. Then Asher's gaze slid across the men, recognition rocking him back a step. He focused on Ghost, and Ghost gave his head a little jerk. Asher nodded. He got it.

Blaze, Ethan, Chance, Kane, and Seth nodded back. They wouldn't have known each other well, being on different teams, but they'd have crossed paths at HOT HQ. Hell, they might even have deployed to the same zones from time to time. Shared a ride in a military bird across the pond to get there.

"I'm moving home, that's what I'm doing," Asher said without missing a beat. "I'm from Angels Cove, across the river. Grew up coming over here for football games and scout meetings. And sometimes church stuff. Hey, EG," he said when Emma sauntered back from the restroom.

"Oh my God, Ash!" she exclaimed, throwing herself at him. He put an arm around her and Rory both. Blaze and Chance went solid, but they didn't interfere.

"You, too, huh?" he asked, dropping his gaze to her belly.

"Yep. This is my fiancé, Blaze Connolly."

Blaze stood and shook Asher's hand. Recognition passed between them but neither admitted it. Then Asher shook Chance's hand, too. "Nice to meet you both."

A round of introductions was made and Ghost asked Asher to sit with them. He shook his head. "I don't wanna interfere with your gathering. Just thought I'd say hi. Couldn't believe it was you."

"It's me. Everything going okay?"

There was no doubt Asher knew what he was talking about. As one of the nine men of Strike Team 6, which had been captured and held for weeks by Sergei Turov when Mendez was on the run, Asher and his men had endured a special kind of hell at Turov's hands. Ghost had been part of the rescue team, and what they'd found had been men nearly broken by deprivation and torture.

Ghost had lied to Mendez about their condition when he'd called to report they'd retrieved the missing team, but he'd had no choice. Mendez had been waiting to find out if his woman lived or died after being shot by Dmitri Leonov. He'd been in no shape to hear the truth just then.

All the men lived, but not all of them had survived. Three men had chosen to leave the service when it was offered. Two had dropped off the radar completely, and one died when he stepped in to help a woman being attacked and got shot. Six men had stayed active-duty, but they'd left one by one as their enlistments ended. Not one of them had chosen to re-up.

Asher nodded. "Doing great, thanks. Bout to open my own business. Heard there was a new range over here, but no idea it was yours. I'd like to check it out sometime."

"You're welcome anytime. You opening a range?"

Asher shook his head. "Nah. Going into private security. Got some buddies coming to help me out."

"I know any of them?"

He grinned. "You know all of them. Cam, Austin, Lane, Reed, and Wilder."

What was left of Strike Team 6. "Man, that's good to hear. Going into business together, huh?"

"Yeah. Figured it was time. People need help, right?"

"They do. Be good to know you guys are close by. Wish you the best, Ash."

"Thank you, sir."

"Nope, it's Alex now. Come see me when you're settled."

"I'll do that. Nice to meet everyone," he said. "Ror, EG, good to see y'all. Glad you're doing well."

"Did you visit Theo yet?" Rory asked.

"Not yet. Just got here."

"Come on, I'll take you to the kitchen. He's going to wet himself when he sees you."

Asher laughed. "That was a long time ago, Ror."

"I know, but it's still funny. Come on, Idgy," Rory called. "You know you want to see this reunion."

"Damn straight," Emma Grace replied.

Ghost dropped next to Diana again, pulled her chair closer just because he wanted the comfort of her warmth. He was glad Asher McCrae was here. Glad what was left of the team was joining him. Losing a HOT team to treachery from within their own government had been hard on those who'd known what happened. You swore an oath and you worked your ass off, believing in your country's ideals, and then someone who was supposed to be serving the nation was actually serving themselves when they gave you up to the enemy.

It was monstrous, and it shouldn't have happened, but former Vice President Mark DeWitt had gotten what was coming to him. Justice prevailed this time.

They'd been sitting around shooting the breeze for probably another twenty minutes after Rory and Emma returned when Callie prodded Seth. He didn't miss a beat.

"Gotta head out," he said, standing and taking Callie's hand as she got up with him. "Nikki has school tomorrow."

Nikki was currently sitting at another table with a friend, but what did Ghost know about kids? It was approaching nine and the drive out to their place was a good half hour.

Beside him, Diana yawned behind her hand. Ghost seized on it. "Us too," he said, standing.

She followed his lead, and they said their goodbyes. He put a hand against the small of her back and guided her toward the door, giving Asher a nod as he passed. Asher sat at a table with Theo Harper. They each had a beer, and they were laughing. There'd been too many soldiers in HOT to know everyone's background, which was why he hadn't known Asher was from Angels Cove.

Nothing much over there they didn't have here. It was something of an artists' colony, with little shops filled with paintings, jewelry, pottery, and other things that he personally had no use for. It was more isolated than this side of the river. Seemed an odd place to set up a security business, but maybe that was the point.

He didn't know what it was like to have a hometown to return to, but he thought he could understand. Especially based on the greeting Ash had gotten from Emma and Rory. Like old friends.

He ushered Diana out the back door and down the steps. The night was chilly, but she had on a sweater. A soft as silk sweater that shaped her curves without clinging. He took her hand. She didn't stop him, didn't pull away.

"Your place or mine?" he asked as they walked.

"Mine's closer."

"Exactly what I've been thinking for the past hour."

She laughed, the sound tinkling into his veins like music. "That long, huh?"

"Since the second you walked in, and I saw you. Hell, probably since I walked into the Dawg, if I'm honest."

He caught her and spun her in front of him, tugged her in close and waltzed her in circles while she laughed. Of course she knew how to waltz. He did because he'd learned as a young officer, knowing he'd be going to official events and not wanting to look like he didn't have a clue. He'd waltzed general's wives, ambassadors, and at least one senator. It *always* came in handy.

But none of those times compared to the sheer joy on Diana's face as she twirled and glided and laughed. He stopped spinning and pulled her into his arms, plastering her against him from breast to belly to hip. Every nerve ending in his body twitched alive.

"I've been patient, Diana, but I need to be inside you again."

"I need it, too," she admitted.

They hurried for the Sutton Building, unlocked the back door, and raced up the stairs. He took her key and inserted it in the lock while he pinned her to the door and kissed her soundly, then caught her as the door flew open. He pulled her inside, kicked the door closed and shot the lock. When he turned, she was on him, ripping at his shirt.

He pulled her sweater over her head and dropped it. They went for jeans, unsnapping and unzipping, pushing down hips, until he was naked, and she only had on a pair of lacy panties and a bra that displayed her breasts like they perched on his own personal shelf. He tugged the cups down until her flesh mounded over them and attacked her nipples with lips and tongue.

"Alex," she moaned.

"You make me crazy," he growled before lifting her up and carrying her to the couch where he sat her on the back of it and dropped to his knees between her legs. She cried out as he buried his face in her sweet, wet heat, her fingers curling in his hair, holding him to her. As if he needed any incentive to eat her up.

Her ankles crossed over his back, her thighs falling open a bit more as her cries grew louder. He sent her over the edge without mercy, drove her to a second peak, and then straightened and would have slammed into her except for the lack of a condom.

"You don't need it," she said, knowing why he hesitated, her voice husky. "Unless you want it, or you need to protect me. I have an IUD and I'm not promiscuous."

Hell, maybe he wasn't thinking straight. Maybe she did that to him. But he stepped between those gorgeous thighs and drove in to the hilt.

"Jesus," he gasped. "So fucking wet and hot."

"Please," she moaned. "I'm so close. Don't stop."

"I haven't moved yet, Princess."

"I know. Still close."

He held her hips to keep her from tumbling off the back of the couch and drove into her again and again. Harder, sharper, sweeter, until she fell apart, her silky walls squeezing him tight as she came. He bent to suck a nipple into his mouth and fucked her stronger while she begged him not to stop.

She came again, her walls rippling down the length of his cock. Two more pumps and he came hard, his semen shooting deep inside her. He held her, her forehead laying against his chest, her breaths panting on his damp skin.

His heart careened like a downhill skier, and his legs were rubber.

"I still don't like you," she said against his skin, her breath tickling him. "But you sure know how to show a girl a good time. Think I might put your number on the bathroom wall at the Dawg."

He laughed and tipped her head back with a fist beneath her chin. "You do that, you might have to share this good time with other women. That what you want?"

Her eyes were twin pools of turquoise. Warm, inviting. Like a tropical sea. "Since you put it that way, no. Think I'll keep having my way with you and enjoying all the spoils."

He kissed her briefly, then pulled out so he could get a washcloth to clean her up. The sight of his cum dripping from her slick heat sent a wave of possessiveness through him. Instead of cleaning her, he swept her into his arms, carried her to the bedroom, and gave her as much good time as she could handle.

They fell asleep tangled together in her bed. Before he drifted off, she mumbled, "Still don't like you."

His arms tightened around her. Her face was against his neck, an arm and leg slung over his body.

"Still don't like you, either."

"Good," she yawned. "I'd hate this to get awkward."

22

I t was too delicious, waking up with Alex Bishop in her bed. Because the man was insatiable. He turned her insides to a quivering mess of neediness and her body to a boneless heap. He licked and stroked and sucked in all the right places, until she flew apart even though she'd have sworn she couldn't possibly do it again.

They showered together, kissing, stroking, soaping each other's bodies before finally rinsing and turning off the cooling water. She vaguely thought her water bill was going to be hell this month, and then she decided she didn't care.

She made coffee while he stuck bagels in the toaster and then spread them with cream cheese. She picked up the remote and flicked on the television to hear the news. Local news was so much nicer here than it'd been back home in DC. Huntsville was growing quickly, but the crime segment was mercifully short in comparison.

Alex set her bagel in front of her and kissed her forehead before returning to fix his own. She sighed as she took a bite. Joel had sometimes made breakfast for her when they spent the night together, but there were no kisses or ass squeezes accompanying delivery.

Alex always touched her when they were together. She didn't know why she kept saying she didn't like him when it was quite obviously a lie she told herself. He repeated it back to her whenever she said it, but he didn't treat her that way. He treated her like she was special. Like he cared for more than getting laid.

Even if it wasn't true, it was nice.

"I forgot to ask," she said as she poured them both coffee. "Did Daphne really order a giant skeleton?"

She knew the answer, but she wanted his reaction. It did not disappoint.

"She damn sure did. And a couple of giant skeleton spiders too. Not that spiders have internal skeletons, but that doesn't stop Halloween decoration manufacturers, apparently."

"I've seen those. Kinda ridiculous, but also probably scary if you encounter it at night. What's her plan?"

"Vagueness about a family event with a bouncy haunted house, hot dogs, and safety demonstrations. For adults and kids both."

"Not a bad idea, really. At least it's not that carnival you were worried about."

He laughed. "No, but it's still not what I wanna think about when I've got more pressing shit going on."

Athena and the militia. Whether or not they'd be invited to the next level.

"We need to talk about what we're going to do next," she said.

He nodded. "Not here, though."

"Agreed. But soon."

"Can you come to the farm tonight?"

A shiver rocked through her. Because she knew what would happen when she went out there. Another hot night of him giving her everything she'd never realized she wanted until him.

"I have nothing pressing going on. I—"

Whatever she'd been about to say died in her throat as a familiar voice emerged from the local news. She whipped around. Viktor's face filled the screen, and her stomach clenched. Tiny beads of sweat popped up on her forehead, between her breasts. He was in town today to cut a ribbon for an organization that worked to deliver clean water to poor areas of the world. The interviewer asked if he had any other events planned. He said he was looking forward to seeing the Space and Rocket Center before he left.

Diana shuddered. Despite Viktor's supposed humanitarian work, it'd been remarkably easy to avoid any footage of him speaking. He wasn't often in the news, except as b-roll while someone else did the voice-over about his philanthropic efforts. Whenever she came across any film of him speaking, she turned it off or changed the channel to a different news source.

She grappled for the remote and clicked the television off, but not soon enough. That insidious voice was in her head, his Russian vowels heavy and dark. Destructive. So casually destructive.

"Hey."

She turned blindly toward the voice speaking to her now. A hand touched her cheek, slid through the moisture on her skin. It hit her that she'd started to cry. Embarrassment crowded into the frame as she ducked her head and wiped the tears away.

"Sorry. I don't know why that happened."

"Princess," he said, his voice soft and soothing. "Come here."

His arms were open, welcoming. She slid onto his lap, fell into those arms, and tucked her head into the crook of his neck. His skin was warm, and he smelled good. Like her French soap, but it wasn't feminine on him. His body chemistry turned it into something uniquely his. Deliciously his.

She closed her eyes. When had anyone ever held her so tenderly? It wasn't real, she knew that, but he was a decent man and she liked how he made her feel protected and safe.

"You don't have to tell me about it. Not yet. But I hope you will one day."

"It's ugly," she whispered, her heart bashing her ribs.

"The things that drive us usually are."

She lifted her head. "Alaska?"

He nodded. His pewter eyes held reams of pain. In

that moment, she felt like she could tell him. Like he'd understand. She'd never told anyone because she hadn't thought they would. Like Viktor had said, she'd gone with him willingly. And though she knew that for the bullshit it was now, she hadn't known it then. It's how men preyed on women, especially younger women who lacked enough experience of the world to recognize the bullshit.

Not that she could have walked into a police station and reported a rape. It absolutely would have gone his way, and she'd have suffered for it. So would her family because she had no doubt he would have made good on his promise to ruin them.

But if she'd had more experience, she would have known not to believe she was at fault. That's the part she hadn't trusted herself enough to refute. He'd said it was her fault, and she'd believed him, at least on some level. It had made her doubt herself and despise herself. Without anyone to talk to, she'd let it fester until she'd had to do something or let it consume her.

She'd chosen the FBI, and she'd been fighting injustice since. But was it ever enough?

"Do you want to talk about it?" he asked softly.

The words jammed in her throat. She wanted to, but she'd held them for so long that it was impossible to speak them aloud. Besides, what if she was wrong? What if she told him and he didn't understand? Or, worse, saw her as helpless and weak? He wouldn't trust her to have his back —not that he did now, but she'd prove it to him if she got the chance.

If she told him about Viktor, it would ruin everything. He'd believe her incompetent.

"No." The word was a razor blade. It hurt. But the truth would hurt even worse.

He pushed her hair back, tucked it behind an ear. "Okay, honey. Just know that if you ever want to, I'm here."

She sniffed and made herself smile. "You don't like me, remember? You don't want to know my secrets. You might have to feel some sympathy for me then."

"Oh yeah, thanks for reminding me. I almost forgot."

His thumb swept the inside of her wrist until she shivered with longing.

She found the strength to slide to the floor and walk away before she did something dumb. Like tell him everything. "More coffee?" She picked up the pot and waved it.

"Sounds good."

She poured some into each cup, avoiding his gaze while she did so. Her phone buzzed. She picked it up, hoping it was Gannon—or even Teddy—inviting her to another militia gathering.

Nothing quite so exciting, unfortunately. "Well, hell," she muttered.

"What is it?"

"Ackerman. My suspension is over. I can go back to work."

"Thought that's what you wanted."

Her gut twisted. "It was. But I feel like we're onto something. I want to be free to investigate, not chasing my tail on orders from people who don't want me involved in the Dashevsky investigation."

"Nothing's happening fast, Diana. Recruiting moves slowly with these movements, especially with something like this. If they're really planning some kind of attack, and they have *his* resources, they won't half-ass this thing. The two I met weren't gravy SEALs. They're most likely intelligence officers in somebody's army or CIA equivalent, and they aren't rushing anything without more intel. This isn't happening in a week."

She grumbled. "You're right. Maybe I'll find something once I have access to the servers again."

"See? There's always a bright side."

"I just really, *really* want to nail that bastard. I want to pin him to a wall and watch him squirm, and I want him to know it was me who did it."

He reached for her hand. Squeezed. "We'll get him."

She almost believed it was possible.

23

"There she is," Clay Ackerman said as Diana walked into the office later that morning.

She tossed her purse on her desk and grinned at him. "Did you miss me?"

Ackerman grinned back. "You know I did. What did you get up to? Trouble?"

"You know it," she said with a straight face. Not that she'd tell him the real trouble she'd been up to, but it was the answer he expected because he laughed.

"Been quiet without you around here, kid."

"Peaceful, you mean." She nodded toward the door that led to the director's office. "Anything going on I should know about?"

"Not much. The usual stuff. Reports of a plot to bomb city hall that we need to consult with local law enforcement about."

"Oh great. The usual suspects involved?"

"You mean that group that thinks the mayor and the city council are actually aliens in people suits?"

"Bingo."

"They'd be the ones. Then we've got some espionage to dig into over in Research Park."

"Exciting."

He spread his hands. "I know it's not what you wanted, but this stuff is important."

"I know it is," she said, feeling slightly guilty at her sarcastic retort. Ackerman always knew how to put things in perspective. All crime was important, and all victims deserved justice. Didn't change the fact she wanted Viktor to answer for all the wrong he'd done. More importantly, she wanted him stopped.

"If there's enough to get him, they'll get him. Think we gave them a damn good start."

"I know." She plopped in her chair and booted up her computer. "It's fine, really. I'm just focused, and I don't like giving up on a case until it's finished. You know that."

"I know. It's what makes you a good officer."

A warm glow kindled in her chest. "Thanks, Clay. So tell me, how's the dating scene going?"

He waggled his eyebrows. "It's going. Got a hot date tonight with a cute gal I met at country line dancing this weekend. What about you?"

She knew what he was asking. It was no secret she and Joel had broken up. And no secret she hadn't seemed heartbroken either.

"Actually, I'm seeing someone."

"Really?"

"I think I should be offended at how surprised you look."

"I'm only surprised because you don't get out much. If you aren't here, you're at home. Never saw such a pretty young woman keep to herself the way you do."

"And I never saw a middle-aged man go clubbing as often as you do," she said with a smile.

"Touché." He shrugged. "No reason to keep myself at home, moping that Amy left me. She's got a new man, so why shouldn't I have fun too?"

"You like going out, and you should. I don't. I'm an indoor cat, Ackerman. You know that."

"Who's the lucky guy? Anybody I know?"

"Do you know everyone in this town?"

"Hardly. But since you don't get out much, figured it has to be someone who works here or somebody we've talked to during our investigations."

"You got me there. It's Viktor Dashevsky. Didn't you see he's in town today?" Her stomach twisted to say it, but she was going for smart-alecky. Of course Ackerman could predict she wouldn't have gone out on her own, but it sort of rankled that he knew that about her. He'd be shocked as hell if he knew about Big Mike's. Or the militia gathering. She itched to tell him, to get his advice, but she wouldn't. He would disapprove, and that would bother her.

"Saw that. The big man himself, in and out like

Huntsville's a cheap whore not worthy of a cuddle and a kiss."

"He didn't have to come at all." It's what she'd been thinking about all morning. "He could have sent a minion, but he came himself. Sure would be nice to know who he meets with while he's here, don't you think?"

"Diana." Ackerman was frowning. "Not everything the man does has an ulterior motive."

Wrong, she wanted to say. "You're probably right. I can't help myself though. I don't trust him."

"Not up to us anymore. We did what we could. They know what they're doing in Washington." He unwrapped a Hershey's kiss and popped it in his mouth. "How's the small-town living thing going? You get engaged to the police chief yet?"

"What? Chief Vance is seventy if he's a day, and he's married."

Ackerman snickered. "Your face, Di. Didn't you tell me you like those Hallmark movies where the big city girl goes to the small town and marries the police chief?"

Her skin was hot. They talked about a lot of stuff while driving around to interview people. Some of it stuff she wouldn't say to anyone else, probably.

"It's not always the police chief. Sometimes he's a Christmas tree farmer. Or he owns a hotel, or maybe he's a broody guy raising his small child after the tragic death of his wife."

"Fine, fine. So no small town romance yet, I take it? Except, wait a second—are your cheeks red?"

Dammit. "It's not precisely a small-town romance. He's not from Sutton's Creek any more than I am. But he lives there."

"You gonna keep me in suspense?"

"Is it any of your business?"

"No, but we're friends, aren't we?"

She sighed. He was her friend. He'd had her back so many times before, and he'd smoothed over her rough edges whenever they talked to people. She was abrupt and cool, and he was the friendly guy people wanted to talk to.

"Of course we are." She pushed her chair back and lifted an eyebrow. "It's Alex Bishop."

Ackerman's eyebrows climbed his forehead. "One Shot Tactical? That guy?"

"That guy."

"Daaaamn, I thought you couldn't stand him. Didn't much look as if he liked you either."

"Apparently, we were both wrong."

She kept telling Alex she didn't like him, but it was a lie meant to protect herself. If she didn't like him, he couldn't hurt her when it was over. They'd thank each other for the good time and walk away.

Her heart clenched. Ridiculous. They'd had sex a few times. It was nothing more than that.

But it felt so damned good that she didn't want it to end anytime soon.

"What happened to change your mind?"

What happened was he kissed her to fool Gannon into thinking they were together at the militia gathering, and her body hadn't stopped wanting him since. Not telling Ackerman that.

"Got to talking in the Salty Dawg one night and realized we have more in common than we thought. And then he kissed me." She shrugged, unwilling to say more.

Ackerman took the hint. He laughed and shook his head as he slid his chair up to his desk and tapped the keys. "Gotcha. Good for you, girl. Nice to see you having fun for a change. You're too young to always be so damn serious."

She liked that he didn't say she was too pretty. That was a man thing to say, but Ackerman never did that to her.

"And you're too old to party like a rock star, but here we are."

"The perfect couple," he said with a grin.

"Butch and Sundance, together again."

"Amen, sister." He banged the keys a few more times, then shoved the keyboard tray beneath the desk and stood, grabbing a piece of paper that emerged from the printer. "You 'bout ready to go kick some ass and take some names in connection to this bomb threat?"

"Nothing I'd love more."

24

"Seriously, Daph?"

"Trust, Alex." Daphne stood with her clipboard in her hand, waving at the field and explaining what her idea was for the family day.

A twelve-foot-tall skeleton stood beside the range with a pod of skeleton spiders ranging in front of it. Daphne had tied an orange and black scarf around the skeleton's neck and rigged up leashes to the spiders so it looked like he—it?—was taking them for a walk.

"You realize this is a shooting range and training facility, right?"

"Yes indeed, I sure do. And I'm telling *you* that participating in the community and providing them a place to learn about how to keep their homes and businesses secure, not to mention the most important thing of all—their families—is a good idea. It's practically a community service, Alex. And it'll bring more business in the long run."

"We don't need more business."

Hell, they already had more than they needed. They'd hired a couple of part time RSOs, but they were going to need more instructors if they kept expanding.

And they didn't need more instructors because that would just be more people poking around and potentially impeding the mission. Not to mention, once Ghost Ops wrapped up, would the range still be there?

Probably not.

Daphne gaped. "You did not just say that!"

"I did. Plan a fun family day if it floats your boat, but not because I want more business."

Her frown was monumental. "Then why would you do it?"

"Because you aren't wrong about the community service aspect. If we can educate people on some basic safety training, it's worthwhile."

She tapped her chin with her pen. "I'll see if I can get the fire department out. And the police. We can have demonstrations—oh, that's brilliant! You're brilliant, Alex!"

He blinked. "I didn't say anything."

"You did. You said you don't want more business, but you don't mind educating the community. We have the space out here, and if we can get the firemen and police to participate, a lot of the education will be on them. It's a win all around."

"How the hell do you plan to pull all this together before the end of the month?"

"Never you mind, mister. I got this."

"Daph, I say this with love in my heart—you exhaust me. Do whatever you want. Just don't ask me to give you money, and don't you dare invite a carnival to set up on the field."

He could see the moment that idea took hold. "A carnival—I bet we could find one."

He put a finger practically in her face. "Absolutely not. The first tilt-a-whirl or Ferris wheel that rolls in here, I'm firing Kane and sending him back to DC to beg his old contacts for a job. You feel me?"

She huffed and snapped her teeth at him. He barely withdrew his finger in time.

"Fine. We'll have our own carnival. No rides, no carnies, just some booths from the local businesses and some games."

He sighed and flicked a hand at her in dismissal as he walked away. Kane hovered near the door like a mother hen as Alex stepped inside.

"Uh, you okay, boss?"

"Wondering if I can ask Diana to send Daphne back to New Orleans. But sure, I'm fine."

"She's a lot," Kane said. "But she means well."

"I know she does." He stopped and faced his team-mate. "If you tell her I said what I'm about to say, I'll liberate your balls from your body with a strand of dental floss and no anesthesia."

Kane nodded, his throat working as he nearly choked on his own spit.

"You okay?" Ghost asked.

"Yeah, uh. Hell of a visual."

"Precisely. Here it is: she makes me laugh. I like seeing her eyes light up with ideas, and I like it that the grumpier I get, the more enthusiastic she is. For somebody who went through all the crap she did, with the shitty upbringing she had, she radiates joy. Some of it's you, but some of it's just who she is. She makes this place sunnier."

Kane's eyes shone with love. Ghost envied him that. He didn't know what it felt like, probably never would. Though thoughts of Diana made warmth glow inside him. Probably just desire kindling to life. Couldn't deny that sex with her was hot and all-consuming.

A thought he deliberately pushed away so he didn't embarrass himself with a stiff dick pushing against his jeans.

"Yeah, she does," Kane said with a goofy grin. "Best thing ever happened to me."

"You're damn straight she is. You ever screw it up, I'm taking her side. Just so you know."

"Appreciate that, boss," Kane said wryly.

"Know your strengths, man. In a personality contest, she's gonna win. But if I need somebody to charge into a nest of tangos at my side, it's you."

"Good to know I have my uses."

Ghost chuckled to himself as he headed for his office.

He knew for a fact Kane would tell Daphne some version of *Alex likes you and your crazy ideas* and he didn't really care. Daphne deserved all the acceptance and love from friends she could get after her life with the O'Malleys. Her father had pitted her and her brother against each other as children, laughing as they tried to one-up each other. When one of them hurt the other, he'd cheered and told the hurt one to toughen up.

As crazy as his own dad had gotten in the depths of his paranoia, he'd never physically harmed either Ghost or his mother. Neglected them. Made them work hard every day to hunt and fish and prepare for winter, where they'd be iced in for months. Going outside during those dark days had courted death at every turn, but he'd done it when ordered to do so.

A wolf howled inside his head, and he shook it to clear the sound. His dad and Daphne's had both been motivated by making sure their kids were prepared for the life they were given. Was that love or not? It was a question that haunted him sometimes, though less often than it used to.

The older he got, the more he didn't give a shit what the motivation was. Harm was harm, meant or not meant. His parents were dead, his mother because of his father's paranoia in taking them so far from the help that could have saved her life, and his father because even after all the prep and planning to stay alive when the government fell apart and anarchy reigned, you couldn't outrun your own demons when they were determined to kill you.

He sat down to go over paperwork when his burner phone pinged with a text.

> **Gannon:**
> Congrats, man. They want to talk to you
> again. They'll be back two weeks from
> Saturday. You in?

He rocked back in his seat. Hell, yeah, he was in. He sent back a response. Then he sent one asking if he could bring Diana or did he need to leave her home.

> **Gannon:**
> Bring her along. There'll be people,
> though not as many as last week. See
> you both at the brewery on Thursday?

Ghost typed an affirmative and then swore. He'd hoped Gannon would have said no about Diana returning to the farm when the Europeans are back. Then he could have told Diana very truthfully that she wasn't invited. Hell, he should have done it anyway. But he kept thinking of her reaction when she'd heard Viktor Dashevsky on the television that morning. She'd gone stiff and distant. There'd been sorrow and fear. Anger. She'd cycled through a range of emotions in a span of moments, and he'd witnessed them all.

Who was he to say she didn't have a right to go after Dashevsky for whatever he'd done? If he made the choice to leave her out of it, he was making a decision for her without her knowledge. He thought of Daphne giving him hell for the decision he'd made when he'd told Kane not to get involved with her, and though he'd thought he was right at the time, it was a shit thing to do. Doing the same to Diana, even if he was trying to keep her safe, wasn't going to sit right in his gut.

Fucking Daphne Bryant and her fucking guilt trips.

Ghost sighed. What the hell was happening to him? Thinking about what people *wanted*, about their emotions, when he was trained to be a military commander who didn't give a shit about emotions. He was trained to get the best results possible with the least cost in lives, and that's what he needed to be doing.

But here he was thinking about *feelings*.

His own feelings were that he didn't want Diana out there again. She was strong, he knew that, and she was a good agent. Taking Diana to a militia gathering wasn't the same as taking Daphne or Callie, for instance. Though maybe Daph was a bad example because she could outshoot most of the people there.

Point being, Diana was trained, even if she didn't have his training. She wasn't stupid and she wouldn't blunder into anything she shouldn't. What'd happened with the four men from the Dawg who'd gotten the jump on her last week wasn't going to happen again.

Because he'd be with her. They'd operate together, a team. They'd have each other's backs.

Didn't stop him from worrying about what he couldn't predict, but they'd go over all the possibilities before they ever drove onto that property.

This was a mission. They were both professionals. Feelings had nothing to do with it.

He bolted awake, heart pounding, his every instinct to leap from the bed and grab the pistol he'd left in the night-stand drawer.

Something stopped him, though. He was sitting upright, muscles tensed and ready, but a voice inside him commanded him not to do it. A scent of flowers and woman stole to him, reminding him. Grounding him.

"Alex? What's wrong?"

Diana pushed onto an elbow, her blond hair sliding over her shoulder to cover her naked breast, her expressive eyes staring at him with concern. He shoved a hand through his hair and subsided against the headboard, breathing slowly. The wolf had been on him again, its jaw closing around his throat. He'd felt the warm blood sliding down his skin, smelled the sharp tang of it.

Always, before the teeth crushed his windpipe and ripped him apart, he woke. Thank God.

"Dream," he said roughly. "Happens sometimes."

She sat up next to him but didn't make a move to invade his space. He reached for her, dragged her against him until she'd slung a leg over his body and an arm around his waist.

"I'm sorry," she said. "Do you want to talk about it?"

Did he? Not really.

"You don't want to hear about the things that give me nightmares."

She traced a finger over one of the scars on his torso. Souvenir of a knife fight in Syria.

"I had nightmares for a long time, but they're gone now," she said. "I think I just channel those feelings into disemboweling Viktor. Oh, and I often wish for a handy lion when I'm doing it so I could feed the pieces to it."

He snorted an unexpected laugh. "Damn, Princess, you're diabolical as hell."

"Remember that when you consider driving to the next meeting without me."

His belly twisted. "Already told you about it so how could I go without you?"

"I'm not sure, but I know you'd do it if you thought you could get away with it."

"I would," he acknowledged. "Unfortunately for me, tying you up and locking you in my SCIF for the duration isn't an option. Because that's about the only way you wouldn't show up."

"True." She moved, the soft hair of her pussy sliding against his hip. He dropped a hand to her ass, cupped the perfect mound of one cheek, let his fingers glide into the wetness between her legs. She gasped a little and widened her legs to give him better access.

The sound sent an arrow of desire straight to his dick. He'd already fucked her twice last night and he was ready to do it again. What made this particular woman impossible to get enough of? That's what he didn't understand.

He'd had her many times over the course of the past few days, and still he wanted her like he was a teen boy getting his first piece of ass. He was forty-two years old, and he'd long ago achieved the ability to regulate his needs.

Not with Diana. With her, he wanted more. Every time he was inside her, it was a revelation. The way her walls gripped him tight, the way she moved, the sounds she made. He couldn't get enough.

He told himself it was the newness of it. The fact they'd clashed so often before succumbing to the heat between them. This thing would burn itself out. Maybe not today, and not next week. But soon, because there was no way he could keep wanting her with this kind of intensity. This kind of need didn't last. It was raw, elemental, not rational or logical. It was instinct.

Her hand wrapped around his dick, stroked him firmly. He would have flipped her on her back and thrust inside her body, but she rolled to a sitting position on top of him, holding his cock while she sank down on it.

"Jesus," he hissed when he was fully seated inside her.

She threw her hair over one shoulder, but it tumbled back in a silky waterfall. He hooked a hand behind her neck and dragged her down for a kiss, his tongue sweeping into her mouth. She rode him slowly, her hips undulating, their bodies moving in rhythm. He was happy to let her have the lead.

For now.

But when the urgency started to build in his balls,

when he needed to slam home inside her and make her shout his name, he flipped her onto her back and drove into her again and again while she took everything he poured into her. Need, loneliness, fear—a lifetime of pain that was his alone. He told himself to throttle it back, that it was too much, that he was pushing her too hard.

"Like that, Alex—oh God, like that," she gasped. "Yes, don't stop.... *Please* don't stop."

Freed, he powered into her, drove her into the headboard until she braced her hands on it to hold herself in place. For him.

It happened fast. Her back bowed, her pussy squeezing him tight, his name tearing from her throat in a broken cry that included a prayer and a curse both. He drew out her orgasm as long as he could—and then he planted deep and poured himself into her, pulse after pulse, until he was drained.

"Oh damn, that was good," she whispered up to him, one hand skimming down his back while the other threaded into his hair and held him to her as he collapsed onto her.

His heart thundered along with hers as he took them over again, taking his weight off her. He draped her on his chest, their bodies still connected, feeling every pulse and twitch of her walls around him.

"Why does that feel so fucking amazing every time?" he said between breaths. "And why do I always want more?"

She kissed his chest, her mouth moving lazily over his

skin. "I have no idea, but it's the same for me. If you'd asked me two weeks ago, I'd have said sex was nice enough but not a big deal."

He ran a hand over her back, down to her ass, gripping a handful because he loved touching her. "Is it a big deal now?"

"It is with you."

Those words should bother him a lot more than they did. He didn't want her growing attached because he wasn't staying once this mission was over.

But for the first time since his boots hit the red clay of Alabama, he wondered if he could.

He fell asleep with Diana lying on top of him, her even breathing lulling him to follow her into sleep.

For the first time in a long time, there were no wolves lurking in the shadows of his dreams.

25

orning came too early. Diana woke to sunlight slanting across her face. She turned to see if Alex was awake, but the bed was empty. A frisson of alarm tingled across her skin before the smell of coffee tamed it.

And then she had to wonder why she'd been alarmed. After last night, did she really think he was planning to kick her out of his bed and his life?

Sex with Alex Bishop was the most incredible sex of her life. Maybe it wasn't that way for him, but she knew it was good. He'd said as much. Plus, there was the fact they still had to work together to infiltrate the militia.

No, he wasn't kicking her out just yet.

But it was a very good reminder not to get too attached. This thing between them, whatever it was, wasn't going to last. He was forty-two and he'd never married. Not the kind of guy to make long-term plans with.

As if she wanted to get married. She did not.

Marriage was stifling and rigid. Her mother had wanted to be an artist, but she'd chosen to marry into the Adler family instead. She'd had to give up any notion of doing something so bohemian as painting pictures when there were dignitaries to entertain.

It might be the twenty-first century, but women still gave up careers for men and children. Diana wasn't willing to change her life plans based on something so unpredictable as marriage. And children?

No. Just no.

She would be a *terrible* mother. Not because she wanted to be, but she didn't know how to be a good one. Her own had not been terrible, but she'd always maintained a distance with her children. Like she loved them, but not so much it was a messy thing.

The floors creaked as someone approached. Alex appeared in the door, wearing nothing but boxers, two cups of coffee in his hands. When their eyes met across the room, his face split in a grin.

"Didn't know if you'd be awake or not."

"I'm awake. Barely."

She scooted upright as he walked over and handed her a cup. She'd pulled the comforter up with one hand to cover her naked breasts, but he tugged it down again.

"That's better."

She eyed him as she lifted the coffee to her lips and

sipped. So good. "You realize it's October, right? And it's chilly? My nipples are going to be able to cut glass in a few minutes."

"I'll lick them and make them feel better."

A sizzle of lightning kindled between her legs.

"That'll only make them colder when you stop."

"Then I'll have to find ways to make you sweat, won't I?"

She knew he could. She leaned back on the headboard —the very one he'd banged her so hotly against last night—and let him ogle her as she drank coffee.

"You know," she said, dropping her lashes for a moment. "You told me last night that I didn't want to hear about the kinds of things you dreamt about. You don't have to talk about it if you don't want to, but that's a very different thing than me not wanting to hear it."

He watched her with those silver eyes that missed nothing. "True," he said finally, voice rough. "Guess I don't want to talk about it."

"Valid. If you ever do, I'll listen. I know you've probably seen a lot of stuff doing what you did in the military."

"Yes. But that's not what I dream about. Not usually, anyway."

She gazed at him, understanding prickling to life. "Alaska."

His eyes were diamond hard. "Alaska." He took a drink of coffee, went silent a moment. "You're perceptive. I didn't expect that."

She arched an eyebrow. "Because I was born a rich

girl, you mean? Because I went to boarding schools and had tutors and an Ivy League education? People are complicated, Alex. None of us fit into neat little boxes."

"No, I guess we don't." He dropped a hand to her arm, traced his fingers up it. "Will you ever tell me who Viktor hurt that sent you on a path to the FBI?"

A pinprick of pain blossomed in her chest. "Ah, so you figured that out, huh? I was probably headed for a career in international relations. But then Viktor happened, and I knew I wanted to fight for justice instead." She drew in a breath. "I'll tell you when you tell me about your dreams. About what caused them. How's that?"

"Won't argue with that deal." He took her coffee cup and set it on the nightstand with his own. "But right now? These beautiful nipples are begging for my attention."

Diana left Alex standing on his driveway, hair tousled, shirtless, coffee cup in hand as he watched her leave. Such a sexy sight. How had she gotten so lucky that she was the woman warming his bed night after night? That she knew what drove him wild, and how to make him lose control until he unleashed all that alpha virility on her body?

She *still* tingled with the aftershocks of what he'd done to her that morning. After he'd taken her coffee cup away, he'd worked his way down her torso until his face was between her legs, making her beg him to let her come.

Then he'd made her get on all fours and took her from behind. She'd exploded around him in no time, pleading for more, and he gave it to her until they were both panting and utterly sated.

Then there was a shower, breakfast, and more kissing before she managed to get out the door. She'd been smart enough to bring a change of clothes so she could dress for work instead of needing to go back to her apartment. She'd been hoping he'd want her to stay the night, and she hadn't been disappointed.

Last night, they'd discussed going back to the militia meeting. It wasn't for another two weeks, so they had time to plan. Alex had downloaded the audio from the bug in Gannon's apartment, but he'd found nothing he could use. The man spoke to people on the phone, and he watched porn. He also made dirty phone calls to someone, probably a 1-800 sex line, and jerked off while he did it.

She'd never been so happy not to be the one listening to the recordings in her life. Brent Gannon was a creep, not because he watched porn or jerked off to phone sex, but because of the way he acted toward women. The things he'd been accused of while still active-duty were terrible. That he'd gotten away with it, simply being forced into retirement rather than being prosecuted under the uniform code of military justice, was infuriating.

Not her circus, but damn.

It was a good half hour drive to the FBI Headquarters

on Redstone Arsenal. She parked and stepped out of her car, hitting the button to lock it.

"Diana."

She jumped at the voice, spinning to find Joel standing there, hands in his pockets, looking moody. He was tall and good-looking, but nothing like Alex. How had she ever been attracted enough to have sex with this man? The idea seemed foreign to her now. When she thought of what they'd done together compared to what she did with Alex—well, it was like the basic no-frills package compared to the deluxe everything included package. Not even in the same universe.

"Hi, Joel. What's up?"

"Heard you were suspended."

A kernel of irritation flared to life. "I had a disagreement over a case and took some time off. You've made it clear you don't care, so why are you asking?"

"I do care," he told her. "I just needed some time to think."

"I see. Think about what?"

"You. Us."

"Us?"

His nostrils flared. "I was angry with you for being so cautious. For pulling me in and pushing me away. But I realize it's just who you are, and if we're to have anything lasting, I have to accept that about you. It wasn't bad between us." He took a step toward her, put a hand out, but he didn't touch her. "I miss you, Diana. I miss the easy relationship we had. It was never messy, never difficult. We had a good time together. I want to try again."

Oh God. Diana swallowed, guilt pricking her. Not what she'd expected. And not what she wanted, either. Maybe she could have accepted if she'd never gotten naked with Alex and found out what real passion was like. But now? Even knowing what she had with Alex was doomed to fail?

She couldn't go back. She'd ride that rocket ship into the stars, and she'd ride it to the ground again while it exploded into a million pieces on impact. But she'd never settle for adequate and safe ever again.

"There is no us, Joel," she said softly. "You said you were tired of me not fully committing to this relationship. And you were right." She put a hand on his arm. "I'm sorry I couldn't be what you needed, but you shouldn't compromise what you want from someone just because what we had was easy."

He stared at her hand on his arm. When he lifted his head, she thought she'd see sorrow or regret. What she saw was so much worse. She took a step back, stunned at the rage on his face.

"You think you're so fucking special, don't you? You forget I know who you really are, Diana Adler. How do you think people would feel if they knew you only got this job because of your connections, huh? Do you think Agent Ackerman would trust you to have his back if he knew you weren't qualified? That it was nepotism put you here with a gun and a badge, and that you can walk away whenever you get tired of playing around at being law enforcement?"

Every word was a blow. It's what she feared people would think, yes. But it wasn't true. And she wasn't going to let him intimidate her.

"Go ahead and tell them all. Make an announcement to the entire building," she grated, though fear pulsed inside. "I'll survive. Because I'm not walking away. I'm here because I believe in what I do, and I'm good at it." Outrage flared hot in her chest, her belly. "How dare you threaten me? For what? Because I didn't leap into your arms and thank you for giving me another chance? Did you really think I was so damned needy I'd come back the moment you crooked your finger? You broke up with *me!*" she shouted, uncaring who heard. "I didn't do this to us, you did. And now you're angry because I'm being honest and telling you that you're better off without me?"

She poked a finger in his chest. The rage in his expression didn't dissipate, but he took a step back. "Go ahead, Joel. Tell them. Tell everyone. I've survived worse, and I'll survive this. Fuck you, asshole."

Diana spun on her heel and marched toward the building, dragging her controlled access card from her purse and pressing it to the reader when she got inside. Her cheeks flamed and acid boiled in her stomach. She didn't want people to think she couldn't accomplish anything without her family connections, but she also wasn't going to cave in and do whatever he wanted just to keep him from talking. How dare he threaten her like that?

Her temper was still at the flashpoint when she reached her desk, throwing her purse down and heading for the coffee pot. Alex had made coffee for her, but she could use more. Maybe she didn't need the caffeine, but she wanted it. It was that or go find Joel and strangle him.

Ackerman was in the break room, pouring a cup of black liquid in a mug. He looked up when she stormed over. "Whoa, what happened to you? Do I need to go kick some ass over at One Shot Tactical?"

"You'd get your ass kicked if you tried. But thank you. And no, it wasn't anyone there."

"Probably right," he said with a grin. "Those dudes are big and badass. But I had to offer."

She snatched a cup, peeled back the tabs on three creamers, and dumped them in. Ackerman poured her coffee while she fumed. Joel had always been so predictably even keeled and dispassionate. But that? It was like that silly movie where the cute little gremlins turned into hellish demons when you got them wet.

He knew her real name because she'd been stupid enough to tell him once when they'd been sharing things about themselves, but she would have never thought he'd threaten to use it against her.

"You gonna tell me about it or you want to be pissed a while?"

She grumbled. "It's personal shit. Joel ambushed me in the parking lot with a speech about getting back together. When I said no, he dropped the nice guy act and said a few choice things that I'm still processing."

"Whoa." He shook his head. "Men can be assholes when they don't get their way. You know that."

"I think lots of people can be assholes when they don't get their way. I guess I didn't expect it out of him."

Ackerman leaned against the counter. "I never understood what you saw in him if I'm honest. Not my business though."

"I thought he was nice. Attractive. Plus, we both work here, which means fewer explanations about workloads that keep you at the desk after hours, or bad moods because it was a shit day dealing with criminals. Clearly, I was wrong about the nice part."

"I'm sorry it happened, but glad it wasn't Bishop that pissed you off. I liked him the first time we went out there. And whether you believe me or not, I could see you were attracted to each other."

She gaped. "You're making that up."

He shook his head. "I'm not. Your nostrils flared and your pupils dilated whenever he was near. He did the same. He could barely take his eyes off you to look at me. Hell, I thought he'd ask you out at some point, but you just kept circling each other every time we went out there."

"Since when did you become an expert in attraction?"

He elbowed her, smiling. "Being single in my fifties and hitting the clubs taught me a lot."

"Apparently."

They walked back to their desks. "Believe me, I know not every woman is attracted to a man my age. Helps to know what the signs are so I'm not that creepy old dude hitting on a woman half my age."

"You're a good guy, Ackerman."

"I try. Think the world would be a better place if we all tried harder."

"I can't argue with that." She typed in her password to pull up the files they'd been working on. Then she looked over at where Ackerman was doing the same. "Hey, how did the hot date with the line dancing lady go?"

He frowned. "It didn't. She ghosted me."

"I'm sorry." She hesitated. "Okay, now hear me out— do you think maybe nightclubs are the wrong place to be looking for companionship?"

"Probably. But it's something to do at night when my house is too quiet. I can't watch TV night after night or read books like you. I'm an extrovert. I need people and noise."

"Why don't you come to the Founder's Fest in Sutton's Creek this weekend? There'll be booths around the square, hayrides, and free concerts in the park. And you can't miss Colleen Wright's ghost walk cemetery tour."

He arched an eyebrow. "You don't believe in ghosts, do you?"

"No, but she does. She's quirky and, swear to God, strangely perceptive about things she shouldn't know anything about. You might meet someone at the fest, and that's so much better than a club, don't you think?"

He shrugged. "Maybe. I'll think about it. You going?"

She couldn't help but smile. "Yep. The One Shot group has a booth. Daphne's idea. I'm going to go and laugh at Alex while he smiles and hands out the flyers Daph managed to get printed practically overnight. He's more anti-social than I am, so it'll be fun."

Ackerman shook his head as he chuckled. "Strange relationship you two have. But you seem happy."

He had no idea how strange it was. Or how fake. Except the sex, of course. That was anything but fake.

"I am happy."

It might be based on a lie, it wasn't destined to last, and the only thing real was the sex and the affinity she felt when she was with him.

But damn if those things weren't fantastic.

And worth the risk to her heart.

26

s soon as he saw her face, Ghost could tell something was wrong. Diana got out of her car and walked toward where he stood on the porch, her expression troubled. He took the stairs down and met her on the grass, pulling her into his arms and pressing a kiss to her silky hair.

"What's wrong, Princess?"

She tipped her head back to look at him. "How did you know?"

"You look like somebody stole your lunch out of the work refrigerator."

She laughed, a soft sound that wrapped itself around his heart. "Never happens because I always eat lunch out. Can't cook, you know."

"Huh, really? Guess I should have asked. Taking a point out of the 'reasons why you're okay' column."

"You're ridiculous."

"When it makes you laugh." He took her hand and led her up the steps and into the house. They went straight to the kitchen where he poured a glass of red wine and handed it to her in one of the wine glasses Daphne had procured on a thrifting trip. Cabernet Sauvignon, because that's what Diana liked. He'd bought a couple of bottles to keep around since he didn't drink wine very often.

"Thank you."

He cracked a beer and ushered Diana onto the back porch. She sank onto the couch, and he sat beside her, leaning into the cushions and studying the landscape beyond. It was peaceful with the trees turning gold and orange, and a soft breeze blowing. It would be dark soon, but right now the light was golden where it kissed the grass. Had to admit he liked it better than living in the DC metro area.

"Bad day at work?"

She sipped the wine. "Work was fine. Mostly. We're working an espionage case at the moment, and a bomb threat to city hall." She frowned. "Something else happened."

"You want to talk about it?" He wanted her to talk about it, but he knew better than to order her to do it.

She toyed with the stem of the wine glass, rotating it slowly back and forth before she finally spoke. "I was dating a guy from work, off and on the past few months. Joel Newman. He's an analyst, not a field officer. He was with me when we saw you and your friends on the fourth of July. We broke up about a month ago, around the time the Dashevsky case moved to Washington. It was his idea." She frowned, stared at her wine. "He was in the parking lot waiting for me when I got to work. He said he wanted to get back together."

It felt like somebody twisted a knife in his belly. He'd seen her with the guy in the Dawg sometimes, and at the Independence Day Festival. It'd always made something tighten inside him to see her with another man. He'd thought it was annoyance, mostly because she'd been in his space.

Wasn't annoyance now. It was possessiveness.

"Do you want to?"

Her gaze flew to his. "No! And that's what I told him. I thought he'd be hurt, maybe, or sad. He was a nice guy. Never heard him raise his voice at anyone while we were dating." She hesitated. "He was angry when I told him we were better apart, and he said some things."

"What kind of things?" His voice was a growl.

She put a hand on his arm. Squeezed. "It's nothing all that bad. It just surprised me, and I keep thinking about it. Basically, he knows who I really am—and he threatened to tell people I'd gotten my job due to nepotism, that I'm not really qualified. It was ugly and mean, and I guess I'm still shocked it happened. I never thought he'd threaten me like that."

Ghost wasn't. People could hide a lot of ugly when it suited them. Challenge their beliefs or their entitlement, and it all came gushing out. Like the people who said they weren't racist but the first time they got into a heated confrontation with a person of color, the slurs came out of their mouths as natural as breathing. People would show you who they were if you let them.

"He say anything else?"

She shook her head. "No. I told him to fuck off and left him in the parking lot. That was this morning. Didn't see him again."

"You know you have to watch your back, right? You wounded this fucker, and he's gonna look for a way to wound you in return."

"I don't think he'll do anything, but I'll be careful. If he decides to blast the building with my identity, nothing I can do about that. It'll make life harder for me at work, but I've faced challenges before."

"Who else knows about your family?"

"The local director, of course. People in HR, probably. It's not a secret so much as I don't tell people my real name. Hell, I doubt many of them would know who the Adlers are. It's not a common name, but it's also not rare. Even then, would they connect me to Uncle Stephen? Or my cousin Julia, the princess? Or would they think it a coincidence, like two people named Bishop or Smith? If the president was a Bishop, would people think you were related? No, they wouldn't." She shrugged. "I'm not ashamed of my name. I just didn't want it to be common knowledge that I'm one of *those* Adlers. It's hard enough being a woman in what's traditionally been a man's job."

He didn't doubt that. Women had finally been allowed to qualify as Army Rangers, but they still weren't allowed into special units like Delta or HOT or SEALs, for instance. Mendez had been forward thinking enough to bring in a few women as contractors. Victoria Royal, now Brandon, was a fantastic sniper who'd done active ops with HOT many times. Just not while wearing the uniform. There were others, too. Miranda Lockwood, now McCormick, was CIA and sometimes went out with the teams. One of the most lethal women of Ghost's acquaintance was Mendez's wife, Kat. Then there was Natasha Black, who was probably the most formidable of them all.

"I can pay him a visit." In fact, he looked forward to it.

She gave him a significant look. "And do what? Threaten to disembowel him if he breathes my name to another soul? That's not going to work—not to mention it's downright insulting. I could have made that threat myself and put enough weight behind it to make him think twice. It would only make him more determined, though. Human nature."

"I was thinking something a little more painful, but okay, point taken."

"What's more painful than disemboweling?"

"Do you really want me to enumerate the ways in which I can cause pain?"

She frowned. "No, probably not."

He pushed a hand over his scalp. "I'll say it again. You need to be careful of this guy, Diana. Don't make the mistake of thinking he's not capable of escalating. People get upset when they're rejected. Mature people deal with it. People who can't handle their emotions have outbursts."

"He'll cool off."

"Maybe." He threaded his fingers in hers, raised her hand to his mouth to kiss the back of it. "It could be nothing but blowing off steam. He might even be embarrassed he lost his temper. He might never say another word to you. Or he could be planning his next move right now."

"I just don't get it," she said, shaking her head. "He broke up with me. He said I pushed him away and wouldn't let him get close, and he wanted somebody who could be there for him. Then today he said he realized he just had to let me be me, and we'd work it out."

"But you don't want to work it out."

Her eyes met his. Held. "No."

"I'm glad," he said, his voice rougher than he expected. Then he tugged her towards him and kissed her. His body lit up like the fourth of July whenever their mouths touched, but he didn't take it any further just yet. "You staying here tonight?"

If she said no, he was going into Sutton's Creek and staying with her. Nobody threatened his woman and got away with it.

His woman?

Yeah, his woman. For as long as they were doing this, she was his. When it flamed out, then it was done. But until then, she was his—and he protected what was his. He'd be there for her after, and he'd protect her if she needed it, but right now it was non-negotiable. She was his, and he was a possessive and protective son of a bitch.

"Do you want me to?"

"Yes." Because he believed in saying what he wanted. Games were for people with too much time on their hands.

"Then I guess I'm staying."

27

Diana stayed the night, and then he planned to stay at her apartment the following night. It was Friday night anyway, and the Fall Fest kicked off Saturday morning. He had to be there because Daphne had gotten a booth for One Shot Tactical. They were doing shifts in the booth so the range would remain staffed, and he was up for the first three hours with Blaze. Daphne would be hanging around all day to make sure things ran smoothly.

He'd tried to get out of it, but one lip quiver from Daphne and he'd found himself grumbling his agreement to give up three hours of his time. When he'd told Diana about it a couple of nights ago, she'd laughed and said, "She played you. She knows you feel guilty for that stupid agreement with Kane, and she's not going to let you off the hook anytime soon."

He'd grumbled some more, because he knew she was

right, and then he got busy taking her clothes off and making her come. Much more satisfying way to spend his time.

Last night they went to the brewery and had a drink with Gannon, chatted for a while, then left him making eyes at a woman young enough to be his daughter. Dude was a tool, but they needed him for that connection to the militia.

They'd gotten nothing new out of him, nothing of interest. Just the usual bitching about conspiracies and people having it in for him, being treated unfairly after the years of his life he'd given to Uncle Sam. The audio from his apartment was salacious for the kind of shit he watched and the things he did, but so far it wasn't treasonous. He talked to people other than sex line operators, but it was nothing interesting. Athena was never mentioned and most of the talk was about shooting guns or meeting up at bars.

Ghost hoped like hell they got to take him down when they got the leaders of the plot against Athena. If they didn't, then he'd have to have a little chat with Gannon about what he would personally do if there was even a whiff of him misbehaving in future. Especially with women.

The man could be a player all he liked. Be a serial dater and fuck whoever he liked, but he needed to do it honestly. Desire had to be mutual, not coerced.

It was after five when Ghost took the stairs up to Diana's apartment and knocked on the door. He heard her walk across the floor and then she was there, pulling the door open, her wheat blond hair shining in the light, her blue eyes warm and welcoming.

She wore tight jeans with ankle boots and a cornflower blue sweater that slipped off one shoulder to reveal bare skin. He wrapped an arm around her waist and pulled her in for a thorough kiss. Her arms went around his neck, her breath sighing from her as her mouth opened and his tongue slipped inside.

He was instantly hard. Ready to tug her jeans off and slam home. He picked her up and she wrapped her legs around his waist, kissing him with abandon as he carried her into the apartment and toed the door shut.

"Damn, Princess, you make me crazy."

"Same."

It was only the buzzing of his phone in his jeans pocket that brought him back from the brink of diving into this woman and not coming up for air until several hours had passed.

"Dammit," he muttered as her long legs unwound from his waist and slid down his thighs. He set her down and she stepped back, running a thumb over her mouth.

"And now I have to go fix my lip-gloss. You better check your mouth for pink," she said as she moved toward the hallway where the bathrooms were, snagging her purse along the way. "I don't think it's going to be your color."

He pulled the phone from his pocket and sent a quick text to Blaze that they'd be at the Dawg in a few minutes. He'd rather strip Diana naked and feast on her, but he'd promised her dinner with the gang tonight. Reason number one why he didn't follow her to the bathroom. If he did that, he'd bend her over the sink and fuck her with the mirror reflecting everything they did.

And that was a hot as fuck idea he was going to have to file away for the future.

He went into the kitchen, tore off a paper towel, and wiped his mouth. Sure enough, there was pink lip-gloss on the paper. He balled it up and tossed it as Diana returned, looking remarkably put together for a woman who'd just had her legs around his waist and her crotch rubbing his dick.

"You sure you want to go?" he asked.

She smiled that gorgeous smile that seemed to turn him inside out lately. "I'm hungry, so yes."

"But I get to eat you for dessert, right?"

"I'm counting on it."

He took her hand and they walked out of the apartment together. "Then let's get this whole dinner thing over with as fast as possible."

She laughed. "You're insatiable, you know that?"

He was, but only with her. It was almost frightening how much he needed to be inside her. How much he liked sleeping in the same bed with her. He'd always liked his space, liked sleeping in his own bed with nobody throwing a leg over him or cuddling up to him during the night. He wanted to be free to move. Free to respond if someone broke in or if he had a nightmare that woke him.

Until Diana. Now he wanted her wrapped around him, her impossibly soft skin against his, her scent in his nostrils as he slept. Maybe he was mellowing with age, or maybe watching his teammates with their women had him thinking about what it'd be like to wake up with the same woman day after day.

"You complaining?"

"Absolutely not. Your tongue is magic. I like it when I'm dessert."

"Damn, now I've gotta think about the most boring things imaginable or I'm walking in the Dawg with a tent in my jeans."

"I can help."

"Don't want to think about you helping, Princess."

She laughed. "I mean I've got something else to think about. A story about Ackerman. He took Colleen's cemetery tour last night. And now he has a date with a ghost whisperer."

Ghost felt his eyebrows climb his forehead. "With Colleen? Isn't she about twenty years older than he is?"

Diana laughed. "Not with Colleen. With Reba. They hit it off. She took a special interest in him on the tour—"

"Wait, she's doing the tour again? She's over the whole falling in the grave thing?"

"I don't know if she's over it, but she was there last night. Ackerman walked with her as Colleen led the tour. Did you know there's a ghostly regiment of Confederate soldiers who ride through the cemetery during a full moon?"

"Can't say as I did."

"Horses and everything. Ackerman said it was quite imaginative. There are a lot of ghosts in Sutton's Creek, apparently. He didn't see any, though. Reba told him that's not uncommon."

Ghost snorted. "No, I suppose not. Amazes me Colleen can make a living doing what she does, but she's nothing if not determined. And entrepreneurial."

"Have you ever been in her shop?"

"Can't say as I have. You?"

"Yes. One of the first times I explored Sutton's Creek. I went in because I was curious. It's really cute. Smells like patchouli, and there are a lot of crystals that clink together as you move through the narrow aisles. She has a lot of stuff that has nothing to do with ghosts. Touristy stuff like postcards and photo books. She can also tell your fortune and hold a seance if you like. Oh, and teach you to communicate with aliens."

"Busy woman," he said as they reached the back stairs to the Dawg and headed up. It was Friday night, which meant prime rib, and the place was packed. Out of habit, he scanned the room looking for threats. The four idiots who'd attacked Diana at the militia meeting were primary on his list, but he didn't see any of them.

The One Shot Tactical group was at their usual table, all the men and women seated and chatting. Diana hesitated a second, but he propelled her forward with a hand against the small of her back. He hated that she still felt like she didn't belong, and he hated that it was his fault.

"Hey, y'all," Emma said. "We ordered appetizers but no meals yet."

Ghost pulled out Diana's chair and she sank onto it with the kind of regal grace he'd come to expect. Her cousin was a princess, but she could have been, too. He was thankful she wasn't. If she had been, this thing between them wouldn't be happening—and his life would be a lot less satisfying than it was sitting here beside her, bumping shoulders from time to time. Thinking about the dirty things he was going to do when he got her alone.

Ghost only half paid attention to what Chance and Seth were saying while Daphne engaged Diana in conversation. He could hear parts of it, though it didn't make a lot of sense. Stickers, something called washi tape—washi?—glue sticks, and a mini-printer. Then he heard *book club* and tuned out. He was glad Diana was participating, even if the entire reason they'd started dating was to team up so they could infiltrate Dashevsky's militia group. Even when this thing ended and he was gone, he hoped she'd remain friends with the other women.

The evening went the way evenings with his guys and their women usually went. They laughed and talked and ate, joking and daring each other whenever there was a thing to dare someone over. Playing *I'm Too Sexy* on the jukebox and dancing to it while pointing to yourself was one of those things. That was Chance's dare, and he did it because of course he did.

Everyone laughed and cheered, and Rory cupped her hands to her mouth and yelled, "Take it off!"

Which Chance started to do until Big Nikki put her hands on her hips and told him in no uncertain terms she'd throw him out on his very fine ass—her words—if he did. Then she scolded Rory because, as half-owner, Rory was supposed to know this was a family establishment.

And it was, though to be fair it was after eight, the band was coming on at nine, and there were no children present. Still, rules were rules. Chance returned to the table to more cheers, giving Big Nikki a wet smack on the cheek as he did so. She rubbed it off and shooed him away like he was a mischievous eight-year-old instead of a grown man.

Though he often acted like an eight-year-old, so maybe she was right.

Beside Ghost, Diana laughed with everyone else. He slid an arm across the back of her chair and scooted closer to her. She turned to him, the look of sheer happiness on her face hitting him square in the gut.

Had he ever seen her unguarded before? He didn't think so, but here she was, laughing with abandon and giving him the full glory of a face that wasn't clouded by sadness or pain.

Fuck.

He wanted to see her happy like this. She carried too much weight on her soul for someone her age. Too much responsibility. Self-inflicted because she didn't share her burdens with anyone.

God knew he wasn't anyone to point fingers, but he'd been carrying his a lot longer. Plus, he had friends to have his back if he needed them. Diana didn't seem to have anyone.

He put his mouth to her ear, noticing the little shiver that rolled through her when he did. "I could eat dessert any time you're ready."

She turned to say something, but he kissed her instead of waiting for a reply. When they broke apart, he knew she was as ready to leave as he was. His gaze collided with Seth's as he swiveled his head to tell everyone they were going. There wasn't any animosity on Phantom's face, but there wasn't approval either. Not that Ghost needed anyone's approval.

Seth nodded as he picked up his beer and sipped.

Ghost took Diana's hand and they stood. "Well, ladies and gents, it's been fun."

"Aw, leaving already? It's not even nine o'clock." Daphne had a gleam in her eyes that said she knew exactly what was on his mind.

If he weren't in his forties, he'd stick his tongue out at her. He figured if he did, she'd stick hers out in return. Then they'd devolve into a chorus of *oh yeah? Yeah!*

"Yep. And it's your fault for making me stand around in a booth tomorrow. Gotta get enough sleep."

"Because you're old. Totally understand."

"Kane, you need to get your woman under control." He was laughing inside, but he said it gruffly.

Kane snorted and kissed her temple. "As you well know, nobody controls Daphne."

"Thank you, baby." She kissed his cheek. "Nighty night, old man. And Diana. You get tired of this old dude, I'm sure we can find you someone far younger and less crotchety."

Diana laughed. "I like him just the way he is. But thanks."

"What are friends for?"

"Come on, babe. Let me get you home before my Geritol wears off."

Diana waved as they walked away. "Goodnight, everyone. Thanks for a fun time."

"Night!" they called out as he dragged her toward the back door.

Five minutes later, he had her naked and spread-eagled, her gorgeous ass sitting on her kitchen island. He sucked her nipples while she moaned, then dropped to his knees and slid his tongue into her wet heat.

Fucking perfect.

28

iana sprawled on her bed, skin damp, breaths coming in pants. Alex lay on his back beside her, one arm thrown over his face. He was not, however, breathing like he'd run a marathon. Time to work on her fitness levels, apparently.

In moments like this, she felt satiated and limp—but also alone because he wasn't touching her anymore.

As if he hadn't just touched her into several back-to-back orgasms. What was wrong with her?

She closed her eyes and told herself to stop being ridiculous and needy.

But then his fingers touched hers, and the gathering tension in her heart ebbed. He threaded their fingers together and gave hers a squeeze.

"I can feel the change in you," he said, his voice a deep rumble in the darkness. "When we're done and you're lying beside me, something happens."

She sucked in a breath, shock and fear twisting together. "I'm fine. Really."

He went up on an elbow beside her. She opened her eyes to find him studying her. She couldn't help the tight squeeze in her heart, or the way her soul stretched toward his like a flower seeking light.

"Where do you go, Diana?"

"I don't go anywhere. I'm right here."

"You go somewhere in your head. I can feel the disconnect."

She sighed and closed her eyes a moment. "I'm reminding myself this isn't real. We aren't building a relationship, and once we get what we want from the deception, it'll be over."

"I think you know by now there's something going on here. What it is, I have no idea. But it's more than a simple deception to get into the militia and find the traitors. Assuming we make it inside, live through what we gotta do, and stop these fuckers from stealing this technology and turning it against the world, then maybe we'll find out we've got something we want to keep exploring."

Her throat was tight. "Maybe."

He dipped his head, his lips meeting hers, and her bones melted. Again. Or was it still?

"Not gonna lie," he said against her mouth, "this isn't what I expected. *You* aren't what I expected."

"Same. I don't even like you."

His fingers slid between her folds, stroked her still-sensitive body until her back arched and she knew she could come again if he kept it up. "I don't like you either," he whispered. "But I'm kind of addicted to making you come."

That was all it took to send her tumbling over the edge, her body shaking as she splintered apart. She already couldn't catch her breath and now he'd stolen what little she had left.

"I could live inside here," he growled possessively, his fingers sliding deep, wrenching more feeling from her. "Just fucking slide in here and stay."

She gripped his arm and held him in place before he could pull away, rode his fingers until the last tremors faded.

"Fuck, baby. So hot for me. So damned perfect." He gathered her to him, tucking her into his body, and dragging the covers up.

She burrowed into the safety of his arms, breathing in his scent. Pine forest, spice, leather, steel, and gunpowder. *Fanciful.*

But true. He smelled like all those things, maybe not simultaneously, but she'd smelled them on him at one time or another. Alex Bishop was the most deliciously masculine man she'd ever been with.

Her phone dinged with a text. Not just any tone, but her mother's tone. Diana sighed and pulled away to reach for it. The screen lit up, invading the cocoon of darkness.

> **Mother:**
> Will you be home for Thanksgiving? I'm
> planning the seating and I really must
> know as soon as possible.

Diana clicked the button to make it dark and dropped it on the nightstand. Then she burrowed into Alex again. He didn't ask, but she suddenly wanted to tell him.

"My mother. She absolutely must know, as soon as possible, if I'm going to be home for Thanksgiving. She's planning the seating and it's critical I tell her right damn now. Probably so she can seat me next to the richest, most connected, most eligible bachelor in attendance."

"Do you usually go home for Thanksgiving?"

There was an ache in the vicinity of her heart. "Not if I can get out of it, no. I'd rather be working. Last year, I went to Cracker Barrel with Ackerman. His wife left him, so we were both alone."

"And you prefer that to being with your family?"

She suddenly felt like an asshole. "I'm sorry. I shouldn't be talking about this."

"Why not? Because my parents are dead?"

"Well, yes. I didn't mean to be insensitive." Not to mention she didn't know what kind of holidays he'd had with his family. He had terrible memories of Alaska, but before that? She wanted to ask but didn't.

"You aren't insensitive, Diana. I want you to tell me things. And before you think everything about my life was hell, I actually had a good childhood until the years we went remote. My parents were good people. They adopted me as a baby, because they couldn't have children, and I had a good life. Even when we first got to Alaska, I had a good life. My dad..." She felt him swallow. "He fought in Desert Storm. It was the nineties, and the Kuwaiti oil fields were torched as the Iraqi army retreated. Toxic fumes filled the air, oil rained from the sky, and he was there in the middle of it. Something shifted in his brain, though it wasn't immediately apparent. He came home, stayed in the Army for a while, then left as he got more paranoid. But I was a kid. I didn't know how bad it was until it was too late. My mom sheltered me from a lot of it. I thought Alaska was an adventure."

She wrapped her arms tighter around him. "I'm sorry."

"It's okay. I got through it."

He didn't say anything more, and she bit the inside of her lip. "You must think me so spoiled and ridiculous. I had everything growing up. Birthdays and holidays were lavish, with extravagant presents piled high beneath the tree at Christmas, and we took family vacations to exotic places every year. I never lacked for anything. If it could be bought, I could have it."

"And things that couldn't be bought?"

She loved that he understood enough to ask the question.

"Well, that's different, isn't it? I have no reason to complain about anything. Ever. I was safe, and I had the best of everything. But until I was four, I thought our nanny was my mother. I made the mistake of calling her mommy in front of my parents—and they fired her. I never saw her again."

Even now, the confusion she'd felt at Melinda's absence was easily called up from the depths of her heart. She'd cried and cried. Her brothers cried too, but not quite as hard as she had.

"I'm sorry, honey. That must have hurt."

"I was a child. I didn't know better, and honestly, if they'd been around more, maybe I would have known they were my parents and not just people with presents who sometimes stopped in to see us between social engagements."

His arms squeezed a little tighter.

Her throat ached. "I had everything when I was a child. I have no reason to be ungrateful. But I'd have taken fewer things if I'd had more hugs, you know? More love. That's all I wanted. Somebody to hold me and love me and tell me I was special. Somebody whose lap I could crawl into whenever I wanted, who would be there with attention and cookies, not with a message passed through a babysitter and a bunch of useless toys."

"It's what every kid deserves. I'm sorry you didn't have it, baby."

She squeezed him back. "And I'm glad you did, but I'm sorry for what you went through when your dad was unwell. It seems so unfair. He served his country, and they couldn't help him?"

"There were a lot of soldiers who got sick in one way or another. And I think they tried, but once he left the

Army and decided to escape what he saw as a corrupt government and the erosion of his rights, what could anyone do? My mother could have refused to go. She probably should have, but she loved him and thought he'd feel better when they got away from everything. When he could breathe fresh air and not hear voices in his head anymore."

"How did she die?" she asked gently.

She felt him stiffen. And then he sighed. "She had a heart attack. She was fifty-two at the time, and she'd been having some shortness of breath and pain in her back. It came and went over the course of weeks, but my dad didn't think it was anything to worry about. Neither did she. She insisted she was fine. But she wasn't. She died in her sleep. We tried to wake her the next morning, and she was cold."

"Oh God, Alex. I'm so sorry." She kissed his jaw, hugged him tighter. He was trembling—but no, that was her. She was trembling for him. For the child he'd been.

"I should have done something," he whispered, his voice sounding more tortured than she'd ever heard it. "Should have insisted he send for the doctor. We had a sat phone. He could have called. *I* could have called, but I didn't. I was too scared of him to do it. And Mom insisted she was fine, it was just some indigestion and change of life stuff. Jesus." His voice was ragged as he pushed away from her and swung his legs over the side of the bed.

Her heart pounded. She didn't know what to do. Go after him? Let him work through it alone?

"Alex. Don't go. Please don't go."

The muscles of his back were taught in the moonlight slanting between the blinds. She thought he might drag his pants on and leave her. But he didn't move. It was as if he was at war with himself.

"Please," she whispered.

Finally, as her heart hammered, he slid in beside her again, dragging her into his arms and holding her tight, his face buried against her neck. Tears pricked her eyes and she squeezed them tight.

She felt him breathing into her skin, felt the quick beat of his heart. She lifted a hand to his head, stroked his hair, dug her fingers in and massaged his scalp.

"Thank you," she whispered. "For telling me. I'm glad you stayed. I like having you in my bed. Also, I might like you just a little bit. But don't tell anyone. I'll deny it if you do."

She wanted to make him laugh. He didn't, but his arms tightened around her for a moment and his mouth moved against her skin.

"I like you too, Diana. More than I ever wanted to."

29

He did three hours in the booth. It wasn't excruciating, but it wasn't his idea of a good time, either. Diana showed up the last hour and wandered around the festival, poking in and out of booths, talking to people, buying things. He watched her move around the square whenever he wasn't talking to someone, studying the liquid grace that infused her limbs, the elegance that oozed from her as she glided along, picking things up with her graceful hands and then taking money from her purse and handing it over.

Every time she'd walk by his booth, she had another bag.

"She's different," Blaze said.

Ghost felt his belly clench. "Different how?" The question was a growl.

"I mean since we first met her. She was reserved, cool, maybe even uptight. That's not an uptight woman."

Diana threw her head back, laughing as Violet did a cartwheel and then raced around like somebody'd injected her veins with pure sugar. Which, considering the half-eaten caramel apple on a stick that Paisley was carrying, that's exactly what was going on. Violet jumped up and down, twirled, and skipped away.

Paisley let her, though she called out for her to be careful, to watch where she was going, and for heaven's sake *not* to run over her Aunt Hettie who'd stooped to open her arms for Violet to run into. One stiff breeze would blow Hettie Woods over, so that was probably a good idea.

"She likes your women. They're good to her," Ghost said. "And she likes this town. Something about Hallmark movies, but I don't watch those so I have no idea."

Blaze snickered. "You don't, huh?"

Ghost gave his best *I am your commanding officer, proceed with caution* look. "Do you?"

"I do. I mean I didn't until Emma came along, but they have this whole Christmas in July thing I had to watch. Trust me, I wasn't about to argue with a hormonal pregnant woman." He shrugged. "They aren't all bad. Some of them are silly, but some can be pretty good. It's mostly small-town shit. Big city girl moves to small town, falls in love with a small-town guy, they have some trouble, things almost end between them, and then it all works out. Though sometimes it's the big city guy who comes to the small town. Or a prince. I've seen those, too."

Ghost shook his head. "Sounds like I'd rather get punched in the face. Repeatedly."

Blaze laughed. "That, too. But hey, if it makes her happy...."

Ghost watched Diana smiling and strolling with the One Shot Tactical women—they'd all shown up at the festival, and Daphne had left the booth to join them for a little bit—and decided that, yeah, if it made her happy, he could probably watch one or two of those movies. Then he'd get her to watch something with him. The one where Santa Claus was a Viking badass drunk with an attitude and no tolerance for bullshit, maybe. Explosions, violence, bad guys getting what was coming to them.

Then again, that wasn't exactly a movie made for cuddling. If sappy Christmas shit made Diana want to cuddle, then whatever.

It hit him like a brick to the side of the head what he'd been thinking. Diana. Him. Christmas.

It was October. Next month was Thanksgiving—which she'd talked about last night. And then Christmas.

He'd still be here for Christmas. The Athena launch had been pushed back to January now. He expected it to get pushed farther. That was the nature of government projects. They never came in on time or under budget.

And right now, he didn't give a shit. Let Athena take months. Let him spend those months between Diana's creamy thighs, finding heaven with every stroke of his body into hers. Every kiss, every touch, every second with her—they were a revelation he wasn't tired of exploring.

Last night, in her bed, he'd told her about his mom's death. He hadn't planned to, but it came tumbling out. There was still so much he hadn't said, but what he'd told her had taken a lot of effort. He didn't talk about it. To anyone. There was nothing anyone could do to fix it, and he'd had time to learn how to deal with the things that'd happened.

Talking about it, reliving it, hurt.

He'd done it, though. And he felt somehow lighter for having done so. Wasn't perfect. Wasn't magically healed. But he felt better for it.

He was used to dealing with his emotions in private, and that had been his initial urge. But her voice, so sweet and gentle, had made him want to stay. To burrow into her and see if it was easier to have someone hold him.

Turned out it was.

He watched the townsfolk moving through the square, feeling almost like he belonged in this place, too. The sun shone down, sparkling in the water tinkling in the fountain. The statue of Jacob Sutton gazed out on the town he'd founded, birds flitted among the trees, and the town council had lined the walkways with pumpkins and gourds to signal the season.

It was Alabama in October. Not exactly chilly, but the days were growing shorter and cooler and there was at least one intrepid vendor with hot apple cider and hot chocolate on offer. Wendy Cochran's booth was selling pumpkin spice lattes, because of course they were, and she had pumpkin spice muffins and hot apple fritters for sale too.

There was also ice cream and sweet tea on offer, because the temps would be in the low seventies at midday. All the bases were covered.

Colleen Wright appeared in a flowing burnt orange caftan with a matching turban. She almost glided through the crowd, stopping here and there, before she slid up to the One Shot Tactical booth.

Ghost eyed her. She eyed him back, smiling. Then she fished a cigarette from her voluminous pocket, a pack of matches, and lit up.

"Ah, that's better," she said after blowing out a cloud of smoke. Her voice was roughened from years of smoking, and her fingers were yellowed around the nails.

"How's business, Mrs. Wright?"

"Please, call me Colleen. Business is great, my dear man. It's my busy time of year. The spirits are restless."

Ghost handed her a flyer. "We can help with preparation. Fighting skills. That kind of thing."

She eyed him. Tucked the flyer into her pocket. "You tease, and I understand why, but this is no joking matter. The spirits have been very clear for once."

"Oh yeah? About what?"

"You."

Ghost put a hand to his chest, feigning astonishment. Colleen's eyes narrowed. Really, he shouldn't tease her. She was a kind soul, just a little kooky.

"What did they tell you, ma'am?"

Blaze was mercifully occupied with talking to a man who nodded a lot and turned the brochure over in his hands as if it could impart the secret to becoming a ninja warrior.

"They told me that you are about to encounter a great deal of trouble."

His gut tightened before he reminded himself she said things to get a reaction. "Oh, really? What kind of trouble? Taxes?"

"Joke all you like, beautiful boy."

He was slightly taken aback at that description. And amused. Nobody had called him a boy in years. Hell, he'd left boyhood behind mentally long before he'd ever grown into a man. That's what surviving did to you. That's what chronic stress and parentification did to a kid. Made you a fiercely independent adult with trust issues.

"I'm sorry, ma'am, but I'm having trouble believing you know something about my life that I don't."

She smiled. "I know. It's often that way. This is the time of year when the veil is the thinnest, and it's only getting thinner as we approach Samhain. The spirits are watching, and they are never wrong. You will face a very dark, very dangerous challenge. If you fail, everything you love will be lost. If you succeed...." She shrugged. "Well, suffice to say you will have everything you thought you could not have."

Anger began to swirl together like a tornado forming out of thin air. It was an overreaction, but he didn't like the way her words hit that vulnerable place within. The words were vague, and yet they called up feelings and desires he had no wish to examine right now.

"It would be helpful if you had details. Who to avoid, what not to do, that kind of thing."

"I know, and I'm sorry. That's not how the spirit world works. I would ask the aliens, but they aren't due to return for another month."

The aliens. Right.

Ghost sighed. Why was he getting angry with this woman? She was good at this stuff. Damned good. But she didn't know anything. She just made predictions that fed off his own fears and worries. She didn't do it out of malice or a desire to extract money. She truly thought she was helping.

"Thank you, ma'am. I appreciate the warning. I'll do my best."

"See that you do. Oh, and when you need her, the Huntress will be at your side. Trust in her."

The Huntress?

Before he could ask what that meant, Colleen stiffened, her head coming up like she'd sensed danger. He followed her gaze to where her bestie, Reba, strolled along with Agent Ackerman. He was talking animatedly, and Reba was watching him with what appeared to be adoration.

"Trouble," Colleen muttered. "I see trouble." She swept away in a cloud of orange, trailing cigarette smoke, and Ghost shook his head.

Blaze had his arms folded over his chest, frowning. "What was that about trouble and huntresses?"

"You think I have a clue? She's weird. Maybe I'm going to meet a lady who likes to deer hunt. Fuck if I know. As for trouble, I'm guessing she isn't happy about Agent Ackerman romancing her friend. Probably worried he'll sweep Reba off her feet and then Colleen will be over there in her shop alone, muttering to ghosts and communicating with aliens without anyone real to talk to."

"Huh, yeah, guess the possibility of Reba finding love and no longer having time for her isn't appealing... Hey, brother, you'd tell us if something was going on with you, wouldn't you?" Blaze sounded worried.

Ghost looked him straight in the eye and lied. "Of course I would. All I've got going on is navigating a relationship I wasn't expecting with someone I thought I didn't like."

It wasn't all a lie, because the navigating a relationship part was real, but he'd come this far not involving his team in the plan and he wasn't starting now. If something changed and it was safer to bring them in, he'd do it. But not yet.

"Okay." Blaze sounded gruff. "You know we've got your back if you need us."

"Know it. Appreciate it."

Blaze looked as if he'd say more, but a couple of guys walked up to the booth, and he had to give the spiel about the range and training facility instead.

Laughter had Ghost glancing up. The women

approached, drinks in hand, happy expressions on their faces. His gaze sought Diana's. She looked back at him with clear blue eyes that made his heart squeeze in his chest.

That's when he understood what Colleen's vagueness meant.

The Huntress.

Diana was another name for the Greek goddess Artemis. She was the goddess of the hunt, wild animals, and the moon. She carried a silver bow, and she was a fierce protector of nature and young women. She was also a virgin.

Yeah, well, maybe his Diana wasn't all those things, but Colleen had seen them together and she liked her riddles.

Damn meddling old woman.

The women waited until the men were gone, then Daphne pulled her clipboard from her bag. "Your time is up in fifteen minutes, gentlemen. Kane and Ethan are on the way. Seth and Chance will take the last shift, and the part-time RSOs are at the range handling the shooters, so unless you desperately desire to return to the range, you don't have to go back until your classes are scheduled later. How has it been going? People interested?"

"Yep," Blaze said. "Told them about the trunk-or-treat coming up, too. Lots of people interested in that."

Daphne preened. "Excellent. I really wanted a carnival, but I think a trunk-or-treat event with the safety demonstrations is timelier, especially since it's only two weeks until Halloween. Next year, we'll do something even better."

He genuinely hoped they would. He hoped the range would continue in some fashion once the mission was over. For the first time since the team had arrived in Alabama, he was starting to think Sutton's Creek might be a nice place to call home once this was over. Maybe.

Kane and Chance arrived, Ghost and Blaze got them up to speed, and then he walked out from behind the booth, relieved it was over. He was a military man, a special ops commander, someone who'd seen combat and done the things he'd had to do to keep his country safe.

He was not a salesman. He could make small talk, but he felt about as unhappy with it as Seth did. Not because it was awkward, but he was always thinking of something else he could be doing. He gave orders and they were obeyed. He didn't talk people into things.

Diana waited with her shopping bags and her drink. Ghost walked over and took the bags from her, wrapped his hand around hers. And then, because he could, he pulled her in for a kiss. She tasted like pumpkin spice coffee. He wasn't a fussy drink kind of guy, but he liked it.

"Thank God that's over," he said when he pulled away.

She laughed. "Was it really that bad?"

"Yes. It was mostly women who came to talk to us, and some of them giggled entirely too much for comfort. They weren't interested in self-defense or shooting at all."

"You don't say." She sounded amused.

"Oh for fuck's sake," he said when fresh understanding dawned. Daphne had left them to it so they'd attract the women into the booth and hopefully sell them on classes. Which then put those women in proximity of her events business on the farm. Brunches. Wedding receptions. Photography.

Diabolical.

"Daph," he said when she came near, and the festival goers wouldn't hear him. "Make me stand around in a booth for three hours ever again and you're fired. Kane's fired, too."

Daphne stuck her tongue out at him. He barely refrained from sticking his out in return. Diana snorted as if she knew.

"You'd be lost without me," Daphne said.

"You can be replaced."

"I doubt that. You're welcome to try."

She wasn't wrong. She was super organized, and she was a whiz with the accounting spreadsheets. Still, it was part of the game to threaten her. "Don't tempt me."

She stuck her tongue out again and walked away.

He turned to Diana. "Are you done shopping, or you want to look around some more?"

"I didn't get a hayride yet, and I still want to get some candles. I was saving them for last because they'll be heavy."

"Okay. You want to go on a hayride?"

"Don't you?"

He looked at the tractor rolling around the square with a wagon attached. There were bales of hay all around the perimeter of the wagon and people were seated inside, looking at the sights. Exposed. Easily picked off. His military brain told him all the reasons why it was a bad idea. He couldn't disappoint her though. This wasn't a war zone, and enemy combatants weren't lurking in the streets.

"Sure. Why not?"

Her smile was worth the indignity of perching on hay bales while a farmer drove them through town. He pulled her toward the place to get tickets.

"You wouldn't really fire her," Diana said.

"Nope. But I give her shit because she likes to get a rise out of me."

"You oblige her with a reaction."

"Yeah. Not sure how it started, but she had a shitty family before she landed here. I think she sees me as some kind of father figure since hers was so bad. So she pushes and tests, and I growl and bitch and threaten. Makes her happy."

Her smile lingered. "Makes you happy, too."

It wasn't a question. Diana got things about him he didn't have to explain. He didn't know how yet, but he sensed they were alike in many ways. One day, she'd explain what had happened to make her hate Viktor Dashevsky so much. He figured that was the thing they shared—a tragedy that changed the course of their lives somehow.

"I didn't start that way, but yeah, makes me happy to spar

with her like she's a teenager testing boundaries. When she first came to us, we thought she was a lot younger. I guess I still think of her as a twenty-three-year-old starting out in life instead of the twenty-eight year old she really is." He squeezed her hand as they rolled up to the hayride line. "I'm glad you made things so she could stay. I know it wasn't easy."

She shrugged, but there was pink in her cheeks. "I never want people to think my accomplishments are due to my connections. I want to succeed on my own merits the way you do. The way your friends do." She sighed. "But sometimes they're a good thing and using them to affect the kind of outcome I never could on my own is worth it. Daphne's happiness—her life—is worth a lot more than my pride."

He couldn't agree more. When he'd first learned about her connections, he'd been pissed. He'd thought she was a spoiled little princess who got her way, and who'd barreled into his mission when she had no business there. He'd wanted to see her fail, and he'd wanted to laugh when she did. Her showing up in tears because the Dashevsky investigation was taken away from her should have been a relief.

Instead, it'd bothered him to see her so shaken. Because Diana was the kind of woman who would sacrifice her pride to do the right thing. She'd cared about Daphne and Kane's happiness even though they'd meant nothing to her.

No, her connections weren't the soft-landing he'd

always thought they were. To her, they were a hindrance. And that said a lot about her integrity.

"I'm liking you a little more today," he teased.

Her smile was soft. "Jury's still out on you, but I think this hayride might help."

He put his mouth to her ear. "And if I lick you until you scream for me later?"

She made a little sound in her throat. "That never hurts."

30

The hayride was ridiculously fun. The wagon wasn't too jammed, but there were a good twenty people seated on hay bales as they rode through the streets of Sutton's Creek. Ackerman and Reba were there, too, sitting next to each other on a bale near Diana and Alex.

Ackerman had winked at her, and Diana grinned back. Then he put his arm around Reba, and that little woman blushed bright red. Colleen, resplendent in burnt orange, had joined the group in the wagon at the last minute, and she glared daggers at Ackerman's back the whole way.

Diana thought, if she were Ackerman, she wouldn't want to piss off a woman who communed with the spirits. Especially not so close to Halloween. He turned around to talk to her from time to time, but she refused to engage.

Reba didn't say much either, probably because she could feel her bestie's ire. But she smiled a lot, so that was good.

Once the ride was over and they'd climbed down, Ackerman and Reba headed off toward the storytellers' tent where there were live music and theatrical performances throughout the day. Diana had attended one earlier because Violet Allen was in it and all the ladies had gone to watch. Ethan had rolled in right as it started and put an arm around Paisley. Diana watched them as much as she watched the kids.

It was sweet how much they loved each other. Beautiful.

The play was about the founding of Sutton's Creek, and it was mercifully short. That's because it featured a phalanx of adorable four- and five-year-olds pretending to be settlers. Kinda like a Thanksgiving play, but less pilgrim and more *Little House on the Prairie*. Without the prairie.

The adults shepherding the kids had looked harried throughout the adorably chaotic performance. One little girl cried, a little boy had so much fun stomping and jumping on the small stage that it'd taken two adults to wrangle him off it so the rest of the kids could be heard above the clatter, and at least three kids forgot what they were supposed to say.

All in all, a most entertaining event. Violet hadn't had a speaking part, so she'd done just fine with her best friend Lily Park at her side as they'd hooked arms and sang *America the Beautiful* at the end. Apparently,

Sutton's Creek didn't have a song of its own, which was probably just as well. At least knowing the words to *America the Beautiful* would come in handy at sporting events and presidential inaugurations. Not that a Sutton's Creek song wouldn't be awesome, but nobody had ever written one.

Diana walked through the town square with Alex, holding hands, and feeling like she was living some kind of small-town dream. There were booths with crafts made by local artisans, and a couple of booths featuring artists from Angels Cove. There was a library booth held jointly with the Angels Cove library, and Paisley was in it taking her turn. Emma and Blaze had charge of Violet, who was currently engaged in petting a goat at the petting zoo.

She and Alex ran into Asher McCrae again, the former soldier Alex had talked to at the Dawg the other night. He seemed distracted when they spoke, and Alex looked concerned.

But Asher gave him a firm look and said, "All's good. Swear it."

"Call me if you need anything."

"Will do. Promise."

After that, they spent a bit more time at the festival and then retrieved her bags and took them to her apartment. Alex caged her in at the island where he'd eaten her for dessert last night, and her pulse immediately spiked. He dropped his mouth to her neck, inhaled her as he kissed a shivery trail along her skin.

Would she ever feel this way again when he was gone?

"Come home with me, Diana. Let's get away from town and the noise outside, sit in the quiet of the country. Make love to the sounds of birds and crickets instead of music and voices and that damn tractor going up and down the street."

She looped her arms around his neck. "I'll go wherever you want if there's more of this when we get there."

He kissed her. "I can promise you, honey, I've got plenty to give you before I let you sleep tonight. You're turning into a bit of an addiction if I'm honest. The taste of you, the feel of you. It's a damned crime no man ever ate you before me, but you know what? I'm just caveman enough to be happy about it."

Heat and want zipped through her veins, sizzled into her nerve endings. She'd never been anyone's addiction before. "Well, I have to admit that I can't imagine anyone else could have done it better. I'm glad you were my first."

He searched her gaze. "You know what you're worth now, don't you?"

"Yes," she whispered, her heart aching. She didn't want to think about being with anyone else, communicating her desires to anyone else. Just him.

He took a step back, and she felt the separation between their bodies keenly. But he kept hold of her hand, tugging her away from the island. "Go. Get what you need for the weekend," he commanded, swatting her ass as she walked by. "I need to get you naked as soon as possible, and then I need to feed you dinner so I can do it all again."

Her body lit up with anticipation—at the promise of more to come and at the sweet sting of his hand against her bottom. Any other man, she'd have given him a piece of her mind. And quite possibly broken his wrist in the process.

But not Alex. His touch thrilled her. *He* thrilled her.

As she grabbed her weekender tote and started to fill it with clothing and toiletries, she told herself not to read too much into this thing between them. It was sex, not love. He'd said she was an addiction, and he'd said whatever they had was more than simply a deception to get them into the militia. It'd started out that way, but it had quickly overflowed the boundaries.

But that didn't make it love. Not like what Ethan and Paisley had. Not like what any of them had. Alex's teammates were all happily in love. It was a beautiful thing, and it showed with every interaction between them and the women.

This thing with her and Alex? It was fun, and it was satisfying in ways she'd never known.

But it wasn't love. Even if she wanted it to be.

The water was warm, fragrant with apple-cinnamon bubble bath that she'd picked up at the festival. Diana sank down gingerly, wincing a little as she leaned back against the hard body behind her, settling into his arms and letting out her breath. He picked up her glass of wine and handed it to her.

She took it with a murmured "Thank you."

He kissed the back of her neck, and a shiver rolled through her despite the warmth of the bath.

"That was fantastic," he said against her skin. "Are sure you're okay?"

"Yes, it was. And yes, I am."

She turned her head and kissed him, her tongue tangling with his before she playfully nipped his bottom lip and sipped her wine. His hand glided up to her breast, toyed with a nipple. She sighed.

They'd barely gotten inside his house before they'd started ripping at each other's clothing, leaving a trail all the way to the bedroom. He'd dropped between her legs, thrown her ankles over his shoulders, and licked her until she sobbed his name.

Then he'd flipped her over and taken her hard, tweaking her nipples, rubbing her clit, driving her to her limits. In a moment of sheer madness, she'd found herself asking him to spank her.

And, oh God, the way his hand stinging her flesh intensified every single sensation ricocheting through her. It *was* madness—and she'd loved it.

"That's my good girl," he'd growled, and she'd shattered. Just shattered around him, walls clamping down, body shuddering, every nerve ending on fire for him. He hadn't lasted another minute before he rooted himself deep and came inside her.

They'd fallen asleep after that, drowsing for a couple of hours before he'd run the bath, poured in the bubbles from her shopping today—not enough, but it was the thought—poured wine, and carried her into the bathroom where the big clawfoot tub could hold them both.

He picked up a cold beer and drank. "I think it entirely possible I'm spent for the rest of the night," he told her lazily. "May have to order a pizza."

"Sounds good to me. Think they'll deliver to the bathtub?"

"Even if they did, I wouldn't let them. Nobody sees my woman naked but me."

"And maybe her doctor."

He laughed. "Smart ass. Maybe I need to spank you again."

"Maybe so. But not today. Probably not tomorrow either, if I'm honest. It was… intense."

"Damn, baby, I told you to tell me if it was too much."

The concern in his voice. It swelled emotions inside her that had no business getting involved. "And I would have, but it wasn't. I wanted it, and you gave me what I wanted. Another box checked, and another first."

"I like being your first. Wish I was your first in everything—and, yeah, that's a very outdated point of view. I acknowledge it, but I'm not apologizing for it."

"And this is also an outdated point of view, but I'm glad I'm not *your* first. Because then you wouldn't know what you're doing as well as you do."

"Valid."

She ran her fingers up and down his wet forearm where it lay beside her. "What was your first time like?"

"Ah, well. You're right. I didn't know what I was doing. I had no opportunity before I got to college, so I was an eighteen-year-old virgin. But girls wanted me, so I learned pretty fast."

She could just imagine. A face and body like his, they'd have been throwing themselves at him.

"Was it at least romantic?"

"Nope. It was a bit of an orgy. Very unromantic. But for a teenage boy? Heaven."

"Hmm. I was in college, too. My first boyfriend. I was nineteen. He was twenty. It was fine, but not what I expected. He didn't know where the clitoris was, and I was too afraid to tell him he needed to focus some attention there. But it got better."

"Just better?"

She sipped her wine. "Good enough. He found the clitoris. That helped."

Alex's phone buzzed. He casually picked it off the windowsill. Then he groaned. "For fuck's sake."

"What?"

There was a sudden banging on the front door, and a voice yelling, "Hey! You two! Let us in! We brought food!"

Diana sat up and turned to look at Alex. He frowned. Hard.

"Is that... Daphne? And Kane?"

"It's all of the fuckers. Every last one of them, minus

the kids. They said to let them in, or Seth is going to disarm the system remotely and they're coming in. We have five minutes."

He looked so annoyed that Diana started to laugh. And when she started, she couldn't stop. Tears began to roll down her cheeks. "I don't know why it's so funny," she wheezed. "Your face!"

He looked at her in wonder, but the corners of his mouth trembled until he was laughing, too. "Damn, you're gorgeous when you laugh. Never saw you let go like this."

"Nothing...this...funny...long time." She wiped her eyes, still wheezing. "I don't know why!"

He typed something into his phone. She heard the whoosh of the message going. "Come on, Giggles," he said, holding out a hand to help her to her feet so she could climb out first. "I told them ten minutes, but I guarantee they won't wait a second longer. Let's get dressed and find out what they've brought us to eat."

He rose from the tub as she was reaching for a towel, but he got to it first. He didn't give it to her, though. He dried her off thoroughly while she worked to get the laughing under control. Then he went to work on himself as she walked into the bedroom to find clothing.

He was muttering when he joined her. "They better have something good, or heads are gonna roll for this."

Diana burst into laughter once more.

Eight minutes later, he was answering the door while

she took her hair down from the messy bun she'd put it in for the bath and combed it thoroughly. She was trying not to look too mussed, but the instant she joined everyone in the kitchen, it was patently obvious they knew what she and Alex had been doing.

"Hey, girlie," Daphne said, giving her a side hug as Luna the Malinois came over, tail wagging, hoping for some pets. Diana obliged with ear rubbing. "Figured you'd be famished what with this one not letting you out of bed and all, so we brought dinner."

"Daphne," Alex warned.

"Headed outside to start the grill," Kane interrupted. "Who's with me?"

Chance and Blaze went, beers in hand, because one man wasn't enough to start a grill. It wasn't quite dark out yet, but twilight was waning. Somebody flipped on the flood light. Ethan and Seth were busy putting drinks in the fridge, and the women were setting out the plates, utensils, and napkins.

"What are we having?" Diana asked. Might as well go with the flow because these people were not leaving until everyone was fed and happy. And, as much as she liked being alone with Alex, she didn't mind spending time with them. She was getting more comfortable every time they were all together. Even if she didn't quite belong, they accepted her because she was with Alex.

Though the women had informed her she would always be welcome, she thought it'd probably be awkward once they were no longer dating. A worry for later, though. For now, she was going to drink her wine and enjoy the fun.

"Grilled chicken," Emma said. "And we picked up some sides from Miss Mary's because she makes them family style. And a cake from Kiss My Grits."

"Where are Violet and Nikki?" she asked as the men all disappeared outside with their beers, carrying platters of chicken and a bottle of barbecue sauce. Luna trotted outside with them.

"Violet is having a sleepover at Lily Park's," Paisley said. "And I'm nervous." She held up her phone. "Hence the reason why I'm going to look at my phone a million times."

"It'll be fine," Rory said, patting her arm.

"I know." She huffed. "I know Trey is dead, and we're safe—but I worry. She's so little, and she had a rough time of it with Trey, so I worry she's going to want to come home."

"But she loves Lily," Callie said. "And the Parks are wonderful people."

"They are. Mr. Park is out of town this weekend and it's Eun-Ji and the girls, but she said they were going to watch movies and make tents in the living room. We talked it through, and Violet knows she can come home at any time if she gets scared. I know that sounds very indulgent, but she still has some attachment issues. Eun-Ji knows to call me if Violet has a hard time."

Callie wrapped her arm around Paisley and hugged her. "I understand. My kid sister is with her trainer and some of the other girls. They're helping to set up for a riding clinic at the barn tomorrow, and they're going to sleepover at their trainer's house because they have to get up early to get horses ready. I know Nikki's practically grown, but I still worry because I feel so responsible for her physical and mental health. Like my parents would haunt me if I let anything happen to her. But I also know I'm doing the best I can. And so are you."

Paisley sniffed. "Thank you. Ethan says she'll be fine, and he's probably right. She's stayed with Aunt Hettie before, and she didn't have any problems. This sleepover with Lily is still a new thing and I'm obsessing over it."

"So, nobody has to go home tonight," Daphne said, coming over with a bottle of wine. "Between this house and ours, everyone can stay if you get blitzed. Well, except Rory and Emma. No getting blitzed for you two."

Rory put a hand to her belly. "What I wouldn't give for a glass of wine. It's waited this long. It can wait until this little boy is born."

"Oh my God," Paisley said, "I thought you didn't want to know. When did you find out?"

Rory beamed. "Thursday. Chance was fine with us not knowing. He never said anything, but I finally couldn't stand it. I'm looking at the nursery and wanting to know what color bedding to get, you know? What kind of toys and onesies that aren't neutral. I was tired of yellows and grays. I want more color! So I asked at our last appointment, and Dr. Shaw told us. And we are *not* naming this baby Albert. Though I do kinda like Bear."

"As in Bryant," Emma said as an aside to Diana.

"Oh. Of course. Roll Tide."

"Yes! Roll Tide," Rory said. "You get it."

They talked babies for a little while before moving on to future plans and events. Diana tried to sit silently and listen, but they kept dragging her in, including her in the conversation. It wasn't forced, but natural. Diana had been around enough people acting unnaturally in her job to know the difference. When people were trying to hide things or putting on fake appearances, it showed up in ways she was very used to spotting.

These women weren't faking anything. They were a genuine friend group, brought together by love for men who were friends and partners. Emma and Rory were the only ones who'd been friends before they'd met their men, but if she didn't already know that she would think every one of these women had known each other for years.

"Okay, speaking of upcoming holidays," Emma said, raising a hand for attention. "My parents have issued the invitation to all of you to join us at their house on Thanksgiving. Before you say no, my mother *loves* to entertain. Like loves it. She desperately wants a full house, and she wants to use all her dishes and silver. The house is big enough, and Theo has already agreed to smoke the turkey and make his to-die-for gravy. You don't have to answer now, but please think about it. I completely understand if you want to start your own traditions with your man and your family, but if you haven't made any plans yet, come spend it with us."

Everyone said they were in without hesitation, though of course they had to make sure their men agreed—though nobody thought they wouldn't. Rory and Chance had already accepted. Daphne was pretty certain Kane had no plans, and Callie and Paisley thought it was a great idea.

"Diana? Do you think you might come?" Emma asked.

Five women gazed at her expectantly. "I, um…"

She thought of her mother's text. The phone calls that were soon to start. The discomfort she would feel if she did go home for the holiday. It was never a real family affair so much as it was a performance event to enhance social standing. Everything was catered, and there were people to serve the meal. Her brothers would go with their wives and kids in tow, and her mother would want to know when she was planning to get married. Worse, she would make sure to invite an eligible pre-approved bachelor or two and seat Diana with them.

She wanted to go to Emma's family home. A small-town Southern Thanksgiving? She could think of nothing better. But it was over a month away. What if she and Alex were sick of each other by then? Would he want to spend a holiday with her? Even if they were still pretending for the sake of the militia, would it be an intrusion to accept an invitation without discussing it with him first?

"Thank you," she said, drawing on all her training in

politeness and etiquette. "I'll have to let you know, but I so appreciate the invitation."

"You know," Daphne said, leaning in, "if you're thinking that you don't know what the state of your relationship will be in a month, I totally get that. But I'm telling you, that man is so into you. I've worked with the guys for months, and I've seen the two of you butt heads —but I've never seen him like this. He's still intense and scary in ways I can't even begin to contemplate, but he looks at you like Mr. Watson looks at a new pink unicorn T-shirt—and that's an awesome thing, let me tell you."

Diana couldn't help the inelegant snort that escaped. She knew all about Mr. Watson and his T-shirts. She'd gotten the lowdown on that when she'd been at the Bookalicious Besties meeting. He had a whole range of shirts with sayings that could be outright funny or risqué, but his favorites were pink unicorns.

Soon, they were all laughing, howling about Hiram Watson and Fern Carter and the epic clashes those two used to have. They'd mended fences, mostly, though sometimes Fern told Mr. Watson he was an obnoxious old queen and he called her a sour-faced biddy with a stick up her ass. Then he'd bring her a box of donuts, or she'd give him unicorn cookies from Kiss My Grits, and all was well again. It was a strange relationship to say the least, especially when they used to despise each other so much.

"To sum up," Rory said, "Diana is a pink unicorn and Alex is an obnoxious old queen with a unicorn obsession."

That started another fit of giggles all around. By the

time the men came inside with a platter of grilled chicken and a dirty platter for the sink, the women were wiping tears and snorting at things that wouldn't usually make them laugh so hard. The thing about laughter was that it was infectious—and it felt good.

They piled up plates with food, then gathered around the dining table that'd come with the house and occupied a rather large room with pocket doors. The men told stories about their service together, though it was heavily censored. Mostly about places they'd been and things they'd seen. Ethan was terrified of spiders, and the others made fun of him, but they didn't prank him with fake spiders. Apparently, Daphne's giant spider skeletons didn't bother him at all because they were outsized and ridiculous.

There were other stories. Missed transports. Wrong directions. Parties where somebody got shit-faced and made a fool of himself.

The drinks flowed and so did the conversation. Diana's head was swimming by the time Rory announced she had to go to bed, but first the kitchen needed cleaned. Everyone pitched in to wash dishes and put food away. Then the party broke up with lots of hugs and promises to do it again soon.

Rory, Emma, and Paisley were sober and could drive, Daphne and Kane only had to go next door, and Seth and Callie went with them to crash in one of the bedrooms there when Alex very firmly pushed them all out the door.

When they were gone and it was quiet again, Alex

took her hand and led her to the bedroom. He dropped his T-shirt over her head, slipped on a pair of pajama pants, and they fell into bed, too tired to do anything but cuddle beneath the covers.

Diana yawned. "That was nice. Even if it felt like an interruption when they first arrived."

"I wasn't pleased, gotta say. But you're right, it was fun. I'm glad they showed up and forced food on us."

"You have a good team. A good *family*."

"They are, aren't they? I'm lucky to have them. This assignment hasn't been what I thought it'd be, but oddly enough I don't regret taking it. Thought I did for a while, but I don't."

She burrowed closer to him, feeling the chill creeping into the air. October nights were much colder than the days. "Emma said something about Thanksgiving. I hope you know I don't expect to go with you—"

"Don't you want to? Or do you plan to go home?"

She felt like being honest. "I do want to, and I don't want to go to my parents' house. But what if we remember we really don't like each other? Do you want to be forced to spend a holiday that's about family with me?"

He rose on an elbow beside her. "Princess, if this is what not liking you feels like, I want to keep doing it for as long as possible. I don't think I'll be over it by Thanksgiving. Do you think you will?"

Her heart squeezed tight, then took off like it had a race to win. "No," she finally admitted. "I don't."

"Then unless you want to go sit around a table with

the Adlers, I suggest you plan to come with me to the Suttons' for Thanksgiving."

"Okay."

"Okay. Glad we solved that."

She didn't think they'd solved anything. But she liked the way it felt to be a part of his life.

31

Ghost sighed in frustration and leaned back in his chair. The SCIF was quiet, but his mind wasn't. The damned dream had woke him again, the wolf's jaws around his throat, the blood starting to slide hotly over his skin. Once he woke, he knew he couldn't go back to sleep.

He was no closer to knowing what Gannon's "big thing" happening at the Arsenal was. He'd listened to hours of recordings from the man's apartment over the past few days, skipping past the jerking off to bad porn, and the even worse sexual encounters that occurred whenever Gannon brought home some woman he'd started fucking on the regular. It was the same woman every time. Or there was more than one of them out there who called him Daddy and squealed like a pig when she came.

He'd checked in with Seth because they still had a bug

at Eagle Defense Systems where Gannon worked on days he wasn't at the Missile Defense Agency on the Arsenal. Seth said there was nothing out of the ordinary. Lots of meetings and phone calls, but all about business. If there was a code being employed to talk about Athena without talking about it, then Seth hadn't cracked it yet because absolutely nothing stood out.

Ghost had sent coded messages to Viper, got messages in return, but he was no closer to knowing who the saboteurs were. It was as if, with the president and her administration focusing on other things, whoever'd been after the technology behind Athena was focusing elsewhere as well.

Or, worse, they'd found a way in and stolen it already, and Ghost and his team were chasing their own asses. That thought kept him up at night almost as often as thinking about the militia and how to protect Diana from harm. Tomorrow, he had to walk into that meeting with Diana at his side and pretend he was eager to join their cause. If they got pulled deeper, then what?

He knew she was competent, but the farther he got into this thing with her, the more he worried about her safety. She was bold and ballsy, and she wouldn't hesitate to storm into danger if it meant she'd get her shot at taking Viktor Dashevsky down. He still didn't know why, and he wanted to.

She hadn't shared, and he hadn't asked. Yet.

He would, but he also knew it meant he had to share some things with her.

It needed to happen tonight. He didn't want to walk in that meeting without knowing what her emotional triggers were. It wasn't safe. For either of them.

They'd spent every night together since the weekend of the festival. Usually at his place, though sometimes at hers. He knew she liked her apartment in town, and he felt like he should make an effort to stay there with her, but he was more comfortable at the farm.

After he'd escaped his father in Alaska, after he'd trekked the two-plus days in ice and snow, dodging wolves and avoiding bears, he'd never wanted to be anywhere that remote again. He'd preferred cities, preferred noise and movement. He'd lived in apartments, never houses, and he'd fallen asleep to the sounds of humanity around him.

Of course he'd gone on missions in remote areas, lived off the land, and survived because that's how he was wired. But he'd always gone back to the city or the suburbs when it was over.

Until they'd moved to Sutton's Creek.

The farm wasn't in town, but it wasn't what he'd consider remote. It was quiet, though, and he discovered that he'd missed quiet. Not the quiet of a mission where he'd been huddled on the ground with his team, sleeping with scorpions and snakes, but the quiet of the country where he could hear nothing outside his windows but wind through the trees and wildlife.

He liked being at the farm. He thought, when this was

over, maybe he'd go to the fishing cabin he still owned in Virginia and live there a while.

Except every time he thought of leaving, of not being in Sutton's Creek, it didn't feel right. What was he supposed to do with himself then? He was forty-two, he'd given up his military career for this mission, and there was nothing left for him except succeeding at what he'd been asked to do. Then what?

He'd built a life here, even if it wasn't quite real, and he liked it. What if he made it real? What if he stayed, convinced the president and her people to let him and his team buy the range for real, and made a go of it? They hadn't done badly. Even if money hadn't been a factor in whether or not the range stayed open during the mission, Daphne and her organizational and planning skills meant they really were in the black without even trying.

She'd been right about the booth at the fall fest, and she'd been right about the trunk-or-treat event they'd held on Sunday. They'd had a huge turnout, and they'd cemented relationships with the police and fire departments. They'd had so many signups for classes that they were going to need to hire more qualified instructors to help them soon.

Besides, his friends were staying. They were entrenched. Even New Yorker Ethan, who'd bitched and moaned about the pizza not being as good as New York, was planning to move into a historic home in Sutton's Creek and raise his daughter with the woman he loved.

All of them were planning to get married, to stay. To

become part of the fabric of a small Southern town, even if it was as far from where they'd started as the moon was from the sun.

What if he stayed, too? He could. Why not?

He stood, put things right in the SCIF, then exited before the team arrived for work. He'd left Diana asleep in his bed an hour ago, kissing her on the forehead and telling her he had things to do, and he'd see her later. She'd murmured at him to have a good day and then turned over and went back to sleep.

He stood outside in the dawn light and breathed the cool air before he went for a run. Daphne's ridiculous giant skeleton and its spider dogs stood sentinel over the range, and the fields were wet with dew. A lone figure moved through the field between the range and the houses. He started walking, moving toward her, until they met in the middle of the dew-drenched grass.

"I thought you were sleeping," he said.

She went into his arms, lay her head against his chest. His heart stuttered as he wrapped his arms around her. He pressed his lips to her blond head, closed his eyes as he breathed her in. The comfort of her. The rightness of her in his arms.

Jesus, what was happening to him?

"I was, but it's lonely without you."

"So you came looking for me. Alone."

She tipped her head back to gaze up at him. "Where else would you be? Your commute is a short walk. And this isn't exactly downtown Chicago in the middle of the night. Think I'm safe enough, though maybe those cows over there might get a little frisky."

He ignored the cows. "I might have gone to town for breakfast. You'd have walked over here for nothing."

"You'd have gone without me?"

"Maybe. I could have brought you something before you woke up."

"I suppose you could have. But I knew I'd find you here. You also forget I could see the bowl on the counter where you ate cereal before you left. Though you're a big enough boy, I suppose you could eat a second breakfast."

"I could. But you could have called me instead of walking over. I'd have come back."

She shook her head. "I didn't need you to come back, Alex. I just wanted to see you again before I have to go to work. It might be a long day. Ackerman called when I was getting dressed to say we've got to drive to Scottsboro and Rainsville. Meth dealers. I'm not thrilled about it, but what are you gonna do?"

"I can come to your place later, be waiting for you with dinner and a bath."

"That's sweet of you. I think I'd rather come back here. Do you mind?"

"I don't. Just figured you were getting tired of never sleeping in your own bed."

"I like my bed. I also like waking up with Wendy Cochran's breakfast sandwiches so close by. But I like waking in the country, too." She swept her arm to encompass their surroundings. "It's peaceful and pretty. And we can talk out here, which we may need to do before tomorrow." She frowned. "Are you sure you don't want to tell the team about the meeting?"

"Are you worried about it?"

She shrugged. "Not exactly. But I've spent enough time with them now to know how much you care about each other. And they're more than competent, Alex. They might be a help if..."

"If?"

Her blue eyes fixed on him again. "You were worried I wouldn't be good backup when this started. I don't want you thinking about that when we need to be focused on what's happening out there. I know Gannon's an asshole, but he's hinted whenever we've met with him lately that something will happen at that meeting. I don't want you thinking about how to protect me and not doing your job. If you know they're ready to help, you might not think so much about me being with you."

Was he that bad at hiding it? He started to explain but she put a finger on his lips to keep him from speaking. "I know you've been dreaming, Alex. I know it wakes you up at night, and I know I have to be contributing to it since you've never wanted me involved. But I can't let you go alone, so please just involve your team somehow if it's going to eat you up inside."

Jesus, this woman. She astounded him and intrigued him—and he thought he might never tire of her company for as long as he lived. And that thought staggered the fuck out of him.

"I am thinking about protecting you," he said roughly. "It's what I do, who I am. Doesn't mean I don't trust you to have my back though. I don't want you there because I don't trust *them*. I never wanted you in the middle of this, but we'll go in together. You're my backup, and I'm yours. We won't go in completely blind. Mendez knows about the meeting. If anything happens, he'll send my guys after us."

He didn't like looping Viper in, especially since deniably was his whole reasoning for keeping those he cared about out of it. But Viper insisted, and he wasn't the sort of man to take no for an answer. He also snorted at the idea of cracking under pressure—or polygraphs.

She smiled. "Does this mean we're a team then?"

"Yeah, we're a team."

"I feel honored. Should we have a little ceremony? Spit in our hands and shake on it? Make pinky promises? Synchronize our secret decoder rings?"

He stared at her. "Diana Corbin, are you making a joke at my expense?"

That giggle he adored escaped. "Maybe." She stood on tiptoe and kissed his cheek. "But also, thank you. I feel like I've accomplished something big, having you think I'm good enough to be on your team."

"I do," he said honestly. "And I know I was a dick to you over the past few months, but the information you gave us was invaluable. We wouldn't have known about the Dashevsky connection as quickly as we did—if ever."

It bothered him to think they wouldn't have made that

connection, but it was entirely possible. Diana was the one with the in-depth knowledge of the Dashevsky Group, and she'd brought it to them when Callie was in danger.

"You'd have gotten there. I have to think Washington would have told you his people were involved, and you'd have put it all together without me. Just not quite as fast."

"You're a good agent, Diana. You always have been, even when I was pissed at you for invading my operation. And I suppose I can admit that I like you a tiny bit more than I used to."

She squeezed him. "I like you a tiny bit more, too. But don't read too much into it, because once you start acting all macho and ordering me around at the meeting tomorrow, you'll be at the bottom of the likability ladder again."

"Chance I'll have to take, I guess."

"Okay, I better get going. Have to meet Ackerman and get on the road. See you later, Magic Man."

He took her hand. "Not so fast. I'm walking you to your car."

"Oh, right. Need to protect me from those cows."

"Tease all you like, but I'm not letting my woman walk back to her car alone when I can go with her. Kiss her properly, maybe cop a feel before she goes."

"Just be aware she's copping one too. If it makes you hard, that's not her fault."

He gave her a look. "Princess, just looking at you makes me hard."

And somewhat unnerved about all the other things he

was feeling inside. He pressed her against the car door and kissed her until they were both feeling the pain of parting.

"Gotta go," she said regretfully. "But we'll take up where we left off when I get back tonight."

"Counting on it, babe."

"Bye, hot stuff." She got into her Beemer, started the engine, and reversed out of the space beside his truck. He watched her go, frowning as her taillights grew farther and farther away.

It was a goodbye like any other, and yet it was somehow unsettling too. As if a freight train barreled down the track, and he'd just stepped into its path.

32

ckerman drove. Diana sipped the coffee he'd grabbed for her when he stopped at a gas station to pee after they'd been on the road a while. She was tired because it'd already been a few hours of riding around to different appointments to interview suspects or meet with law enforcement. Not to mention she'd stayed up too late with Alex. Impossible not to when being with him felt so damn good.

Even after the epic sex they'd had—the kitchen, the bathtub, his bed—the instant he'd kissed her this morning, she'd ached for him. She could have easily dragged him back inside and done the whole thing again, but Ackerman had been waiting.

And then there was the part where Alex had called her his woman. Wasn't the first time, but every time he said it, the words burrowed just a little bit deeper into her heart.

"Late night?" Ackerman asked after she yawned again.

"A little. You?"

"Believe it or not, no. Took Reba to Miss Mary's for dinner. Colleen joined us. Uninvited, I might add."

"Oh dear. I wouldn't take it personally though. She's just afraid of losing her best friend and business partner."

"It's not that serious. I like Reba. She's sweet. But I don't see us marching down an aisle. Haven't even gotten past first base yet."

Diana had a sudden picture in her head that she really didn't want. "No, no. We are not discussing anyone's sex life here. Boundaries, Ackerman. Boundaries."

He laughed. "Gotcha, kiddo. Speaking of sex lives—without talking about any of that stuff—Joel bother you anymore?"

"No. Thank God."

After that crazy display in the parking lot, he hadn't approached her again. She'd been waiting for somebody to ask her if it was true she was related to the deputy CIA director—or to a freaking princess—but nobody had. If Joel was planning to blast her family name to everyone at work, he hadn't done it yet. She didn't know why since he'd been so vicious about it.

Alex had told her to be prepared for him to do something to wound her for rejecting him. But short of outing her family connection, what could he do? Tell people she'd refused to take him back?

"I talked to him."

Diana's head whipped around. "You did what?"

Ackerman shrugged. "Talked to him. Not a threat or anything. He came up to me. Wanted to tell me something."

Oh shit.

"And? Did he?"

"Said something interesting about you."

Her heart thumped. "Okay. And? Do you think I'm not qualified anymore? Don't want to be my partner? Think I'm just a nepo baby pretending to work for a living?"

"I think you're plenty qualified, Diana. I could tell when you showed up that you had a fire in your belly. I've never been worried about your ability to do the job."

Her eyes stung. "Okay, well, thank you. I appreciate that."

"I could wish you'd told me, but I understand why you didn't. Kinda disappointed you told that douchebag, though."

She sighed. "It was a moment of weakness. Don't tell me you've never made a bad decision."

"I've made plenty of them. Probably gonna make plenty more before I'm through." His hands flexed on the steering wheel. "Shit happens in our lives, you know? And we don't always get it right. I was too distant with Amy, too often gone. I thought I was fighting for the right things. But maybe I wasn't. Maybe I'd been wrong all along."

Diana's belly clenched. She didn't know what to say to that. Ackerman was always the friendly one in this partnership. The happy one. Even after his wife left, he'd sailed into being single and embraced it wholeheartedly. Not immediately, but faster than she would have thought possible when a ten-year marriage ended. They didn't have kids, so the break was complete. Amy had moved to Atlanta to live with her sister, and she wasn't coming back.

Diana wasn't stupid enough to think Ackerman wasn't affected by the divorce, but he was the kind of person who tended to get on with it. It wasn't even his first divorce. Amy was number three, in fact. But Ackerman was practical, and he didn't dwell. She'd always admired that about him.

"What is life except making decisions and then questioning if it was the right one or not?"

"True. Soooo, about this decision to date the guy in charge of One Shot Tactical. Still think it's a good one?"

She frowned. "They're all partners in the business. What makes you think Alex is in charge?"

He shot her a look. "Seriously? He's the one who acts like he calls the shots. No matter what any of them say, you know as well as I do these former military types still follow structure. According to their service records, he's the ranking guy."

The false service records. What would Ackerman think if he knew what Alex was really capable of? "I know. But we don't talk about his military days, or the range."

They were getting into delicate territory with this

conversation. When Callie Crowell had been a target of Dima Smirnov and Viktor, Diana had worked alone with Alex and his team. She'd used her knowledge of their operation to gain access, and she'd met with them inside their SCIF without Ackerman involved. He'd known she was working on something, but he hadn't known what. She had not been authorized to tell him.

"How well do you really know this guy, Diana? He's charismatic, I'll give you that. And he's clearly turned your head. But who is he really? Why is he here?"

A shiver skipped down her spine. "I guess I know him a little better than you know Reba. We're just dating. Having fun. Like you said, nobody's making a trip down the aisle. It's fun, and he's a lot more entertaining than Joel ever was."

"By entertaining you mean...?"

"Be quiet," she said, blushing as he laughed.

"Okay, fine. I hear you. Alex Bishop is a good time. Joel was a steppingstone on the way to a good time."

"I wouldn't put it quite that way, but yes, Alex is a marvelous time."

Ackerman shook his head. "Just be careful, okay? Feel like that guy has more going on than meets the eye. Not sure all of it's good."

She turned her torso toward him. "Are you kidding me? Just a couple of weeks ago, you told me 'good for you' and 'you go, girl'. What happened? Did he glare at you or something? Is Reba swooning over him when she should be swooning over you?"

"Nah, nothing like that. I had those thoughts then, but I didn't mention it. Thought it wasn't my business. Still isn't, but you're my partner so I couldn't keep it to myself."

Diana sat back in the seat and sipped her coffee. "Geez, Ackerman. Way to give me whiplash. But I hear you. I'll be careful."

Though she feared it was already too late for that. Her heart was involved, whether she wanted it or not. All she could do was hang on for the ride.

The scenery in eastern Alabama was beautiful. The trees were turning, the mountains stood lush against the landscape—not mountains like the Rockies or the Alps, but smaller ones, foothills of the Great Smokies. There were green fields, and blue, blue sky that seemed to go on forever. She didn't get out this way often, but she loved it.

The warm afternoon sunlight made her sleepy. Ackerman turned on the radio and country music filled the car.

"Damn," she said, yawning. "I need a nap."

"So take one. I got this. I'll wake you when we get to the next stop."

"I'm going to try to stay awake, but if I fall asleep, then I'll owe you one."

He laughed. "You can try, but I don't think it's gonna happen. All those late nights with your new lover boy. Surprised you made it this far."

"I'll remind you that you said that when you start staying out late with Reba."

"Sure, sure. You can do that."

Despite her best efforts, she fell asleep. There were dreams. Of Alex, of his friends, of her parents and her brothers. Joel was there, too, chasing her down a hallway. Colleen was there, telling her the spirits were restless.

And then there was Viktor. Not his face, but his voice. It was near, in the darkness, the Russian vowels dropping heavy and thick. Her Russian wasn't good because she'd dropped out of that course of study after what he did to her.

She'd taken Italian instead. She should have studied Arabic or Greek, but she'd already decided not to pursue international affairs. She could order food, buy clothing, and enjoy a vacation in Italy. She could not work in the Russian embassy, nor did she want to.

Not anymore.

The dreams kept coming, and she felt as if she were fighting her way through a veil of thin black silk. It never lifted, but she could hear things. Voices. And she felt hands on her, lifting her, carrying her. It must be the movement of the car, but it felt so real.

When she finally woke, when her eyes snapped open, panic flooded her system. Her heart galloped, sweat beaded on her skin, and her chest felt so tight she didn't think she'd be able to draw breath. It was dark, and she lay on a bed. She tried to sit up, racking her brain for how she'd gotten here. What she didn't remember.

Was she sick? Had Alex come to get her and taken her home?

But no, when she tried to move, her wrist was caught against something. She pulled, but nothing happened. It took her a moment to figure out that her wrists were bound, chained to something solid—quite probably the headboard—and she was in utter darkness. She blinked and blinked again, hoping the darkness would clear. Had they done something to her eyes?

Logic told her no, they hadn't. Not anything permanent anyway. Her eyes didn't hurt. There was no wound.

"Ackerman," she wheezed.

They'd been together, driving to Scottsboro and a meth investigation. Had it gone wrong? Had someone taken them prisoner? Where was Ackerman? Had they hurt him?

"Ackerman," she said again, her voice only marginally stronger. "You... here?"

Her head throbbed. Her heart still raced. And nothing but silence greeted her inquiry. She was alone, or Ackerman was here but still passed out—or worse—and nobody was coming to save them. He could be hurt, dead, dying.

She didn't think she was dying, but she felt like hell.

She jerked against the restraints, searching for weakness, but they were tight. It felt like cuffs. She moved her hands, bending the fingers of one toward her wrist—and encountered steel.

Fear ripped from her stomach to her toes and back up

to her brain. Where was she? How long had she been there? Where was Ackerman?

"Hey," she called out. "Anybody there?"

No one came. She heard nothing in the darkness, no sounds of movement. She focused on her senses. The air smelled like... nothing? It wasn't dank or earthy like a cave or a basement. It was the nothingness of the indoors. She sniffed again. The very faint odor of onions reached her. Or maybe she was imagining it.

But if there really were onions, then this was a house. She was on a bed, but she hadn't wanted to assume. Beds could be dumped into cellars or warehouses, too. But her surroundings didn't echo like a warehouse. She reached above her head, searching for the headboard.

It was iron, and she was anchored to it by a short chain that ran through the cuffs. She followed the chain with her fingers, scooting upward to see if there was any weakness, any kind of place where the chain might slip through the bars of the bed.

But search though she might, there was nothing. Frustration pounded into her.

And fear. Because what was this? What were they planning to do with her?

She dozed again, because the drugs hadn't worn off completely, finally waking when she heard the scraping of a key in the lock. Light flooded into her prison, shining on her from a flashlight that someone shone in her face. She squeezed her eyes closed and brought her arms up to shield them.

"*Ona prosnulas,*" a male voice said. "*Prevedi yeye.*"

She's awake. Bring her.

Russian hadn't entirely deserted her then.

Rough hands grabbed her. A key snicked in a lock and the chain slid free. The cuffs remained, however. The man dragged her to her feet.

"You will walk," he said.

"I can't see. It's too bright."

"Put a hand over your eyes." His tone said he couldn't give two shits less.

Diana did as he instructed, covering her eyes as much as possible as they dragged her into a dimly lit hallway. She was forced up a set of stairs and then another, stumbling to her knees again and again, being hauled roughly to her feet so she could keep going. When she emerged into a huge living area with low-slung leather couches and artfully placed lamps, her gaze was first drawn to the giant windows that reflected the interior. It was completely dark outside, which meant she'd lost an entire day. Or maybe it was more than a day.

Oh God, the militia meeting.

She was going to miss it, and Alex would go alone. What if something happened to him?

"Ah, Diana, it's so lovely to see you. How have you been, my dear?"

Her gaze jerked to the source of that voice, her stomach knotting. Viktor Dashevsky—Russian oligarch, fake humanitarian, man who would be king if he could manage it—lounged in one of the fat club chairs, a highball glass in one hand, ice cubes tinkling softly as he lifted it to sip the amber liquid. Bourbon. She could smell it from where she stood.

"What have you done with Ackerman?" she growled. It was the only thing she could think to say. If she loosed her tongue and said what she really wanted, she would be screaming.

Viktor arched an eyebrow. His gaze slewed to the other chair where a man sat with his back to her. She hadn't noticed him, but now he stood. Turned.

Her heart dropped to the floor as everything she thought she knew crumbled to ash.

"I'm sorry, Diana," Ackerman said.

"Why?" she gasped, betrayal scouring every inch of her. Rewiring her understanding, her belief in people. "Why would you do such a thing?"

He frowned, his gaze dropping to the glass in his hand. "President Willis is weak. She won't take a hard stand against our enemies. You know it as well as I do. If we don't do something, we'll be overrun. Our nation will suffer, and people will be forced to fight foreigners on our own soil. We'll be invaded by the Chinese or the Muslims —or, hell, the Mexicans—if we don't do something to take back control of our government."

Diana could only gape. And then she laughed, a bitter sound that was wrenched from her soul. "Oh, of course, because being invaded by the Russians is infinitely preferable to any of those people, right?"

Ackerman's frown grew deeper. "We're cooperating

to make a better world. A stronger world where we stand for what's right against those who would tear us down. Mr. Dashevsky is a great humanitarian, and a believer in ruling with strength and compassion. He's helping us to take back our country, not invading us. That would be impossible. America is too strong for that."

Her heart hurt. Absolutely hurt. She'd had no idea he was filled with hate toward people who, for the most part, were just living their lives the same as he was. There were bad people everywhere, of every color and religion, but that didn't make an entire group evil or intent on invasion.

"You have no idea what you're doing, or who this man really is," she told him, jerking her chin at Viktor. "No idea."

Because, for all Ackerman's delusional thoughts, he couldn't really support a man who trafficked in humans and fomented war so he'd have a place to sell his weapons. Could he?

"Yes, yes, my dear," Viktor said, sounding bored. "You have always had it in for me since that moment when you seduced me. You wanted access to my money and my power, but I didn't fall for you as you'd hoped. I did not make you my wife, as indeed I told you I would not. You have only yourself to blame."

Her throat closed tight. She couldn't speak. The absolute unreality of the situation hammered at her like a sledge, destroying everything she thought she knew. She would tear him apart with her bare hands if she could. Spit on his remains.

And yet the chance of it happening now was next to nothing. Not with Ackerman on his side instead of hers. Her belly churned with acid as she tried not to succumb to hopelessness.

"Liar," she growled. Her knees buckled as the man standing behind her kicked her legs out from under her. She fell hard, breaking her fall with her hands, but unable to save herself from hitting hard because of the way they were bound in front of her.

"Hey." Ackerman sounded concerned. "You said you wouldn't hurt her."

"She is not hurt," Viktor replied. "And it is up to her whether or not she will be. Boris, do not strike Ms. Adler, please. And remove those cuffs. She is no threat to us like this."

The man behind her roughly removed her cuffs and took a step back. Diana pushed herself to a sitting position. She did not rise because her limbs felt weak. She glared at Viktor, and then at Ackerman, who broke eye contact first. Good, let him marinate in guilt, if indeed he felt even an ounce of it.

He'd been her friend. They'd spent countless hours together, talking about life. Going to Cracker Barrel, eating breakfast, sharing Thanksgiving. She'd been there when Amy left him, and she'd teased him about his dating escapades later on.

None of it had been real. At least not for him.

"See, my dear, I can be reasonable. And I will be reasonable, I promise you."

"What do you want from me?" She glared at Viktor. Because he had to want something, or she wouldn't be there.

He twisted the highball glass in his hands, the ice clinking. "I wish to know everything you know about Colonel Bishop and his friends."

"I don't know anything."

Viktor raised a finger. "Do not lie to me, Diana. Tell me the truth and leave nothing out, or I shall be forced to let Boris persuade you. His methods are not nearly as kind as mine."

33

t was pushing eight o'clock and Ghost still hadn't heard from Diana. They didn't text or call each other throughout the day, because they weren't the kind of people who needed to cling to each other, but the longer the day got and he didn't hear from her, the more that feeling of standing on a railroad track with a train chugging toward him intensified.

There was no reason for it. Diana would have told him if Gannon had contacted her. The people she'd met and cultivated at Big Mike's, when she was trying to infiltrate the militia on her own, weren't as connected as Gannon was. Even still, she'd have called or texted if one of them had contacted her and asked for a meeting.

Wouldn't she?

Doubts began to circle his brain. She'd seemed worried about him leaving her behind—but what if she'd been working her own angles all along? What if she'd left him behind because she'd gotten intel that sent her on a different path?

No. Diana wasn't stupid. She knew they had to go together. Hell, just that morning she'd urged him to involve the team. She wouldn't have done that if she was planning some kind of meetup on her own. He didn't believe it for a moment.

He trusted her. It had happened slowly, over weeks, but he trusted her like he trusted his guys. She wasn't stupid and she wasn't reckless. Even if he didn't know what drove her, he knew she was smart and determined. She wanted to take Dashevsky down, and she wanted to do it right.

So where was she? Why hadn't she been in contact?

He picked up his phone and sent a text. It was possible she was just busy, that time had slipped away from her.

"Hey, boss. Locking up and heading to the Dawg," Ethan said, peeking into his office. "You going with?"

He hadn't intended to. He'd been planning to wait for Diana, but without any communication from her, he had an urge to head into town, wait for her there. If she got in late, she might want to crash in her own bed, afraid to disturb him in case he was asleep. He'd send another text, tell her where to find him. If he didn't hear from her by the time the Dawg closed, he'd head home again.

He didn't like that idea, though. He needed to know where she was. He wasn't going to be settled until he did. He'd never felt like he needed to know where a woman he was fucking was before—but this was more than fucking. He knew it, even if he hadn't admitted it yet.

"Yeah, I'm coming."

He logged out of his computer and turned off the light, following the guys out the door. They were talking, laughing, discussing the events of the day. They were happy men, and he was glad for that.

Try as he might, he felt disconnected, unsettled. Wrong.

"What's going on, Ghost?"

His head snapped up to meet Blaze's questioning look. They were standing in the parking lot. His men were watching him. Not one of them moved toward their cars.

"Nothing." And then, because it was eating away at him, he told them. "Haven't heard from Diana yet. She and Ackerman had to drive to eastern Alabama today, but I thought she'd have texted to say she was on the way back by now. Or had to stay overnight somewhere if they weren't done. Just a little preoccupied with why she hasn't gotten in touch."

The men exchanged a look.

"And does that seem normal to you?" Seth asked. "Diana taking off and not letting you know where she is?"

"We aren't up each other's asses all day. She has a job. I have a job." He said it gruffly, but even as he heard himself say it, it sounded like an excuse. Denial. Because he didn't want to be that teenage boy who messed up again. Who missed the signs and made a mistake he'd never stop thinking about. *You should have used the sat phone when you had the chance. She might not have died.*

"Think it's time?" Chance asked.

Ghost started to ask time for what, but the guys were looking at each other, not him.

"Prolly so," Kane said. "Seth?"

Seth cleared his throat as he fixed Ghost with a stare. "We know what you're doing. We know where you've been going, who you've been talking to, and what you and Diana thought you were going to do alone. We know, we're pissed, but we forgive you. We know you didn't want us involved out of some misguided attempt at protecting us, but you're wrong, man. So fucking wrong. And you damned well know it. We're a team. We came here to do a job, and we're gonna fucking do that job. We're gonna do it right, we're gonna win, and then we're gonna settle down and raise our kids with our family— that's you and all of us, by the way—because that's how this is gonna go. Any questions?"

He was staggered. Just fucking staggered. He stared at them. They stared back, faces set, expressions stern.

"Did you bug my fucking house?" he growled. "My phone?"

Seth frowned. "Didn't have to."

"Then how?"

"Because we're not stupid, you dumbass," Blaze practically yelled before he quieted down and added, "Dumbass, *sir.*"

Kane snorted at the amendment. "That's right. Not as dumb as we look."

"Hey," Chance objected. "Not all of us look dumb. That's just you, Demon."

"Asswipe."

"Douche."

"Focus, children," Ethan said, snapping his fingers. "We're busy telling our lovable but idiotic teammate and leader here why he didn't fool us, not fighting about who looks the dumbest."

"We know about the meeting tomorrow," Seth said, cutting to the chase. "And we know that Diana not being back yet is setting off alarm bells in your head. Could just be that she's out of range and it took longer than they thought. Could be any number of things. But we're fucking tired of pretending we don't know what's happening. We're here, we're involved, and we aren't taking no for an answer."

Ghost blew a breath. Raked a hand over his head. These fucking guys.

But he loved them, dammit.

"How do you know these things? If you didn't bug me —or her—how?"

"First, I wouldn't do that," Seth said. "Okay, I would do that. But only if it got bad enough I had to. Didn't need to, though. The bug at Eagle Defense Systems was the first clue. Gannon talked about you. About meeting with you. To someone on the phone."

Ghost frowned. "You didn't tell me that when you gave your reports."

"Because I'm not an idiot!" Seth was yelling now. "I told *them*. Wasn't gonna clue *you* in that I knew you were up to something. I lied and said there was nothing on the recordings."

"Lying to your commanding officer," Ghost said mildly.

"Sue me."

"All it took was knowing you were meeting with him," Chance added, "to realize you were trying to cut us out. I'm gonna guess it's because we're making lives here, and you're worried that involving us puts us in the crosshairs of Washington if something goes wrong. And while I care very much about what I'm building with the woman I love, the kid we have coming, *none* of that is gonna matter if Viktor Fucking Dashevsky gets his hands on the project!"

And now Chance was yelling. Fucking hell.

"Did any of you ever think maybe I'd really gone rogue?" Ghost demanded. "That I wanted to join up because my fucking father was a separatist and I understand the life? What if I'm a believer, huh? You think of that? Just because you think you know me doesn't mean you do."

"Fuck no," Ethan said. "Not for a minute."

The rest of the guys chimed in with emphatic *fuck nos* of their own.

"Didn't know that about your father," Blaze said. "But

even if we did, not one of us would think you'd be involved in that shit show other than to try and be a fucking hero who'd sacrifice himself to save the rest of us. Which, for the record, we didn't ask you to do. So, no, never occurred to me you were actually a believer. Diana either. Woman has too much of a grudge against Dashevsky to fall in line with that crap. It's either that or she missed her calling as an actress, because there's no way the same woman who gave us information—helped us—when Callie needed protecting or when Daphne needed sheltering, believes for a single damned minute that a militia movement tied to a Russian oligarch is what she needs to be doing with her life. No fucking way. And neither do you."

Ghost huffed a breath, and then another. "You fucking assholes," he growled. "I didn't want you involved. I want you to have those futures you're planning, to make lots of babies and be happy. You deserve it, more than most, and I didn't want to drag you into anything. I'm not authorized to do what I'm doing. It's not sanctioned. If we get caught being involved with these people—"

He sucked in another breath, forced down the emotion threatening to well up. "I don't want you going down with me. I won't put that burden on any of you."

Ethan was closest. He slung an arm around Ghost's shoulders. "You dumb fuck. Respectfully, of course. None of us are going down. The trick is not to get caught, right? So we don't fucking get caught."

Blaze put a hand out. The rest of them piled on. Ghost

kept his hands at his sides, fighting his impulses, fighting the urge to order them to stand down. He was still their commanding officer. They were civilians only in name, but they were HOT until they died.

"Waiting on you, Alex," Blaze said.

He groaned as he put a hand on theirs. "You assholes. You should go home and cuddle your women and leave this to me."

"Not happening," Kane said cheerfully. "Anything happens to you, I'm not explaining to Daph why I didn't have your back. She's fond of your cranky ass for some reason."

"Count of three," Seth said. "Where None Dare," they chanted in unison before breaking the circle.

They were headed for their cars when Ghost's phone buzzed in his pocket. He snatched it out to see if it was a reply from Diana, but he didn't recognize the number.

> Using Clay's phone. Sorry, we were in a
> dead zone. My phone died. Day ran late,
> so staying in hotel. Will text in the
> morning. Love you!

Darkness swirled in his soul. Anger—and an impending sense of a loss that would kill him if it happened—churned in his belly.

All he had left was instinct, and his instinct told him the text was wrong. Completely wrong.

Diana wouldn't call her partner Clay. She wouldn't say she'd text in the morning when she had a phone—

Ackerman's—and could call him for a quick conversation now. And she definitely wouldn't say *love you* in that casual, flippant way. She would have said she still didn't like him. That was her style. Not *love you* when they'd never used those words before. They had a language that was theirs alone, and this wasn't it.

He dragged in a breath, and then another as certainty settled bone deep. "Something's happened," he called to his team. "Diana's in trouble, and we need to find her."

Five faces hardened as they moved toward him. Five men vibrated with anger. Not for him, but for her. She was one of them, and they took care of their own. He loved them more in that moment than he'd ever thought he could. Brothers. Comrades in arms. *Family.*

"We need a plan," Ethan said.

Chance was already moving, unlocking the door to the range. "Then let's get to work."

They filed inside and stalked toward the SCIF. They'd use every bit of technology and know-how they possessed to find Diana. Then they were going after her, no matter where she was.

Nobody took one of their own.

Nobody hurt a hair on his woman's head and lived to tell about it.

He would annihilate them. No matter what price he had to pay.

34

They'd drugged her again. That was her first thought on waking chained to the same bed as before. This time by only one wrist. The other…

Well, she assumed it was the same bed anyway. She lay in the darkness, cataloguing her pains, remembering.

She'd refused Viktor's command for information. But he'd let Boris lay hands on her, and she simply wasn't strong enough. She'd tried, but the pain…

Ackerman was no help. He'd protested, but Viktor ignored him. So he'd stood by while Boris beat her and he'd done nothing. That had nearly broken her.

She hoped Alex would forgive her, but she'd had to make a choice when the pain was too great to bear. He'd once said she wasn't trained like him, wasn't capable of suffering deprivation and surviving hardship.

He'd been right, of course. She might have been ignored as a child, her emotional needs not met the way she'd needed them to be, but she'd never suffered a moment's deprivation in her life. She was *pampered.*

She'd worked hard to be an FBI agent. She'd been driven. The things she'd gone through in training—well, that wasn't real hardship, was it?

Her face was swollen, and her head hurt. Boris had only hit her in the face once before Viktor stopped him.

"Let us keep her pretty face intact. She may yet be useful."

She didn't know what that meant, but it'd chilled her to the bone.

"Tell them what they want to know, Diana," Ackerman had said. "Just tell them and be done with it. Alex Bishop doesn't care about you. He's a traitor, a dangerous man. He's using you."

"Fuck. You." She'd spat blood at him. And then Boris jerked her upright and twisted her arm behind her back, shoving it so high something had to break.

And it did. She felt the moment her wrist snapped, and she screamed at the pain. But the beating didn't stop. It continued until she found herself speaking, telling them what she knew. Not everything, but she hoped it was enough to satisfy Viktor.

Either it had worked or she'd passed out, because she was here in the dark with only the sounds of her own breathing and the throbbing in her head. Tears welled behind her eyes, made everything hurt that much worse. She didn't want to cry. If she started, she might not stop.

Ackerman had betrayed her. Viktor had stormed into

her life again, pretending he'd never hurt her in the first place. That she had seduced him and been vengeful because he hadn't married her. It infuriated her and made her feel hopeless at the same time.

Why did powerful men get away with such things? Why were they able to hurt others and nobody held them accountable? They lied, changed the story, pretended to be good people, pretended to care about others, and yet all they did was take and take and take.

And nobody ever believed the victims, the ones who said they were hurt by this man. No, people took his side, believed him because he was rich and powerful and why would he need to rape a woman when he could just pay for sex if he really wanted to? No way would he engage in human trafficking because that was a criminal offense, and he was such a wonderful guy who gave money to help those less fortunate. Plus, he was already rich, so where was the incentive?

Those were the things people said, and it sickened her. Ackerman believing that Viktor Dashevsky was more competent than President Marla Willis simply because he was a man. Never mind that Viktor was Russian and a friend of Putin's. That didn't stop men like Ackerman or Gannon from thinking the woman was somehow the one who was dangerous. The woman who'd been elected by the people to lead them was the bad guy in their estimation, and she needed to be stopped. Even if it meant climbing in bed with a rich foreigner and handing him the keys to the kingdom.

She lay in the dark and felt the tears slip from the corners of her eyes to her temples and into her hair. Why had she bothered? Why hadn't she just done what her mother wanted and married somebody rich and connected so she could be a socialite wife and not have to worry her pretty head about these things? Why had she thought she could make Viktor pay for his crimes?

"No," she whispered. "No."

It wasn't over yet. She was still alive. She still had a shot so long as she was breathing. No matter how hard it was, how impossible it seemed, she wasn't finished.

She thought of Alex, of the things she'd read in his file. Of what he'd told her about his childhood. She hadn't heard it all, but she'd heard enough to know he had survived against long odds. And then he'd joined the Army and survived that as well.

If he were the one chained to this bed, he wouldn't be crying. He wouldn't be thinking about how awful the world was and how the bad guys always won. He'd be making plans to survive, to take the bad guys down when he escaped or his team arrived to rescue him.

Not one of those One Shot Tactical men would give up the way she felt like doing. They'd been shot, stabbed, beaten, and they'd lived to fight another day.

She had to live too. She'd only just started to feel like she belonged, like she was part of something bigger than herself, and she wasn't ready to give that up. Not without a fight.

Footsteps sounded in the hallway outside her room.

She dragged in a breath, and then another, willing her heartbeat to slow down. She had to survive this. She had to live to fight another day. She had to be strong, and she had to believe rescue was coming.

The door to her room rattled. She held her breath, her heart racing, hoping they'd found her, that she was safe.

It scraped open on hinges that needed oiled. But it wasn't rescue that stood in the entry.

It was death.

35

"The last place her phone pinged a tower," Seth said, pointing at the screen. "Scottsboro."

"What about Ackerman?"

"Same. But they took a government vehicle today which means a tracker device."

Government vehicles often had GPS trackers to monitor things like speed, location, and idle time. It was ostensibly to track efficiency, but it also kept employees accountable. You weren't supposed to run personal errands in a government vehicle, and GPS meant people abusing the system would be caught and dealt with.

It also meant they could track Ackerman and Diana's path.

Seth was busy typing commands, pulling up menus, and finding what he needed. Nobody said anything as they waited.

"Car's currently in Scottsboro. At a motel," Seth added.

Ghost felt like his chest was going to explode as emotion assailed him. "No. It's not right. She wouldn't fucking send me a text if they were at a motel in Scottsboro. If her phone was dead, she'd borrow a cord or buy one and she'd charge the damn thing. Then she'd let me know she wasn't going to make it back tonight with more than a stupid text. And even if she borrowed Ackerman's phone, she'd fucking call for two minutes to explain. That text isn't even in our language."

His men looked at him. "Uh, language?" Kane asked.

He swore. Turned around and punched the wall. He wanted to shout, but that wouldn't help a damned thing. Wouldn't find Diana and wouldn't end this nightmare.

He spun back to find them still watching, eyes a little wider, sympathy writ large on their faces. He knew they all got it because they'd been in the same position he was in now. Jesus, he'd never anticipated this. Or how much it would fucking *hurt*.

"Yes, our language. You have a language as a couple, right? If Daphne texted and said she was looking forward to a quiet night in because she was tired of talking to people all day, would you believe it or would you think it sounded wrong?"

"It'd be wrong. She likes to talk."

"Exactly. Diana doesn't call her partner by his first name, even if it's shorter to type, and she doesn't say *love you*. We don't—haven't—*fuck*." He drew in a breath, gathered his thoughts. "It's not something we've ever said, and it's not something she would say in a fucking text like that."

"I believe you," Seth replied. "But this is where the car and the phones are. Let me see if I can pull up any surveillance cameras.... Okay, yes, there are two in the parking lot and the motel has CCTV in the halls. I'll get to work on it."

He was about to lose his fucking mind. Every minute felt like a minute wasted when he should be on his way to wherever Diana was. It was entirely possible he was wrong, that she really was in that hotel, sleeping after a long day, and he'd have to shift his beliefs about what he thought was going on between them. Maybe he was the only one who wanted more out of this relationship, and she'd just been doing it to create the illusion they'd needed so they could work together to infiltrate the militia.

Fuck.

Twenty minutes later, Seth spoke. "Got something. Sending it to the overhead." The video from one of the parking lot cameras appeared on the screen. It was a wide-angle view, but good enough to tell what was happening. "That's the government vehicle."

It was a basic white sedan that pulled into the lot and went around the back of the motel where the second camera picked it up.

"That's Ackerman," Ghost said as a man got out of the car. He was on his phone, gesturing as he talked. Diana didn't emerge from the passenger seat. "Can you zoom in?"

"On it."

A few seconds later, Diana came into view. Her head drooped to one side, her hair curtaining her face. She was very clearly asleep, but it didn't seem quite right. She hadn't shifted, and Ackerman hadn't gone around to wake her. He also hadn't walked inside the motel to check in.

A black Tahoe with tinted windows drove up a few moments later and pulled into the spot beside the govvie. It blocked the view of the sedan from the camera, but the sedan was still there when the Tahoe pulled out. Diana was no longer in the govvie, and Ackerman wasn't there either.

"They would have crossed the field of view if they'd gone inside," Ethan said.

"I'm looking for another camera on a nearby business," Seth told them. "But I think we can confidently assume they got into that Tahoe."

"Need that plate number," Ghost growled.

Seth tapped the keys. "There's a fast-food place with a camera, but it's too far to get a good look." He typed some more. "Come on, come on," he muttered.

Ghost was practically holding his breath, his gut churning, fury burning behind his eyelids. He needed to *do* something. Needed to find her and tell her he'd been a fucking dumbass, that she'd done something to him and he needed her in his life however she'd have him.

"Got it. Running the plate. Thank fuck we have this system."

Ghost knew what he meant. The SCIF and the access to government systems they had was due to the mission. If they didn't have it, this entire thing would take a lot longer. Too long. Diana could be dead by the time they figured out where she'd been taken.

Had somebody followed her and Ackerman? Attacked them at the motel? Meth was big business, and some dealers took serious offense at attempts to eradicate their hold on an area.

But his gut told him no, that Ackerman was involved in whatever had gone down. The man had been standing around like he was waiting for someone, talking on his phone and gesturing. Then the Tahoe drove up and he was no longer there. Neither was Diana. Had she gotten into that vehicle willingly, or was she drugged and they'd had to put her inside?

"It's a rental," Seth said.

For the first time since this nightmare began, hope started to blossom in his chest. "Please tell me it has GPS."

Seth's grin was shit-eating. "Hell, yeah, it sure does. Gonna call up a satellite and find out where that bitch went."

If Washington noticed they were using NRO* assets, he didn't fucking care. All that mattered was finding

---

* National Reconnaissance Office, maintains United States reconnaissance satellites

Diana so he could hold her tightly and tell her everything he felt. Ask her to make a life with him. Because he wasn't ever gonna tire of those clear blue eyes gazing up at him in wonder when he joined his body with hers. It felt like nothing ever had in his life.

It felt *right*. More than that, being with her felt like home. *His* home.

Excruciating minutes passed before Seth had an update. "The Tahoe is sitting on Gunter Mountain at this address."

He called up a Google Earth shot and zoomed down until they had a visual. It was a big house set on a bluff with a view of the Tennessee River and Guntersville Lake.

"Who owns it?"

"Checking now."

"None of this makes sense," Ethan gritted. "I thought Ackerman was a nice guy. Hell, spoke to him at the fall fest last weekend and he was just so friendly. Diana seemed to really like him. Only person who glared daggers at him was Colleen, but that's because he was with Reba."

"Diana does like him," Ghost said, anger churning in his belly that she'd very likely been betrayed by a friend. But why? Fucking why?

"Whoa. That doesn't make any sense at all," Seth muttered, typing.

"What?"

"It's a five-million-dollar estate. Bought with cash

three months ago." He hit enter, looked up. "By Brent Gannon."

"There's no way he has that kind of money," Ghost said, thinking hard. "But he's got his dirty fingers in the middle of this shit. Everywhere we turn, he's there. He paid for it, his name's on the deed. But there's only one person with that kind of money who he'd be involved with."

"Viktor Dashevsky," Ethan breathed.

"Holy fuck," Kane said.

"Damn," Blaze added. The others looked pissed.

But Ghost was happier than he'd been in hours. He had a name, a target, and a mission. And he wasn't waiting a moment longer.

"Suit up, men. We're making a mountain assault."

"Fuck yeah," Blaze said. "Let's go get our friend. Nobody takes one of our own and gets away with it."

"A-fucking-men," Seth growled. "We'll get her back. Swear to God."

They would get her back. The alternative was too bleak to contemplate.

36

Boris was dressed in a black assault suit. He had a gun at his side and a knife in a belt at his waist. He wore jump boots and looked like he was planning to wage an all-out attack on an enemy.

Her, probably.

Diana yelped as he jerked her off the bed. Her broken wrist was agony, sharp and stomach-churning. He unlocked the other cuff keeping her anchored to the bed and then dragged her toward the door. Her ribs ached, hurting when she breathed too deeply. He'd bruised them with punishing blows earlier.

"I can walk on my own," she snapped. "You're going too fast."

"Shut up," Boris growled, dragging her up the same stairs as before, shoving her into the living space. The kitchen was dimly lit, but it didn't interfere with the view beyond the windows like the brighter lights had hours ago. It was still dark, but there was a band of pink on the horizon. Dawn was coming.

Boris shoved her into a chair, and she cried out as her bruised hip hit the side of it.

"Ah, did you sleep well, Diana?"

She jerked her head toward the sound. Viktor stood there with a cup of coffee in his hand, smiling like she was a houseguest rather than a prisoner. He wore dark jeans, a maroon polo, and a gray jacket. He also had a camouflage ball cap on his head. Like he was planning to go hunting or hanging out with a group of good old boys.

"Lovely, thank you. Your hospitality is stellar, as always," she spat.

He laughed. "Such a fiery girl. Perhaps I should have married you. Made you my wife and enjoyed your body every night. It was quite fun, what we had. Don't you think?"

She seethed. Just seethed. "Oh, certainly. Best rape ever. Also my only one, so it's possible someone else could have done a better job."

It made her sick to say the words, but even if he pretended what had happened between them was something different, she wasn't going to play along.

"You are wasted in the FBI. You could have joined my group, could have commanded battalions. But no, you would rather waste your time chasing criminals. Such small thoughts, Diana. You never could see the bigger picture."

She heard voices. Two men emerged from the darkened hallway. Ackerman and Brent Gannon strode into the room.

"I should have known," she said as Ackerman met her gaze. "You and this douche. All that hanging out in clubs, serial dating women. You and Gannon. Peas in a pod. The whole time, you were buying into his bullshit. Neither one of you is worth the air you breathe, you know that?"

Ackerman's expression hardened. "You don't understand anything. And why would you? Your family's in the middle of everything that's wrong with Washington. And yeah, I knew who you were all along. Joel didn't say anything to me. He's too much of a pussy to do anything but threaten you so you'd take him back. Guess he didn't reckon with Bishop having a bigger dick though."

Sadness pierced her anger. "I really thought you were different, Ackerman. I thought you were one of the good ones. All that talk about not being a creep, the way you never made me feel less of an agent for being a woman. You always treated me like your equal. Was it all an act?"

His face reddened. "I liked you, kiddo. I did. But this is bigger than you. Bigger than me."

Gannon looked smug as he eyed her. "You really thought I was a stupid fuck who had no idea what you wanted from me, didn't you? All that flirting, promising, and then you roofied me so you and your boyfriend could search my apartment. Didn't do any good though, did it? All you ever hear on that bug you dropped is a bunch of porn and people getting off."

Her stomach clenched. All this time, she'd thought she

and Alex had a chance, but these people had been one step ahead of them the whole way.

"As lovely a reunion as this is," Viktor interjected, "we have things to accomplish. Is Bishop still expected at the gathering in a couple of hours?"

Gannon nodded. "Yes, sir. I texted him. Told him to come alone. That this is a test, and she'll be fine if he does as we say."

"And how do we know he cares enough about her to do it?" Viktor said.

"We don't. But he'll show. Either he cares and wants her back, or he really wants into the movement."

"Hmm." Viktor sipped his coffee. "Yes, well, I want him and his men. Boris? Are you prepared to sweep up his team?"

"My men are waiting. We'll take them all before the day is through."

"Excellent." Viktor set the cup down. "I do love when a plan comes together. Now—"

The lights went out and silence descended. But only for a moment.

"Where is that fucking generator?" Boris grated. "This should not—"

"Hands up, asshole, or I'll blow your brains all over these beautiful countertops."

37

iktor Dashevsky's mountain house was ridiculously easy to infiltrate. Probably because he didn't expect to spend much time there and hadn't upgraded the security yet. There was security, but nothing that would keep out a determined black ops team. There was an iron gate meant to keep out unwanted visitors, and a camera on the gate to record those who drove up to it as well as perimeter alarms.

But Ghost and his team didn't turn into the driveway. They left the big Suburban they'd brought on a side road nearby and went through the woods, disabling any cameras they encountered, until they emerged near the house. There was an alarm system on the house, but also easy to disarm. Seth hacked in and silenced it, then unlocked the doors with a keystroke.

On the way over, the team had studied the architectural drawings. They intended to search the lower floors before heading up, but the sound of voices coming from the kitchen area changed the plan.

The big dude in the assault gear put his hands in the air as Blaze jammed the barrel of a rifle in his back. Ackerman, Gannon, and Dashevsky stood in shocked silence, hands in the air. The team relieved all of them of their weapons and zip-tied their hands together behind their backs.

Ghost relieved the commando of his—there were a few—and wrenched his hands behind him to zip-tie him before Blaze dropped the barrel of his rifle.

Everything had happened fast, but finally he was free to go to Diana. She huddled in a chair, her eyes big as she watched them. They'd grease-painted their faces and geared up like they were about to face Dashevsky's entire army, so maybe she didn't know who'd come to her rescue. It was entirely possible she hadn't recognized Blaze's voice when he'd threatened to blow the big dude's brains onto the granite countertops.

"Diana," he said softly, going to her and dropping to one knee at her side. He cupped her cheek, fury blazing hot at the swelling and blood on her beautiful face.

"Alex, oh my God," she cried, throwing herself at him. He caught her and she yelped.

"Baby, where are you hurt?" he whispered.

"Everywhere. My wrist is broken. My ribs might be cracked. Oh God, it all hurts—but you came. You're here."

"I'm here." He held her to him, not too tightly, and thanked God she was alive as she dropped her face into his shoulder and pulled in deep breaths. Like she was trying not to cry.

He wanted to sweep her up in his arms and get her out of here, but he had things to take care of first.

"Colonel Bishop," Dashevsky said. "We can make a deal. Don't be a fool, man. You can lead a revolution, be richer than you ever dreamed."

"Surest way to make me shoot you here and now is to keep talking," Ghost said. "I'm not interested, Dashevsky. In anything you have to say."

"I know who you are. Who all of you are. You will never know a moment's peace if you don't make this deal. You think I can be contained by your government? You may walk out of here today, but I will find you. They will not keep me, and I will be free. That's when I will come for you."

"What makes you think you're walking out of here alive?" Ghost asked. "Any of you except her? You think I'm gonna let what you've done to her stand? That you will *ever* threaten the people I care about again? Not happening, motherfucker. Excuse me, honey," he said softly to Diana. "I need to deal with this."

He disentangled himself from her arms, leaving Seth to watch over her, and stalked to Viktor, putting his barrel against the man's temple. "The plan, douchebag. All of it. What you intend to do with your army, what precisely you're after at the Arsenal, and what you think you're gonna do when you get it. Tell me how the plan works, who's involved, and I'll consider not putting a hole in your head."

"You're making a mistake," Dashevsky said.

"No, but you're about to if you don't talk."

———

Sirens screamed up the side of the mountain by the time Ghost took his pistol from Dashevsky's skull. The man's eyes flashed as those sirens wailed into the courtyard.

"I will not forget this," he spat, his accent thicker and coarser than when Ghost and his men had arrived.

"Neither will I." He leaned in closer, until Viktor's eyes grew very wide. "Do you know why they call me Ghost?"

"I don't care."

"You should. I can walk through walls, Viktor. Through iron bars. I can find you before you even know I'm coming, and I can end you. Today, I found you. Be thankful you're still alive. You won't get another chance."

Police in full tactical gear boiled into the house a moment later, taking custody of the men who were restrained. Ghost stood beside Diana's chair, his hand on her shoulder. The team fanned out behind them. Diana climbed to her feet when Viktor was hustled out, her face lined with pain. It killed him to see her like that, but he had to let her have this moment.

"You know what, Viktor?" she asked as the man holding him stopped so she could have her say.

"You are still nothing to me, Diana," Viktor said, sneering at her. "Less than nothing. You are not important."

"Not what I asked, but okay." She leaned toward him, her beautiful face bruised and swollen. "You shouldn't try to be an evil mastermind when you don't quite have the brains to pull it off. And you definitely shouldn't kidnap and torture an FBI agent if you don't want to spend some time in the prison system."

"I will not spend any time there," he snarled. "And I will come for you. All of you."

"Oh my." She laughed, a tinkling sound filled with happiness. "Threatening a federal agent and a special military team with law enforcement as witnesses. I'm not sure it will go quite how you expect, but maybe you're right. Maybe you'll be released back into Putin's loving arms. He isn't going to like it when he understands how you planned to make yourself king of the world, is he?"

For the first time since Ghost and his team had captured these men, he saw real fear on Dashevsky's face. The law enforcement officer holding him hustled him away, and Ghost put an arm around Diana. She sagged into him, trembling, and his eyes stung with emotion.

Fucking hell.

"Proud of you, Princess. That was fucking amazing."

"Think I'm going to pass out now," she said. He guided her into the chair and Kane appeared with a medical kit. Ghost held her good hand while Kane examined her wrist, checked her eyes for concussion, and administered a pain killer.

"Sorry," she said. "Sorry."

"What are you apologizing for?" Kane responded. "This is what we do for our fellow soldiers. You fought the good fight, and now you let us take care of you."

The team gathered around. Diana closed her eyes and gritted her teeth. As the sun came up over the mountain, the bruises and blood on her face were more apparent. There was a knot above one eye. Ghost shook with rage. He wanted to storm after those men and do what he'd promised he wouldn't when he'd made the deal with the voice on the other end of the phone.

"I didn't mean to tell them," she whispered. A single tear slid down her cheek. "Dammit, I swore I wouldn't cry."

"Go ahead," Seth said softly. "I damned sure would."

She cracked an eye at him, one corner of her mouth lifting as if she wanted to smile. "Not you," she said. "No way."

"Way. Nobody likes to be in pain, and some shit hurts worse than others."

"It's true," Chance said. "Crying is allowed in black ops. Hell, it's encouraged. Beats spraying gunfire at a wall while screaming like a Viking warrior."

"I dunno," Ethan said. "That option sounds kinda fun."

Diana laughed, and then winced. "God don't make me laugh. Hurts my ribs."

"We need to get you an x-ray," Kane said. "Fortunately, I know a good doctor who is also discreet."

Diana turned to Ghost. "I t-told them who you were, what I knew about you. I'm sorry I wasn't stronger. B-but Boris broke my wrist, and the pain didn't stop, and I'm not you. I couldn't take it."

Ghost dropped to his knees beside her again, lay his palm against her good cheek, caressed her as gently as he could. "You're alive, Diana. That's all I fucking care about. You held out as long as you could, and swear to God I wish you hadn't even tried. I'd rather you were unhurt and that you'd told them every damned thing they wanted to know. Because it doesn't fucking matter. Dashevsky's going down. It's real. You got him, baby, just like you wanted."

Her eyes widened for a second. Then she shook her head. "I didn't get him. You did."

"We helped. Without you, it wouldn't have happened. And I don't mean because he kidnapped you, either. Your investigation, your determination. It's you who started the chain reaction. Kidnapping you was the nail in the coffin, but it would have happened another way if not today."

He wished it had. He'd give anything not to see her in pain. She looked broken, but she wasn't. There was fire in those eyes. Good.

"Maybe you're right," she said, sounding weary. "Can we go home now? I'm hungry, tired, my body hurts, and I need a bath."

Ghost lifted her in his arms, careful not to jostle her.

She was precious to him, and he wasn't letting her go until he had to. "Yeah, we can go home."

She lay her head against his shoulder and closed her eyes. He strode out of that house filled with anger, but also with happiness. Diana was alive, she was in his arms, and the future was ahead of them.

"Still don't like you," he murmured in her ear. "But you're growing on me."

She tipped her head back to look up at him. "Same, Magic Man. Same."

38

The sun was over the horizon as Alex carried her outside into the cool morning air. Her jacket had disappeared somewhere between yesterday and now, but Alex was warm. Still, she wanted to stand on her own two feet and walk out of this awful place herself. Even if it hurt.

"Put me down," she said. "Please."

"Diana, I can carry you—"

"No, I want to—I *need* to walk out of here on my own. I don't want them to see me and think they broke me. I want Viktor's last memory of this moment to be me standing free while he's in cuffs."

The police were still outside in the courtyard, talking on radios. Viktor and Boris were in one car. Ackerman was in another, his head bowed. Gannon was in a third car, staring straight ahead.

"Okay," Alex said, kissing her temple. He set her on

her feet. It hurt like hell, but she straightened her spine and stood staring at those cars, at the men in them, and felt nothing but rage. Viktor turned his head to look at her, glaring, but she only lifted her chin higher.

"You have not won," she murmured.

Alex gave her hand a light squeeze.

One of the cops walked over to Alex and shook his hand. It wasn't until she started to pay attention to the people milling in the courtyard, really pay attention, that she realized what she had not before.

These men and women—because there were a couple women in camo like the rest—weren't what she'd thought. Their patches identified them as the Air Force Office of Special Investigations. She'd worked with OSI before. And maybe she shouldn't be surprised to see them because Athena came under the purview of the Air Force and the newer Space Force. It was natural they'd be involved in an operation to protect the project.

"Thank you, sir," the man said. "Appreciate your help on this one. If you could, uh, wait a few moments? The major would like to speak with you."

"I have a couple of minutes, but not more. I need to get Agent Corbin home."

"Yes, sir. Understood, sir."

The airmen started to get into cars and SUVs. One by one, the cars carrying her attackers moved down the drive toward the road. One did not move, however. When the other vehicles were gone, the men sitting in the front seat of the remaining car got out. One opened the back door.

Brent Gannon climbed out and another man unlocked his cuffs.

Diana blinked. Alex didn't seem surprised, nor did his team, as Gannon walked toward them, rubbing his wrists.

"Agent Corbin, I apologize for what happened to you, but I'm damn glad you're alive."

"I..." She turned her head. "What is going on? Did you know about this?"

Alex met her gaze. His was troubled. "Not until he called me when we were on the way here. Still not happy you let this happen, Major Sharpe."

Sharpe?

"I'm sorry, sir. Viktor Dashevsky didn't inform me of everything, as I told you when we spoke last night. I only learned he'd arranged with Agent Ackerman to abduct his partner after it was done."

"But you wouldn't have stopped it even if you had."

Gannon—Sharpe's—eyes sparked. "This was an active investigation, sir. I've been embedded for months now. We were close to getting what we needed. And now we have, thanks to all of you."

"At what cost?" Alex growled.

Diana put her good hand on his arm. The other throbbed, but the painkillers Kane had injected her with were helping. "This is the job," she said, looking at Sharpe. "We're investigators. We do what needs done. I assume you're wearing a wire?"

Sharpe inclined his head in answer. "Thank you for understanding, ma'am."

He grinned at her. He was strangely a lot more hand-some than he'd been as Gannon. Younger, too. Not by much, but enough. As if peeling off that role had returned him to his natural state. Whatever that was.

"I'm impressed you roofied me, make no mistake. I didn't see that one coming."

"You were a bit of a pig as Gannon. I thought you probably deserved it."

He looked a little ashamed. "Not a nice man, that Colonel Gannon. Quite a pervert, actually. Sorry for the porn and the noises you had to listen to, by the way. But Gannon's finished for now. Hope I don't have to resurrect him, but you never know. In the meantime, the militia leaders are rounded up, Dashevsky is in custody, and we're on the way to exposing his organization for what it really is. In part thanks to your groundwork, Agent Corbin."

"Sir," one of the airmen called. "We need to be on the road. The transport is arriving in an hour."

"Be there in a moment." He turned back to Diana, Alex, and the team. "We're taking Dashevsky and his men to Guantanamo. They'll be held there to prevent, uh, interference from certain quarters. You don't have to worry about him getting out or coming after you. It won't happen. His reputation will be destroyed when the truth is known. Nobody will demand his release."

Diana felt the shock to her bones. It wasn't what she'd anticipated, wasn't how she'd wanted it to go down—because she'd wanted to be the one who faced him across a table and levied charges—but it was damned good. Probably even better than she'd hoped for.

Viktor Dashevsky would no longer traffic in humans. He would no longer foment war and sell illegal weapons. Others would rise to take his place, because that's how humanity worked, but she'd go after them, too.

Because that's how she worked.

"Thank you, Major."

He held out his hand. She put hers in it and they shook. He was careful of her, because of her injuries, but there was respect in his eyes.

When he turned and went back to the car, he got in the front seat and one of his men got in the back. Then they headed down the drive.

"Never had a clue," Seth said. "He's good. Sure explains why we never found anything we could really use, though."

Alex humphed. "That's a man who disappears into a role, for good or bad. Right down to that ridiculous notebook entry about Greek mythology. He was prepared for anything. Not a fan but have to admit we need people like him. Reminds me of Ian Black," he muttered. "Really wish I could make him pay for all that porn and squealing. Bastard played recordings, varied enough that it sounded real. So he says anyway."

"Maybe some of them were real," Diana said.

Alex shuddered. "God, I hope not. Nobody should sound like that."

A big, black Suburban ambled up the drive with

Chance behind the wheel. The doors opened, the guys peeled off weapons and stowed them in the very back. Three of the guys climbed into the back row. Alex helped her into the middle row, then got in beside her. She was weary and in pain, but she was strangely happy too.

He threaded his fingers in hers. She leaned her head against his shoulder and closed her eyes.

The doors shut, the engine revved, and they were moving. Going to Sutton's Creek.

Going home.

39

After Emma Sutton examined her, took x-rays, set her wrist, and gave her horse pills to knock out the pain, Diana begged Alex to take her to the farm instead of her apartment.

"You'll be closer to the doctor here," he protested.

"I want to be alone. With you. I want to sit on that pretty screened in patio with my coffee and listen to the birds sing. I want to go for walks in the field and woods, without having to talk to anyone except you. I don't want to run into Colleen or Reba, or anyone else, and make polite talk about things that don't matter. I'm tired, Alex. Heartbroken over Ackerman, if I'm honest. I just want to be by myself for a while."

"Okay, honey. Whatever you want."

He took her back to the farm, drew a bath for her, and then dried her carefully and put her to bed with a tray that had scrambled eggs and toast. She fell on the food because she hadn't eaten since lunch the previous day. When she was done, he took the tray and put it in the kitchen before returning with a big cup that had a lid and a straw.

"Water," he said, setting it on the bedside table.

"Will you hold me? Please?"

He looked troubled, and her heart thumped. Were they through? The militia was no longer a reason to stay together, Viktor was in custody, and the only thing that remained was shepherding Athena to the launch date. They didn't have to be together for that. It was possible he was just being nice in letting her stay until she'd recovered.

"I want to," he rasped. "But I don't want to hurt you. If I jostle you at all…"

Relief sank into her bones. "You won't. Just hold me for a little while. I'll fall asleep and you can go."

He sighed. Then he started to peel off his clothes. He'd showered in another part of the house while she'd soaked in the tub. The greasepaint was gone, and he wore a navy T-shirt and jeans instead of black assault gear. He shucked it all except for his briefs and climbed in beside her, slipping an arm around her so she was nestled in the crook of his shoulder. She wanted to turn on her side and cuddle him, but her ribs and hip on the right side were too sore. Her left wrist was in a cast, and her cheek was tender where Boris had hit her.

In short, she was a mess.

"Thank you for coming for me," she said as the food

and medicine started to soften her muscles. She hurt, but she would sleep. Thank God.

"Diana," he said, his voice sounding strangled. "I'll always come for you. You're one of us now."

"I like that," she whispered. "How did you find me?"

She felt his lips on her temple. "It's a long story. I'll tell you later. After you sleep."

"Okay."

When she woke again, he was gone. She managed to get out of bed on her own. She shuffled to the bathroom to take care of business. When she got a look at her reflection, she winced. Her eye was black, there was a bump on her cheek, and she looked like hell. She managed to smooth her hair down with Alex's brush, then found her bag and pulled a robe over the T-shirt—his—that she wore. She held her forearm straight up and down as much as possible because Emma had told her to keep it elevated. It looked like she was walking around waving hello to everyone.

If anyone were there, which they were not.

Thankfully. She couldn't handle people right now. Not when her feelings were still so raw.

"Why are you out of bed?" Alex demanded. He halted abruptly in the door to the bedroom, a tray with a bowl and crackers in his hands.

"Emma didn't say I had to stay in bed. She said to rest and keep my wrist elevated."

He frowned. "Diana. You've been hurt."

"Yes, I'm aware. Answer me truthfully. If you were in

the shape I'm in, would you stay in bed all day or would you want out of it?"

His frown grew stronger. She could see the moment he caved, though.

"Okay, fine. But if you start to feel tired, you're getting back in bed."

"Yes, sir."

He arched an eyebrow. "That easy?"

She shrugged. "Maybe it is."

They went to the small breakfast nook that looked out on the backyard, and he put the bowl of soup down, got her a ginger ale, and took a seat with her. She ate as much as she could, then pushed the bowl away.

"Now will you tell me how you found me?"

He reached for her hand, tangled fingers with hers. Warmth blossomed in her soul.

"When you didn't call or text, I finally texted you. The response came later, from a burner." He took his phone out and showed her. "I knew it wasn't you. Tracked the govvie you and Ackerman took to the motel in Scottsboro, then tracked the Tahoe that picked you both up. Seth found the location and discovered the house was in Gannon's name. Seemed a no brainer. We were on the way when Gannon called and revealed he was undercover OSI. He didn't try to stop us because he knew he couldn't, but we agreed to work together."

She looked at the message, at the flippant way someone had typed *love you*. Was it Ackerman? Maybe. She would never know. She lifted her gaze to his, surprised when it was blurry. She swiped the tears away as he squeezed her hand.

"Baby. Don't cry. Unless you really want to."

She tried not to laugh. It hurt to laugh. "Maybe I do. I still can't believe Ackerman did it. That he willingly delivered me into Viktor's hands."

"Did he know about your family member?"

His gaze was sympathetic. She dragged in a breath. Then another. "Oh, Alex. I have so much I need to tell you. Ackerman didn't know. And it wasn't a family member Viktor hurt."

Be brave.

She squeezed his hand. "It was me. Viktor Dashevsky raped me seven years ago when I was still a graduate student."

"Diana." He moved his chair beside hers, wrapped an arm around her. "Fucking hell, I'm so sorry."

She could feel him trembling with suppressed anger. For her.

"I never told anyone. Until now. Well, I might have said the words to Viktor when Boris was listening, but that doesn't count."

"Baby."

"I couldn't tell anyone when it happened. Nobody would have believed it." She told him the story while he listened, his teeth grinding from time to time. She knew what it took for a man like him to hear that someone had hurt a person he cared for—because she truly believed he did care for her now—and know he couldn't fix it. That he couldn't make it go away or make the person responsible pay. But Viktor was going to pay, and that was something she would hold onto for the rest of her life.

He'd hurt people, but karma had come calling. Maybe not soon enough, but it was there all the same.

"Diana. I'd fucking kill that prick if I could rewind the clock a few hours."

She disentangled her hand from his and put it against his cheek. "I know. But what's happening is even better. Guantanamo. He won't leave there alive. Even if he did, he'd disappear once Putin got his hands on him. Viktor's days of harming people are over."

He turned his cheek and kissed her hand, then bent to kiss her mouth. Gently, though she wanted more. Her body responded to him even if she was incapable of following through at the moment. He made her nipples tingle, her pussy ache. Her heart pound. She craved him.

Loved him. So much.

"I still don't like you," she whispered when the kiss was over. Her heart hammered, but she told herself she had nothing to lose. Nothing at all. She would tell him, and whatever happened would happen.

He put his fingers to her mouth, stopping her from saying the words she wanted to say.

"I don't like you either," he said, his gaze holding hers. "I fucking love you."

She smiled as joy flooded her heart. "That's what I was going to say."

He grinned. "I know. But I thought it was my turn to

say something important. I love you, Diana Corbin. Adler. Don't much care what you call yourself, but I hope you'll call yourself mine. My wife when you're ready. My partner. My lover. My soul. You're already those things to me whether you marry me or not."

She covered his mouth, stopped him from speaking. "I love you, Alex Bishop. Magic Man. And I'm definitely going to marry you. Eventually. Can we live here? Or, if we can't because the government wants to sell this property to developers or something, then can we buy a place nearby and stay right here?"

"Yeah, I guess we have to stay, don't we? Our family is here."

"They sure are. You, the guys, the ladies and kids—I feel like this is where I belong. We'll have to visit my family sometimes, put up with their stodginess, but they won't object to you because you're a military hero. Even if they do, I don't care. Not changing my choice."

"Not changing mine either."

"I wish I didn't feel like utter shit," she sighed. "Because I would so jump you right now."

"Not if I jumped you first."

She slapped a hand over her mouth so she didn't laugh. When she finally felt like she'd smothered it, she dropped her hand. "Dammit, I don't want to laugh. I do but I don't. I can just see the future though. We're going to try to outdo each other forever, aren't we?"

"Competitive high achievers like us?" His eyes sparkled. "Nah, never happen."

They smiled at each other like idiots for a while. Then she sighed and rubbed her thumb over his lips. So many things she wanted to do to him right now. And couldn't.

"Take me outside on the porch and sit on the loveseat with me so I can snuggle up to you?"

He tucked a lock of hair behind her ear, caressed her cheek. "Yeah, I can do that."

40

The summons to Washington came two weeks later. Diana's wrist would still be in a cast for another month at least, but her ribs had only been bruised and her black eye was now an alarming shade of green. In other words, she was doing better.

So much so that she insisted on going to Washington with him. He dreaded the flight, waiting in the airport, standing in security lines, and all the other mess that went along with travel. He dreaded it even worse with Diana not being completely healed yet.

But he needn't have worried. A government jet picked them up at Huntsville and delivered them to Reagan National a couple of hours later.

A car waited for them. Ghost wasn't sure where they were going—the Pentagon, HOT HQ, the FBI, the White House—but instead the car took them north and west, to

Langley. Diana's expression was carefully controlled, the cool mask once more in place. The only heat came from her hand on his. They said little because they weren't alone.

They'd spent the past two weeks together, quietly going about their lives. Diana hadn't wanted to go out in public, so they hadn't. He cooked or ordered in, and they watched television or talked. He went to the range during the day, but he returned to the farmhouse often to check on her.

They slept in his bed, tangled in each other, and they'd even managed a little bit of gentle lovemaking as her injuries healed. She wanted more, but he was the one who'd been refusing to take it up a level. For now.

The women had waited precisely three days before they started asking to see her. She'd seemed surprised, but she'd agreed with a quiet eagerness that made his heart glad. Seeing her surrounded by those five ladies, fussing over her, talking about books and the gossip from Sutton's Creek, had soothed a worry he hadn't realized he'd been holding onto.

Because she had friends who cared about her. It wasn't just him who saw beneath the reserve and the caution to the woman beneath. Diana was herself with them. Maybe not as much herself as she was with *him*, but she was getting there. Emma, Rory, Callie, Daphne, and Paisley would never desert her. She would realize it for herself as time went by.

"I guess we're seeing Uncle Stephen," she said when the car approached a gate leading to the Central Intelligence Agency Headquarters.

They were taken through several layers of security and then shown into a small conference room with a large screen at one end. A few moments later the door opened, and the Deputy Director walked in. He was accompanied by the FBI Director, the Secretary of the Air Force, Major Sharpe, and General John "Viper" Mendez.

Stephen Adler took one look at his niece and shot Ghost a look that would have flayed him alive if it were a weapon. Diana wound her fingers with his and stepped closer. Adler noted their body language and sighed.

"I'm happy you're well, Diana."

"Getting there," she said. "Thank you."

"Have you seen your parents yet?"

"I thought it best if they didn't see me like this."

He nodded. "Probably right. Perhaps some heavy makeup at Thanksgiving or your mother will have a heart attack."

"Not coming but thank you."

The CIA Director entered the room then, accompanied by the Vice President. "Everyone's here. Excellent."

Introductions were made all around and then they were asked to sit. Ghost pulled out the chair for Diana before sitting beside her. She reached for his hand under the table, and they locked fingers.

The briefing that took place then was something Ghost would never forget as long as he lived. Judging by

Mendez's granite expression, he wasn't pleased with what he was hearing, either.

"So let me get this straight," Ghost said when the Director finally stopped speaking. "Athena is a boondoggle at best and an outright fabrication at worst. For the purpose of finding traitors in our own government and bringing them to justice. My team and I volunteered to give up our careers in the Army and move to Alabama to protect the project. But it was never real. There is no shield that will protect this country from nuclear or EMP attacks. We just pretended there was so the cockroaches would come out of the woodwork."

"At this time, there is no viable shield," Vice President McEwen confirmed, much too cheerfully for Ghost's liking. "But Athena *is* real. It's something that's been under development for years, yet it's never left the development phase. We're decades away from such a thing. The best we have is GMD, and that's imperfect, but we won't stop trying. Your country thanks you for all you've done to find and stop the threat to our security. You also have the president's personal gratitude. And you, Major Sharpe."

Ghost was unable to speak he was so pissed. Months spent protecting a project that wasn't ever going to fall into enemy hands and be a potential world ender. Months being told he was on the most important mission of his life, trying to protect this nation and worrying about his friends. And the families they'd been forming against orders.

Orders that should have never been given in the first

place. What did it matter if Blaze or Chance married the women carrying their children? If any of them married the women they loved? It should have never mattered, and yet these people had thought it acceptable to toy with all their lives.

He gritted his teeth, his jaw aching with the pressure of not saying what he really wanted to say to these men. These puppet masters.

Taking orders was part of being a soldier. And yet this entire mission was an outrageous presumption on their part. He could see from the looks on Mendez and Sharpe's faces that they were as shocked as he was. As angry.

Diana must have sensed his mood because she squeezed his hand beneath the table. "I assume Viktor Dashevsky will remain in custody?" she asked, chin notched high, voice set to cool command. A freaking princess in a roomful of peasants. God, he loved her.

"He will," Don Lewis said. "And those who were protecting him, feeding him information, are being dealt with. You will see some resignations from Congress in the next few weeks. Some CEOs from defense companies will no doubt be replaced as well. Make of it what you will, but that's all I'm authorized to say."

"Why did you move the investigation to Washington?"

Lewis exchanged a look with her uncle. It was Adler who spoke. "I asked him to. We were hearing alarming things about Dashevsky's activities in Alabama through Sharpe. He had his eye on you, Diana. After the botched Stinger acquisition this summer, he turned his attention to finding information about who had interfered. It naturally led him to you, and Colonel Bishop and his team."

Her nostrils flared but that was the only sign of irritation. "Thank you for telling me. Though it would have been nice if you'd told me then. I'm not a child, and my job isn't a hobby. The same as yours isn't."

He inclined his head. "You're correct. I apologize."

"Was Joel Newman your idea as well?"

Adler's mouth flattened. Lewis cleared his throat. "I needed to know you were safe. I assigned Joel to get close to you."

"Well," Diana said, sounding queenly, "I suppose I shouldn't be surprised."

"He's been reassigned. The threat to your identity isn't something you need worry about."

"I'm not worried. I'm an Adler and I don't much care who knows it anymore. It doesn't define me. Only I do that."

Ghost leaned toward her because he didn't give a good goddamn what these men thought. "I love you," he whispered.

She turned her smile on him. "I love you, too."

"My men's military records," Mendez said. "How did that breach happen?"

The CIA Director looked pained. "An insider in the Pentagon who supplied information to Trey McCann. That person is being prosecuted for the dissemination of classified information."

"It should never have happened," Mendez growled.

"Agreed," the Director said. "We're working to make sure this kind of thing doesn't happen again."

"Your records will be restored," McEwen added. "We can't acknowledge this mission, of course, but you'll all be given promotions on paper and paid your full retirement accordingly. Anyone who wants to return to active duty—including you, Colonel Bishop—will be welcomed back and given new assignments."

Ghost didn't even have to think about it. "Thank you, sir, but I'm going to enjoy my retirement. Believe my men feel the same, but I'll inform them of your offer."

Mendez nodded, and Ghost knew his friend understood. What had been intended before was no longer what Ghost wanted. The offer to return wasn't going to restore what he'd given up—and he just didn't want it anymore. He wanted Sutton's Creek, Diana, his friends, and the life they'd built there.

The meeting ended shortly thereafter. The VP left accompanied by Sharpe and the Secretary of the Air Force. Don Lewis had his own car waiting. He chatted briefly with Diana, alone, and then she talked to her uncle before she returned to Ghost's side. They joined Mendez in his staff car and were ferried into Washington, to a swank restaurant in Georgetown where Kat Mendez waited for them. She kissed her husband and then flung her arms around Ghost, telling him how happy she was to see him after so many months.

"You're looking gorgeous as usual," he told her.

She arched her eyebrows. "You mean I don't look like

the harried mother of an elementary school child? Bless you."

Ghost introduced Diana, and Kat immediately hugged her. "Oh my, you are even more lovely than he led us to believe. It's so nice to finally meet you."

"Thank you. It's nice to meet you as well. I know that Alex thinks of you both as dear friends."

He did, but he hadn't quite said those words. Diana was being Diana. Polished, smooth, and intuitive. She dazzled him every day with how well she knew him, and how deeply in love with her he kept falling.

The evening was far better than the day had been. They had dinner, drinks, and talked for hours. Elena Mendez was staying with a friend for the evening, so her parents did not have to race home. At the end of the night, they parted ways reluctantly, with many hugs and promises to get together again before too much time passed.

"We will come to Alabama soon," Kat said. "Isn't that right, Johnny?"

"We will. I want to meet Colleen and hear about the aliens and how to communicate with them through the Piggly Wiggly produce aisle."

Ghost snorted. "You'll hear about a lot more than that, believe me. But that's one of the crazier things for sure."

Mendez put his hand out. Ghost took it. "Proud of you, Alex. Wasn't easy what you did and wasn't right what they did to you and the boys. If I'd known..." He shook his head. "Well, that's politics for you. Always about the expediency of the moment and never about the people it might hurt."

They shook firmly. Ghost had a lump in his throat. "I'm not sorry," he said, wrapping an arm around Diana. "Without this assignment, I wouldn't be standing here with the woman I love or thinking about the future we're going to build together."

Kat put her arms around Mendez's waist, and he dropped an arm over her shoulders. "Love is always worth the risk," he said. "Without that, we've got nothing but an empty home and duties that pile up. Make no mistake though, we're replaceable. The job continues whether we do or not. That's why family is number one."

"Amen," Kat said.

Mendez and Kat got into the car that was always waiting for him, and Ghost and Diana took a taxi to the Marriott. The next day, they were up early and boarding the jet for home when Ghost had a revelation.

"Shit! I didn't ask about the farm. I was too pissed to think straight. I don't know if I'm going home to tell everyone we've gotta start over again."

Diana wrapped her arm in his as they settled side by side in the plush leather club seats. "It's taken care of."

He turned to her, studied her sparkling blue eyes. "What do you mean it's taken care of?"

"When I talked to my uncle, I told him that he'd better use all his influence to make sure you and the guys could buy the farm and keep One Shot Tactical going. He promised he would."

"You believe him?"

"I do. He feels guilty about managing me, for one thing. But more than that, he's an Adler. If he gives his word, he'll keep it. The Adler name is something he takes seriously. He'll make it happen."

"You're amazing."

She smiled. "So are you."

"What did you talk to Lewis about?"

"Work. I'll be returning when I'm healed. With a promotion, though an appropriate one for my position. Not a family-influenced one."

"Are you worried people will say it was anyway?"

She shrugged. "A little, but like I said, I define me. I won't deny my connections, but I'll make sure people understand I'm competent at what I do. I won't take any bullshit from anyone."

He lifted their joined hands and kissed her knuckles. "That's my girl."

Her gaze dropped. "Ackerman's awaiting trial." Her voice was almost whisper soft. "I won't have to testify. He's confessed to everything and made a plea deal for a shorter sentence. He'll be out in ten years."

"Are you okay with that?"

"Surprisingly, yes. I hurt for the friend I thought I knew. But the man who stood by while Boris beat me? He can spend the next ten years rotting in a federal pen and worrying how to repel advances from big men named Bubba. He's damned lucky he didn't get sent to Guantanamo with Viktor, but I guess he had information somebody could use."

"With you on that one. He's lucky I didn't kill him. I wanted to."

"I know. I'm glad you didn't, though. Revenge is easy. Letting justice take its course? A lot harder sometimes. I know I won't forget what he did, but then again neither will he. He ruined his life, and for what? The idea that our president was a weak-willed woman? Presidents change. The next one could be everything he's hoped for. Not that he'll ever get to vote again."

He frowned. He heard the pain in her voice, and he knew she would grapple with the betrayal for years to come. "I never told you about my dream."

She turned her head, studying him. "You did not."

He sighed and leaned back against the seat. "When I was fifteen, I couldn't take it anymore. My mom had been gone for over a year, and my dad was getting worse. Paranoid, delusional. He would wake me in the middle of the night, throw me outside with nothing but my coat and boots, tell me to survive. Somehow, I did. It wasn't winter yet, though it was always fucking cold. But I knew, as soon as the ice settled in, I wouldn't be able to make it if he threw me out. He wouldn't listen to reason, and I'd freeze to death under the guise of making me tough. I knew if I didn't get away while the snow was still minimal, I'd never do it. Because I'd started dreaming about escaping, making plans. One night, when he was drunk, I finally did it. Took the supplies I'd been hiding and left."

"Oh, Alex." She gripped his arm.

"I know, baby. But I'm here. I survived. It took three days. There were wolves, they got my scent, started following me. I saw them lurking in the forest, and I was scared, but I kept going. At night, I climbed high up a tree to evade them and any bears that prowled. I made it, and they didn't attack me—but I dream they did. I dream about the big alpha wolf. He was white, and he was the one I saw the most. I dream he's on me, his jaws around my throat. One rip, and I'm done."

"Oh, honey. I'm sorry. But I'm so glad it didn't happen that way. I'd be lost without you."

He caught the tear that slid down her cheek. "Don't cry, Diana. I'm okay. I just have that dream when I'm stressed and I feel like shit's closing in. I've felt that way with this mission, and that's when it returned. Wanted you to know. It might come back, it might not. But you might also have your own dreams of danger closing in. If you do, you can tell me about them. They won't get better if you keep it inside, and they may not anyway. But having someone at your side makes all the difference for getting you through the darkness when it comes."

"I will tell you if it starts," she said. "I love you, Alex. Everything that happened these past few months led me to you. I can't complain about that."

He kissed her cheek. "We're a team."

"We're a team. I will always be at your side, ready to take on the world for you."

"I know you will. I think you know there's nothing I

wouldn't do for you, no one I wouldn't fight to protect you."

"Yes."

"Still don't like you," he teased.

"I don't like you either."

"I love you," they said in unison.

41

"Diana!" Miss Mary's smile was big when the bell over the door announced Diana's arrival. "I've got that casserole you ordered in the back. Luther," she called, "get Diana's cheesy potato casserole. She's here to pick it up."

"Thank you, Miss Mary. Looks like you're pretty busy today."

"Shoo-wee, child, yes. It's always like this right before Thanksgiving. We cook a lot of food, sell a lot of casseroles." She mopped her face with a bandana she kept tucked into where her apron tied at her waist. "This may be the year I decide to retire."

Diana grinned. "I've heard that you say that every year, and then every year you keep on going."

Miss Mary laughed. "Well, I probably do. Ain't getting any younger. But I like cookin', and folks seem to like eating, so I just keep doing it."

Luther brought out the casserole, and Diana paid for it, chatted a bit more, and then went to the doctor's office to hand it off to Emma Sutton.

"Hey, Diana. Is that Miss Mary's cheesy potatoes?"

"It is indeed."

"Mmm, smells divine. I'll just pop it in the fridge and take it to Mama after work. You didn't have to bring anything, but she appreciates it."

Diana shrugged. "Your mother is so sweet to invite all of us over tomorrow. Therefore, I agree with everyone else that the least we can do is bring some dishes."

"Honestly, I'm glad it's potluck. Mama will do her famous dressing and the mashed potatoes—oh, and the pumpkin pies—but everything else is taken care of, and that's going to make the day so much easier. She'll fuss on her table settings and making sure everything is perfect anyway."

"I'm sure it will be."

Emma studied her. "How are the ribs doing?"

"So much better. Hardly any pain unless I twist a certain way."

"Good. Another week for the cast and we'll see how the wrist is. Did you make an appointment with physical therapy?"

"I did."

"What a good patient you are."

Diana nodded to the other woman's protruding belly. "How are you and Baby feeling?"

"I feel great, honestly. Blaze fusses at me, but I'd go

crazy if all I did was sit around. Honestly, men have weird ideas about us sometimes, you know?"

Diana laughed. "You mean like we're delicate and need looking after?"

"That's it," Emma said with a laugh.

They talked a while longer and then Diana consulted her watch. "I need to run to the library. Paisley called to tell me that Louise Penny mystery I wanted is available."

Emma smirked. "Couldn't say no to Mr. Watson, could you?"

Diana shook her head. "Who can? He's kind of adorable—and pushy too. Plus, he named his book club How I Met Your Murderer. Who can say no to that? But I'm a Bookalicious Bestie first and foremost."

"We've got the best books," Emma said.

"Damn right. I've read *all* the two-dicked blue aliens now. They go fast, and they're such fun."

And Alex approved of how absolutely horny they made her, which was a plus. Though he had yet to really let go with her. Still too worried about her injuries. It'd been almost a month now, so he was going to have to get over that *real* soon.

"I know. Who would have ever thought those would be the feel-good happy books I'd want to read when the world was too much to deal with?"

They looked at each other. Both of them said, "Nikki," at the same time. Then they laughed.

"Poor Callie. I don't think she's stopped blushing yet." Emma made a shooing motion with her hand. "Okay, you, get to the library or I'll make you talk to me until my next patient arrives."

They shared a quick hug and then Diana was on the way to the library. She waved at Miriam McClinton as she passed the baby store, Little Blooms. She'd already bought presents for Emma and Rory's babies, and she'd probably buy a few more soon. Judy Simpson was locking up at the Sutton's Creek Bee.

"Hi, Ms. Simpson."

"Oh, Diana! How's our resident Fibbie? Solve any crimes? Did you check into that illegal gambling ring I told you about?"

Diana kept her expression as neutral as possible. "I'm good, thank you. I did ask Mr. Warren about the gambling, but he assured me they were playing Left Right Center with dollar bills. Then he showed me the dice, and I have to say I don't really think there's anything illegal going on there."

Judy's face twisted. "Well, then. Sneaky of him. But don't you worry, I'll get to the bottom of it."

Diana waved and kept walking. When she reached the library, Colleen Wright was coming out the doors, a stack of Danielle Steele novels in her arms.

"Diana! How are you, dear?"

"Wonderful, Mrs. Wright. How about you?"

"Oh, just peachy." She leaned in. "Poor Reba though. She was practically inconsolable when she learned that terrible Mr. Ackerman was arrested. He was the first man to ask her out in quite a while. I'm trying to cheer her up with some books."

"I'm sure she'll be fine with time." Diana hesitated. "Clay was a nice guy who hid who he really was from a lot of people. I'm so sorry he hurt Reba's feelings."

"Thank you for saying that. I tried to warn her. The spirits never liked him. But I couldn't come right out and say it, could I? She would have thought I was interfering."

Diana thought of Colleen sitting behind Ackerman in the wagon, glaring, or joining him and Reba for dinner uninvited. But she didn't point out any of it. "You are very wise."

Colleen patted her arm. "Well, I must be on my way. Happy Thanksgiving to you and that handsome man of yours."

"Thank you! Happy Thanksgiving."

Mr. Watson was the first to greet her when she walked into the library. Today's shirt was butter yellow with long-sleeves. It said *THAT'S A HORRIBLE IDEA....WHAT TIME?*

"No unicorn today?" she asked.

"I have some new ones I'm saving for next week," he told her. "Are you coming to book club next Thursday?"

"I am."

"Excellent. If you care to bring that gorgeous man along with, please do. If nothing else, we can sit him in the corner and gaze upon him."

"I'll keep it in mind."

Diana got her book, talked to Paisley about tomorrow

at the Suttons, and then drove back to the farm. She'd been staying there since Alex and his team found her. She was going to have to let the apartment go, but she'd do it after Christmas. She wanted to be able to stay in town with Alex during the festivities if they wanted. Too much making merry at the parade or a fun night at the Dawg? Go to the apartment.

She also wanted to find another tenant before she gave notice. Alex had told her it was up to her what she wanted to do, but she knew she wanted to live at the farm with him. She had zero doubts that Uncle Stephen would come through on his promise.

Alex walked out on the porch as she parked beneath the tree. She went up the stairs and he greeted her with a kiss and a glass of wine.

"Mmm, delicious," she said taking a sip as they held hands and walked inside. He would have led her to the kitchen, but she tugged him toward the bedroom instead.

"Diana," he said softly as she pulled. But he'd dug in his heels like a stubborn donkey.

And she'd had enough. Just enough. She set the wine on the nearest surface and started pulling off her shirt.

"Babe, what are you doing?"

"I think you know, Magic Man. You've been sweet, you've taken care, and you've made me come. You've come too, but it's all been so sedate. Like two people afraid to tell the other what they want in case it's too shocking or raunchy."

She dropped her shirt on the couch, unhooked her bra

—thank heavens for a front clasp—and dropped that too. His eyes glazed as she hefted her boobs in her hands, tweaking her own nipples while he watched. The front of his jeans started to bulge.

"I need the man who isn't afraid to unleash his passion on me, the man who will lick me into a screaming orgasm and then cram me full of his cock until I can't breathe for want of him. I'm dying here, Alex. I need you to touch me like I'm not going to break."

She unzipped her pants, shoved them down and kicked them off. Then she shed her panties until she stood completely naked. His jaw had dropped open, the pulse in his neck throbbing.

"Diana," he said hoarsely. "I don't want to accidentally hurt you."

She went to him, hooked a hand around his neck, and pulled him down to her. "You idiot. If something hurts, I'm going to tell you. And if it feels fantastic, I'm going to tell you that too. Just stop treating me like I'm made of glass. I'm so happy here with you. I love Sutton's Creek, love that people accept me and know who I am when I see them in town, and I love that we're going to a big family Thanksgiving tomorrow with all the people we care about the most. But right now, I need a really, really good fuck, okay?"

"Christ, Princess. The things you say."

She wasn't sure what he would do, but then he took her mouth like a storm.

Later, when she lay in bed panting, her pussy tingling

from the aftershocks, her body limp and satisfied, she propped herself on an elbow and slid her gaze over his magnificent form. The man was cut. Mouthwatering. Made to stare at. Mr. Watson was right about that, but Diana was the only one who got to see the full package. Lucky her.

"Satisfied?" He quirked a grin.

"Supremely," she said, stretching like a cat. "So, have we solved the dilemma? Will you be giving me the full dick experience from now on, not the limp dick one?"

He snorted. "Limp dick? Never, and you know it."

She kissed his chest. "Well, no, it's never been limp. I was talking more about the rating system."

He threaded his hands in her hair, dragged her down to him, kissed her until she was ready to climb on and ride him again. "I love you, Princess. If the full dick experience is what you want, it's what you get."

"Mmm, I love the full dick experience. And you, who possesses said dick."

He laughed. "Makes me wonder which of us you love more. Me or my dick."

She wrapped her hand around him. "I love you equally."

He rolled her beneath him and slid inside, fully hard and ready. "For answering correctly, you get a prize."

"Oooh, what kind of prize?"

"This kind."

He pulled out, slammed back in, and Diana forgot to breathe. Again.

But it was worth every toe-curling moment.

Ghost sat on the huge wraparound porch at the Suttons' house with his guys while the women were inside helping Mrs. Sutton put away all the dishes that the guys had washed before coming out here.

Doc Sutton and Theo were watching football. Ghost and the team would join them soon, but they'd somehow all gravitated to the porch with their beers.

Ghost had snagged the porch swing and he used one foot to propel himself back and forth rhythmically. He'd told them about Athena when he'd returned from Washington a couple of weeks ago. They'd been predictably angry, but it'd been Chance who'd laughed first and said, "Fuck 'em. And thank God for 'em too. Because I have Rory. Wouldn't have met her if we hadn't moved down here."

The rest of the guys quickly agreed. Ghost was pissed at the manipulation, but he couldn't disagree either. Life in Sutton's Creek was better than anywhere else he could have gone. This was it for him now.

Diana, his team, their ladies and kids, and Sutton's Creek.

"Still can't believe it's ours," Kane said. "They're really calling the property and all the equipment a bonus for services rendered?"

"Yup," Ghost said. He'd gotten word from the president's chief of staff that morning. Apparently, Stephen Adler had come through with even more than Diana had asked for. She'd been ecstatic when he told her.

He'd pulled his guys aside after they'd arrived at the Suttons earlier and told them in one of the fancy parlors Mrs. Sutton had decorated with antiques and oil paintings. They'd reacted the way he had: happy, shocked, hopeful.

The future was theirs now. One Shot Tactical would keep providing training and services—and hell, it was probably gonna grow if Daphne had her way. Which she would because she was good at it and there was no reason not to expand.

"We're free," Blaze said. "We can get married, raise our kids, and make our lives here permanently."

"Fuck yeah," Ethan replied.

"This has been a perfect day," Seth said.

"How so?" Chance asked. "Not disagreeing but want your perspective."

"Not just the range, but this." Seth waved a hand. "Us. We're have the love of amazing women, we love our jobs, ain't nobody gotta bug out in the middle of the night for weeks downrange, and we just had a kick-ass Thanksgiving dinner in a gorgeous house with wonderful people. I couldn't have imagined this would be my life when I sat in that briefing room almost a year ago and agreed to give up everything for an unknown mission."

"Yeah," Ghost said, sipping his beer. "It is perfect, isn't it?"

A sudden burst of laughter had them all looking up. Six women walked onto the porch, smiling, giddy, carrying drinks and talking rapid fire. They came over to where the men were and split up, each woman going to her man, sitting in his lap or next to him. Diana sank onto the porch swing beside Ghost, her beautiful face glowing with happiness.

"Daphne had an idea," she said. "You have to hear it."

A chorus of female voices drowned out his groan.

"Okay, I'll bite," Ghost said. "What's the scheme, Daph?"

She stood as if she were about to give a speech. Then she grinned and spread her hands. "Gentleman, you are about to hear an idea that's going to sound crazy but hear me out. We have the venue. We have the time to plan. We have the opportunity to throw the biggest, best wedding and/or reception this town has ever seen. Next May, assuming everyone is on board, we can get married. All of us, at once, like a Jane Austen movie, only it's six couples and not two—we get married and we throw a party. It doesn't even have to be the formal wedding, if you want to get married in a church first, and then we hold that big bad party on a gorgeous day in May. There will be bands. There will be dancing. There will be tremendous food—"

"Will there be goats?" Ghost drawled.

"No goats! No way." Daphne shuddered. "Just a big old party to celebrate all of us marrying all of you."

"Personally, I love this idea," Emma said. "You are my sisters and I want to celebrate with you. We've waited this long, and our little girl will be a couple of months old by then. Also, Mama thought it sounded fantastic. I could already see the wheels turning in her head when we left to tell all of you."

"Nobody will forget anybody's anniversary," Rory added, her arms around Chance.

Ghost looked at Diana. She was grinning. "You like this plan?" he asked her.

"I think it sounds perfect. If anybody wants to get married before that, or after, or not at all, we can still hold a big party."

"Dammit, Daphne, I think this might be your best idea yet," Ghost said, taking Diana's hand and kissing it. "Because I am so marrying this woman."

"Really?" Daphne asked. "You like it?"

Everyone said they did. That it was perfect. And why the hell not? Throw a big old party, invite the whole town.

"Wait—maybe we should consult Colleen," Kane said. "Find out if the spirits agree. Or the aliens."

"About that," Seth said while everyone laughed. "I stumbled on a Reddit forum. There's a group of hobbyists likes to fly drones at night. They attach lights and take video because they're trying to create viral vids for YouTube. They show up in Sutton's Creek every few weeks because Benson Chambers is part of the group, and they fly over the fields near his house."

Everyone was quiet for a long moment. Then they started to laugh.

"But hey," Emma said when the laughter died down.

"There are things she hasn't been wrong about. You have to admit that."

Ghost tucked a lock of hair behind Diana's ear. "True. She said when I needed her, the huntress would be by my side. And here she is. My very own goddess."

"Sweet talker."

"Marry me in May?"

She kissed him. "Wouldn't miss it for the world."

Thank you for reading Alex and Diana's story!
I hope you enjoyed it as much as I did.
Wow, this was a wild ride!

If you want to read a bonus scene about the big group wedding, sign up for my newsletter so I can let you know when it's available:
www.lynnrayeharris.com/newsletter

My next series will be set in Angels Cove, so you'll be seeing all these beloved characters again as Asher McCrae and his men move to town and work with the Ghost Ops team from time to time. The first book, **CODE NAME: GABRIEL**, will be up for pre-order soon! As always, if you're on my newsletter list, you'll get all the info first.
(If you're wondering if Theo Harper will get a story, I have to say there's a good possibility it will happen!)

If you enjoyed this book, please consider leaving a review.
I appreciate you!

HOT WITNESS

An enemies to lovers, hidden identity, motorcycle club, military protector romance from *New York Times* Bestselling Author Lynn Raye Harris.

Eva Gray has a secret. Eight years ago, her sister entered the Brothers of Sin Motorcycle Club and never came back. Seven years ago, she vowed revenge, even if she had to change everything about her life to do it—her look, her name, her face.

Now she's stalking the Brothers and looking for weakness. She's close to achieving her goal, so close she can taste it. But a prominent federal judge is now in ICU, and Eva's the only one who can prove the club hired the hit.

Jake Ryan was once a Brother, but he got his life together when a judge gave him a choice: prison or the military. He took the military and he's never looked back. Now, as a member of the lethal Hostile Operations Team, he's accustomed to working on the side of justice.

So when he's asked to infiltrate his old gang to protect a witness and get evidence, he doesn't hesitate to do his duty. But little does he suspect that Eva Gray is a girl he once knew or that she's on a mission of her own. A mission that could see them both dead before they're through.

When the warrior meets the vengeful virgin, nothing and no one is safe…

**BUY HOT WITNESS TODAY
at www.lynnrayeharris.com**

BECOME A HOTTIE!

If you love HOT — if you can't wait for the next Special Operator to get his own book — Lynn's Facebook group is the place to be! Discuss all things HOT with fellow readers and fans as well as the author herself.

JOIN TODAY at
https://www.facebook.com/
groups/HOTReadersAndFans/

WHO'S HOT?

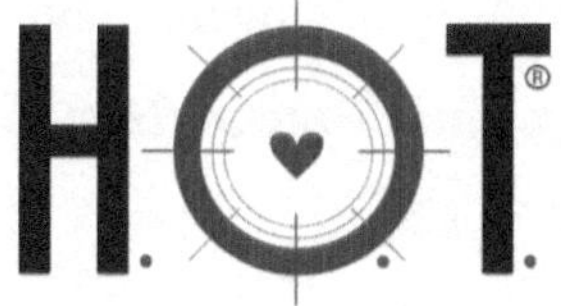

HOSTILE OPERATIONS TEAM®
★ STRIKE TEAM 1 ★

Matt "Richie Rich" Girard *(Reckless Heat & HOT Pursuit)*

Sam "Knight Rider" McKnight *(HOT Mess)*

Kev "Big Mac" MacDonald *(Dangerously HOT)*

Billy "the Kid" Blake *(HOT Package)*

Jack "Hawk" Hunter *(HOT Shot)*

Nick "Brandy" Brandon *(HOT Rebel)*

Garrett "Iceman" Spencer *(HOT Ice)*

Ryan "Flash" Gordon *(HOT & Bothered)*

Chase "Fiddler" Daniels *(HOT Protector)*

Dex "Double Dee" Davidson *(HOT Addiction)*

Commander

John "Viper" Mendez *(HOT Valor & A HOT Christmas Miracle)*

Deputy Commander

Alex "Ghost" Bishop (see Ghost Ops, *ALEX*)

Freelance Contractors

Lucinda "Lucky" San Ramos, now MacDonald *(Dangerously HOT)*

Victoria "Vee" Royal, now Brandon *(HOT Rebel)*

Emily Royal, now Gordon *(HOT & Bothered)*

HOSTILE OPERATIONS TEAM®
★ STRIKE TEAM 2 ★

Jake "Harley" Ryan *(HOT Witness)*

Cade "Saint" Rodgers *(HOT Angel)*

Sky "Hacker" Kelley *(HOT Secrets)*

Dean "Wolf" Garner *(HOT Justice)*

Malcom "Mal" McCoy *(HOT Storm)*

Noah "Easy" Cross *(HOT Courage)*

Jax "Gem" Stone *(HOT Shadows)*

Ryder "Muffin" Hanson *(HOT Limit)*

Zane "Zany" Scott *(HOT Honor)*

Freelance Contractor

Bliss Bennett *(HOT Secrets)*

THE HOT SEAL TEAM

Dane "Viking" Erikson *(HOT SEAL)*

Remy "Cage" Marchand *(HOT SEAL Lover)*

Cody "Cowboy" McCormick *(HOT SEAL Rescue)*

Cash "Money" McQuaid *(HOT SEAL Bride)*

Alexei "Camel" Kamarov *(HOT SEAL Redemption)*

Adam "Blade" Garrison *(HOT SEAL Target)*

Ryan "Dirty Harry" Callahan *(HOT SEAL Hero)*

Zach "Neo" Anderson *(HOT SEAL Devotion)*

Corey "Shade" Vance

Freelance Contractor

Miranda Lockwood, now McCormick *(HOT SEAL Rescue)*

BLACK'S BANDITS
HOT HEROES FOR HIRE:
MERCENARIES

Jace Kaiser *(Black List)*

Brett Wheeler *(Black Tie)*

Colton Duchaine *(Black Out)*

Jared Fraser *(Black Knight)*

Ian Black *(Black Heart)*

Tyler Scott *(Black Mail)*

Dax Freed *(Black Velvet)*

Thomas "Rascal" Bradley

Jamie Hayes

Finn McDermot

Roman Rostov

Mandy Parker (Airborne Ops)

Melanie (Reception)

Freelance Contractor

Angelica "Angie" Turner *(Black Out)*

GHOST OPS

Blaze "Shadow" Connolly *(BLAZE)*

Chance "Wraith" Hughes *(CHANCE)*

Seth "Phantom" King *(SETH)*

Kane "Demon" Fox *(KANE)*

Ethan "Dragon" Snow *(ETHAN)*

Alex "Ghost" Bishop *(ALEX)*

ABOUT THE AUTHOR

Lynn Raye Harris is a Southern girl, military wife, wannabe cat lady, and horse lover. She's also the *New York Times* and *USA Today* bestselling author of the HOSTILE OPERATIONS TEAM ® Series of military romances, and 20 books about sexy billionaires for Harlequin.

A former finalist for the Romance Writers of America ® 's Golden Heart Award and the National Readers' Choice Award, Lynn lives in Alabama with her handsome former-military husband, one fluffy princess of a cat, and a very spoiled American Saddlebred horse who enjoys bucking at random in order to keep Lynn on her toes.

Lynn's books have been called "exceptional and emotional," "intense," and "sizzling" — and have sold in excess of 4.5 million copies worldwide.

Connect with Lynn Raye Harris online!
lynnrayeharris.com & hostileoperationsteam.com

facebook.com/AuthorLynnRayeHarris

instagram.com/lynnrayeharris

tiktok.com/@lynnrayeharrisauthor

goodreads.com/lynnrayeharris

bookbub.com/authors/lynn-raye-harris